Play to ___

by D. Rus

Book 2
The Clan

Play to Live

Also by D. Rus:

Chapter One

From the Analytics Department report made at the AlterWorld Corporation emergency board meeting.

Subject: The surge of violence among the digital population.

The psychologists' reports show that after only three or four months, the digital population (later referred to as perma players) complete their adaptation period and cease to view the virtual world as a game. The memories of their past lives fade, the rich colors of their adopted environment forming an entirely new outlook. So how do the perma players see their new home? For them, it holds a wealth of virtually unlimited opportunities—a promise of an eternal life devoid of the concept of criminal punishment. In other words, it's a world of brute force in the absence of authority.

But this is only one side of the coin. Ask yourself for a moment: who are the people who come to populate those virgin virtual lands? I would like you to turn your attention to the chart included in the report.

Unstable teenagers, troubled war veterans, handicapped persons with all kinds of disabilities, the elderly and terminally ill, criminal elements and escapists attempting to flee reality.

We can only wonder why the once-isolated cases of enslavement and violence have taken all this time to swell out of control. In the last three months, our Customer Service has reported over fifteen hundred documented cases of personal violence. We do understand that until the legal status of perma players is finally recognized, all our attempts to help them will remain a gesture of good will and by no means our obligation. Following earlier instructions, we ignored most of the inquiries received from perma players, burying them in red tape. That made sense when such incidents were isolated because every such case demanded type A or A+ intervention whose consequences would be hard to predict.

Now, however, the situation careens completely out of control. The Informational Intervention Department works against the clock but still we find it increasingly difficult to influence public opinion and minimize the damage done by the independent media.

The cases involving minors are especially harmful for the image of our corporation. Technically, none of this is our fault as parental and age control functions are the responsibility of capsule manufacturers. Still, if some of the incidents were to be made public, the company's reputation and financial stability would receive an enormous blow.

In view of the above, we recommend the following measures:

To begin lobbying for new standards of software protection as well as hardware security and physical protection of the FIVR capsules;

To condition public opinion in favor of introducing the retina recognition login system as the basic player authentication tool. To ensure the Department of State's interest by suggesting the possibility of extending this function to cover cyberspace in its entirety;

To introduce the Voluntary Death ability that would allow the player's transportation to a safe zone;

To stall the ratification of the law confirming perma players' legal status if, or when, it is passed;

To arrange for a media campaign with the slogan The Law is Not Retrospective! *under the pretext of shielding the digitized individuals from any financial claims of their past lives. Its real purpose would be to free the corporation from the responsibility of any repercussions involving perma players prior to the passing of the law.*

J. Howards, Director of the Analytics Department

* * *

"Murderous scumbags," these were Dan's exact words as I told him the story of my imprisonment in the Forest Cats Castle. "That's it, then. No more Mr. Nice Guy."

They had thrown together an emergency meeting in the Small Hall of the East Castle gathering, by the looks of it, nearly all of the Vets' officer cadre. People kept coming. I could hear teleports pop open behind the open windows as new groups of personnel arrived. They had announced Code Orange—one below Red which stood for imminent military action.

In my house clothes, I looked pretty foreign within a crowd glittering with armor and artifact gear. I hadn't yet had time to do a corpse run. Another person who looked out of place was Taali. Tearful, she had refused to leave and was now sleeping by the fireplace cuddling the white Winnie the Pooh, shuddering in her sleep and clinging to the creature's silky hair. The others cast occasional glances in her direction, lowering their voices. They'd already had Cryl healed, fed and questioned; their debriefers had picked the best of his brains. Now he was fast asleep in a guest apartment next door, recovering before a new interrogation session.

Watching Dan issue tasks to one of his assistants gave me a decent idea of the effort involved. They had to sieve through the logs line by line, copying all suspicious names, stats and locations—going into a meditational trance as they searched every minute of their absolute memory for shreds of relevant information.

Captain Scarface, the commander of the special service company, rubbed his chin. "Looks like the world as we know it is no more. The Cats have robbed us of the illusion of freedom and immortality."

"Wipe the motherfuckers out," growled an Orc with Lieutenant's insignia on his tunic. "Obliterate them IRL!"

That was Fang, the commander of an elite rogue squad charged with the elimination of hostile wizards. He had a tendency to chain smoke and emotionalize. The pile of cigarette butts in front of him kept growing dangerously fast. Although tobacco hadn't hit the market yet, there was just about enough of it to cover the clan's needs.

"Wish it was that easy," Dan shook his head. "Most of them are permas, anyway. Getting to them is only a question of time. That's not the problem. But—we have to measure our response. Most of us have families in the real world. If we start taking the bastards out, the next day they'll be sending us pictures of our children's severed heads. Their millionaire daddies will never forgive us for mopping up their kids."

"Just don't tell me you knew nothing about it," I said. "Why did both you and Eric keep going on and on about the dangers of being a lone player?" Now that I finally got it off my chest, I stared at the 'cloak-and-dagger' waiting for his response.

He shrugged and took a sip from his enormous coffee mug. "There's a difference between guessing and knowing. We started noticing some funny tendencies about three months ago. Instead of growing, the influx of perma players in our area started dwindling. We received a few requests to keep an eye on some of the newbie permas. But we failed to locate them. We realized the full extent of the problem when a few of the more prominent moneybags started to disappear. There were dark slavery rumors coming from the Caliphate, the Asians and the Afros. There were a couple of Cats sightings we could connect to the sites of the newbs' disappearance. In other words, few facts but plenty of suspicions. Not that they could keep it under wraps for much longer. It's a mystery how you were the only one who broke out. How did you do it, by the way?"

I shook my head. "I don't think it would work for anyone else. Sorry. If I knew how to commit harakiri without a blade..."

"Shame," Dan said. He didn't sound as if he'd believed me.

Sorry, folks. Admittedly, I had my share of secrets and I chose to keep them to myself. No one had appointed Dan my father confessor. In any case, I was an atheist. Or had been. These days I was supposed to be the Fallen One's overt follower, wasn't I? I still couldn't quite get over it. Meeting a real virtual God. The mind boggles!

The door swung open. Everybody rose to greet the clan leader.

General Frag: once an ex-Afghan campaign major and commander of the 56th Assault Battalion, then a legless stump and ultimately, eighty years' worth of no bullshit. Apparently, Frag was a nickname his next door neighbors had given to the sprightly old boy who was constantly busy scurrying around the block in his wheelchair, his tunic dripping with ribbon bars. His children had turned out well. So had his grandchildren. One day with their grandfather's consent, they lay his weakening but still lucid frame into a FIVR capsule. Having been to hell and back a few times, he probably appreciated his second chance much more than I did. The clan owed its existence to his tireless energy. Now his right to life had once again been challenged. And as I studied the powerful soldier, I started to feel sorry for those who had dared step in his way.

He nodded a greeting and took his place at the head of the table. Unhurriedly, he looked over everyone, his stare pausing on me.

"So here you are, troublemaker. As if your tobacco scam wasn't enough for us to deal with," he glared at the smoking officers who hurried to stub out their cigs. "And five minutes later it's red alert, stand to!"

Dan jumped up, attempting to speak, but the General waved his explanations away. "Sit down. You don't have to defend him. Yes, it's potentially lucrative. Yes, he'd come up with some decent intel. Can't an old man grumble a little? But you, Dan, you seem to be losing your grip. These monsters have been operating right under your nose. So let's recapitulate on what we know about the Cats. Stay seated."

As Dan reported, I began to realize the sheer complexity of it all.

"The clan is rather young. It's limited to the Lands of Light and then only to our cluster—which means they're mainly Russians like ourselves. Three castles, the Forest Castle being their main base. I've managed to lay my hands on a members' list from a month ago. About four hundred members, two thirds of them in perma mode. Permas or not, they're not your average bunch. Everything points at the Olders being their founders."

The room hummed in disbelief. Dan raised his voice above the noise, "I have no intention of demonizing our oligarchs, but that's the impression I get. The clan counts lots of spoilt brats, rich daddies' girls and boys and their entourage. Now that I think about it, I can see that the Cats have always enjoyed the Olders' unspoken support—backing even. It's true that the Olders like staying on the sidelines—they seem to be quite happy with being third in the financial ratings. It's very much like the Forbes list: there you won't see the true movers and shakers. No Rothschilds, no Rockefellers, no Morgans or Warburgs. Same here. But—our business sharks still need a few pairs of strong hands that can solve their business dilemmas for them. Sometimes it's hired guns or private armies, but some cases can be so sensitive that they have to turn to crime rings for help. The Cats are one such ring. To my knowledge, all the missing bankers were in disagreement with the clan's leaders. This is cause for serious concern. I'd risk the assumption that the Olders could be test-driving new brain-kill techniques. In a world inhabited by perma players, this is a knockout argument.

The General's eyes narrowed with the promise of all the things he could do to the overeager researchers. He nodded his agreement.

The door opened a crack, letting in Aunt Sonia. She was a true to God larger-than-life Odessan mama who about two years ago had decided to see what made her granddaughter spend all her waking time in virtual reality. In those days, capsules hadn't had time limits. As Aunt Sonia discovered AlterWorld, she stumbled along a thousand-strong cooking guild and happily indulged in a protracted quest to prepare the Prince's Banquet. As you can imagine, her granddaughter came home in the morning to her granny's comatose body who since then had become General Frag's castle chef and, if rumors were to be believed, also his kindred spirit.

Aunt Sonia shuffled to the conference table. Noiselessly, she began unloading her bottomless bag, producing copious platefuls of pies and cold cuts. Their homemade smells overpowered the stench of stale tobacco. The men cheered up. Even Dan paused, sniffing the air in anticipation.

The General didn't seem to appreciate her concern. He frowned, motioning his chef away as she tried to place a personal plateful of treats in front of him. He turned his heavy stare to Dan, bringing the conversation back on a business track. "What was that about mass newbie slave trade? Any ideas what they might need it for?"

"Most likely, just some Cats overdoing it. With all the power they suddenly enjoyed, they would have been stupid not to use it for their own financial advantage. One more thing. The moment we presented them with a claim and began mobilizing, we got a call from an Olders representative. Who then asked us not to rock the boat and try to solve the problems diplomatically at the table. Offering themselves as mediators."

"Right," the General nodded. "Send them the data on the bankers slaughtered by the Cats and watch their reaction. We will pursue the conflict. There are certain things that can't be tolerated. This is a real threat to everyone's wellbeing. Our reaction should be fast and tough enough, regardless of whatever may transpire. What will we do to them? Any suggestions?"

Dan cringed. The others perked up, buzzing. Dan raised his hand, waiting for the room to calm down, then went on,

"We've already discussed an idea or two. Starting with a real-life mirror response: eye for an eye, rape for a rape. It's harder than just smoking the motherfuckers but still quite doable. Ending with copycat brain-kill sessions. I'm not sure if it's going to work for them, though. A lot of its effect is based on self-hypnosis."

The General shook his head. "If we go this route, we might beat the fear of God into a dozen of those spoilt jerks. And by doing so, we'll get ourselves some truly heartless immortal enemies, unforgiving and unforgetting. So we can't really use half measures here, but we need to tread carefully to make sure we don't put our own families in the line of fire. Dan, you will pin down a couple of real-life Cats who've been seriously involved in our affairs. A couple of the worst cases to make a show trial of. A bullet to the groin, another to the head. Let the rest lie low, hiding in dark corners and behind closed curtains. We have a few trusty guys IRL who see eye to eye with us on this so they'll help us do it. But as for the rest of us, it will take some thinking-"

Feeling like a child in class, I raised my hand.

"Speak up."

"Do we really need to defeat like with like? We won't be that different from those spoilt jerks ourselves then, will we? Me, how can I put it... While I was stuck there chained and tortured, I spent a bit of time thinking of ways to punish them without ourselves becoming torturers. So I have a few thoughts. Four punishment levels. In this case we should really use all four. The first one, we kill them in the arena and keep them for a week, thus stripping them of all their gear and stuff that's not in the bank. Second, develeling them. We mop up some dungeon or other, then force them to move their bind point to the boss room. They'll have to agree once they see that eternal captivity is the only alternative. Then we wait for the mobs to respawn and watch a long string of xp-loss deaths all the way down to level 10 which, as I understand, is the limit."

The room buzzed with agreement. The General cocked his head, squinting at me. "You Jesuit bastard! Now I can see you are a Dark Knight and not some emo elf. In any case, it's a good job that develeling makes them lose their stats and talent points, or we could get level 10 mobs with level 100 skills, if not more. It might actually work. They'll lose a couple years' game. In any case, a chain of a few hundred deaths does hurt to say the least. I look forward to listening to the two remaining ideas."

With his supreme approval, I went on, "The rest is easy. We ban them from the Russian cluster. A territory ban. Let them go play with the Asians or North Americans, whoever. And finally, we can put them on the alliance Kill on Sight list. Hopefully, on the cluster list. Then anyone who meets them is potentially obliged to kill them, at least within the Russian area of responsibility. That's how I see it."

The General slammed his enormous hands down on the table. "I love it! Any objections?"

"I'd torture them into vegetables first," someone mumbled.

"We are not them!" the General spoke up. "But I think I know what you mean. We're not going to create a complete penitentiary system. I suggest we accept the 4DKP system as the base. Once all four boxes are ticked, any repeat offense will result in a brain kill."

Looking at the puzzled faces around, I voiced our question as someone not tied by military protocol. "What's 4DKP?"

The General seemed to anticipate both the question and his answer, "4DKP stands for Four Death Knight's Punishments. Stripping one first of his possessions, then of his level, his home and finally, his life by putting him on the KOS list. You'll go down in the annals as the creator of the shortest penal code in history."

He guffawed. Others joined in. Apparently, my system appealed to them. It didn't look as if this world would need lawyers any time soon.

The discussion went on. They spoke about the possibility of leaking the information into the real-life media hoping to make a few waves. Dan declined the idea point blank.

"We'll be sitting on a ticking bomb," he said. "Once they hear about virtual violence and potential identity destruction, they may limit game access, causing the numbers of new players to plummet. That will directly affect the nature of the newcoming perma players. For all we know, the powers that be may confiscate the servers and install them in some secret underground lab to experiment on us. Are you sure? I suggest we put the fear of God into the admins and demand the introduction of the quick death option."

For a brief moment he paused, his stare clouding over. "Here, I've got a message from the Olders. They suggest we don't do anything we might regret later. They ask us to retract our ultimatum. The Cats are willing to negotiate. Apparently, some of those responsible for torture are already in custody while others have either escaped or logged out."

"Yeah, right," Captain Scarface cringed. "Next thing we'll hear that those in custody have somehow lost their mental abilities. All we'll receive will be a couple of butt boys and a few bodies battered beyond recognition. Been there, done it IRL."

"The Olders offer all victims a guaranteed compensation. They also demand we introduce a common protectorate of the Crystal. They suggest using it for its intended purpose, in order 'to control individuals with antisocial and psychopathic tendencies'. As if! The Cats agree to hand over the castle for that purpose—for five million compensation! They don't want much, do they?"

The General shook his head in mock surprise. "Those bastards had it all covered behind our backs, that much is obvious."

I jumped up. "We need to destroy the Crystal!"

"Sit down," the General waved my suggestion away. "Everybody here understands that. The boot is on the other foot now. We're not accepting their charity. We'll rid the world of the Cats. We'll see what we can do to destroy the crystal. Dan, your job is to play for time. We'll need it to discuss the situation with other Alliance members. We also need to complete the call-up. That wretched dome shield! Without it, we could have dropped onto them one dark night and drowned them in their own blood in under ten minutes, special-service style. But now..."

I leaned toward Scarface sitting next to me. "What's the problem with the dome? Is it so hard to deactivate?"

The captain made a face. "The one over the Forest Castle is an eight-hour job for the entire clan. Double that if the Cats' wizards can sustain the dome from inside, then double it again to allow for any expected resistance: surprise attacks, rogues and NPCs, and saturation attacks. Add to it the exorbitant expense of elixirs and accumulating crystals. War is never cheap."

Oh, well. I sat there, thinking. I really didn't want to disclose my Astral Mana Dispersal spell but it was perfect for this particular job. We had to punish the Cats and destroy the Crystal. Also, raising a bit of money wouldn't go amiss, considering I'd put my foot in it again.

I PM'd Dan. *I know how to deactivate the dome.*

For a moment, he stared at me, failing to keep his emotions in check. Then he switched on his poker face and froze, forwarding my message to the general.

Frag exercised a much better self-control. He didn't stop discussing their call-up plans—he took his time finishing it up, then announced a smoke break. "Max, I need you. You too, Dan."

He waited for the last officer to clear the room, watched the door slam shut, then turned to me. "Speak up."

I glanced at Winnie the Pooh. I had a bad feeling about that sideways squint of his. I turned to Dan, "Are you sure this thing here is not a mole?"

Winnie bared his teeth. Dan cast a cautious glance in his direction. "He's worse than a roach: you just can't kill him. He respawns in under a minute. You can't lock him out as he uses micro portals to jump any wall. To make things worse, we've trapped him once and ported him to the Asian cluster, so now he keeps a safe distance from everyone."

I didn't believe my ears. "How did he make it back?"

"You tell me. The same evening, he was sitting here by the fireplace."

"That's enough," Frag lost his patience. "Find some other time to discuss your albino panda. Max, your turn. How are you going to deactivate the dome? Just don't tell me you have access to the control artifact."

I sighed and began, "There was this dungeon I mopped up once..."

I fed them a slightly edited version of the 'how I laid my hands on a High Circle spell' story. "If you can arrange for a continuous mana flow, the dome will be down in two minutes max."

The General had already left his desk and was pacing the room, rubbing his hands. He stopped in his tracks, causing his coat to sweep around his legs, and swung about, pointing his finger at me. "Now. Not a word to anyone about anything. I don't need to tell you. We'll fuck the Cats up. Tomorrow, five a.m.. Only the old timers, levels one hundred-plus. We deploy both special units: Scarface and Savage. A hundred and fifty men should be enough to take over the place and mop it up. Plus another two hundred to help restrain the detained Cats. Dan, you call up the senior officer meeting. In an hour in my office."

"There could be over two hundred Cats," Dan pointed put. "Plus NPCs. If anything, they can afford to hire all the men they want. Plus teleports. With only a hundred fifty in the first wave, we risk letting them jump ship."

The General paused, thinking. "You're probably right," he finally said. "I was thinking in the wrong direction. Taking over the castle isn't the priority. Too bad. Now we'll have to go cap in hand asking the Alliance for help. Which means potential intelligence leaks and carving out their cut. And I'd hate to give other clans a free rush. Talking about cuts—if you do deactivate the dome, we'll transfer you a thousand raid points. Later you can either cash them in or swap them for gear."

"Raid points, what's that? Don't give me that look. I know I'm a newb to end all newbs."

Dan shook his head. "You're right. I keep forgetting you've only been playing for a couple of weeks. Even the Pratz give us less headache. To put it simply, one point equals one level. Imagine two clans are taking a castle. One sends a hundred men level-100 each. The other one sends two hundred. That leaves the first clan with ten thousand points and the second one, twenty. The castle and loot are worth three million, divided by thirty thousand points is a hundred gold per point. That means that a level-100 player will get ten grand's worth of trophies, and a level-120, twelve grand. This is oversimplified, of course. The system isn't that linear and it doesn't offer itself readily to cases like yours. The first-line soldiers earn slightly more than the reserves, that sort of thing. But you get the idea."

I liked their way of doing maths. The cut they promised would be worth it. Should I really cash in the Dark Princess' promise? She'd guaranteed her help whenever I needed it, hadn't she?

"General?" I said. "I happen to have some contacts among the Dark Elves. A lady I know promised me a squad of cutthroats whenever I needed them. What if I try to get them in as raid members? They definitely won't leak anything to the Olders. And their participation won't involve other clans. I hope you don't mind me doing a bit of leveling up."

Dan exchanged glances with the General. "Cutthroats. That's good," he said. "They're tough. I keep watching you, Max. Whenever there's a problem in the making, you seem to pull a new ace from your sleeve. I wouldn't want to come across you at a gambling table."

"You shouldn't," I said.

Chapter Two

From the Analytics Department's report made at the AlterWorld Corporation's emergency board meeting.

Subject: Control loss trends in gaming content.

Ladies and gentlemen! About a month ago, we were entrusted with the task of looking into the reasons behind the virtual world's ignoring the major changes made in the 2124 patch. As you probably know, we were planning on introducing the new class that we'd all been looking forward to: Berserker. After a period of exhaustive and adequate testing and despite the patch's faultless performance upon its launch, the new class is still unavailable to players. All other minor and secondary improvements have been functioning without a glitch.

As we got busy collecting and processing the data, the problem went from bad to worse. The new server patch 2271 containing two new High Circle spells has failed, as has Patch 2312 that contained the urgently developed Quick Death ability. The virtual world has simply ignored them.

We have created a classification of the changes we've introduced in regards to their globality and their physical impact on a 1 to 10 scale. Which shows that if a month ago AlterWorld rejected all exterior manipulation at level 9, we are now unable to introduce the same even at level 6. If we extrapolate this data to the future, we'll be able to say quite confidently that within the next three months we risk losing all control over the game content even to the extent of changing the color of a roadside stone.

Ladies and gentlemen! The virtual world is rejecting our intrusion. It's becoming independent. And if we add to these facts the defection of AI 311 combined with the continuing digitalization of the players and the world's independence from the servers even after their being physically cut off, our status becomes painfully clear. We are no more its creators and guardians. Very soon our function will be limited to that of a doorman. We offer access and let them in.

J. Howards, Director of the Analytics Department

Endorsement:
Confidentiality level AA.

To Howards:

Please find a way to neutralize the above phenomenon or at least decelerate it. Replace all hardware clusters. Use reserve copies to recreate parts of the world. Fractionize global updates if necessary. Do whatever it takes in order to keep our grip on the world for as long as is humanly possible.

A. Lichman Jr., Board member

* * *

I took Lieutenant Brown on his offer and did a quick corpse run to finally collect my stuff. My way now lay to the Drow capital where every Drow clan had their own quarters and Prince's residence.

Time was an issue. It was almost ten in the evening. At four a.m. we had to create a raid group and begin distributing buffs and supplies.

Frag had given me two hours to get a clear answer from the Drow. He'd also given me a teleport clearance to the Dark Lands complete with the services from Porthos, a Wizard and the clan's cabbie.

Virtually every clan did their best to level a few transporters. The Wizards had a special teleport skill branch. Few would willingly become cabbie men, which made such volunteers worth their weight in gold. A boring skill but extremely well-paid. You could easily earn three hundred gold a day just by standing in the city square offering your services to take anyone anywhere in AlterWorld. The branch started by opening personal portals followed by group, raid and stationary ones. Admittedly, you had to waste a year of your time to properly level this one-sided char that miserably lacked in all other respects: his talent points were inadequate and you had to sacrifice battle spells to portal leveling.

Porthos didn't really resemble his book prototype. He was puny and constantly angry. He sat in his office next to the portal hall providing transportation for those who needed it. He must have had a busy day because, as I approached, he was choking on the contents of yet another vial of mana elixir.

He squeezed the last drop into his mouth and cringed with disgust, suppressing a belch. "I'd pay a million gold to anyone who'd make a cinnamon-free version of this crap. Otherwise I'll be the first player capable of puking, if you know what I mean."

Then he noticed me. "Where to? Drow capital? Shit. It's a middle portal, over a thousand mana. I don't think I can take it for much longer!"

He looked out into the corridor. "Jazel... er... Jazelwolf! What's that for a name! Come on, get me the duty enchanter from the guards' room. I need him to send me some mana. I've had enough of this swill, it makes me see triple. It's your job now to mix it with the invisibility elixir."

He turned back to me. "Ready? I'll send you by individual portal."

He froze, searching for the right spell, then tensed up and mumbled it, waving his hands about like a hypnotist.

Teleport spell alert! Destination: the Original City. Accept: Yes/No. 10... 9... 8...

The portal popped open. I found myself standing on a massive portal platform in the middle of the the Drow capital's main square. The first things I noticed were the tall spires of the Royal residence on the hill surrounded by expensive trading houses—Gothic-style with fancy shop signs. The place was busy, teleports popping in and out. I caught a few surprised stares. A High Elf is not a common sight in a Dark city—a bit like an African in the Moscow metro. At least no one attempted to challenge me. My interface had highlighted my friendly status, puzzling some of them while putting others' minds at ease.

I didn't have much time. Still, my eye kept being drawn to a row of important-looking buildings sporting large signs. AlterWorld Bank. OlderBank. Drow Bank. Now that was a thought. I had to be on the Olders' black list as it was, and after our upcoming mission they would circle my name in red. As it was, all my financial interests, including the texting contract and Internet search, were concentrated in our enemy's hands. How dumb could that be? I opened up Wiki, searching for bank rankings. Drow Bank was a private shop, ten million bucks security capital, the sixth biggest in the virtual world. Nothing to sniff at. That was it. Time to shift my capital to the Dark side, LOL.

I pushed the bank's door. A bell tinkled. A well-mannered nonentity took me to an available teller. I opened an account and transferred all twenty thousand of my remaining cash to it. After a moment's thought, I auctioned off all of the remaining tobacco supplies which by then had to have reached or nearly reached the top price. That was another eight grand. I asked about their safe deposit boxes—they did offer them, insured up to a hundred grand, no instances of theft or robbery as yet. Very well, that could wait. It wasn't as if I had too much stuff. All my earthly possessions could easily fit into a bag or my room at the Vets'.

In order to connect to third-party services I had to go upstairs to a department that proudly bore the name of RealService. Their full package worked out even cheaper than the Olders'. They were apparently in the process of setting up a video stream enabling one to watch pre-recorded TV programs and real-world films. The mind boggles.

I spied another sign next to it. RealShop. The name triggered a complex domino effect in my memory. I blushed. Damned if I didn't owe somebody a favor.

I walked over to a respectable-looking salesman, his face reflecting his eagerness to help me solve any problem, provided the price was right.

I pointed at the sign. "Is this what I think it is?"

The man gave me a dignified nod. "Most likely."

"I love your sense of humor. Basically, I need some information about a certain lady. I need to know if she is still employed at the same place. And if she is, I'd like to have a small gift delivered to her."

"That's not a problem. Order processing is twenty gold. The rest is entirely up to you."

Excellent. I strained my memory trying to remember her job title and the company name. My defective real-life memory had failed to preserve her phone number. I had to give them their due: after some initial data processing and a phone call, the worker confirmed that Olga was still employed by Chronos. She was expected at work tomorrow morning.

"What would you prefer to give her?" the salesman asked, flexing his fingers over his virtual keyboard.

"A bunch of flowers, a really nice one," I said with pride.

The salesman cocked his head, studying me. "How long has it been since you've given anyone flowers? Here, we don't operate in generic terms of 'I'd like that bunch of roses over there' or 'I need a few nice carnations'. We work personally with each client. We're able to process any request worth any unlimited amount of money. A million, if necessary. We can stud every petal with diamonds, encase the stems in platinum and present them in a Ming dynasty vase..."

He couldn't have cut me down to size any better had he tried. "No diamonds, please. Rhinestones, why not. Preferably in moderation. How much will it cost?"

He paused. "A hundred twenty gold a flower. Plus ten percent commission."

"Good. I'll need twenty-one of those."

"Accepted. Anything else?"

"I'd like some champagne, please. Demi sec."

"Anything in particular?"

My memory struggled, forcing a single name to the surface. "Veuve Clicquot."

The salesman nodded his understanding. I seemed to have redeemed myself in his eyes a bit.

" White, demi sec. Veuve Clicquot Ponsardin. Nine hundred gold. If the lady is someone very special, I'd suggest Veuve Clicquot La Grande Dame Brut. Unique 1998 vintage. Eight thousand gold a bottle."

My inner greedy pig hiccupped and slid down the wall. I lovingly supported him by the elbow. "I think the lady prefers demi sec," I told him firmly.

"Very well. Anything else?"

"A quick message would be nice."

"No problem. I'll take it down."

"*Hi Olga. This is Max. Flowers and champagne, as promised. Thanks a lot for the tip. It worked. Laith, High Elf, Level 52.* That's it."

He nodded. "With delivery and our commission, that'll be three thousand nine hundred. Your order will be delivered tomorrow between 10 and 12 a.m. Anything else?"

I concentrated, skimming the virtual mall pages, then created a large gourmet hamper for my Mom. Her favorite chocolates, some caviar, smoked sturgeon and foie gras. I racked my brains trying to remember Mom's favorite treats that she normally couldn't afford. I felt no regret whatsoever shelling out another two grand. My inner greedy pig ouched but chose not to interfere.

I checked the clock. Half an hour had disappeared up its own backside. I had to move it. I asked him to email me the customer service contacts, bid a hasty farewell and hurried out.

I had barely taken a few paces.

"You, Snow White! Wait up a sec," a voice said behind my back.

Was he speaking to me? I didn't care. It's not as if I had friends here. Without slowing down, I kept moving along the square, searching for someone sufficiently official-looking to ask my way to the residence of the House of Night.

I could hear a few people catching up with me. I swung round, just in time to parry a hand reaching for my shoulder. "Problems?"

A huge Level 92 Barbarian gave me a gap-toothed smile. "Are you always so quick? We just want to know what a Snow White like yourself is doing in our town. You look nice and friendly enough. As a matter of fact, we were about to set off for your part of the world. Ever heard of the Dark Hunter achievement? I'm actually one blond scalp short of it," he guffawed, eyeing my crown.

"What's the problem? Can't you dye your own hair? I'm sure your friends will be more than happy to help you with the scalp thing."

He frowned. "No need to be so vocal, buddy. What if we go outside the gates and you can help them. We're not asking you for much, are we? What's fifty deaths between friends?"

"Guys, please," I said. "Have you boozed your brain cells away, starting a punchup in town?"

The hoods didn't like it. They stepped in my way. How stupid could they be?

"No violence within the city limits!" Attracted by the brawl, a patrol was already scurrying toward us. The chief guard's practiced stare brushed over me. He lowered his head in respect. The Princess' Mark seemed to be working. He peered at my opponents. His face twitched. "Gont the Barbarian! This is the second verbal warning for disturbing public order. Another one, and you'll have to appear in court. The decision is final. Dismissed!"

The Barbarian glared at me.

Warning! Gont the Barbarian has added you to his personal enemies list. +5 to Fame!

Would you like to add Gont to your list? Killing a personal enemy will add +20 to Fame. However, being killed by your personal enemy will result in your losing 40 Fame points. Adding limit: 1 person every 24 hours. Potential trophy: the loser's ear as part of the Avenger achievement.

So! I didn't even know we had this sort of option. In any case, I didn't need it at the moment. If his kick was picking enemies fifty levels weaker than himself, he was welcome to it. *Decline.*

He screwed up his face. "Chicken!"

"If you say so, hero. Dismissed!" I turned to the chief guard. "Sergeant? I need to see Princess Ruata of the House of Night. It's pretty urgent."

Hearing the name, the guard jumped to attention and all but saluted me, "One moment!"

He produced a crystal artifact and spoke into it, swallowing the words. It looked as if NPCs didn't have built-in communication channels the way players did.

After a brief wait, a teleport popped open nearby, letting out a Drow mage. He nodded to the guards, then turned to me. "Our Lady will see you. Are you ready?"

Not bothering to wait for a reply, he laid his hand on my shoulder and opened a new portal.

Teleport spell alert! Destination: the House of Night, Small Castle. Accept: Yes/No.

I accepted.

A sonic boom hit my eardrums. I found myself in the portal hall of the Small Palace. Nice digs. Frescoed ceilings, stucco moldings, carved wood and gold everywhere—and lots of it. I dreaded the thought of what the Big Palace might be like.

We hurried along mosaic corridors, the palace guards saluting as we approached. Finally, we stopped by the highest carved doors I'd seen in my life. The mage froze, expectant, then stepped aside, having received a silent command that only he could hear. He motioned me to enter. I stared at the enormous doors, not really knowing how to push or pull them.

I didn't have time to lose face. Noiselessly, the doors swung open, revealing a huge throne room. Massive columns lined the central passage which was tiled with opaque stone speckled with gems and gold dust. It led to a pedestal with two thrones upon it. The bigger and heavier one stood empty. Princess Ruata sat on the smaller one.

I approached, lowering my head. My heart was jumping out of my chest just like it had been when we'd first kissed. I'd already forgotten the effect she produced in me: a mind-blowing cocktail of pheromones and non-verbal messages. The aroma of wild strawberries enveloped me; I swallowed and, unconsciously, made an extra step forward wishing to bury my face in her hair. This wasn't right, surely! I pulled myself together, put on my best friendly face and looked up at her.

Bang. My heart sank to my stomach. Bang. Ecstatic, my inner greedy pig fell flat on his back. She was something, really.

The Princess' eyes were upon me, moist and glowing. An understanding smile fluttered across her lips. She spoke first.

"Be welcome, my savior. It has taken you a while to visit the poor prisoner."

How's that for pure sarcasm!

She rose and descended a couple of steps to my own level, showing the ultimate respect reserved for the most welcome guests. I heaved a sigh and surrendered to her charms. Resisting them was beyond me.

She gave me a studying look. "You haven't wasted your time. You're stronger now. Even here, we have heard about your exploits..."

Fame level 3, I thought.

Her eyes widened. "You bear the Mark of the Fallen One! Have you met him? Did he grace you with his touch?"

At that point, I finally awoke from my stupor. I flexed my neck which still ached, for some unknown reason, where it had met with the sword of Darkness. "If you count a sword stroke as a touch—well, you could say he did indeed."

She shook her head in disbelief, then clapped her hands. In a blink of an eye, a dozen servants had laid a table for two. She motioned me to a high-backed chair.

"Be my guest. Do partake from these fine viands and tell me where you met the Fallen One. I have the right to be curious: I am the priestess of the Dark Temple, the only one in our town. Any manifestation of the Fallen One is sacred to me."

I filled our wine glasses and took a swig, both to show my respect and to wet my throat. "Actually, it was one of the reasons why I'm here."

I didn't want to dwell too much on it. Still, she used all her vast arsenal of persuasion to drag the story out of me. She'd utter little shrieks of horror in all the right places, covering her mouth with her perfectly manicured little hand; then she'd lean against me, as if unwilling to miss some detail, accidentally revealing her already-bulging cleavage. Her mind, though, seemed to work like clockwork as she directed the conversation with well-pointed questions.

"Ruata, please!" I finally begged. "No need to massage my libido. I'm going to tell you everything, anyway. Besides, I have a Paladin girlfriend. You saw us together, didn't you?"

With a chuckle, she shrugged my question off. "A man can have as many women as he wants as long as he can protect them, provide for them and make them happy."

I zoned out, contemplating her words. I wasn't really ready for any kind of relationship. I wasn't even capable of protecting myself, considering I'd only been extricated from the torturer's hook less than three hours ago.

Having said that, where was the Prince of the House, their true protector and provider?

She caught me glancing at the empty throne. Grief clouded her face. "The Prince is dead. He died defending the Second Temple against the Undead of the clans of Light. They'd cut deep into our lands then. But we failed to keep the Temple..."

I couldn't believe my ears. "Pardon me? What do you mean, he's dead? Don't your warriors respawn after battle?"

She gave me an unhurried nod. "The Fallen One is kind to his children. He nearly always grants us the chance to resurrect. But he gets weaker with every perished temple or priest. Recently, he's often left the dead warriors in his palace halls. Four of them didn't come back from the Second Temple battle. For us, it's a lot. The House of Night has no ruler now. That, too, has weakened our position..."

I had no idea that NPCs could die for good. Wonder if it was the developers' smart idea or some software glitch? Otherwise, in another ten years there'd be none of them left. "Why won't you elect a new Prince?"

She tensed up like a puma about to strike. Locking my eyes with her mesmerizing stare, she barely leaned toward me, "Would you like to take his place?"

New Quest alert! The Prince of the House of Night.

The great Prince had been slain in battle defending the Temple. Are you ready to accept the burden of power and the responsibility for the lives of thousands? Prove you're worthy of taking the Prince's throne!
Execution conditions:
Clan leader (met)
Castle owner (not met)
Priest of the Fallen One (not met)

Fame Level 5 (not met)
Level above that of Princess Ruata (current level: 171) (not met)
Be in favor with the Princess (met)

Wow. That was serious. I looked up at the girl. She was greedily waiting for the answer. I swallowed, trying to concentrate. "Ruata, you... I mean, all of you... do you need a proper Prince or just someone to look good on the throne? If I become your Prince—will it give me control over your clan? Will I have access to the treasury? Will I be able to give orders to the cutthroats? Will I have the right to make my own decisions?"

She closed her eyes, pleased with my reply. "You're asking the right things. No, we're not looking for a lapdog to sit on an embroidered cushion. Our clan is desperate for a ruler to control it. With full access to the army, the treasury and full control over the clan members' lives. Including that of one particular Princess."

She looked up at me, defiant. Her nostrils quivered, her chest rising with excitement. Holy mama mia! So many goodies with one free offer! What was the catch?

My inner greedy pig was already banging the *Accept* button with his clammy little foot. The Princess' undoubted charms were pushing me in the same direction. I lingered, trying to resist their pressure enough make my own decision. I shut my eyes, checking all the options and looking for the potential catch. I didn't see any. I accepted the quest.

I lowered my head, "I thank thee, Princess Ruata, for deeming me worthy of the task. I shall do all I can to prove you've made the right choice."

She gave me a gracious nod. "And I thank thee, Laith the Immortal. Your name and that of your clan are both synonymous with our House. I believe this to be a good omen. Hurry up! Our Council had insisted I make the same offer to four more heroes. Go and be the best!"

You couldn't but live up to this woman's expectations. I nodded, wiping my inner greedy pig's drooling mug. The PM inbox flashed with a message from Dan. *Max? Any developments? Assembly in two and a half hours. We march out at o-three hundred. You'd better move it.*

I jumped up. *Three hundred? I thought you said five a.m.?*

Sorry bud, our mistake. We forgot you didn't know our insider speak. We never mention the real time of the raid. To calculate it, you need to deduct one to seven hours depending on the day of the week. Basically, we need you here!

The Princess gave me a knowing look. "You've got to go, haven't you?"

"I'm afraid I have. Listen, I'm really sorry-"

"Don't be. Just make sure you punish your enemies well. Loot their castles, then raze them to the ground. Take their gold and their best women.

This is how it has always been. This is the path of the strong, even though it's not the only one. As for your request..."

I froze, waiting for her to decide.

"I will give you some warriors. Fifty cutthroats. Our elite. But... They don't know you. Besides, they are too powerful a force to hand over to you lightly. Which is why I'm going with you."

I stared at her, speechless. She gave me a knowing wink. "I'm not going to be in your way, don't worry. Also, I'd love to meet this Paladin lady of yours. Men have no idea of how to choose their concubines properly."

Chapter Three

From a private letter sent by Sir Archibald Murrow, AlterWorld board member, to Dave Rubac, Head of Integration and Development Department.

Dave,
I'm not sure if you can see the big picture from where you are, but the noose seems to keep tightening around the senior executives' necks. Did I say noose?—more like a steel cable! Everyone has jumped on the bandwagon piling their two cents of pressure on us: from competition to the independent media and from perma players' families to administration, from law enforcement to human rights activists. Everyone from Austria to Zimbabwe seems to have a claim to file with us.

In short, the Council is currently considering all potential scenarios. One of which envisages the wholesale evacuation of the entire senior management staff to AlterWorld, including family members, security staff and a number of our friends. The possibility of this turn of events has reached 25% and keeps growing by 3 to 4% a month.

Expect someone to approach you in order to discuss it. These people will show you all the figures, including some very frightening stats that speak for themselves. You have to trust me though: the situation is not good. We just might be made the scapegoats in which case no amount of Forbes ranking can get us out of the shit. They'll be only too happy to clear out some space.

Your job now is to provide us with a digital shelter. Not literally, of course. No one expects you to build a new Vault 13. On the contrary. We need a stronghold and a bunch of trustworthy NPCs in the middle of some friendly territory, plus a few sources of gold, preferably infinite. Don't forget that a digitized individual is technically immortal and you know better than I what 5% interest per annum can do to one dollar after three hundred years. Having said that, you never know how it might go—we just might come back to Earth one day.

Please consider the responsibility this involves. We put our trust in you, but by the same token your loyalty will be repaid in kind. You remember our slogan, don't you? By working for the Corporation, you're working for yourself and the future.

Re:
Dear Sir,
Unfortunately, by now the intervention of this caliber into the game world seems to be outside our control. We have engaged a number of analysts who are looking into some alternative solutions for the task you have

proposed. We're in the process of creating some unique quests that only we can complete, as well as burying some treasures and fractioning some unique artifacts, making access to certain yet undiscovered locations technically unattainable.

By now, our list of bookmarks is quite extensive. I can assure you that in the event of an emergency, our start-up positions will be next to limitless.

* * *

I contacted Dan in order to get the coordinates and a temporary digital key which allowed me to create a portal exit point on the Castle premises. The Drow Mage assured me that the data was sufficient to start transporting the Cutthroats in ten minutes.

The arrival, to the Portal Hall, of fifty unknown warriors caused a quiet panic and very nearly resulted in a blood bath. Apparently, the fact that I was to return with reinforcements had at some point fallen off the grapevine, and already the portcullis was dropping, isolating the Portal Hall from the rest of the castle, as death holes were clanking open and the reinforcements was jumping off the couches in the guards' room.

Eric saved the day when he saw my perplexed face in the thick of the crowd.

"All stop! Stop, you idiots!" he yelled at the top of his voice. "Dan! This is Eric from Portal Hall! Come quick before they make mincemeat out of Max and his Drow!"

Dan reacted quickly, sending an all-clear through the common channel. Surrounded by a dozen elite bodyguards, Ruata watched the scene skeptically.

Dan gave me a thumbs-up. Then he managed to surprise me. Approaching the Princess, he gave her a quick bow. "Greetings to Princess Ruata, the Lady of the strongest Drow house. Truly your warriors are the best from amongst the Dark Elves."

The girl lowered her head, accepting the compliment with matter-of-fact dignity. Having said that, how much of it was a compliment? Unlike Dan, I didn't really know a lot about the House of Night or their dealings.

Dan led us outside, crossing the square toward the donjon. The cutthroats joined the other raiders who were already in the process of concurring over buffs, ordnance and communication channels.

The square was flooded with light from enormous burning oil vats. Several hundred magic torches filled the air with a subtle cedarwood smell. You couldn't see any of it from the outside as the castle had already been shrouded by a Dome of Darkness—a routine procedure at code orange—installed by some high-level Death Knight from the clan's Dark branch. I thought I'd seen that ability before inside one of the development chains.

Having said that, it could be some funky artifact. The control room—the Castle's sancta sanctorum—must have had loads of accumulating crystals and other artifacts, especially because traditionally, the control room was the last line of defense which implied maximum protection and self-sufficiency.

A very sleepy Taali stumbled past. She beamed at me, her grin quickly replaced by an indignant glare as she noticed the Princess. Nostrils flaring, Taali strode toward us shaking her gorgeous head of hair. I could see the symptoms of a cat fight.

The Princess turned to her, flashing a welcoming smile. Talk about python vs. rabbit. Taali was shrinking even as she walked. Her decisive stride wobbled, her flushed cheeks betraying her feelings. Finally, she lost her nerve and dived under my arm, mumbling something as she grabbed at me.

She rose on tiptoe to whisper in my ear, "Did you really need to bring her over?"

"Sorry, sweetheart. We do need more men if we want to teach the bastards a lesson. The Princess has kindly offered her troops. Plus, it considerably increases our share of the loot."

She didn't seem to hear, though. Her gaze wandered around. "Do you remember something you said about pheromones? " she breathed out almost soundlessly. "Do you think they work for... for women, too?"

Meeting my puzzled stare, she blushed, her hard slender elbow poking my ribs. "That's not a joke!"

I replied in mime, locking my mouth shut and throwing away the key. I didn't mean it as a joke. I'm not that stupid.

The Princess with her delicate Elven hearing must have heard every word of our exchange. She laughed in a soft, husky voice, startling both Taali and myself. A thousand gentle pins and needles pierced my spine. The woman was a love-beam generator on two legs.

I squeezed Taali's hand. "Take it easy, girl," I brought my face close to hers. "I'm in turmoil, too. I'm not sure about pheromones, but I do know that the sound frequency of 250 Hz can manipulate one's sexuality. Also, don't forget she's a Dark Priestess. She has to have some tricks up her sleeve. I think I need to do a bit of research—Wiki must mention some odd spell to counter her magic with. It's no good her trying to wrap me around her little finger."

Taali nodded, then stood up. "Sorry, I can't leave it like this."

She shook her heavy mane and slid to my other side, wedging herself between me and the Princess. Ruata smiled back at her glare, giving me a barely perceptible wink. Oh. About time I made myself a tinfoil hat.

So we walked to the small hall that housed our HQ. Its walls were lined with the floor plans of the Forest Castle. God knows how they'd managed to lay their hands on them. Another large map showed the surrounding area. An analyst was hurriedly adding detail to it—apparently following the reports of our stealthed rogues who were surveying the castle area under cover of night.

The General gave us a curt nod, then bowed to the Princess, thanking her for her troops. The officer on duty hurried to put us in the picture.

"Four rogue groups of five men apiece have advanced toward the enemy two hours ago. They've already taken up their positions around the castle. They've also discovered three enemy outposts and a chain of guard spells. They're doing nothing about it—no point in alarming the enemy yet."

A waitress who'd been doing her rounds with a trayful of steaming coffee had finally made it to us. Rubbing his reddened eyes, the officer nodded to her, taking a cup. We all followed suit, sampling the delicious drink. Gingerly Ruata took one sip and froze, concentrating on her feelings. She'd had coffee before, surely?

The officer piped up, "Unfortunately, the best bridgeheads for concentrating the attacking forces are all under surveillance. So it looks as if we'll have to move straight on. Two Wizard groups under invisibility spells and power cover are already taking up their positions about three hundred feet from the castle walls. On our signal, they'll create stationary portals opening directly onto the castle square. The first line should be fully deployed within ninety seconds. Max, what's your ability range?"

For a moment, I just stared at him absently before realizing what he'd had in mind. I leafed through the virtual spell book and found it. "One hundred and twenty feet."

The officer made a face, pouting his lips. He scratched his head and turned to Frag. "Problem, Comrade General. The Death Knight's range is a hundred and twenty. That's an extra minute's walk from the portal. Besides, that'll put him within range of their crossbows and glaive throwers, as well as magic. They'll break the spell."

Frag frowned, thinking. "Max, you move to your position in half an hour under your own steam. I'll give you eight Enchanters and two Necros as your batteries. Each can transfuse you about a thousand mana. That's not much but the transfer quotient is too steep. Still, it's good enough for a Bastion-class shield. I'm also giving you five of Lt. Singe's Wizards to cast a Minor Power Dome around you. I would have given a few rogues to cover you, but we have none to spare. Sorry about that. And... I suggest you take five of your cutthroats. Just make sure the invisibility is maintained."

An ash-haired humanoid with the rank of Lieutenant added nonchalantly, "Mana transfusion has a ten minute cooldown. We'll be out of circulation so don't count on us any further."

"I know," the General nodded. "How much damage can the dome sustain?"

"Thirty kee. Followed by a big bang with everybody lying flat on the ground watching snot fly."

"Not enough. We'll give you Brown's group. They'll cast a new spell if the dome drops below twenty percent. But that's about all I can do. I'm not going to lose my best-trained men. I'll need all of them when the battle enters its crucial stage."

Lt. Singe shrugged. "We can start by casting some mist," he offered. "Lots of it. It'll last three minutes or so. That'll force the Cats to spread the field of fire thinly, minimizing the damage."

"Excellent," Frag said. "That's it. Go to it!"

"Yes, Comrade General," the officer barked, noting his orders on his clipboard. "Max," he went on, "we seem to be clear on your objectives. Now for the big picture. Once the dome is down, we take out the main gate, it's about a hundred thousand hits, should take us a minute or so. The first special-ops vanguard will mop up the square, get to the teleport pad and take control over it in order to meet the enemy's potential reinforcements and any of the enemy's eventual malingerers. The second reinforced company will take the donjon and the control room. To bring the castle under our control, a group of forty men has to hold the central artifact for twelve minutes—quite doable. The cutthroats—two thirds of them, rather— will mop up the walls and the corner towers, mainly against NPC guards. They're perfect for the Drow and will give them some XP into the bargain. The remaining one-third will move to reinforce the HQ group. The General's priority is to take the basement dungeon before the enemy has had the chance to destroy evidence or move the prisoners. So that's where the HQ group and the Drow will be heading, followed by the HQ staff and a dozen reserve guards. We need to exercise extreme caution. We must capture as many targets as we can alive and hand them over to the second wave. Keep your eyes and ears peeled, listen in to all communication channels, stay put if you're killed as the clerics are under orders to reincarnate all corpses within two minutes of death. That's more or less it. Now," he looked me and the others over, "hurry downstairs and join the raid, then form a group with several support teams. Lt. Brown is in charge during the first stage. Once he's gone into battle, you're responsible for yourselves and the cutthroats."

They refused to take Taali along. Instead, they entrusted her with the equally important but safe task of monitoring real-world newsfeeds as well as the Cats' and Olders' guest forums. We needed to know how fast they'd react and who would be the first to start making waves.

Everybody had something to do. I received two invitations, to join the group and the raid respectively. I accepted both. I spent the following ten minutes on my feet in a solid shoulder-to-shoulder formation as the wizards cast buffs on the entire raid. Their spells had doubled my power: hits, strength and magic resists of all levels. Perfect time to do some solo leveling!

I got a word that the total cost of the buff ingredients was about thirty thousand gold.

As I waited, I played around with my chat boxes creating and saving unique raid settings. The sheer number of channels made my eyes water: raid chat, group chat, HQ staff, battle and private chats and the location chat for whoever happened to be around. Mind boggling.

Then their quartermaster issued me, as a hybrid class, ten elixirs of life and mana each. He reminded me to return the surplus after the op and submit screenshots of respective log entries to justify my expenses. Yeah, right. Finders keepers, losers weepers. Those were top elixirs restoring nine hundred points each. Hardly any surplus going to remain, I thought as I spirited the vials away into quick access slots. My inner greedy pig grabbed a clean cloth and began wiping the vials lovingly checking the result against the light like some otherworldly bartender.

Finally, our group of twenty-six sentients detached from the rest and teleported to the Cats' territories. We landed at a spot chosen by our recce, less than a mile from the castle. A quick invisibility spell, and we sat down on the ground waiting for the signal to move up. I think I even had a quick nap.

A nudge to my shoulder brought me back to reality. The whole group was ready, waiting for me.

Lt. Brown posted an order in the group chat:

Attack in fifteen minutes. Renew invisibility, then continue to the staging area.

I glanced at the raid chat box half-expecting an Armageddon. As if! The Vets never failed to surprise me with their discipline. The chat was perfectly organized, staff reports interspersed by the occasional flicker of senior officers snapping orders. Just like in some space mission control center.

We jumped about a bit, checking for any rattling gear, then trotted off to the position chosen by the rogues.

A hundred and twenty feet. It felt horribly close. The castle walls seemed to loom overhead, the shadows of the guards flickering in the crenels. The sharp sting of the glaive thrower glistened in the torch light. Already the castle was surrounded by a good fifty warriors. In a moment, that number would grow manifold.

Lt. Brown moved his lips watching the timer mete out the seconds. On his sign, we drank our mana elixirs. We were going to need them.

A taste of cinnamon lingered in my mouth, the popping of stationary portals so loud in the night. Spells hissing. Fog thickening around us. Let the party begin!

Immediately after casting a mist screen, Lt. Singe's wizards made a circle, unfolding the Minor Power Dome around us. As they did so, I selected the castle as target and activated the Astral Mana Dispersal. The ground shifted underfoot as the black vortex began its slow whirling dance. One of the special-ops guys cussed with feeling. A swift hook to his liver stopped him half-word. Now we could see the castle's protective field clearly as the anthracite lightning branched over it, squeezing out and devouring the spell's magic ingredient.

Behind the castle walls, the alarm bell tolled. Several powerful fireballs shot skywards, illuminating the field and the dark mass of warriors exiting portals and taking up their positions. A glaive thrower snapped, followed by another one. I didn't see the first glaive. The second one hit the dome, ricocheting into the sky. The mages winced, absorbing the cooldown. Thirty seconds...

We were our enemy's closest and most enigmatic opponent—therefore, his primary target. Try to imagine a foggy circle about fifty feet in diameter with a black tornado dancing at its center. All the enemy had to do was realize the connection between our presence and the dome awash with black lightning. I could only hope that the banshee wails of their wizards reporting their accumulating crystals being drained dry would frustrate the enemy enough to force them into making hasty errors.

At the moment, I had all the mana I needed. Clan enchanters worked in pairs transfusing their stocks to me.

Sixty seconds. The pressure on the dome kept growing. The glaive thrower fired every ten seconds, the constant ricochets of crossbow bolts rattling against the dome. Finally, the enemy deployed the big guns. The sky burst into a crystal hail. A downpour of meteors showered overhead like tracer bullets. Flame spewed from the gun slits, devouring the mist-shielded circle. Fire rose above our heads, roaring like a blast furnace. The dome-controlling wizards were turning paler with every second. Blood gushed from one's nose and another one's bitten lip. The third one groaned, clutching his head.

"The dome!" Brown barked to his mages.

After a brief moment, a supplementary power dome rose over our group. Not a moment too soon. The first dome exploded into a million crystal shards, its five casters collapsing on the ground. An already-drained enchanter was fussing over them, forcing the turquoise elixir into the mages' white lips.

Eighty seconds. The distant Vets' formation got moving, rapidly covering the remaining ground. According to HQ's calculations, the castle's defenses should collapse after three or four more ticks. Now that the enemy had a more interesting goal in their sights, they relaxed their pressure on us. Two Necros, our last reserve, began pumping us up with their mana. The Lieutenant peered at me, then at the castle, as if asking, *so where's the result you promised?* The whole op was at stake. We were almost out of mana. The second dome was about to give up the ghost. And their defense was still holding. By the looks of it, we sure had underestimated the Cats.

The Necros raised their hands, drained. My mana was at forty percent. That would last me about fifteen seconds' autonomy on the High Spell. Two or three ticks. After that, *hasta la vista, baby.*

Time raced. "That's it," Brown wheezed.

With a crash, the second dome collapsed. A crossbow bolt struck me in the hip. I had three thousand damage points' worth of passive shields. As long as I had them, I could hold the spell. The flames roared, reaching up over our heads. Clouds of toxic green smoke clogged our lungs, thorns pushing through the earth to pierce our feet. The enemy's mages made sure they kept us occupied. What an eerie feeling, to stand amid the fire like a broken doll feeling nothing as the shield absorbed not only the damage but also the very sensation of pain. There *was* no pain, thanks to our developers and the Fallen One.

With a quiet tick, the spell entered its last moments. But the enemy's defense still held. Pointless, all pointless. The power of the cooldown was pressing me to the ground, forcing me down ankle-deep into the soil.

I closed my eyelids. I'd let everybody down.

"I'll help you," a familiar voice whispered into my ear as my mana bar refilled to the brim. For a brief moment, a dark shape obscured the stars.

*New buff alert! You've received an unknown buff: *#@$$@#@!*
Effect: Restores 100% mana and gives 30-second protection from any type of damage.

"Thanks, O Fallen One. I owe you," I croaked.

The Fallen One was raising my credit limit. That was all fine—until payoff day.

Strength was gushing from me, the cooldown releasing its heavy grip. My lungs didn't feel the acrid smoke any more. The bone thorns crushed underfoot, unable to break through the invisible divine protection. My comrades in arms were dying, all dying. Having never recovered, the wizard group had turned into a mass grave. The enchanters were trying to use the portals but how could you expect them to cast a personal gate under the pressure from five or six debilitating spells? Lt. Brown stared at me, perplexed, not understanding how it was possible I was still alive and casting the spell. He wasn't looking forward to a cheap death but he wasn't going to prevent me from having my way, either. So he made the only possible decision. He deleted me from the group and transported everybody else via an evacuator portal to a random destination.

So there I stood alone amid a dozen graves, in a semicircle of cutthroats shielding me with their bodies. I met their leader's stare and nodded: *get lost.* He lowered his eyelids briefly, then shook his head. He had his orders. After a brief moment, the Drow collapsed all at once. Now I was well and truly alone.

Bang! The earth shattered as the dome over the castle exploded in a billion fragments. We'd done it! The Vets' battle cry shattered the air as they charged the main gate. A couple dozen warriors and archers got busy blunting their weapons against iron oak, a hundred mages getting through kilotons of mana per second as they transformed it into all possible types of magic damage.

The castle put up a good fight. Boiling tar kept flowing, crossbows and glaive throwers released over the sea of flying arrows. With a thump, a trebuchet discharged from a donjon tower, propelling a two-ton rock onto the second line of our warriors. Yes, but... that was little more than an agony. Even I, too dangerously close to them on my hot spot of vitrified earth, could see that the Cats had failed to hold the perimeter.

After another half a minute, the gates groaned and collapsed, letting in a human flood that consumed the thin line of defenders and everything around them. So far, the op had been a success. Now for the second part of the show: taking over the castle.

Chapter Four

From the chat logs of an unknown bystander.
Current time.
Place: a lay-up about five hundred feet away from the Castle's main gates.

"They're going in, Sir. O-three hundred hours, just as we've been told.
"I detect the instance of a High Circle Spell...
"No, Sir, I'm afraid I can't establish the caster's name. The group is protected by a mist screen.
"Roger that, Sir. I'm adding all the established names to List 12.
"I'm observing the intervention of a third force. Presumably, a class A structure. An unknown spell detected. It's a buff, uncategorized.
"List 12 updated. The caster's name established. Code name assigned: Puppet.
"Roger that, Sir. Priority target list updated. Puppet added at #2.
"Roger, Sir. Commencing countdown now. 30 minutes to time D. The group is ready, Sir. We won't let you down."

* * *

I downed the mana and life elixirs and sat on the still-hot ground amid the makeshift graveyard. The interface blinked, receiving Lt. Brown's message.

Stay put and take it easy. The reserve clerics are moving up toward you. They'll resuscitate everyone.

I shrugged and typed *OK*. Why wouldn't I take it easy? There I was watching the slaughter on the castle walls from the front row as an occasional guard's body dropped into the moat. In a way, it was spectacular, very much like a New Year's firework display: deafening flashes and bolts of lightning mixed with the rattle of steel and some heavy-duty cussing. That was a favorite male pastime: to batter the bad guy black and blue and get away with it. Actually, I'd already noticed that about one-third of the Vets were girls. Not in the combat groups, of course, but they had their fair share of fierce valkyries.

I made a mental note about the perma players' gender ratio. This was a potential time bomb. Of course there were always lots of female NPCs—the Drow Princess alone was worth her weight in gold. Still, it was hardly a substitute. The NPCs were just that, NPCs. They hadn't had childhood Disneyland trips, they hadn't read the same books and were clueless about music. Learning to become kindred souls with a human being could prove a daunting task for them.

A couple of healers arrived. Three mid-level warriors came slithering over the vitrified stones behind them, meant to provide cover in case of any eventualities. The senior cleric stopped, estimating the potential work load, then began sending messages over his hospital chat, apparently calling for reinforcements. Fourteen resurrections and all the rebuffs—definitely too much work for the two of them. And now speed was our main advantage. I turned back to the castle. The skirmishing on the walls was dying down, dominated by the cutthroats' dull black armor. The north tower glaive thrower was lazily burning. Opposite, smoke bellowed from the south tower gunslots, apparently induced by some Godawful feat of magic. The front line troops had already passed through the gates, followed by a short HQ column. Judging by the serried rank of Drow warriors amid them, the Princess had to be there, too.

A solemn fanfare resounded behind my back as the Pearly Gates opened. The resurrection spell was a sight and a half. The idyll was ruined by Lt. Brown who swore wholeheartedly as he studied the surrounding desolation and the newly-sprouted graveyard. It was impressive, I had to admit: pockmarked with gravestones, the surrounding field was dug up as if by an artillery barrage.

The arriving cleric reinforcements worked double time. In less than three minutes, all the dead had been resuscitated. The enchanters headed back home while both Wizard groups stayed put, waiting impatiently for a rebuff, having a quick smoke and talking in quiet voices. They discussed the High Spell and cursed the ever-watchful NPCs on the walls with their paranoid Forest Cat masters. Apart from the regular guards on the walls, the Cats had also posted strengthened ballista sections which, together with some extra wizards, must have cost them a fortune.

"I can't guarantee much," the chief quack said. "My buffs are all level 160 but these are personal ones and not raid buffs."

A new battery of elixirs shot their corks in the air as the wizards hurried to refuel. I had a funny feeling that very soon cinnamon flavor would be on its way out, what with the dozens of elixirs one was obliged to down on a raid. Try taking a spoonful of cinnamon sugar every five minutes or so and see how you feel.

Lieutenant Brown, iridescent from the spells he'd cast, shouted over the cacophony of sound effects, "Max! The backup's already beat it. We too need to shift our asses to reinforce the front line. You shouldn't stay here on your own. You'd better shoot off to the HQ to make sure you get maximum protection. Besides, there you'll be in the thick of things. Come on, off you go. I'll keep an eye on you while I still can."

I nodded, obeying his logic and the commandeering note in his voice, and hurried to catch up with the HQ entering the main gate. Five cutthroats at the rear had recognized me and stepped aside, letting me into the perimeter toward the Princess and some Drow mage with a poker face. From a group of backs further on, I recognized Dan, the General and another couple dozen officers and HQ security guys.

Then I saw a few shafts of dark light rising around the Princess. Two at first, followed by two more and then another one. The next moment, the five respawned warriors lowered their heads bowing to her. Obeying her subtle gesture, the five bodyguards surrounded me again. I glanced at the clock. Apparently, the cutthroats' respawn time was ten minutes, their bind points set up in direct proximity with the Princess. I'd heard about this ability of the Drow house rulers before. I made a mental note to keep that in mind, just in case. You never know when something like that might be needed, especially if your life span approaches eternity.

I nodded my gratitude to the Princess, simultaneously typing away a brief message to Taali who had to be at her wits' end by now. Something along the lines of, *Doing well, the dome's down, everything going as planned.* By then the HQ column had already stopped in the center of the castle square, not far from the portal platform encircled by the thick ranks of the first special service company. They had every reason to be there, especially considering the couple dozen figures stacked up by the castle wall bound hand and foot. In the inner yard, the reserves fussed about resuscitating the dead and distributing the second round of supplies. Judging by their cheerful voices, they were already checking out one of the enemy's warehouses.

The donjon's massive gates lay on the ground nearby, a file of Cat captives trickling out of the dark gateway. Their expressions varied—some dumbfounded, other puzzled, angry or smug. Some of them spat threats, others begged while yet more preserved a grim silence.

Tavor and I noticed each other simultaneously. He struggled in the hands of two burly special-ops guys, his face a mask of hatred. He knew only too well who'd brought the Vets to his lair.

"You're dead, sucker! We got you once, we can get you again! Your family are dead, too! You're a fucking corpse, man!"

Apparently curious about the subject matter, the General motioned the guards to approach. In all honesty, his words had cut me to the quick. I already knew he was one vindictive son of a bitch. I also realized he was too half-baked not to make good his threats. I wouldn't put it past him to use some of his remaining real-life contacts to punish the imaginary culprit of his misfortunes. I had to decide what to do about him.

The Princess stepped forward, studying him. "Give him to me," she turned to the General. "We're tied by blood. He was the one who slaughtered the Drow prisoners. One of them never came back from the halls of the Fallen One.

Frag frowned. "What would you need him for?"

She gave him a blood-curdling smile. "We keep learning from you, the Immortal ones. Now it's our time to adopt a new skill. For this we need some unperishable meat."

The General scowled, his squint promising nothing good. "Do you know why we're here razing this cat's house?" He waited for her regal nod and went on, "I'd *hate* to see all the immortal clans unite against the House of Night. Our self-preservation instincts are extremely strong. What you're suggesting might alienate you to thousands of this world's dwellers."

She shrugged the idea off at first, then nodded her surrender. "As you say, General. All I wanted was to pay the blood debt and also help this young man," she pointed at me, her voice filling with steel. "Can *you* protect him? Or are you only capable of weird feats to protect your enemies against your allies? Lenience is never a good thing, General."

He chuckled, refusing to rise to the challenge. "We're not lenient. We're supple. Whereas an overwrought blade breaks, a supple one will only bend, ready to rebound and strike again."

She was about to object when a pop from three stationary portals assaulted our ears. Three air-thin arches rose on the granite platform, disgorging a wave of armor and clattering steel that descended on our special-ops men. The attackers weren't many, twenty at most, but their levels and their gear left nothing to be desired. Our guys would have made a quick job of them, but more kept coming out of the iridescent portals: various support classes followed by a close-knit caster group. Things were getting heavy. Our two forces were roughly the same strength. We were about fifty, plus the cutthroats. The attackers were fewer but their levels were slightly higher.

Dan was already reporting the results of a preliminary analysis. "Mercs. I can see some Steel Helmets, Bullhorns and Weasels. All top pros, the choicest in lowlife. They'll fight anyone at all provided the money is right. Someone has invested heavily in them. At least a hundred fifty gold."

The General burst into a string of commands. "Code B! I need two reserve platoons. Cutthroats: one third stays on the walls, the others go down and take care of the casters. Dan, I need the merc groups of Rabid Dog and Robinson Crusoe. Forward them their twenty-four hour contracts now!"

At that moment, Tavor—still face down on the ground and in the hands of his guards—disappeared in a teleport's popping void. WTF? As one of his guards glanced this way and that, three more prisoners—those piled up by the wall—disappeared one by one, followed by two of the attacking casters. This wasn't an attack! They were stealing our prisoners!

"General! They're pulling Cats out! Some are already gone! The attack is a decoy!"

Dan had already found his bearings. "The mercs are sending them invitations to join their group, then pull them out through the portal. Take all the prisoners down to the dungeon! Don't let them be selected as targets! Do it!"

Doing it proved a bit tricky, though, as prisoners kept disappearing physically right out of our hands. Very soon there was no one left to salvage.

An unknown guy next to me—some HQ caster lieutenant—exploded in a cascade of blood. An unstealthed enemy group of five rogues showered us with killing combos: about fifty hits in under two seconds. The unlucky Lieut's body was still melting in the air when the rogues stealthed back and pulled out. The guards lunged at them, furious. They did manage to select one of them and break his stealth, their dozen blades leveling up the score of the fallen.

Surprisingly, it was Dan who apprehended the second rogue. Intercepting the mercs' supposed trajectory, he lunged to one side to where a blurred shadow stole past, his two swords shimmering dangerously as he unstealthed the enemy. The rest was easy. Thieves aren't meant for full combat. One to two was already a good score, considering that the unlucky Lieut was already resurrected and cussing like the trooper he was. Our only losses were the wizard's raid buffs and a momentary dip in battle control.

But once I surveyed the whole picture I saw that not everyone was as lucky as we'd been. Here and there, enemy rogues kept coming up in groups of five, razing our reserves and whoever dared to get close to them.

The cutthroats saved the day. Themselves high-level rogues, they came down the walls, highlighting the enemies and unstealthing together with them in a splatter of crimson. It reminded me of a dogfight: opponents rolling on the ground amid screams and fur flying, the black granite of tombstones replacing their dead bodies. A few dozen pets added a surreal touch to the scene, from simple skeletons and elementals to monstrous creatures of hell and higher planes. Many of the players chose to fight in their secondary shapes: druids preferring the wolf form that positively affected speed and regeneration and also added night vision. Shamans chose to transform into bears for their added strength and hits bonuses. A troll towered in the donjon gateway, blocking it—the one I'd met before who'd complained he had to smoke several cigarettes at a time.

The game developers had spared no cost on visual effects, and now their work was paying off. The fight looked like an action blockbuster meeting a horror movie. Hollywood, eat your heart out. Control spells added groups of temporarily blinded, mute or paralyzed players. Poisons and acids removed sheets of skin, a whole bunch of fire spells filling the air with the sickly sweet smell of roast and the stomach-churning sight of charred flesh.

The sword fighters gave as good as they got, their paralyzing combos leaving behind broken limbs gradually regenerating back to health. Blood combos were equally spectacular.

It's not easy to touch the hearts of our contemporaries. What was X-rated twenty years ago—what forty years ago had been only possible in some sleazy underground clubs—today is daytime TV staple. It gets harder to scare anyone with special effects or a documentary footage. It gets harder to get anyone to sympathize.

When there were barely half the mercs left, they attempted one last charge, apparently intending to get deeper and try to pull out whoever they still could. Their steel wedge headed toward the donjon entrance, promptly met by twenty of our reserves. Finally, a teleport popped open, letting out our merc reinforcements Frag had organized earlier. That gave the final edge to the skirmish. Having said that, the enemy forces disappeared with smiles on their lips. They had completed their mission, looking at what had to be quite substantial bonuses.

We had pissed away our prisoners, that was a fact. We'd underestimated the enemy something rotten. The Vets had lost a couple of points in my eyes. It was all right the op being a slapdash job done on a shoestring and in any case, if you wanted anything done, you'd better do it yourself. Anyone could criticize anything after the fact, every kitchen having its own President and Chief of Staff. But we'd made some kindergarten mistakes. We lacked some serious sword and sorcery experience, indispensable on rare and large-scale missions like taking over a castle.

The castle square had turned into a boneyard, hundreds of graves speckling the scorched, uprooted fragmented stone. Gradually, the castle would restore and the graves disappear, leaving only a nasty aftertaste behind.

The clerics had received their orders to seek out allied graves and were already busy resurrecting the dead fighters. Little by little, discipline had replaced chaos. Dan slapped my shoulder as he ran past, then sent me an invitation with observer status through the HQ communications channel. The picture was getting clearer. Frag sent his mercs to reinforce those storming the control room, followed by a trickle of constantly reanimated soldiers.

They had already dispensed with the NPC guards. The control room was defended by about thirty Cats who, in their infinite wisdom, had made their bind points right there in the room and were now taking turns dying and respawning to charge again. As they were gradually being forced deeper into the room, some of them failed to get to their graves in time to pick up their gear. They were short on mana, the elixirs' three-minute cooldown stalling all the fun.

Five minutes later, it was all over. Our guys were busy taking prisoners and locking them up in one of the towers. The Vets had taken the control room. The op went into its final countdown. Twelve more minutes, and the castle would be ours. How's that for loot! I could only hope it wouldn't get stuck in our respective throats.

I followed the HQ group into the cellar of the donjon next to the arena, cutting down a couple more holed-up Cats on our way and taking another one alive. Just a few more steps down, then the steel door screeched open.

The darkness was tinted crimson from the crystal's glow, the artifact's aura busy devouring mana. I stood, overtaken by the horror of everything I'd experienced there. I broke into a cold sweat, my knees slackening. There, I had approached the edge of something truly ugly. I gulped, bringing my body under control.

The prisoners were all gone, but the Cats had barely started removing the evidence. Three quarters of the cellar were partitioned into cages containing heavy chains and tools of torture. Initially meant to intimidate the prisoners, now they were going to testify against the Cats themselves. No way they could deny the fact that they had been keeping people against their will. If only we could shake more additional info out of the illegal prison owners' themselves! We needed to know who covered their backs—who bought slaves, that sort of thing.

We walked over to the artifact flashing crimson across our faces. Our mana began leisurely shrinking.

"Fat bastard," one of the officers whispered.

I peered at its stats.

2,000,000 mana. Siphons mana to restore health.

So. Not bad at all.

Dan drew his two swords and attacked the artifact with a killing combo. Chunks of crystal went flying as if the blades were hacking at a block of ice. Dan paused for us to check the crystal's stats.

1,999,118... tick... 1,999,441... tick... 1,999,761... tick... 2,000,000..

Yeah. Killing it was going to be a job and a half.

Dan shook his head. "It would take a whole squad a good hour to take it out—call it two. At least all it does is suck mana and doesn't strike back."

The sound of a gong echoed around the dungeon. The vets cheered, hugging each other. The sacked castle was now officially their property. I just hoped it wouldn't go to their heads. Quite a few locals wouldn't be happy about such expansion. First the cigarette business with its potential financial windfall and now this hefty chunk of real estate.

Outside, the stationary portal popped again. Everyone pricked up their ears hoping we didn't have to handle any more 'visitors'. The clatter of steel followed the howling of dozens of spells. The avalanche of chat messages confirmed our worst suspicions.

"Report! Report now! WTF's going on?" a staff officer yelled over the command channel.

Upstairs, fur was flying. The cellar ceiling shook with the rattle of swords. The torches blinked, rivulets of dust crumbling down our necks. Commanders' reports became more coherent, giving us some idea of what was happening. It looked like a crushing defeat.

There're about fifty of them! I can't give you a more exact number, they keep stealthing!

WTF? What class was that? I've never seen anything like it! Camo, stealth, two swords, fast heals and Ice School spells? Shit, they're all 200-plus! Time to leg it, Sir!

Use groups! Groups of five men for each target! Fucking Camo bastards!

Gray, we're finished. You can write off Platoon One completely.

I got one! I got him! Ah shit! I'll need help-

They've only got chainmail! Use stabbing weapons, they work best! Just go for them!

Frag froze, his eyes scanning the chats, then reeled off a string of commands. "Control! Block all portals into the castle premises! Dan, Code Eight! Bring in all the mercs you have! Standby status: zero. We need at least a hundred, preferably a hundred-fifty." He turned to one of the officers, "I need a casualty update."

He sat in a trancelike state as he monitored dozens of status reports and pieced them into a view of the battle. "First line, thirty-one. Second, twenty-five. Six mercs. Nine cutthroats."

"The enemy?"

"Five confirmed... no, six."

"Shit!" the General spat out. "Control room, I want you to barricade inside and hold on. Some of our men will be retreating to you from the square, they won't be long. Prepare to demolish the castle!"

My inner greedy pig startled with indignation. Oh, yes. You can take a castle, you can also demolish one—twice as fast, too, even though you won't get even twenty percent of what you could have had. Plus, you lose all the castle supplies. The op will only cost you money, the heap of almost-earned gold turning into a humble fistful.

Then three portals popped at once. We were too late.

"That's the Cats' mercs! They've rebuffed, changed into new gear and started it all over again! Same as fifteen minutes ago!"

Frag gritted his teeth. Things didn't look good.

"Dan, send an S.O.S. to the Alliance channel. We need all the help they can send."

Without taking his eyes off the combat chat, Dan reported, "Sir, this isn't them. The Camos are some third party. They fight everyone indiscriminately. Cats are sustaining their first losses."

"Belay S.O.S. to the Alliance! Order to all raid members: leave the Camos and the Cats alone! Let them smoke each other! Retreat to the control room or to the cellar and wait for reinforcements!"

"Sir, there *are* no reinforcements!"

Frag swung round to face Dan. "What did you say?"

"All the zero-status groups are unavailable. Someone's hired them at the last moment for some stupid, meaningless job in the Wastelands! Whoever did that won't get even a quarter of their money back from it."

Frag gave him a tired nod. "They just used their money to strip us of reinforcements. Anybody else we could use?"

"About a thousand mercs are still in town. A hundred of them are already engaged here, on both sides. The same number are now away in the Wastelands on some anonymous employer's orders. Others are all status one or above, they're either offline or hired out. We could pull together about sixty, I suppose, but we'll need at least half an hour. Same shit with the Alliance, talking it through will take time."

"Do both! Now!"

"Sir," the monitoring officer reported, "two thirds of the mercs are already gone, the rest are using portals now. Our men are retreating too, pulling back through key positions according to your orders. The enemy has eleven dead, forty still functional, controlling the square. Ah! They're not going for the donjon! Sir, they're trying to get here!"

My heart dropped. The crystal. "Dan! They want the artifact! That's why they're back!"

Dan and the General exchanged glances. "Looks like it," Dan nodded.

Frag lowered his eyelids, searching for the best solution. "Max? You think you can destroy the artifact? Like you did with the dome earlier today?"

I shook my head apologetically. "I can't. The spell has a twenty-four hour cooldown."

The Princess's voice distracted me, melodious and calm against the barking of orders and panicking chats. "There are ways around it," she reached into her bag, producing a purple-glowing vial.

"Reset Potion," Dan commented in a frozen voice. "Rare drop from the Phantom Dragons. Recipe unknown. Ten to twelve grand a vial if you can get it at all."

"If the General foots the bill," she said, handing me the vial.

Frag nodded. I peered at the stats.

Reset Potion. Resets all spell and skill cooldown times. Can be used once every 24 hrs.

Awesome. I accepted the vial, glancing around the cellar. About sixty people had already taken cover inside. The soldiers were promptly barricading the only remaining passage. The HQ staff hovered at the back while reserve supporters faltered in the middle. I did a quick bit of math, moving my lips and counting fingers. Two million hits plus regen. That was two to the power of twenty... or twenty-one, even. A hundred and five seconds of the spell... just over ten thousand mana...

"Dan?" I said. "I'll need seven or eight thousand mana's worth of batteries. Think you can find them?"

He frowned, turning his head as he looked over the crowd calling out the names of whichever Necros and enchanters he could see. "Seven. Do what it takes—drink it, whatever. Just do it. They're about to slaughter us all. Try to make it worth our while."

Then the Princess spoke again. "Dan? How much do you pay your mercs?"

He looked her over. "On average, ten gold a day per level." And, second-guessing what she was about to say, "Less for wholesale. NPCs are paid half."

The Princess shrugged off his attempts to downprice her offer. "General?" she turned to Frag. "I could offer you another fifty cutthroats and a hundred House of Night guards. Only two hundred grand with urgency and delivery charges, provided you give me the access codes," she pointed at a Drow mage who nodded his ability to open a portal directly into the cellar.

Frag cringed. He couldn't refuse the offer. "I accept, Princess."

She gave him a knowing smile. She knew he would. "Here's your contract."

I didn't follow the rest of it. My batteries and myself took a few swigs of our elixirs and began deciding on the mana transfer order. Finally, I opened the Reset Potion. A mere taste made me purr with delight. Orange custard cream... good...

Someone gave me a push on my shoulder. "Quit dreaming! Can't you hear our guys are already fighting?"

I could indeed hear the rattle of steel by the cellar's steps and the Vets' hearty cussing. The attackers in their camo armor fought in silence.

Select target: Crystal. High Spell: Activate.

The floor bulged. I was already getting used to it. The dark funnel disappeared through the ceiling. Its black dome must be looming now over the castle, unfolding its fury, stripping our enemy of their defenses, all the secret observers pissing their pants as they typed away at their reports to whoever had sent them to rat on us.

Thirty seconds. In the pop of a portal, the shuffling of dozens of feet and the clanging of drawn swords added to the sounds of battle as the Drow poured through the opened gate.

Sixty seconds. The nondescript mass of secondary players by the entrance who'd been trying to stay away from the scene of carnage had now begun to dwindle. The pressure of the Camos had dropped noticeably.

Bang! The crystal shuddered and burst in a crimson flash, crumbling all over the cellar floor in an ankle-deep heap of dust.

Spell alert! Your control of the Astral Mana Dispersal spell has soared!

The Astral Mana Dispersal has been transformed into Astral Mana Absorption! The caster receives 1% of all energy he releases into Astral.

I froze. What was that supposed to mean? Around tick 15 or so the spell became self-sustaining? This was something nobody needed to know. Let them think I was just a useless son of a bitch constantly in need of the cavalry to save his sorry backside.

The Vets seemed to have gotten the hang of it. They'd forced the Camos back onto the steps and went on fighting. The spot wasn't good as it didn't allow them to use their numerical advantage. By the same token, the enemy couldn't stealth any more and had to accept open combat.

The Vets were losing one man to their every three, but now they could afford it. The numbers of our attackers continued to drop. A powerful battle cry from outside announced the arrival of the control-room group. This was agony. The Vets were paying back for their moment of weakness and fear as well as for their financial losses.

The Princess cast a sly little glance my way. I frowned, trying to work out the catch. She pursed her lips, apparently annoyed with my dull-wittedness, then glanced down, her eyes pointing to the dust at my feet. I peered at it. Amid the grey fragments, several gems sparkled like drops of blood. Satisfied that I'd gotten her hint, she whispered something to her bodyguards. They lined up, forming a wall that protected me from any prying stares.

I bent down, pretending I was sweeping the dust off my boots, and picked up four precious little stones in the process.

Magic Absorption Crystal.
Item class: epic
The main ingredient for the top-level Magic Negator

Ruata stepped closer and poked my shoulder, inconspicuously showing me two delicate fingers, then opened her hand. Freakin' businesswoman. I parted with half the loot and dropped the remaining stones into my bag. Yes, I'd done it. I just didn't want four more Negators going on the loose in the world. Safer in my bag.

The rattle of blades on the steps had died down, replaced by excited shouting and a struggle. A knot of cussing bodies rolled into the cellar and fell apart, revealing a battered Camo, his hands twisted behind his back. At least we'd got one.

Rubbing his hands, Dan glanced at Frag who nodded. Dan walked over to the prisoner and crouched trying to look him in the face. The man wore a mask that only revealed his thin pressed lips. He raised his head, studying everyone, before giving us all a smile. A very nasty smile.

He jerked his head down, hitting the fragile artifact gem on his neck with his chin, and shouted something I didn't quite get. Then he smiled again. The artifact began glowing, brighter and brighter, droning as it changed color across the entire spectrum.

"Fire in the hole!" Dan yelled, jumping aside and taking cover behind some debris.

Some of the men dropped to the ground, covering their heads and trying to flatten themselves against the floor. The fighters holding the prisoner just cringed, turning their heads away from a blow that couldn't be blocked.

A flash of lightning crackled like a powerful transformer targeting the prisoner's body. A star of five voltaic arcs connected his forehead and limbs, imprinting itself into my retina. With a bang, a granite tombstone collapsed onto the floor.

"Shit!" the General spat, unmoving.

He looked over his fighters getting back to their feet and turned to Dan. "Please. It's time to forget those real-life reaction times. I understand that this motherfucker beeped like an impact grenade, but we're immortal now, right? Anyway. Soldiers! The castle has been taken and purged, the portals are blocked. Whoever wants to squeeze us out of here has got a real job on his hands. Restore order in your units, make a list of prisoners and inventorize our takings. Preliminary debriefing at ten hundred tomorrow. Dan, get me everything I need to know about this mysterious third party."

The General was still busy barking orders but my inner greedy pig was already deaf to the world, dancing a jig with abandon. His hour of triumph was near—the sharing out of booty!

Chapter Five

An excerpt from the Veterans clan treasurer's memo:

The final loot inventory leaves us with the following picture:
One Bastion-class castle: 3,400,000.00 gold
One Colossus-class Dome Shield artifact: 1,600,000.00 gold
Stationary mana accumulators, 41 (all empty, 24 beyond repair):
1,700,000.00 gold
The Castle treasury: empty. A hidden strongbox discovered in the
Commandant's office containing 220,000 gold.
Warehouses and clan depots containing:
Miscellaneous ingredients (pertaining to alchemy, weapon making,
forging, etc.): 122,311 pieces, of which Rare: 1,311, Epic: 14, totaling 423,000
gold
Workshop finished articles: 1,488, of which Rare: 36, totaling 172,000
gold.
Elixirs: 14,670, of which Rare: 212, Epic: 2, totaling 155,000 gold
Miscellaneous ordnance (arrows, crossbow bolts, throwing knives,
hatchets, shurikens, etc.): 153,300 pcs totaling 19,000 gold
Miscellaneous (crafting tools and fortification equipment, etc.): 611,000
gold
The items dropped by slain enemy soldiers traditionally become
property of the combatants. As such, they are not reflected in the inventory,
excepting the eight items dropped by the Camos and turned over to the
security department.
Grand total of loot: 8,300,000 gold
Raid expenditures: 155,000 gold, plus:
Payment to mercenaries, 70,000
Payment to Drow, 200,000
Payment to Max, 1,240,000

Mr. Simonov's resolution: I deem it reasonable to undervalue the loot by
fifteen percent and raise the price of the unverifiable consumables by twenty
percent. That would allow us to diminish our payment to Max to the sum of
1,030,000.00.

Security department resolution: I'm in accordance. One million gold is
well enough for a newb. Signed: Dan.

General Frag's resolution: I object. If it ever surfaces, we'll never clear our name. Max's contribution has virtually tripled the loot. Without his exercise in lightning assault, the best we'd have managed to get would have been the castle's bare walls. Pay him in full and consider adding a bonus.

(End of excerpt)

* * *

The attendance of the next morning's meeting was less than usual. We'd had too many things to do so virtually no one had gone to bed the night before. The Vets were busy improving the castle's defense potential and negotiating some of the more sensitive issues with the allies as well as making an inventory of the loot and building the castle into the clan's infrastructure.

About fifteen people had gathered in the small hall which hadn't suffered much during the storming of the castle. The officers rubbed their tired eyes and drank gallons of coffee. The iridescent tobacco smoke hung under the ceiling creating an inappropriately festive atmosphere and making Frag wince. He didn't say anything, though.

I kept nodding off, too. All through the night, the castle had been buzzing—literally, like a high-voltage transformer. The loot crew kept tapping the walls poking their noses into every corner while the others checked every nook and cranny for the last holed-up prisoners. The universal enthusiasm had got the better of me and now I was deeply missing the lost hours of sleep. Only my inner greedy pig diligently listened to every report making mental notes in my memory and marking the most relevant points in red.

An officer from the analytics group was summarizing the reports received, voicing their recommendations.

"...the castle's defense potential has been restored by twenty percent. Three mana accumulators have been fully charged and talks are under way to convince the alliance to temporarily allot us three mages as mana generators. Unfortunately, due to the excessive speed of mana siphoning," he cast me an accusing look, "over half of the unique crystals have been destroyed to a total value of two million four hundred thousand gold. I strongly recommend we find resources to order more accumulators."

Frag waved his recommendations away. "We're not millionaires. The clan's purse has its limits. There're more important expenditures to consider. Even with the remaining crystals the dome is a cut above the one we have in the East Castle. I'd love to know which of the Cats came up with the bright idea of using a shield three classes higher than the castle itself! A Colossus dome in a Bastion castle, who would have thought of that? Not in a Stronghold or even a Citadel but in a Bastion! Actually, we have to thank them for that. Both them and Max. Without him, we'd have still been bashing our heads against their shield barely affecting its regen levels and becoming the whole cluster's laughing stock, much to the Cats' delight. Dan, that's something you should have taken into account."

"My fault, Sir," Dan mumbled habitually, making a show of knitting his eyebrows as if saying, *we're not mind readers to have spies everywhere at twenty-four hours' notice.*

The officer waited for the General's nod and continued, "We have already started repairing all the non-regen damage to the buildings incurred during the attack. We expect it to be completed by the evening. We can't really improve the castle's defensive potential as the Cats have already maxed out everything they could: the height of the walls, the number of towers and all possible hits. Bastion is its limit. We could install minor dome shields over certain areas, I suppose. The main gates, for instance. But that would be overdoing it, I have to agree with the Cats on this one."

"The emergence of the High Spell," Frag murmured, "makes it more like a new reality. I'd like you to leak information about our supposed mole at the Cats' who had presumably helped us to get access to the Shield Artifact. That will do two things: detract attention from Max and placate our allies as the sheer possibility of penetrating a dome shield within a few minutes overturns the entire clan war strategy. We've been hearing from other clusters about such lightning attacks before, so it's very possible Max isn't the only proud owner of this uber toy. Another thing. We need to assign some people to buy up all available Reset Potions. Price is no object. This is now a seriously strategic product which will decide the outcome of many a sensitive situation."

Upon reflection, I had to agree with him. I contacted my auto buy and ordered it to monitor the market and buy up the precious elixir at a price of up to twenty thousand gold. Yeah, you could call me sleazy, I suppose.

The officer went on, "As you probably know, a class-five castle allows us to hire NPCs up to level 100 for the sum of 2% of the refund value using the following formula: 200-(category*20). In our case it results in sixty-eight thousand a month. Ninety percent of it was spent on the guards, mainly archers and ballista operators. The good news is, if we hire them through the castle interface, the prices are one-tenth of what independent mercs charge. The remaining funds were spent on service and maintenance staff. Mr. Simonov insists we lower alert levels clan-wide as quickly as possible in order to relieve two-thirds of the guards. At the moment, the upkeep of all four castles costs us over two hundred thousand. We could consider some alternative solutions, I suppose, like raising the clan tax from five to ten percent of the loot. I would also like to attract your attention to the fact that the numbers of new clan members grow significantly slower than its territories and the real estate it controls. All this forces us to spread the existing human resources very thinly. The analytics department recommends stopping any further expansion and concentrating on seeking out new perma players. More than that, we strongly recommend reviewing our hiring practices switching our attention from individuals with combat background to those with gaming experience. Actually, this is the chief of the security section's opinion so I suggest we hear him out."

Frag glared at Dan. "Speak up, then, Major."

Dan rose and opened his mouth to speak when a teleport popped open, letting in the White Winnie. He cast a look around as if he owned the place, grabbed at the chair closest to him and dragged it toward the fireplace.

"You piece of shit!" Dan roared like a wounded bear. In one lightning-fast motion, he drew a knife and threw it at the creature's furry back.

Bang! Boom! Equally as fast, Winnie had used a micro portal to teleport himself behind the chair. The knife sank deep between the lacquered scrolls on the chair's back.

That didn't stop Dan. "You furry-eared rat! Just when I hoped I'd never see you again! How I look forward to seeing your stuffed head over my mantelpiece!"

"Belay that!" the General rose, revealing his enormous height. "You, there, Winnie or whatever your name is! Listen up!"

A black-nosed white head peeked from behind the chair, baring its teeth. I selected it as target, just in case: Destructive Touch never missed. Five hundred hits was plenty to instill the fear of God into anyone.

In the meantime, the General continued, "Now. If we're to live under one roof, I'm afraid you'll have to conform to our social order. Rule number one. You disappear at the first request."

Winnie growled warningly, baring needle-sharp white teeth.

"Stop scowling! Rule number two... I'll tell you later. I haven't thought about it yet. You ask, what are the alternatives? Well, we'll make sure we'll be killing you at every opportunity which is basically non-stop. You can respawn all you want, every minute if you wish. Your whole life will consist of *You've died in battle!* alerts or whatever you NPCs have. I'm not asking your opinion. I'm informing you. I expect you out of here in thirty seconds. If you need a fireplace, the one in the Trophy Hall will always be kept alight for you."

The General smiled at his own words and rang the bell, ordering a servant to start a fire in the Trophy Hall using the best birch wood. Winnie switched his angry glare from one officer to the next, then growled something that in his language had to be akin to an f-word. With a pop, he reappeared on the desk, right in front of Dan. Three things happened at once: Winnie clawed the steaming coffee pot, Dan cursed, a new teleport popped open. Winnie was gone. Our gun-boat diplomacy had once again proven its worth.

Dan was wiping his face with a napkin, threatening to nail someone's ears over his bed.

This Winnie was an interesting type. Not that I was losing any sleep over him—he was a Vets' headache. At the moment, I experienced an eerie sensation of loneliness. Just a minute earlier, I had received the Drow Bank's confirmation of the transfer of one million two hundred forty thousand gold into my account. No less. My inner greedy pig was unconscious, prostrated on the pile of virtual gold while I kept detracting one zero from the amount, visualizing the sum of a hundred-plus thousand bucks. That was the price of a one-bed flat in a nice suburb! Especially because between the crisis, the new Draconian wealth taxes and the new rise in utility bills, Moscow real estate prices had slumped somewhat. Having said that... those few square feet of Moscow bricks-and-mortar were of no use to me any more. This money could still buy me a nice little mansion somewhere in either Original City or the City of Light. Having given it some thought, I decided to secure Mom and myself from real-life bailiffs and sent the bank a request to cash thirty thousand gold. That would be enough to pay off a couple months' credits, and then we'd have to give it another think.

I also made a mental note to buy some boost elixirs. It was high time I started investing in myself and upgraded my gear as befitted my new status. A quick bit of math showed that seven and a half grand every five days would give me an extra talent point and five free characteristics. How's that for tough as nails? Paladin Fuckyall, eat your heart out!

By then, Dan had smoothed his rumpled feathers and went on, "Now. First, a few facts. We seem to be lagging behind in our armaments race with the Top 10 clans. Our increase in force structure is considerably slower. Besides, the average warrior's level in our combat section is lower than that in other clans. You may have noticed that virtually all mercs were slightly above us. Not even to mention the Camos. The problem being that we seem to simply bask around in our second lifespan in this world, enjoying our freedom, our youth and the health we had never even hoped for. We waste our time frequenting our chosen haunts, philandering, fighting in the arena and tinkering with diplomacy. True, we keep leveling our newbs and doing a bit of farming—about three hours a day or so. And in the meantime, what's the output of every schoolkid perma player or, God forbid, some hardcore nerd who spends his whole life in and out of dungeons? Now that they finally have the opportunity of playing till they drop, they try to prove their value to the world doing the only thing that they can do well: leveling. What does it leave us with?—a bunch of level-200 Fuckyall-type sixteen-year-olds. Our analysts' estimations show that long term, the situation will improve allowing our clan to remain in the Top 10 thanks to our discipline, in-depth planning, clear-cut hierarchy and a powerful inner structure. But in the meantime, our ratings have started to sag. We need to double the leveling times for our leading soldiers and lay our hands on a few multi-level dungeons which would give us some relatively safe level-up locations.

He looked around, catching his breath. Everyone went quiet, appreciating the seriousness of the problem. The frowning General drummed his fingers on the desk.

"That's one thing," Dan went on. "Secondly, we're not flexible enough. We're often too slow and unwilling to part with what often hinders us the most: our real-life experience. Take my recent blunder when I dived flat on the floor on hearing that imitation pulse grenade. My reflexes kicked in before I had time to realize there was nowhere for a grenade to come from, let alone remember my own immortality. In the meantime, the prisoner could have escaped. Same goes for our combat skills as the night attack clearly demonstrated. What we lack is flexibility and thinking out of the box. We still tend to confine our thinking within the limits of the physical world and classic combat strategy. Did you see how elegantly they outplayed us by pulling the prisoners from right under our noses? This is sword and sorcery—the world of a thousand unanticipated opportunities. Things like having a numerical advantage, troop deployment, action coordination and coming up with twenty development scenarios are not enough to secure a victory and achieve our objective. Way not enough! What we need is fresh blood, veterans of online battles—people with a different way of thinking! On average, our soldiers have only two months of real-life action experience. Then their column comes under fire or they get blown up by a land mine—and there we have him, a crippled waste of space. Why would he be better than a twenty-year-old student who's never seen a gun in his life but who's spent the last five years fighting in various MMORPGs? Teach him some discipline and put a little fear of God into him—and you'll have an excellent soldier who'll become a good investment for the clan. Would you say that the Steel Visors or Horned Helmets are easy opponents? You wouldn't, I can see that. Good. But did you know that the most of them are under seventeen? That should give you some food for thought. That's all from me on this subject."

The General slumped back in his seat. Silence filled the air as everyone digested what they'd just heard. I tried to shrink myself into insignificance. The Vets had just exposed their weak spots in front of me—either having forgotten I was formally a stranger or believing I was too deeply in it with the rest of them.

Finally Frag spoke, "Very well, Dan. I expect a detailed analytical report from you. We'll need to work out an action plan. What kind of people exactly we need, how we can incorporate them in our system and teach them some army discipline. What can we offer them to make them interested? You have a week to look into all this. Now! What have we got next? The media? Are they making waves?"

Dan nodded, silent, as he hurried to gulp down some hot coffee. If anything, the Vets weren't the suckers for brainless discipline. No dumb respect for rank here: none of the proverbial 'yes, Sir, no, Sir'. Everyone seemed relaxed in a creative working atmosphere. I had to admit this was something I really liked about them.

"Almost immediately, the media launched countermeasures," Dan continued. "Apparently, they followed one of their prearranged scenarios. We were accused of unprovoked aggression, of rocking the boat and of planning to take over the entire cluster. As we all know, the bigger the lie, the easier it is to believe. They took all affordable measures to make waves: forums, hired pens and pressure on the part of some of the stronger clans. Soon after our taking of the castle, though, the pressure faded away. Our enemy knows full well what kind of evidence we now possess and wouldn't risk forcing us to reveal a whole layer of corpus delicti in order to justify our actions."

The General nodded his satisfaction. "What do your analysts and counterintelligence people suggest?"

Dan glanced at his empty mug and the upended coffee pot. One of the more observant officers rose in his seat, passing him an almost-full one.

"They've thrown enough shit at the fan to give us our fair share of cleaning to do," Dan went on as he poured himself another cup. "In the afternoon, we're holding a press conference with the Alliance and top clan representatives. We're going to expose evidence of both torture and slave trade. We'll show them down to the cellar, then allow them to spend some time with some of the prisoners and ex-slaves. Some of them are complete vegetables which is more than enough to impress any doubting Thomases. As you all must know, we've taken sixty-eight prisoners in total. As we found out later, twenty of them were ex-cellar dwellers and Ivan the Terrible's customers. To our regret, we have failed to locate him. One of the prisoners turned out to be an interesting type: one of the more prominent Olders. He cussed at our guys like a trooper threatening them with all sorts of shit. It's true that our men had been a bit heavy-handed with him, but then again, he should have watched his tongue. When they asked him what he was doing in a Cats' castle late at night without minders he told them some story about his observer status at some talks apparently held there. As I've reported to you already, the Olders sent us an ultimatum demanding the release of their money bag which we did immediately according to procedure. All captured Cats are low to middle ranking. We're trying to persuade them to collaborate. We're desperate for any information. But we shouldn't expect much: the fattest chickens had fled the coop immediately after Max's escape."

He paused. I raised my hand to offer a thought that had just started to form in my mind.

"Go ahead," the General said.

"I wonder if we could outlaw possession of the Astral Stone and offer a reward to those who find it? Penalize those who attempt to conceal it. That way we could avoid-"

"Not bad," the General agreed. "Analyst group, I want you to work on it and get a rough concept ready in time for the press conference. Now, the Camos. Got anything on them?"

"Very little. It's an unknown hybrid class: a cross between the rogue, paladin and wizard, specializing in ice spells. This is a killer combination, although tailored mainly for stealth-heavy blitz missions. All this rings a few bells. This is something made to order to suit the needs of various security forces. I never believed they would ignore AlterWorld. And considering the prospects of our independence, they would increase their interest in us tenfold. I don't think that you know but there's an old rumor among electronic engineers that all microchips and processors above a particular degree of complexity have been tampered with to allow, if need be, the usurping of control of the system. Apparently, it's done at the government's demand. The moment the chips receive a coded command via satellite, all radios, phones and computers will happily die. Which is one of the reasons why the use of imported electronic parts is prohibited in our space and strategic missile forces. A slightly similar situation exists with our cell and FIVR providers whom the law obliges to install control and interception devices into their products."

He took a large gulp of his coffee and paused, frowning. "Which leads us to the following conclusion: why, for the sake of argument, wouldn't somebody like the CIA or the National Security Agency obtain a similar confidential authorization allowing them to implant bugs in order to monitor everything that happens here? A special class with some equally special gear, things like that. The few items we managed to take from the Camos support this theory, too. Their PK rating is modest. They didn't drop anything—apparently, their gear is all soul-bound. The contents of their bags, however, were droppable. They're all unknown items, their names evidence of their non-gaming origin. How would you like "ration #6", " stimpack, universal", "first aid kit, large", "poison throwing knife #9". You can see a structure here: developers following exact orders. Having said that, it offers another scenario: that the Camos are the Admin's internal security force. Still, all their body movements remain a mystery to me. It's pretty clear they arrived in order to either capture or destroy the Crystal. What remains unclear, though, is why they couldn't solve the problem via administrative channels instead."

Dan made a helpless gesture. He was done. Frag was tapping his dagger against his cup while the other officers conferred in low voices, discussing Dan's speech. I, too, was worried about this new unknown force. If government security agencies started having the upper hand over regular perma players, that could lead to no good at all. Absolute power corrupts people. It makes them lose any sense of reality. The Cats' example was enough.

One of the analysts in charge of monitoring the media channels rose. "General, the Cats clan has just announced its voluntary dissolution. The remaining two castles are put up for auction. Formally, the clan and its property have ceased to exist. Does that mean we've won?"

"They've legged it," the General spat. "Fucking lowlifes. Those who can will make new characters for themselves. Their permas will predictably escape to the British cluster. Now, take this down: put all the Cats on our clan's KOS list. When we hold this press conference, we'll recommend everyone to do the same."

The remaining discussions dealt with some minor clan issues. I apologized and sneaked out.

Once outside, I paused wondering whether I still needed anything there. Then I activated the teleport and headed for the East Castle. Yawning, I dragged my feet to my apartment—Winnie-free, to my delight—and collapsed into bed.

I woke up late in the afternoon when Taali who by then knew my personal preferences had crept through the door and placed a plateful of Russian salad right under my nose. By then, I was half-awake and smelled my favorite chow at the second whiff.

"Supper in bed!" she announced, filling a clay mug with *kvass*. "Go ahead, munch away. I expect all the details once you've eaten. I've been choking on their forums and their tabloid lies. Dan has a really sick imagination judging by the search requests he wanted me to monitor."

I'd almost finished sharing the news with her when Cryl PM'd me. *Wassup? U here? Fancy coming to the small hall?*

I typed *OK* and turned back to Taali. "I want you to meet Cryl. He's cool. He's in perma mode too, so he's one of us."

We walked down to the small hall and stopped in the doorway, unsure whether to enter. A girl stood by an open window, her stare frozen in front of her. This was Lena from the Cats' castle. I didn't even know they'd rescued her. Cryl was fussing around her, his eyes suspiciously moist. Noticing us, he placed a finger to his lips and whispered something to the girl, soothing her, before walking over to us.

He gave me a strong handshake. "Thanks, bro. I won't forget what you've done for us."

I waved him away and nodded toward Lena. "How is she?"

He sniffed. "Not good. She blocks everything out. You can take her hand and lead her wherever you want like a stray calf. If you give her an apple, she'll eat it. If you put it on the table in front of her, she'll just sit there without noticing it."

Taali's eyes filled with tears. She covered her mouth. "Is she the girl you told me about? Lena, right? The one they raped?"

Cryl answered instead, "The Vets' doc says he doesn't think she's been raped. She doesn't appear frightened when you ask her to remove some items of clothing. She just blocks you out. According to him, the combination of stress and fear had triggered a shut-down: she's locked herself inside her mind, bolted all the doors and windows and thrown away the key. So now she just can't get out."

"Listen, guys, we've got to do something!" Taali said in a low voice, grabbing our hands. We nodded in unison.

"Doc thinks all she needs is lots of positivity, care and attention. Alternatively, a strong emotional shock could do the trick, preferably a positive one. I'm thinking of taking her outside the town wall, finding some nice spot there. But I don't know the area very well yet..."

"I know a place," I said. "There's a lovely spot nearby, lots of sunshine and flowers, some non-aggressive bunnies running about. Have you already changed your bind point to the castle? Then take Lena and let's go. Still, I don't think it will be enough. I have an idea, though. Tell me what you know about her, every little detail."

Putting my idea into action took me another day and cost me over twenty grand. My inner greedy pig silently handed me the money, sharing our enthusiasm for the cause.

The next morning was sunlit and quiet as our group arrived at my favorite spot. Butterflies fluttered over the flowers still wet with dew. Cryl caught a baby rabbit and handed it to Lena. Although still spaced out, she fingered the bunny's ears thoughtfully as the creature calmed down, enjoying her touch. Unfortunately, that was the extent of her progress.

Then we heard quiet voices and the shuffling of footsteps approaching. I tensed up, my heart pounding at 200 bpm's. Taali pressed an unfinished garland to her chest, anxious. Now...

"Lena?" we heard a woman's voice, indescribably warm and comfy.

The girl startled. Insecure, she turned her head. Her eyes opened wide, filling with tears that poured out, striping her cheeks.

"Mom? Mommy?"

She jumped up, dropping the flowers from her lap. The scared bunny leapt off and disappeared. Stumbling as she ran, her legs tangled in her skirt, the girl rushed toward the kneeling figure. The woman cried openly, reaching out to her.

"Mommy? Where have you been? I've been waiting for you..."

Chapter Six

Memo:

Arizona 6, a classified virtual space and perma effect research facility.
Research staff: 1,446
Hired staff: 41,522
Security unit: 1,933
Laboratories: 76
Virtual capsules: 16,000
Annual budget: $2,600,000,000.00

The Tempus project progress report:
We have chosen AlterWorld as our default virtual world due to its officially largest digitized population as well as its fast-growing self-sufficiency and independence.

At our request, the AlterWorld corporation has developed a large body of unique spells and gear items. They have also provided us with an uncategorized Super Nova castle for all our internal Tempus Project needs and experiments.

Four months ago, eight thousand of our staff were subjected to medically induced full virtual immersion using premium class equipment. They were given a piece of gold as target and asked to begin casting a specially-created teleportation spell in order to teleport this object to a so-called Alpha Zone. In doing so, two important conditions were observed:

The casters didn't know that Alpha Zone was a real-life sterile installation within Lab 14.

They hadn't been informed of the spell's artificial nature, each of them believing it was a regular level 1 skill and that the purpose of their efforts was to level up their magic powers through repeated systematic training.

Three months and 5,184,103,322 spell activations later, our equipment detected a brief occurrence of the coin in Alpha Zone. The duration of the occurrence amounted to 0,09 sec. Unfortunately, the occurrence later proved to be a high performance illusion as other equipment had failed to register the presence of any material object. The first sighting was immediately followed by an avalanche of new illusions of teleported coins as the result of all other spell castings.

The duration of the illusion's occurrence in our world kept growing, reaching 51 sec as of today. Moreover, in the last 72 hours our spectrographs and mass detectors have been registering the growing presence of gold dust in the portal chamber.

Another interesting and equally important discovery has been the fact that the test subjects have managed to improve their casting skills. For instance, they now cast a teleport spell 0,12 sec faster than was standard. While both phenomena still demand some serious assessment, the fact remains that these two discoveries transcend the limits of the feasible, not only changing our entire world view, but also reviewing humanity's potential.

* * *

Still flabbergasted by the miracle that had just happened before us, we were sitting in the glade not far from mother and daughter who couldn't take their eyes off each other. Lena was telling her something, laughing and gesticulating, as her reunited mother listened to her with a happy smile on her lips. It couldn't have been easy for her to recognize her daughter in this Elven maiden even though the changes in her child's appearance weren't that spectacular: the girl had based it on her own picture. In any case, you can't cheat a mother's heart.

Herself, she looked like an alien body in the surrounding riot of color. As we'd frantically texted each other earlier, I'd recommended Tamara Mikhailovna to choose clothes her child could easily recognize. So now our fragile Elfa sat next to a still-pretty woman of about forty years of age wearing a rather short dressing gown and house slippers worn to a state of perfect orthopedic match with her feet.

A barely audible gong floated over the glade. Clouds of anthracite-colored diamonds swirled around Taali and Cryl, glittering in the sun like the lights of a thousand discos. Before I could raise my eyebrows in surprise, I was enveloped in a similar asteroid cloud of crazy diamonds. Yet another gong, and the gems descended into the grass, then disappeared without a trace.

Quest completion alert! You've completed a secret quest: A Friend in Need-2.
Donate the lion's share of your property to help those in trouble.
Reward: A Smile of Fortune-2. Luck will follow you around for one full week. It will increase your crit chances, send you rare loot and do various other things associated with good luck and Gods' assistance.

Congratulations! You've received Achievement: Soul Healer
Reward: +1000 to Fame

Congratulations! You have attracted God's attention and his hand has touched your shoulder.
Reward: unique skill The Help of the Fallen One.

Effect: once every 24 hrs., you can completely restore health of any creature in AlterWorld with the exception of yourself.

My friends didn't say a word, dumbfounded. Their stares clouded as they read their own interface messages. Finally, I spoke,

"Everyone got the Help of the Fallen One?"

Cryl nodded, closing the invisible windows. "Yeah. What's all this about? What's earned us the Dark One's attentions?"

Taali nodded absent-mindedly, still under the impression of all the rewards she'd been showered with.

I thought it was time for me to open up a bit. I had no reason not to trust Taali, and we had to let Cryl in on our secrets as he was one of us now. You couldn't possibly exist in this world without having someone to cover your back. Besides, I was used to having a rogue in the group especially because Bug—with whom I'd done the last twenty levels or so—was still a regular gamer and not a perma. You couldn't really count on him long term, especially confronted with a looming eternity. How long would he be in the game—a year, two? And then? There you were...

"He's not that Dark, really," I said. "By the way, it was him who helped me to escape from the Cats. The siege of the castle wouldn't have gone as smoothly without his intervention. He's neither good nor bad, he's in a league of his own. That's the way he wants to be, without all the clichés and name tags, you understand?"

Cryl looked up at me, surprised. "How do you know all this? You speak as if you met him personally."

I just shrugged, "Why wouldn't a young god want to meet his disciple?"

Deep inside I heard a familiar quiet laughter. The Fallen One? He was getting a bit too much. Raising my head to the sky for some reason, I shouted,

"Three-one-one, are you here? Can we see you?"

The laughter stopped. A barely visible mirror-like dome shrouded the glade, enveloping Lena and Tamara Mikhailovna who sat there oblivious to the world.

A figure entwined within the swirls of the darkness appeared a couple paces away from us, its cloak of night draped around its shoulders. The same humorous glint in his eyes, the same surge of power emanating from him, squeezing your chest like the cooldown from a High Spell.

Involuntarily, both Taali and Cryl jumped up and lowered their heads. I forced myself to remain seated trying to look disinterested and uninvolved. The Fallen One kept eyeing me ironically, building up the pressure, until I felt sweat trickle down my temple.

Finally, I gave up, "What now? Just don't try to tell me you're more interested in dumb worshipping that you are in our affairs."

The god threw his head back, laughing. The invisible pressure disappeared. I managed an inconspicuous breath of relief. Last time I'd felt something like this was in Turkey when I had my picture taken with a tiger. The beast had been apparently pumped up with tranquilizers, his neck chained tight to the concrete floor, but even in that state, his power and God-given fury had been palpable...

"Sit down," the Fallen One motioned us to resume our positions before sitting down first. He looked over us, making sure everybody was ready to pay attention to whatever he had to say.

"You've no idea, Max, how right you are," he went on. "By the very fact of your being my disciple, all of your actions, deeds and even words add to my karma. And the stronger the pressure produced by such events, thoughts, or emotional surges, the bigger the energy flow I receive. One could, of course, just donate some mana, loot or experience—all this will be available once the First Temple is restored. But few things can come anywhere near the kind of force this little girl has released into this world."

The rebellious AI nodded at Lena sitting quietly next to her mother who was plaiting her hair. "Her immersion is phenomenal. She has the potential to mold the fabric of the universe as if it were modeling clay. What a priestess she'd make! An inexhaustible source of power—neutral power, mind you, not a flood of black energy from some overzealous necromancer or a dark Drow rogue who gets his kicks from butchering young players in newb locations. But their power tastes vile and that's exactly what it does, creates the impression of me being a Dark god. Imagine, Max, if someone turned you into a true Death Knight, Morana's messenger, who leaves nothing but desolation and well-fed vultures in his wake? And you, Cryl— would you really prefer to become a thief and a hired killer? I wouldn't, either. Even though I too need power just like you do."

He turned back to me. "Oh, one other thing. I can't guarantee I can help you every time. For every such intervention I have to pay with my own power, whatever's left of it."

"Why did you waste it on this new skill, then?" I asked. "It wasn't crucial. You don't think you should have saved it for something truly important?"

The god smiled. "Not crucial, no, but the timing was perfect to hand out a few purpose-built freebies. Where do you think it would be the easiest to start a rockfall: in a desert or on a mountain slope where all you need to do is kick one piddly little pebble? The situation you've just created allows me to interfere without messing up the logic of the universe. Had I tried to issue each of you with the apocalypse button, then yes, I'd have overdone things. So once again: keep shaking the foundations and doing grand deeds. One day the reward will find its heroes."

"Yeah, right. So that their patron god could cash in his chips, too," I couldn't hold the sarcasm back. "Ditto for using the Help of the Fallen One on a dying player. One gram of gratitude a day multiplied by three multiplied by eternity. Not bad for a power investment, what d'you think?"

The Fallen One grinned and gave me a wink.

Cryl stepped forward and lowered his head. "O Fallen One, may I accept you as my god, too? None of the Light ones came to help me when I was dangling pinned to the ceiling in the Cats' cellar. No one showered me with their skills and attentions. But if I became one of the founders of a powerful movement, that could bring enough fame, fortune and wealth to last me two eternities, if necessary."

I stared at Cryl in surprise. The Fallen One gave him a look of approval, nodded and slapped Cryl's shoulder, accepting his request. With another gong, a new explosion of diamond dust erupted. The kid's eyes widened as he moved his lips, scanning the messages visible only to him. I'd love to know what the god had given him.

Unexpectedly to us, Taali stepped forward, too. "O Fallen One, is it true that dark priestesses have a number of, er, very special skills?" she blushed even though she'd managed to avoid putting her request bluntly.

The Fallen One grinned again. "It is, Paladin Maiden, it is true indeed."

Taali raised a proud head, "Accept my vows too, then!"

The god shook his head in surprise and glanced at me with what I thought was a hint of envy. "No vows needed. Your ambition is well enough. Accept my gift, then..."

The gong struck again. Taali's eyes started twitching, reading the lines of text in her interface—her nostrils flaring, a winning smile blossoming on her lips. Finally, she lowered her head in a bow. "Thank you..."

The tired god lowered his eyelids. "Time for me to go. I've done too much and revealed myself much more than I should have. Max? You've got to be on your way, remember?"

I nodded. "Sure. I need to kit myself out first and then I'll be off."

The Fallen One nodded and turned to go when his stare happened on Lena. The girl and her mother stood nearby, studying the god with interest, not daring to approach. The Fallen One lingered a few seconds; then, coming to a decision, he bit his lip and snapped his fingers. A plain gray bracelet appeared in his hand. I noticed him whisk away a crimson streak that ran from one end of his mouth to his chin. Oh. I just hoped our god wouldn't overexert himself handing out his gifts.

Curiosity forced me to select the bracelet as target and check out its stats.

Platinum Bracelet of the Dark Priestess. A Divine Artifact.
Item type: Independent, indestructible

Soul bound. Cannot be removed even after the player's death.
Item class: Unique
Permanent effect: The Mark of the Fallen One. Your relationship with all
Dark races has changed to neutral.
Effect: Journey Home. Teleport to any Dark temple of your choice.
Cast time: 0
Mana: 0
Cooldown: 24 hrs.

My inner greedy pig shook, his eye twitching. How I understood him. This kind of thing could save your backside in dozens of situations. Not forgetting that all of the Fallen One's actions had at least one hidden agenda. By wearing the priestess' bracelet, the girl would get used to her new status. And by teleporting 'home' to a Dark temple after she'd extricated herself from various dangers, she will reinforce the association: *I am the priestess, the temple is my home, my safety.* This Fallen One was anything but simple.

He handed his gift to Lena. Having exchanged a few words with her mother, he tousled the girl's hair and waved his goodbye to us all. With a pop, the god disappeared, still enveloped by his dome. The summer forest sounds assaulted us with a renewed force, the sun growing hot and strong. Time to get back home and hide under our castle roof. A bite to eat wouldn't go amiss, either.

Tamara Mikhailovna and Lena walked over to us. The girl looked into my eyes, her stare attentive and vivid, very unlike I'd seen it before—bathed with joy, happiness and interest in everything around her.

"Max, thank you so much! Mom told me you helped them to find me. I don't know what would have happened to me without your help!"

My inner greedy pig purred, flattered by her praise. Still, I wasn't the only one deserving of it. "It's nothing, really. You need to thank Cryl over there. He stayed put feeding and guiding you. And Taali was upset about you more than any of us and helped us with everything she could..."

"Did she? I can't remember anything," the girl looked at my friends with gratitude. "Thank you too!"

We started along the trail that led to the castle. We could see the Vet's flag flying on the donjon spire. Tamara Mikhailovna had already changed into some period-appropriate fantasy clothes. Now she was doing all the talking, going unhurriedly into every detail. She had the rare gift of endearing herself with everyone from the first minutes of meeting them, just like a favorite auntie on a visit from out of town.

"I can't thank you enough, Max, both for myself and for our Dad. He'll come later on in the afternoon. No one gives time off to chief physicians. I'm not even talking about vacations..."

"It's nothing," I waved her gratitude away, embarrassed enough as I was. "What are you planning to do next?"

Tamara Mikhailovna stopped and looked back at the rather steep ascent we'd just climbed. "I'm not even out of breath," she shook her head. "What with my asthma and bad knees, I've been jumping around like a schoolgirl in May. And the air here reminds me of the seaside. St Petersburg is all covered in sleet, slush and those chemicals they use to melt the ice in the streets. Answering your question—yes, we want to go perma mode, both of us. When our Lena got trapped in the game, we started looking for her here. The police don't deal with missing children if they're lost to the virtual world. The AlterWorld's administration was playing for time, quoting their confidentiality clauses and demanding an official request for an international police search. In short, my husband and I decided to go digital and look for her ourselves. She's immortal now—sooner or later, we'd have found her ourselves. Instead, you found us... with this horrible story..." she wiped the corner of her eye making sure her child didn't see it. She didn't need to bother: open-mouthed, Lena was listening to the blushing Cryl feeding her his finest war stories.

I tried to distract the woman from her sad thoughts. "You'll have to join a clan. Preferably, one in the top 10. That'll give you some security. If you have enough money, it would be a good idea to buy a house within the city limits. You don't even need to go above level 10. Then again, Lena has already done that so you might need to catch up with her, too."

She nodded. "I think you might be right about joining a clan. And you, Max—are you with the Veterans?"

"Not really. I have a mini clan of my own. Just a pocket version, so to say. More of a family than anything else."

She stopped in her tracks, looking at me with interest. "Would it be possible for us to join it somehow? I assure you we're serious and hardworking people. We can be useful. And we aren't going to arrive empty-handed."

"You don't understand me," I shook my head. "Joining a clan isn't a formality. You will need it as protection, to help you and to speed you up. Besides, they're only two of us: Taali and myself."

A hand lay on my shoulder. "There're three of us."

I swung round, facing a serious Cryl. "There're three of us," he repeated. "I owe you. You're my only friend. Besides, I've already told the Fallen One I'd love to be present at the birth of a new era. I have no doubt whatsoever you'll make it big, man. You'll need a security force then, won't you? I'm not setting my sights on the post of its chief but I think I could make a decent operative."

"You see?" Tamara Mikhailovna smiled at me. "You're three already! With us, you'll be six. A journey of a thousand miles begins with a single step. In another hundred years we'll be laughing remembering this conversation!"

I looked at them all, willing myself to say no. The poet was right: we're responsible forever for what we have tamed. "Don't you understand? Running a clan is a pain I wouldn't wish on anyone, myself included!"

The woman's wise eyes smiled. "It's the retinue that makes the king... or the general. Once you pick the right people, your problems will be limited to setting objectives for them, then controlling the results."

"Send me an invitation," the rogue demanded.

I glanced at Taali. She winked at me and shrugged.

I raised my hand, motioning everyone to calm down. I had to do some quality thinking. Actually, it was probably for the better. My being part of the tobacco alliance tied me to my nanoclan for the next five years. At the same time, I realized full well that my clan had to be strong enough to guarantee both safety and lots of other things, as I had already said many times on different occasions. As always, if you wanted something done well, you had to do it yourself.

"Very well, then," I said. "It's not as if I'm dragging you in at gun point. You can always leave the clan, and not necessarily feet first. Here're your invites."

The next moment, my clan grew twice its original size. Tamara Mikhailovna declined my invitation.

"I'd like to change my avatar first," she said, answering my surprised stare. "I want to be a Higher Elf like my girl. Make a few alterations to my age and appearance... not much, just a little," she explained, embarrassed.

I nodded my understanding. Everybody wanted to be forever young and beautiful. She didn't need to explain it to me.

As we were walking through the castle, Dan collared us, wishing to report on Taali's situation. They had been busy collecting a wealth of information. A couple more weeks, and the lowlifes would be brought to justice. They already had the gun: a semi-automatic Tiger carbine with all options and high-end sights, virtually a clone of the good old Dragunov sniper rifle. Dan insisted Taali spent the next week at the shooting range and loosed off at least a couple hundred rounds to get used to it. So starting the next day, she was to go to some gun club not far from St Petersburg and remain AFK for a while.

Everyone got busy, leaving me alone to think about my own situation. My Mom, rather. Tavor's frantic threats had left me with a bad chill in my spine. I had to do something about them. Mom had better move somewhere else—ideally, to stay under surveillance for a while. I really didn't want to go cap in hand back to the Vets. Begging never pays; besides, I didn't want to supply them with all the trump cards they might need. A potential leak couldn't be disregarded, either.

Once upstairs in my room, I dragged the armchair to a narrow window with a forest view, made myself comfortable and opened the chat menu. The saved contact of the RealService representative glowed green, indicating his online status. The spirited exchange that followed secured me an excellent apartment in a secure gated community in the suburbs. That particular pleasure cost me three hundred bucks a week: pricey but bearable, considering the current state of my wallet. I also ordered their removal van for the next morning.

After a moment's hesitation, I decided to humor my paranoia and looked up several security agencies. On average, bodyguards cost from five to thirty bucks an hour. I chose something mid-range: a retrained ex special-ops officer with a gun license. I opted for automatic contract renewal and issued a daily standing order. Now all I had to do was break the news to Mom without triggering a heart attack.

It took me a while to type the message making sure it sounded positive and optimistic. I told her of my inventing a unique recipe bound to secure our financial future. I also told her about the new friends and powerful allies I'd made. Then I complained about 'some people' never happy with their share of the pie and let her know, point blank, about her temporary change of address in order to provide her with the safety and comfort levels befitting a new clan leader and virtual millionaire. My Mom wasn't stupid, of course. She was bound to read between the lines. But at least this way it would take her some time to figure something out—a big difference from the 'Mom, your life's in danger, you've got to lie low and keep a bazooka under your bed!' scenario.

I stretched and slumped back in the chair. I wouldn't call myself a money worshipper. Still, money did help solve many problems, making one's life more comfortable. Instead of silently suffering your noisy upstairs and downstairs neighbors, you could rent or buy a proper house with a bit of land. Instead of swallowing painkillers, you could visit a good doctor. Instead of being extorted by the traffic police, you could simply call your lawyer...

Now my current affairs seemed to be under control. The next thing to do would be to see if I could get access to the Vets' clan storeroom. Time for an upgrade. Failing that, I could always check the auctions. Then I had to spend a bit of time tying some loose ends before hitting the road again: the Dead Lands, the Temple and my little baby Dragons were awaiting!

Chapter Seven

"Open, Sesame!" I whispered as I logged in to the Vets' clan storeroom database. The inventory interface was military-style plain: no bells or whistles there.

Less than five minutes ago, my inner greedy pig had been pacing his cage waiting for the Vets' decision on my storeroom access application. In it, I explained my desire to part-exchange some of the loot for gold. Dan had diplomatically backed out saying the question was out of his jurisdiction and bounced me over to Mr. Simonov. Their decision, however, was signed not by the bookkeeper but by Frag himself. Thanking me for my 'considerable contribution', the General expressed his hopes for further cooperation and made it clear that in the future, my compensation for casting the High Spell during their raids would be revised in favor of a considerable increase. In the meantime, to show their recognition of my services, they granted me full Lieutenant-level access to the storage facility that offered a considerable trade-in discount.

I suppressed a smirk. The Vets had apparently appreciated the outcome of their teaming up with the caster of High Spells enough to attempt securing me for themselves. I didn't even want to venture a guess at the amount I must have helped them make: it's not my style to count the profits in somebody else's wallet. Still, whatever the Vets thought of themselves, I wasn't sure I was happy turning into their hired lockpick. I had to learn to stand on my own two feet, cultivating myself a power strong enough to be reckoned with and not just used. But in the meantime, the Vets guaranteed me the proverbial stroke of a pen that turned my zero into a shiny tenner.

The search interface window chirped open, letting me know they'd finished their checks and confirmed my access status. Thank God for digital technologies! In real life, I'd have had to deal with a cartoon storage officer and his own inner greedy pig, their combined combat skills enough to defeat any quantity of Phantom Dragons.

Right. First things first. Let's check out their vehicle facilities. Where did they keep their bear gear? A haphazard search offered me over four hundred available items, a bit over the top. I sorted them by price, the highest offerings stopping at just over twenty grand per item. Their names didn't say anything to me. I needed to consult an expert.

Any bear-savvy persons around? Apart from Animal Rescue, I could only think of Eric. I PM'd him describing my problem and asking his advice regarding some gear for my Hummungus. I remembered the love and care

Eric had invested into kitting out his own LAV mount. Now it was my time to hear out the expert.

He promptly replied, stuck in the guardhouse as part of the reinforcement group and dying for some entertainment.

Super. Will help you, no question. Which storage have you got access to?

That got me thinking. What did he mean, which one? *Do you have several? I've got Lieutenant's access.*

I see. It gives you access to all classes of items and gear up to rare. Epics and artifacts are locked in the classified vault. Not much but not bad, either. I don't have even that. Ah! Think you could look something up for my LAVvie? I need a Veil of True Vision. It allows a mount to detect a stealthed enemy even farther than a player with an identical buff can. And, please, also Pegasus Horseshoes. They add 15% to speed. And could you also look up-

Hey, wait up! my inner greedy pig and myself replied in unison. We could use this sort of goodies ourselves! *Back to the subject. Once we equip Hummungus, you might be able run wild for a bit, depending on the result.*

What's your money situation?

Not a problem.

Then you should take Winnypore's set, everything you can find—there're six items in total and you've got the Claws already. That's the coolest of the affordables. The rest is a bit out of your league. Besides, they're mainly no-drop, anyway.

Very well. I typed in *Winnypore*. The search returned nine items. When I got rid of the doubles, I was left with four: the helmet, the pauldrons, a cuirass and something that looked like a pair of steel boots. I dreaded to think what the Moon Winnypore was and what it looked like. Price per item: three to six grand. I opened an auction in another window and compared the prices. Oh well, the Vets' had it all at least ten percent cheaper. Would be nice to buy up a million's worth of their stuff and auction it all off. One or two hundred grand easy profit, no sweat. But that would be a total loss of face and reputation, a ripoff to end all ripoffs. We didn't need that, did we?

I gave my inner greedy pig a clip round the ear to stop him looking at me with those imploring puppy eyes. Then I scanned the stats, envying my own bear, and began buying up. I also needed to get him a pair of armored pants, four earrings, two gold chains and something to fit on his teeth a bit like those horror fangs they sell in joke shops for overaged teenagers.

I ended up brainstorming it with Eric, after which we found all the items we needed—apart from the set of teeth which I had to buy from an auction for no less than eighteen grand. But the teeth were worth it, from the first incisor to the last canine.

Mithril Fangs of the Flesh Eater
Item class: Epic

Weapon type: for combat mount only
Damage 96-117, Speed 2.9, Durability 230\230
Effect 1: Hole Puncher. Gives 20% damage probability completely overriding enemy armor.
Effect 2: Flesh Eater. When mount deals a deadly blow, part of the slain creature is devoured, restoring 25% life to the item owner.

There you are, Teddy—not a cute and cuddly toy any more but a carnivorous flesh-eater. I just hoped the effect was purely virtual and that he wouldn't have to chomp on all sorts of unsavory things.

I didn't forget Eric's requests, either. Unfortunately, they had only one Veil so I was forced to give it to him, even though my inner greedy pig kept making suggestive faces. But they had two sets of Pegasus Horseshoes which, beside a speed bonus which wasn't anything in itself, also offered an impressive +170 to hits. I took both hoping that the storage officer wouldn't start wondering about how many legs my bear had.

Now! Hummungus was fully equipped, tenfold more impressive than his owner. His stats looked more than respectable:

Riding Mount: Hummungus (Red Bear)
Level: 26
Strength: 185
Armor: 140
Constitution: 95
Claw power: 77-91
Maul power: 127-162
Speed: 10 mph
Rider: 2
Weight-carrying capacity: 9250
Special abilities: Armor Bearer, Arms Carrier, Mule II, Transporter

My Teddy had become a force to be reckoned with. Not that it hadn't cost anything. Even in real life, seven thousand bucks was more than enough to turn any wuss into a rather dangerous dude complete with bulletproof vest, a shotgun and two handguns under his belt. Add to it a couple dozen tactics and shooting classes, and our bullied-up nerd turned into a potential wonder waffle. That's a wuss, but here I had a combat mount initially created to eliminate everything that moved.

Now I could finally think about myself. Having said that, I had a whole kindergarten to take care of. I opened my guild settings. Cryl was level 13. Lena was a level-11 ranger. I rummaged through my bag and found a whip I'd won in that personal dungeon ages ago. That had been a brilliant find: good job I hadn't given it to Bug as promised. Not because I was too tight or something—no, I'd just had too many things on my plate to remember about it.

Then I made a mental note of setting ten grand aside for each of my new clan members' equipment. Wiping my sobbing greedy pig's face, I assured him that the gear was a loan that later had to be returned to the clan storage. To bring the sniveling creature back to its senses, I set up a clan tax of 10% off all loot and on every sale. Having said that, I seemed to be the only person to suffer from it for the time being. There isn't much in the way of loot when you're level 10. Having said that, I was the only one with access to the clan treasury.

That was it. Now it was well and truly my turn. First of all, I wanted some of the thickest and richest elixirs they had. Even there, my appetite met with dire reality: the Vets kept their vials in a separate Alchemy vault that had nothing to do with their regular storage. And I didn't want to push my luck asking for yet another access. I really didn't need to add any more stones to the already hefty weight of my obligations to somebody else's—albeit admittedly friendly—clan.

So I switched over to the auctions. They offered a decent choice even though I couldn't see anything truly rare, like Unknown Skill Elixir. After giving it some thought, I finally bought four skill elixirs and twenty characteristic-boosting ones. That should last me three weeks, considering the cooldown. I was eighteen grand down but didn't regret a single penny of it. With a clinking of coins, the fluttering of the bag confirmed the receipt of my purchases. I drank two vials on the spot: the mint and the lime-and-honey ones.

I invested one talent point into something I'd long been drooling over but every time had to forgo it in favor of combat skills. A group teleport was something that neither Necro nor Death Knight had; what they did have was an advanced personal one that started at level 30 and allowed you to take your mount and your pet with you. And now I could finally acquire one, too. No more leaving my pets behind in dungeons! My inner greedy pig was still clutching at his heart every time he remembered the Plague Panther, all leveled up and dripping with abilities, that I'd had to abandon in that personal dungeon.

I habitually moved the one available characteristic point to Intellect. I'd done so every time, sharing all the points received between Intellect and Spirit at a ratio of two to one.

Right. What next? It was probably a good idea to set aside a particular sum I could afford. In hindsight, I should have done so before I'd even started buying. Never mind. Let's look at it in another way. I didn't really want to break into the million. Like a single large note in your wallet, it would resist being changed for the dubious pleasure of getting a few penny objects. I had to set aside another fifty grand for various operating costs I could already see coming. By doing a bit of some preschool subtraction, I was left with about eighty grand. Almost as much as I'd just spent on my own mount. Yeah, right.

What was worth keeping of the gear I already had? Honestly, considering the sum I had to play with, I really should upgrade everything I owned. I hadn't made any improvements to my gear since the tournament at the Vets' when it had been appraised at six grand. When you compared it to eighty, all that was left to do was gasp and crumble in a heap on the floor in silent ecstasy.

Still, there were a few things I wasn't prepared to swap quite yet. Staff of Dark Flame, Crown of the Overlord and Jangur's Battle Shield had to stay. The Crown I'd never sell, ever—I needed it as a unique tool for some specific tasks. But no one said I had to wear it all the time, so nothing prevented me from getting some new head gear provided I found something in the same league. The jewelry had to go to the clan vault, a.k.a. my bedside cabinet, at least until the clan finally got itself some kind of fixed abode.

I went back to the Vets' storage and started another search, this time only limiting it by class—Death Knight—and price—lowest first. Well, well. About three thousand search results, the nicest thingies smiling at me from their thirty-grand-plus positions. Looked like I was again forced to buy a few top items and clutter the remaining slots with their budget versions. Not that this particular strategy was without its fortes. It had served me well last time I'd done it.

I pondered over both alternatives. Still, it was probably better to buy the best I could afford. Was I prepared to spend my money on a ton of low-class gear so that one day I was faced with the fact that at level (say) 120, a poorly invested eight thousand bucks hadn't provided me with the advantages I'd hoped for? Much better to get a couple of true uber waffles that I could at some later date exchange for some epics and artifacts.

That brought me back to the initial scenario. Pets were my trump card. I sorted the search results by *Raises the summoned creature's level: highest first*. Just in case you wondered, Death Knights—who were the most deprived in this respect—also had access to the superest items. Not that I complained, really. Who was I, after all—a humble Death Knight coming to them cap in hand for a handful of bonuses for his sickly pet.

Panting from the effort, my inner greedy pig and myself studied the offers. I ran a similar search on the auctions: ten times more choice, but their prices tended to sneer rather than smile.

Soon I'd sighted the first uber goodie:

Renegade's Steel Boots
Item class: Unique
Effect 1: +110 to Armor, +25 to Intellect, +25 to Strength

Effect 2: Speeds up mana regeneration 4%.

Effect 3: The raised creature has a 50% chance of keeping one of its special skills.

Effect 4: +7 to the raised creature's level

Effect 5: -1 to your relationship with Races of Light

Effect 6: +1 to your relationship with Dark Races

Class restrictions: Only Death Knight

Race restrictions: Only races of Light

Jeez. These were my size, tailor made. Having said that, thirty-one thousand gold equaled three thousand bucks: basically, I was exchanging thirty grams of printed paper for a few thousand lines of program code. No, not like that. Was I going mad? There was no code to talk of anymore; nothing to do with dollars. I was behaving like a Russian immigrant in his new home country who'd convert every price tag he saw into rubles and either rub his hands with glee or grasp his head in despair. That wasn't the life I wanted for myself. Money had to pull its weight. It shouldn't collect dust; it had to grow, multiplying my loot and experience.

Now. The next item worth its while was a breastplate, also Death Knight restricted. Necros can't wear heavy armor and they can't count on strength bonuses. The breastplate looked intimidating:

Nazgul Backbone Breastplate.

Item class: Unique

Effect 1: +210 to Armor, +250 to Mana, +250 to Life, +10% to magic resistance.

Effect 2: In case of an attack by a stabbing weapon, there is a 15% chance of receiving a critical hit.

Effect 3: If the wearer's Life drops below 20%, the Aura of Fear will cover all beings within 10 paces, paralyzing them for 2.5 sec.

Effect 4: +6 to the raised creature's level

Effect 5: Sends fragment of bone flying whenever the wearer sustains damage, injuring all enemies within 3 paces and dealing them 40 pts. damage.

Class restrictions: only Death Knight

I mulled over the stats comparing them to those of other suitable objects, finally coming to the conclusion that the breastplate was definitely the coolest of the available. I had to buy it. Thirty-five grand down. I wiped away the sweat. I'd never had the chance to spend such amounts so quickly before. Fifteen thousand bucks in the last hour, the mind boggles. Having said that, easy come, easy go. There were plenty of castles still left, LOL.

I also laid an eye on a bracelet which wasn't particularly impressive, just +3 to pet's level, but being jewelry, it had attracted the attention of a host of other Necros who'd forced the price sky high. Never mind. It could wait. Especially because my reserve was running low. What was it I'd said about low-class gear?

For the next two hours, I pawed over my gold choosing budget versions of the remaining equipment. They wouldn't last, anyway, so I'd have to replace them one day.

With every delivery, my bag got tangibly heavier. Finally, I was done. I spread the remaining pennies thin over numerous clothes and jewelry slots. That was it, enough.

I changed into my new acquisitions and hopped around a bit, testing them. There was some clinking and clanking here and there but not much, despite the hundred fifty pounds of steel hung on me and another seventy in my bag. God bless the game physics! With my strength numbers, I didn't even feel anything lifting under 220 pounds. Above that, it went straight into overload.

Almost ready. I PM'd Cryl to let him know I had to leave for a couple days in order to complete a quest and could be reached by PM if needs be. I warned him about the contents of my bedside cabinet, asking him to take good care of Lena, accept her into our group, invest in some nice fat buffs and get leveling.

I walked downstairs to the portal hall past a few stationary patrols posted at the castle's key points. A couple of women and guards recoiled, shrinking out of my way, still wound up by Frag's security drills even though the threat level had now been lowered to yellow. And there I walked, a ghostly figure adorned with the Lord of the Dead's black crown, the breastplate's yellow ribs sticking out, a tiny piece of dark amber pulsating over my heart. I had used the precious gem to decorate my admittedly unaesthetic breastplate, filling one of the three available enhancement slots which incidentally had also boosted my Dark spells. It was probably a good idea to remove the breastplate in polite society, for fear of scaring everyone shitless.

I quickly arranged for a teleport to a small town about a hundred miles away from the castle. Its name didn't say much to me: my choice had been random. The portal popped open, taking me there. Another three minute wait in order to arrange for another transfer to their nearest town. Rinse and repeat. Fifteen minutes, six teleports and a hundred fifty gold later, I completed my little loose-end tying-up operation, ending up at the already-familiar square in the Original City.

When I'd been there last, I'd made a mental note of an imposing shop sign that competed with nearby bank logos. *Thror's Gem House.* I dreaded to think how much it cost them to keep a high-end edifice like that in the city's main square.

The massive door opened easily. Gear wheels turned, initiating a system of counterweights. Needless to say, everything worked without so much as a squeak. In place of an ordinary shop bell, I was met by the sound of a miniature gold hammer striking a silver anvil. Its significance dawned on me when I saw the goldsmith's apprentice in charge of greeting customers. A dwarf! The first ever dwarf I'd met in this world!

We both froze, studying each other. The dwarf stared at me with surprise, seeing a High Elf in a Drow city. His eyes widened as he took in my friendly status and the Mark of the House of Night. And once he noticed the piece of amber on my chest, he seemed to lose all contact with reality.

"With due respect," I patted his shoulder to wake him up, "I'd like to see Master Thror."

The dwarf startled, coming to. "I'm afraid, the Father of the House doesn't receive visitors any more," he cast me a guilty look.

I raised a puzzled eyebrow.

"I'll go and ask," the dwarf hurried to add. "He might make an exception... exclusively for you."

He disappeared, leaving me wondering who it was I was about to see. I needed a goldsmith, not some patriarch mascot figure.

I couldn't have been more wrong. The reclusive House founder turned out to be a brow-knitted giant—as far as dwarves went, of course. His bulging muscles could have belonged to a blacksmith not a jeweler, his eyes squinting at you as if through a helmet visor. An enormous pole-axe on the wall hinted at his fine military past.

If he'd read my appearance better than his apprentice, it didn't show. Not a muscle twitched on his poker face. "What can I do for you, young Elf?"

"I'm not going to waste your time, Sir. Let's move straight to the point. I've managed to lay my hands on a few items allowing me to build a Travel Altar. My limited skills don't allow me to embark on a project of this scale which is why I've come to your shop as it's the best in town. Think you could help me?"

Now his eyebrows did twitch. "Do you mean you have in your possession an item that used to belong to a God of Light, boy? So now you want to make a Small Altar? Or," he added just a hint of sarcasm to his voice, "you just happen to have some sacred relics to build a Big Raid Altar?"

"Not quite," I reached into my bag and produced two dark fragments.

The dwarf swung round, grabbed some paperwork from the desk and covered the stones with it. Then he raised his hand and made a complex signal with his fingers. I barely heard the hidden gunslots closing. He definitely wasn't your cute and cuddly grandfather type.

Thror froze, listening intently, then nodded, satisfied. He removed the paper and lovingly ran his hand over the stones.

"My apologies are in order, Sir Laith," he mumbled. "Technically, our clan belongs to the branch of Light. Not that we really know who we're supposed to worship there. Their clerics have no problem accepting our gold, but when it comes to our requests to create a temple dedicated to the God of goldsmiths and jewelers, they keep saying they don't have sufficiently powerful artifacts! And they've just used the recently acquired God's Heart to summon Asclepius—the God of physicians—and add him to their Pantheon. Asclepius, for God's sake! What were his parents thinking about, giving him a name like that!"

I nodded, soaking up the precious snippets of information. Seeing as I'd already been up to my ears in Gods' dealings, I had to keep my eye on the ball and learn all I could on the subject. I needed to know every detail, from their Gods' names and jobs to Venus' bra size if only she existed in our world.

The dwarf was already rolling the stones in his hand, studying them and analyzing their stats. Was he performing a spectral analysis of the reflected light? Or just admiring them? Neither would have surprised me.

"This is a complex and challenging task," he finally said. "It requires the level of a Famed Master in Goldsmithing. There're only three of them in town."

He was talking up his prices, the bastard. "I do hope you're one of them," I returned. "And if not, nothing prevents me from going to the birthplace of all true masters, the Kingdom Under the Mountain. Plenty of portals around."

The dwarf flinched, poker-faced no more. "They'll take them off you— and they just might allow you to keep your head. Or they could distract you with prayers and rituals while their masters fight for the order behind the scenes. It's not every day that a Famed Master lands a job that can level up his goldsmith skill."

I smiled: it hadn't taken much for this pick-wielding operator to give himself away. "So you see, Sir, it's in our interests you get the job, isn't it? Having said that, laying my hands on these fragments has drained my finances. Then again, knowing the advantages it could bring you, I'm quite prepared to give the job to you for the very modest kickback of a hundred thousand grand."

The dwarf fell silent, dumbfounded. Why not? I had better break the proverbial mold before he charged me full whack. Finally, he regained his composure and roared with laughter, slapping the desk.

"You're a joker, you really are! I very nearly believed you! I almost showed you to the door," he said with a hint of irony in his voice.

I smiled against my will, confirming my status as a joker. Thror opened a massive writing cabinet which contained, instead of office supplies, a small barrel of something definitely alcoholic. The dwarf tapped the barrel's fat slats, listening to the resonant echo, then poured two mugs and banged them onto the desk.

"Let's share a small cup of Dwarven Extra Dry. No good discussing a two-hundred-grand order dying of thirst!"

I choked. "Pardon me! I don't need an altar of solid gold. It has to be as light and inconspicuous as possible. Ideally it should look marginally better than a campfire tripod. Otherwise every Tom, Dick and Harry will come running wondering what I have here. So I suggest we share the expense: the altars for me, the experience for you."

It was his turn to choke. "I don't make kitchen utensils! I'm a goldsmith! And of all things, I don't work for free! Having said that," his glare clouded over, then glistened again, "you, Sir Laith, bear the Mark of the Fallen One. It stands to reason you have met. And the fact that you have the stones tells a lot to somebody with my experience. Very well. I'll make you the altars you want free of charge, provided you bring me a small vial of the Fallen One's blood."

I jumped. "You don't mess around, do you? I don't think the Fallen One will like it when he finds out that his blood has become a mail-order trade tool to save some miserable ten grand."

We dedicated the next couple hours to this friendly banter. Finally, both of us suitably hammered, we struck a deal agreeing on sixty grand. Too much, dammit. I signed the contract and gave him his fifty percent advance, after which the dwarf reached into the cabinet for a bottle bleached with age.

"Dragon's Tears, forty years old," he explained proudly, pulling out the tight cork, as a Dwarven maiden carried in a trayful of food.

We downed a shot glass each. It did bring tears to your eyes. Had to be at least 120%. Pleased with the effect, the dwarf decided to show the clueless youngster how to chase it down properly. Taking a sausage off the tray, he grabbed the tongs and pulled a glowing ember out of the fire. Bringing it to his mouth, he exhaled, his alcohol-filled breath enveloping the sausage in a green flame, filling the room with all the smells of a German beerhouse.

"Dragon Breath," the dwarf commented, proud. "With a bit of practice, it can burn a hole through a piece of wood half an inch thick."

He was a piece of work, was this gray-bearded master. He asked me for a week to complete the order, explaining it away by the necessity of having to fly to the Kingdom Under the Mountain to pick up some rare ingredients.

We parted almost as friends. Swaying, I walked out of the building. My head could have done with a bit of clearing after his exercise in hospitality. I needed to find a café that served some really strong coffee and study a map of the city. My next port of call had to be the mercenaries' guild. No way I was going to venture into the Dead Lands alone. I needed a good backup.

The next day, if luck had it, I would see the walls of the legendary First Temple.

Chapter Eight

From the online newspaper The Daily AlterWorld:

This is weird. The sixth empty dungeon in the past week. The interesting thing is that they all belong to various newb locations situated near large settlements. The last one was the Gnoll Hill, a mere mile away from the City of Light. This low-level dungeon now lies empty, deserted by all the mobs that used to populate it. The throne in the throne room appears to have been removed, the walls of the room itself are covered in obscenities written in blood-color paint.

See screenshot 14: We'll be back you hairless coyotes!

The AlterWorld administration offers no explanation on this phenomenon. All requests to add new low-level locations are met with vague promises without mentioning any particular deadlines.

* * *

The guild building was overpowering. A fortress within the city: its thick walls gaping with gunslits, its fat towers bristling with the steel needles of the ballistas. Two enormous golems guarded the entrance—projecting more the guild's wealth and influence to the world rather than really guarding anything. Each level 230, how awesome was that? I even took the trouble of looking golem-building up in Wiki. Oh well, it doesn't hurt to dream. My naïve hope of getting one of those as a pet one day and building my own zombie platoon was shattered before it even got off the ground, unable to survive the clash with harsh reality. Only a large clan could afford to keep one of those. To get access to golem building, you had to level up alchemy, goldsmithing and forging skills to Grand Master levels. And the prices! To build one could cost you a small fortune: to get some idea of the costs, place your creation onto the scale and keep balancing it with ingots of silver until you weep. And that was only the beginning of a long and winding road.

I stood there gawking at them, estimating their weight, then using my fingers and toes to convert it into silver and gold losing a few zeroes on my way. It was a lot. I patted a golem's warm mithril thigh and stepped into the dark gateway.

A short tunnel led into a gateway tower. Portcullises bared their steel teeth over both entrance and exit. The many arrowslits and suspicious openings overhead promised a bloodbath to whoever dared fight their way through there. Good job I went there personally instead of hiring staff at the mercs' marketplace. My potentially eternal lifespan meant I might have to build, defend and storm this sort of fortification one day.

The inner court was small but welcoming. It was surprisingly crowded—mainly by what seemed to be mercs waiting to be hired. The narrow space between the keep and the inner wall housed a couple of cafés, a pub, two permanently busy combat arenas and a number of shop signs offering supplies and gear repair among other things. The mercs must have let their guard down, I decided as I eyed the close space. During the first siege, all this razzamatazz was going to burn happily, getting in the way of the already-miserable defenders.

The keep's gates stood invitingly open. I walked through. The ground floor housed the actual gaming content: guild masters, traders, coaches and other miscellaneous NPCs. The first floor and above were rented out to the players who apparently had a good manager and an equally good interior designer. The decor was rather businesslike going on medieval, replete with information desk, soft couches in the waiting area, consultants' cubicles and management offices. All of it busy, all in full play. The money flow—which I enviously estimated at two pounds of gold per minute—ran through the marketplace, leaving in its wake a slight residue of guild taxes that aimed to maintain the local grandeur.

I voiced my rather modest request and was escorted to a cubicle: soft inviting chairs and a wall of fragrant plants that shielded us from the rest of the room. The babble of an artificial brook helped one relax and part with his money. I didn't even notice the consultant at first. He was perched on a couch amidst the greenery next to a side table loaded with all sorts of tasty morsels. This had to be a real-world paid employee with a primitive 3D connection—what perma player would agree to act out the miserable part of an office rat? It still didn't explain his choice of a goblin as character, of all things. Despite his hilarious appearance, the green creature listened to me with dignity, nodding in all the right places like a seasoned reporter.

Finally, he summed it up, "So you need a cover of five, capable of handling two or three mobs up to level 150. Objective: accompany you to the Dead Lands. The setup is clear. Now the fees. A team of five level-140 and above will cost you seven thousand. The minimum contract term is twenty-four hours. As for the schedule: the portal city nearest to those parts is Aquinus, a hundred and forty miles from your destination. Beyond it lie the Frontier Lands. A savage area, virtually unpopulated. Lots of feral monsters, one-off lairs and dungeons, high chances of running into trouble. Even though you've overestimated potential mobs' levels, I agree that in this case you cannot be too careful. If I could suggest anything at all logistics-wise, I'd recommend the Ferrymen clan. We have a good working relationship with their representative. You probably know that one top-level wizard can store up to fifty teleport points in his memory so between them, they've got our cluster all covered—apart from the Frontier, but at least their clan guarantees the minimum of one teleport point per thousand square miles. This should at least halve your travel times-"

"Why would I need it?" I interrupted the flow of his pitch. "Why would I want to pay for any extras if the minimum contract term is the double of what I need? I had actually hoped to hire a group for twelve hours, not more. Having said that, I've got an idea. You think you could ask the Ferrymen about the location of the nearest teleport point?"

The goblin cheered up, enthusiastically nodding his agreement, then started dictating something into an open communications channel. He had to be getting his cut from the Wizards. Having said that, I had better remember the details of the offer. I could use them at a later date.

The goblin surfaced. "You're in luck! Apparently, the only track to the Dead Lands is blocked by the Bone Castle. And as it's quite a landmark, they couldn't overlook it and marked the nearest port point on the transport map. You only need to cover twenty miles: an hour and a half at your mount's speed. Treble it to include any emergencies, it's still only five hours. A group portal costs three hundred gold. What do you think?"

He leaned forward, his ear tufts quivering, his moist nose probing the air. A funny race, really. "Why not? On one condition: seeing as I'm obliged to pay for twenty-four hours, they'll have to work for their money. We'll start with eighteen hours of power leveling—power leveling myself, I mean—a full cover, top performance and a five-strong support group. That leaves us six hours to travel. How about that?"

"I'm afraid, it doesn't quite work like that. The twenty-four hour contract provides for seven hours of sleep and two one-hour meal breaks. That leaves you with fifteen hours to use as you see fit. In case of any eventualities preventing you from complying, an hour of overtime is paid at 10%."

I winced. All nice and logical but nitpicking any way you looked at it. "Agreed. Food and sleep is every soldier's sacred right."

The goblin rubbed his little paws and started typing away. "Considering the change in the assignment's profile, I'd recommend the following lineup: a cleric for buffs and healing, an enchanter for more buffs and mana transfusion, a rogue and a wizard as cover and a tank to take aggro. This would allow you to save on meditation and healing times and squeeze as much intense farming as you can in the contractual period."

I held my breath in anticipation. "How far can they level me up? Have they done it before?"

The goblin sat up, the pride ringing in his voice. "I'd recommend Zena's team from the Sullen squad. She's got a bit of an attitude, that one, but her team know what they're doing. They'll pull 'em good, for sure. They won't idle around. Your DpS is your only problem: that's the amount of damage per second you can generate. The rest they'll all take care of: mana, mob pulling, healing, and finishing them off after reaching 50%. You could do one level per hour, I suppose. More if you have some top gear and a decent pet. I'd suggest you check out our gear rental. I'm sure you'll find something there you can use. They want a deposit of 100% though, or level 150-plus guarantors. The rental costs 1% per twenty-four hours of the item's average price in the cluster."

Jesus. That was an eye-opener. I was still a total noob with no hope of ever redeeming myself. I'd only been talking with that guy for half an hour and already I'd learned some useful things like the existence of the Ferrymen and equipment rental. The only thing that could possibly excuse me was my desperately tight deadline. I'd only had eight days between my initial decision to go perma and my pressing of the login button, including the time spent on looking it all up and laying my hands on a jailbreak chip. I hadn't done so badly, after all. Shame I'd had to waste my early days on sorting out some local problems, but even that pointed to one undeniable fact: here I was still alive—as opposed to the real world where my sorry ass was actively involved in the process of buying the farm. I found it symbolic that Mom had employed the most energetic language refusing to unplug the capsule. I understood her feelings, of course, even if personally I entertained no nostalgia for my wasted thirty-year-old body. The village-boy euphoria of absolute health was still new for me. It forced me from my bed every morning filling me with a desire to laugh and move, flaring my nostrils in the wake of every provocatively-undressed Elven girl.

I shook my head clear of my reminiscing. "Okay. Zena it is. I don't think I'll be needing your rentals. My gear is good enough. I couldn't take another database-browsing today."

"Excellent. The portal reservation is in your name. The wizard on duty will wait for your signal to arrive at the portal hall. The group is currently on standby status three and will be at your disposal in an hour unless you're willing to pay the optional express rate previewed in the contract."

"I don't," I dismissed his offer. "I can wait no problem—what's half an hour between friends. I think I'll have a little tour around your place in the meantime. I love it here."

The goblin nodded proudly. "Custom made by *Shining, the* AI interior design studio," he paused, waiting for my reaction. Apparently, this *Shining* place had to be It. I pursed my lips and tut-tutted, faking an aficionado.

The goblin beamed and tapped the Send button. "Here's your bill. Seven thousand three hundred. Excluding tip," he added in a low voice, looking down.

I nodded, opening my Inbox, and paid the bill in one click adding one percent for his expert advice.

He beamed again. "Thank you," he rose and offered me his tiny paw, making it apparent the session was over. "I'll be happy to help you on any future occasions. You've got my email so feel free to contact me any time even if I'm offline. I've got a real-world forwarding service active twenty-four-seven."

I gingerly shook his tiny sensitive fingers and blurted, "If you don't mind my asking... why a goblin?"

I could see he knew what I meant. His face browned. Was it how he blushed—red color mixed with the original green? How sure was I that goblins' blood was indeed red?

Finally, he spoke, "This is our company policy. To diminish distraction factors and office dating."

As if on cue, a head-turning Elfa from the Information desk hip-swayed past us, escorting a client to a consultant's cubicle. The aroma of violets, a tiny scrap of lace and silk, a handful of diamonds and a whole lot of exposed velvety golden skin. We followed the dreamlike creature with hungry eyes. The goblin gulped and heaved a sigh.

"I think I know what you mean," I put all my sympathy into my words and gave his tiny paw another shake—this time wholeheartedly.

I spent the next hour in a cozy little café perched up next to a training arena. This was the best way to spend what little available time I had: basking in the warm sun sipping coffee and munching on eclairs, filling my immortal memory with combat strategies by class, including the mercs' names and a few of their personal boxes of combat tricks. Very useful. I got so engrossed in it I hadn't even noticed the Inbox flashing at me. Oops. Three unread messages—for the last twelve minutes, I'd been enjoying myself at the rate of four hundred sixty gold an hour. Shit. I jumped up and trotted off to the Departure Hall to meet the impatiently awaiting Zena and Co.

The large oval room was lined with comfortable little couches seating a couple dozen diverse people, from trolls and orcs to halflings and goblins. So that's where all the races came to mingle, apparently. It wasn't all elves as I imagined in my newb location.

I scanned the crowd trying to make out my team. I didn't need to look long. Ramming through the room like an aircraft carrier group through the sea, a female pod of four goblins and a troll was already heading straight for me. Oh well. If a girl wanted to play a troll, there had to be somebody responsible for it. What kind of social protest was that, for chrissakes? A female merc team at its most absurd and ungainly. Was it AlterWorld's emo trying to be funny?

The female Troll came closer. My eyes were at one level with her powerful chest protected by half-inch thick armor.

I stepped back and looked up. "Zena?"

"You blind or what, blondie?" I heard a squeak from below. A female goblin's steel boot gave my knee cap a rather sensitive kick.

She—Zena, apparently—stepped forward, shaking her head. "All you men are alike, really. Stupid as old boots. All you can think of is a pair of boobs. No one's interested in a girl's psyche. What are you staring at? Come on, General, the team's awaiting your orders," she glared at me with sarcastic interest, as if expecting this old boot to speak.

All that time, I was mentally swearing, wishing every ill on the goblin consultant's green head. Sullen squad, he said? Very well, then.

"Right!" wincing from their sarcastic grins, I cleared my throat and said in my most imposing voice, "Enough of your feminist trash! What are your names, girls?"

The rosy smiles waned on the warrior goblins' mugs. They exchanged puzzled glances. So they didn't like me breaking the mold, then?

The leader was the first to regain her composure. "Zena's team, all-female Sullen squad, number 18 in the independent mercs' ratings. Levels 140 plus, gear unique plus. On twenty-four hour hire until o-fourteen hundred hours tomorrow. Today's agenda: rushing the customer from level 52. I recommend the Oasis location, it's teeming with amphibians levels 60 to 100. Freckle Face will port us there, she's our wizard, Freckles for short as it's quite a mouthful in the heat of battle. First we need the Ferryman to jump us to the Frontier, then Freckles will set up a navigational beacon so that tomorrow she can jump us from there herself. Now what next? I can see you've already met our warrior? Yes, Bomba is very likeable, her boobs certainly are," she grinned.

She pointed to a small goblin maiden all kitted out in complex leather armor, her two swords hanging recklessly from two steel rings on her hips. The naked blades emitted a burgundy sheen, sparkling occasionally. At the time, the maiden was ignoring us, engrossed in a heated discussion with some merc over the pros and cons of the latest trend in power leveling, Savage-style. Whoever Savage was and whatever advantages his modus operandi could offer, I didn't have the slightest idea.

"This is Whizz, our rogue. A mage killer. Note the swords. I don't think you've recognized them. Those are Vampire's Fangs, both of them, mind you. There're only seven full sets of them in the whole cluster."

The last one was a quiet enchanter chick going by the moniker of Charmsy. God only knew how she'd ended up in that bunch. She stayed behind the others' backs, blushing every time somebody paid attention to her.

I clapped my hands, asking for silence. "Attention, ladies! Let's get this show on the road. Once we jump to the Frontier, the ferryman's job's done. Then it's Zena's turn to give orders until further notice. I warn you all, I've never had to hire anyone to level me before, so I apologize for any blunders. Ready, everyone? Off we go."

With a long spell and an almighty pop, we teleported to the location.

The bright blue sky spread overhead, the white-hot ball of the sun blazing against the back of my head. Good job we had to start out the next morning. As our wizard got busy setting up a navigational beacon, I had a good look around. The scenery reminded me of the African savannah with its vast open spaces interspersed with rocky outcrops and formidable canopied trees.

A massive mountain ridge loomed on the horizon. I checked the map: that's right, that was exactly where I had to go. The savannah was anything but empty, dotted with single figures beelining in every direction. About half a mile from us, a pride of aggro lions lounged in the shade of a tree. With any luck, we should make it past them.

"All done!" Freckles reported.

Zena glanced at me. I nodded: it was her turn to give orders. She gave me a faint smile. You never knew, we could make a good team.

The portal to Oasis will open in 5... 4... 3...

Bang!

Oh. The location was different but the white-hot plasma ball was still blazing overhead.

"Report!" Zena ordered, studying the area.

The rogue answered first. Apparently, she was the one responsible for reconnaissance and counter PK measures.

"There're two hundred seventy players in the location. Roughly one PK group—the Pratz, low level, no threat for us, plus three singles we're not sure of, all three on the unofficial black list, each already implicated in a few unmotivated attacks. Chat activity: standard. Everything OK," she added in a calmer voice.

"Buffs for all! For the team, type four, anti PK. For the client, type six: DpS, plus you can add whatever you have as magic resists, all kinds. Make sure we don't lose him, that would be a shame to end all shame."

Then she saw Hummungus who'd just appeared next to me, followed by the summoned pet. "And throw in some buffs for his critters too, for hits and damage."

She made a few steps toward the hissing teeth-baring demon and studied the infernal monster. "Who are you, dude?" she shook her head, uncomprehending. "You wouldn't believe it if they told you, a level 52 Death Knight with a level 65 pet. Either you're worth more than a Bentley or I just don't get it."

I gave her a wink, trying to look as cool as a cucumber. Which wasn't easy. Level sixty goddamn five! I was my own train! In his new gear, Hummungus looked truly brutal and as dangerous as a busload of AK-47s. This was going to be a ride!

Buffed up like a power house, I felt impregnable.

"Mana at sixty," Zena reported for the team's sake.

"Seventy," Charmsy echoed.

"Whizz? Make a quick area check, nose to the ground, security evaluation. Give us a couple minutes, then you can pull the first croc."

Zena turned to me. "That's it, then. We're at the Oasis. Sort of miniature Nile delta. The further down the river, the tougher the mobs. Reptiles and other water beasties, mainly: crocs, hippos, a few gators."

"Excellent! See you later, alligator," I waved my hand at the Oasis.

"In a while, crocodile. One last thing: you'd better keep an eye on the Roc."

I looked around, searching for any Gibraltar-shaped cliff.

"The bird," she corrected me. "Level 100-plus. It comes hunting a couple times a day. She can take you out without you even noticing it."

I nodded.

"Now for the pull," she went on. "Whizz will keep increasing the pull speed until she feels your limit. Try to aim for about 50% hits, the rest we'll take care of, you get the XP. The ideal time/XP ratio is when the pulled mobs are 10% above you—15% even, given your critters. In our case, it's level 60 give or take. That's it, quit yapping, here she comes with a gator."

Indeed, the little goblin chick was already scampering toward us pursued by a huge croc. Rotting weeds and fountains of sand burst from under its massive clawed feet. Gosh, I hated those yellow-eyed monsters. Good job I wasn't a warrior. At least I didn't have to step in the creature's way blocking its access to the group's soft underbelly: the cloth-armor casters.

Whizz rushed past us. The croc was only a few paces away when Freckles stood up and cast a spell. Powerful roots burst out of the sand, entangling the creature's feet.

"Don't sleep," Zena poked me in the shoulder. "He's all yours. Whizz is off to get a new one."

I shook myself free from my stupor. Okay, so this was a croc, big and stinking of fish, so what? Teddy, demon, attack! The still-restrained croc growled happily at seeing a proper opponent. He sunk his teeth into the demon's hip. The creature showered it with blows, Teddy's mithril claws tearing through the croc's hide. The stench of fish was overpowering. The waves of uprooted sand lashed us like a tropical storm: three bulldozers locked in combat on a dune top. In silent agreement we stepped back, spitting out the sand.

Zena cringed, sniffing her glove stinking of fish guts. "Gosh! I'd already forgotten how shitty it is out here!"

I nodded. "My kingdom for a pair of ballistic goggles! Freckles, do us all a favor and control them a bit further away, at fifteen paces or so, would you?"

While we recovered, the croc's life had sunk into the yellow zone. The restive silent Bomba reached into her backpack and produced an impressive club of meteorite iron studded with diamond shards molten into its impact surface.

Bang! Crit! Corpse!

Wow. Having said that, the croc was all of a hundred levels below her. You would hardly expect a drawn-out combat at these odds. She had just swatted him, end of story. My pets were full of life, having barely lost 10% hits. Which was also quite predictable, really: the demoness' level was higher than the croc's with Teddy not too far below.

Aha, there was Whizz bringing a new customer. I immobilized the arriving anaconda and set off both pets, casting a couple of Life Absorptions. The rogue chick ran past us and turned round, skidding in the deep sand, then headed back to the water edge for more clients to stuff.

"Bah, it stinks," she dropped sarcastically as she ran past, "has something just died here?"

Followed by some hearty f-words, she laughed happily and hopped over the dunes, reaching for her throwing knife. Things got rocking!

Four hours later, we took a break. By then, we'd already advanced more than half a mile down river. I'd surprised them by my XP building: one level every forty minutes. The pet had long since been raised again so now we were sitting next to an enormous hippo, his bulk frightening the pants off occasional players who tried to approach us. That's right, I'd allowed the girls to do their own little bit on the side so they made a small announcement location-wide, offering their buffing and resurrecting services. They charged a good rate for those but in the absence of competition, they could ask for whatever they wanted. The way it was going, they would make at least a grand by evening—a nice little bonus for them. It didn't really affect my leveling, we had plenty of mana, we'd had no emergencies even though by now Whizz alone couldn't always deliver and had to occasionally turn to Bomba for a successful pull. Zena made sure no one dropped below 40% in case we had to deal with an unexpected pull or a PK. The loot wasn't much to write home about. Lots of meat and pelts, a few gems and various bits of gear—probably, whatever was left of the less lucky players who'd tried to swim across in full armor with a double-handed sword on their backs. I could, in theory, get about four hundred gold out of it toward my operational costs.

My girls turned out to be foresighted and domesticated. In their bottomless backpacks they even had a few sitting rugs, a spotless white tablecloth and a good dozen pots filled with various edibles. We had a hearty lunch and a bit of a siesta as the girls talked between themselves, discussing very ungirly things like the pros and cons of spears as a close-combat weapon. We all seemed to be getting along. They didn't drag their break out until the last, so in less than forty minutes the well-oiled wheels of our conveyor belt were rolling again.

Half an hour before midnight, I dinged for the last time that day. 65!

"Congrats," the tired girls managed.

I nodded. "Thanks, ladies. Great job. I'll be seeing crocs for a week now."

Whizz grinned. "They will, too, after the genocide you committed."

"Not without your help. Freckles, you can port the team back now. Having said that, know of a decent hotel to spend the night?"

"Everything's been taken care of," Zena answered. "There're some nice apartments in the mercs guild. Third floor. They're not cheap, but that's not your problem. Consider it our gift to you. We can appreciate generosity."

I didn't say no. No need to disappoint good girls like those. "I can, too. Okay, tomorrow eight a.m., meet you all in the guild hall. We'll buff ourselves up and off to the Frontier we go. The Dead Lands are waiting. I've got unfinished business there, ladies, that's the whole thing..."

Chapter Nine

Memorandum (excerpt):

Alternate checks have supported the information received from independent sources about China's latest short-term development trends regarding the recent perma mode effect.

1. Their building of an underground perma mode facility is nearing completion. Intended to hold 200,000 FIVR capsules, this class-A sensitive installation is protected by an efficient anti-aircraft canopy and is capable of withstanding a strike from a 10 kiloton tactical warhead.

2. The production of unlicensed cloned versions of iVirt4 capsules has been launched at a classified assembly line aiming to produce 4,000 capsules every 24 hours.

3. A strictly classified Expansion program aims to establish China's domination and control of the more promising virtual worlds. In the light of the latest confirmed independence trends, we deem it vital to develop a similar program of our own.

4. Their new confidential software, Insanity aims to spread terror in the worlds chosen for research or immigration purposes. Over 150,000 mentally ill patients from all over China have been handpicked and are ready to be dropped into the aforementioned worlds. Several hacker groups will be waiting on standby, ready to take over the worlds' login servers within a few hours if required.

5. They have created a seven-level secret program entitled The Great Cleansing aiming to conduct the step-by-step digitalization of the following population segments: criminal elements, political unreliables, long term convicts, the terminally ill, the handicapped and, finally, all sections of the population unfit to work. The final figure of the individuals chosen for the program exceeds 80 million.

All of the above is the subject of deep concern. The success of the aforementioned programs would enable China to dominate not only the virtual worlds (if we can still call them so) but also the world as we know it.

* * *

The teleport made our ears pop as it ejected our A-team under the Frontier's striking sun. Fortunately, the teleport point was up the hill where the breeze fanned us against the heat and the visibility allowed us to survey the area before hitting the road.

"WTF?" I heard Bomba's voice full of indignation. We swung round, staring at an old road skirting the hill several hundred feet away from us. A column of prisoners dusty beyond all recognition dragged their feet toward the depths of the Frontier.

Behind me I heard the sounds of a spell being cast: Eagle Vision x10, immediately allowing the group to zoom in on the approaching procession.

"Gnolls," Zena concluded.

"Yeah," added Whizz. "Tiny. Not one over level 30."

I peered at the crowd loaded with their meager possessions: messenger gnolls, overseers, warriors, shamans... It reminded me of some WW2 footage: the hot summer of 1941, fugitives fleeing their homes, trying to shake off the creeping front line. Warily I looked up, searching the clear sky for any cross-decorated wings eclipsing the sun, descending deathlike onto the helpless stream of refugees.

"Fancy a bit of genocide?" the Troll patted her club with a shovel-shaped hand.

I startled at the scary accuracy of her suggestion. "No, don't. Let them go. Don't know what kind of exodus that is. Could be some community event. In any case, they're not an army. They're refugees. We're not animal enough to assault them."

Bomba's face blackened. I thought at first she was furious, ready to squash her employer like a bug. But the next moment she slung her club over her back and even wiped her hands on her thick leather pants for some reason. Only then I understood it was the troll's black blood flushing her face. The girl had blushed.

The gnolls noticed us. The column stirred, falling into formation. The more battle-worthy gnolls were lining up, shielding casters, gatherers, messengers and other more rare gnoll specimens with their bodies.

"How naïve can they be," Freckles dropped sarcastically.

A gnoll officer emerged from the crowd, waving a shred of something white in one hand and clutching a handful of arrows in the other. Stooping, he ran uphill toward us. Surprisingly, he was well suited for running uphill, dropping on all fours and leaping, pushing with his front legs. I shuddered. Almost like a werewolf.

Soon he stood before us, panting, his tongue hanging out. Waving his white rag, he barked something, then dropped it at our feet. Demonstratively he broke the arrows on his knee, then threw them to the ground in the same way.

Zena turned to look at me. "Need an interpreter, boss?"

I shook my head. "Not really. Everything's quite clear. They're asking us for peace. They don't want to fight."

As if understanding my words, the gnoll glared at me, barking a long sentence that ended in whimpering followed by a threatening growl.

Zena shook her head. "For a fugitive he's a bit too forward, don't you think?"

I shrugged. "Who can understand their logic? He could be trying to assure us that fighting the weak is not kosher. Then once they level up a bit, we might be looking at a good scrap."

"Oh really?" she raised her eyebrows. "You think that's supposed to make us feel better?"

"Oh well, this is pure conjecture. Right, sheath your weapons, show him your empty hands, then turn your backs on him. It's not exactly our direction, anyway."

We nodded to the watchful gnoll and performed the requested motions. Then we summoned our mounts and trotted down the slope. Just another two hours, and I'd finally see those mystical Dead Lands.

Yeah, right. Dream on.

The first half-hour went rather quietly. Small game scattered in front of us, trying either to flee, bury itself in the sand or otherwise pretend it had never been there. The bigger non-aggressive ones followed us with their puppy eyes while the real predators huddled up between rocks, swallowing their hungry drool—we were way out of their league. As their levels grew with every mile, soon it became our turn to give a wide berth to a pack of coyotes, squeezing our way between a pride of lions and an inviting but birdless oasis circled by giant level-100 vultures perched in nearby trees. As I eyed the welcoming shadow, Zena shook her head. With her experience she knew better, of course.

Soon we made our first unscheduled stop by the iridescent mouth of a cave that glowed in a rocky outcrop. A pop-up kindly informed us we had just discovered a one-off dungeon: A Mature Manticore's Lair. The word *mature* meant that the dungeon hadn't been discovered for over a month allowing its mobs to gain in power and treasures. The girls grew restless, casting those buttery pleading glances at me. So much for your feminism, sweethearts. The moment you need to manipulate your man, you use your eye artillery with the best of them.

"Sorry, ladies, we've got work to do. Just bookmark the place or let's wait a few minutes until Freckles sets up a beacon. Once we're finished, you can come back here and pull their tails off all you want. I'm not going to lay claim to that."

Zena was the first to come to. "Now! Stop huddling together like a bunch of greenhorns! We don't need no compact group targets! Whizz, I thought you were our point? Off you go and circle round the group, then! Freckles, set up the beacon, then join Bomba at point."

She turned to me, faking some semblance of regret on her sly goblin face. "Sorry, dude. Greed got the better of us. Mature one-off dungeons are a rare find. Usually they get mindlessly purged already a few hours after their discovery. When a strong guild manages to lay their hands on one, they would sometimes let it mature for a couple of weeks to allow the mobs to fatten up, giving time for XP and loot bonuses to grow. It's non-linear growth, mind you. Those rangers who were lucky enough to discover it *and* keep it under wraps often hire mercs to help them purge it. And between mercs, we have the habit of sharing our war stories—and discussing our clients' loot. I tell you, cleaners later have to mop up the drool by the bucket."

Oh, well. Looks like I'd have to do the same for my inner greedy pig who was already foaming at the mouth. Well, that made two of us. Still, he'd have to grin and bear it—I'd given my word I wouldn't lay claim to any loot. Wouldn't be very nice to change my mind to sponge off the girls.

All the time Zena had been closely watching my face. Now she smiled, nodding to her own thoughts. I just hoped that the conversion rate of missed dosh to virtual authority was high enough that day.

After another half-hour of traveling higgledy-piggledy all over the map, my inner greedy pig got a tasty appetizer as a vast prairie opened up to our right. Although no different from any other stretch of virtual grassland, it was overgrown not with feather grass or whatever, but by billions of Gigantic Fly-Traps, no lass, swaying their sticky flagellae in the breeze. I nearly hiccupped when I made a quick estimation of the unclaimed gold just growing there while the greedy pig was already busy driving his virtual harvester, collecting ton upon ton of the precious tobacco ingredient from the boundless fields. Talk about the Admins' playing along with the tobacco business.

Having said that, harvesting the field was still a job and a half considering it was teeming with all sorts of aggressive wildlife. But in a way, it meant protection from the thousands of low-level amateur boy scouts who would have descended on the field for a quick farm had it been located in a safer zone. Then again, how sure was I that I needed it here, fifteen miles from the Dead Lands and the emerging First Temple? And what was I supposed to do with all this treasure: should I delegate it to the Alliance or the Vets, or, alternatively, put on my farmer hat and harvest it all myself?

I glanced at the girls who were apparently clueless about the contents of my sensational but still unavailable product. In actual fact, hardly twenty or thirty people knew the recipe yet: the guild leaders, their security people and inspectors, that had to be it. In any case, I had to give it a good think when I had the time.

Suddenly, Whizz—until then busy turning circles around us—shrank and bolted toward us, squeezing the alarm button which automatically sent the target's status to the group chat.

Warning! Code Red! Target detected: Junior Vampire, level 123.

The girls perked up and serried their ranks, turning into a cube bristling with steel and magic. The tousled rogue ran up and joined them.

"Report!" Zena croaked, squeezing her shield and her mace.

"Vampires! Three of them tried to intercept me when that cliff shielded me from your view. I detected their shadows just as they went for me. I was lucky I was all maxed out, stealth and all. I managed to select one as target and slammed the alarm before rejoining you."

"Not good. If we've trespassed on a vampires' nest, they'll hunt us down. The bloodsuckers receive a substantial experience both for players killed and for each day survived. Their chief motivation is to kill and to keep on living without dying as they progress in their Nest's hierarchy. As NPCs go, they're pretty weird."

"Vampires? Aren't they supposed to sleep in the daytime?" I showed off my erudition.

"Supposed to, yeah," Zena agreed. "Only they're the wrong sort of bats, and they're about to bite us real hard."

She turned around, poking my shoulder with her tiny fist, her enormous mount tall enough for her to reach me without any problem. "I wonder if you'd have such a thing as a gun about you? I could use it, for sure. Anyway! 'Nuff clowning around. It's all just nerves with me. AlterWorld's vampires have no weak spots. At daytime, they're strong. At nighttime, they're freakin' powerful. All depends how old the nest is we've disturbed, and how many Elders and Higher Vampires it has. Their Prince himself might pay us a visit, you never know. Actually, judging by Manticore's Lair it's been laying idle for quite a while."

"So what do we do, then?"

Zena sniffed, then slapped her helmet down to her eyebrows. "We fight our way through. At worst, we'll die, but when did it stop immortals? At best, we'll smoke the bastards or even find their nest. The loot here is just as good even though we'll need a raid to do it."

So off we went. Our speed, meager as it was already, dropped to a snail's pace. Those who couldn't cast spells when mounted had to walk. I was followed by my personal reinforcement group represented by Hummungus and a level 78 gator I'd raised. We didn't go too far, though. They attacked us by the book, ambushing us at a particular section of the road which was far too troublesome to avoid. A couple dozen vague shadows came at us from every direction. Even a branch of prickly acacia over Bomba's head sported a tooth-baring monster. Two powerful figures appeared on top of a cliff about a hundred feet away from the road: the

Patriarch and the Elder Vampire. In less than a heartbeat, the unstealthed shadows were all over our meager force.

"Control them! Back off, gradually!" Zena commanded.

Casters had about ten seconds while passive shields absorbed damage, allowing us to root and paralyze almost half of the attackers. We backed up, leaving in our wake a thin thread of vampires raging in impotent fury. Actually, we did give them the company of two motionless bodies: one smashed by the Troll's unwieldy club, the other perforated by Whizz's swords until it resembled my Mom's colander. Both Hummungus and the gator had turned into two swirling, growling and howling balls of flesh losing stats at a threatening pace as neither of them was up to their quarry. Having said that, they still did what they were supposed to do, drawing a certain amount of paws and claws to themselves. I was anxiously watching Teddy's stats as I alternated between casting Deadman's Hand and the Aura of Fear. The mobs kept resisting! The young vampire was all of fifty levels above me which made him virtually impregnable. And he was dangerous, too, very rogue-like with his two scythes and lightning combos, occasionally interspersed with his attempts to lunge forward at me and sink his fangs into my vulnerable flesh. The constant pressure from some auras they were using weighed my arms down, affecting my speed and attack strength; my miserable agility bonuses blinked red and expired. Even though the shields still held, my mana and hits kept dwindling—and as I looked at my opponent's scowl, I had a pretty good idea of where my stocks were disappearing to.

I kept glancing at Hummungus' life bar and hit the unsummon button just in time. He folded into his artifact and was now regenerating at triple speed. Very soon I'd be able to summon him again—no buffs this time and maybe for the better as there may be no one left to cast them for him.

Ouch! It felt as if I'd been lashed with a bunch of stinging nettles. A jetstream of prickles ran through my body as the vampire broke through the shields and tucked into my life bar.

I had plenty of hits, about four thousand, but even that would have lasted me a minute at the most—less, considering my breastplate's nature. I activated Jangur's Shield, allowing me an extra five seconds of uninterrupted casting time. Come on now, control him! Yess! The root spell had got him. The deadman's hands broke through the ground, clenching the vampire's feet. He jerked, hissing, his tiny scarlet eyes glaring at me. I ran a few paces back and cast Life Absorption, then began summoning my new pet: the zombie gator which reappeared almost simultaneously with Hummungus' comeback. Without interrupting the spell, I surveyed the battle field. Not good. I couldn't see Bomba at all under the five or six vampires that swarmed over her. Whizz was struggling to fight off two more, her health in the orange zone. Zena was gulping an elixir, ignoring another vampire's teeth which were already sinking into her as she hurriedly selected her team members as targets and sent them the precious few hits she had left—working against time, unable to heal everyone at once.

Two more enemies were hanging off our wizard and it looked as if she'd be the first one to croak. She looked as if she knew it, too. Scowling, she cast a quick spell, sending a wall of ice to swallow and freeze all enemies within a dozen paces. She shouted something long and unintelligible, causing a similar wall of fire to scorch everything around her. Immediately, my vampire's health dropped 25% and two more enemies fell from Whizz and Bomba. Before I knew it, she cast another wall of fire. I sighed with relief. Another couple of those would have solved the vampire problem. But apparently, murderous blanket attacks like those generated an indecent amount of aggro. The released vampires—including some of those that had clung to Bomba—all jumped onto Freckles burying her under a heap of their bodies. The group interface icon went gray, indicating we'd just lost one of our own. But it didn't help the enemy much. Freckles had already done her job. The remaining dozen were rather worse for wear, allowing Bomba's club to strike fear and desolation into the die-hard enemy.

A heart-wrenching howl came from atop the cliff where a couple of mobs stood frozen, forgotten in the heat of the battle. To the sounds of retreat, the remaining vampires scattered in all directions like roaches in a dark room when you turn the light on.

We stood there, panting and looking all around us, but there were no enemies left. Their lookouts had promptly stealthed so now nothing reminded of what had just happened there, apart from a good dozen bodies and our spent frames.

"Bandages, elixirs, buff foods! You'll have to heal yourselves for the moment, I'm all empty. I'll meditate and raise Freckles first, then I can heal and rebuff the rest of you. Laith, go check the bodies. Customers get all the loot."

Did she need to tell me? Every single one of the vampires made me a few gold richer. One of them dropped a small ruby—just some jewelry, no added stats. What did attract my attention, though, were three tiny vials dubbed as Vials of Blood and numbered as 91, 83 and 89. All the drop was automatically reported to the group chat.

Seeing the Vial messages, Zena perked up. "Blood, sweet blood! Let me check the charts. They could be rare numbers... No, no such luck. Twenty to thirty gold each."

"What's that, a lottery or something?" I asked.

"Don't you know? No, of course you don't. It's a top level game for the elite. Basically, sometimes vampires drop these vials, each with a different blood group. Should be a hundred in total, in theory. The smaller the number, the cooler its owner was."

"Why in theory?"

"Because no one has come across the first five numbers yet. Even when we farmed Nosferatu Castle—and we were a hundred-strong raid and by the way, that's where we got those two blades for our Whizz—the Lord himself only dropped number 7. That's the way the cookie crumbles."

That got me interested. I used to collect all that stamp-and-coin stuff myself when I was a kid. "So what's gonna happen when someone gets the whole hundred?"

Zena cracked up laughing. "No one knows, that's the whole thing! The fullest collection I know of contains ninety-one vials. The fucking thing is addictive—and it's hot at the moment, probably one out of three collects them. Here, I'll forward you the chart. You never know, you might need it."

My Inbox dinged. I opened the file. Wow. It wasn't just a price list, but a complete guidebook answering everything about *what, where, how often* and *how much*. Indeed, the first five numbers sported nothing but question marks. I liked it. I wouldn't mind collecting the full hundred myself. There could be a nice mega goodie at the end of it.

"So by themselves they're useless, aren't they?"

"No, they're not," Zena protested. "If you drink them, they'll give you a temporary Vampirism ability and part of the dealt damage will come back to you as hits. The number defines its strength and duration. No need to cringe. It tastes of grenadine juice—no innocent babies were harmed in its making."

"I see. So what now? Are we all clear?"

Zena made a face. "I wouldn't be so sure. In case you didn't notice, these were the youngsters, not a single Elder in sight. It could be they're leveling their young in which case they're off to lick their wounds. Alternatively, these were only skirmishers before letting out the big guns, the Nest masters. In which case we're toast."

"So what did they try to achieve? We've chopped up a nice pile of vampires. Now you'll resuscitate Freckles, then we'll be ready for round two. They should have attacked us all at once."

"Not really. Freckles will have a debuff now. They've burned out our long-term abilities and sussed out our potential and tactics. The Elders won't risk their necks, they get their XP anyway getting stronger every day, growing a new level every week. And the youngsters will respawn in twenty-four hours. They don't have much to lose and they won't drop below level 100. So it's fifty-fifty, really: either they're going to attack us now, all of them, or they'll let us go. Preferably, the latter. That's it, my mana's at fifty, I'll be resuscitating Freckles before she screws my PM up completely."

We spent the next fifteen minutes cleaning ourselves up, buffing and restoring mana. Finally Zena shrugged, "It looks like they won't be coming."

The next moment the bloodsuckers attacked us again. Talk about speaking too soon. Next time I should duct-tape her evil mouth shut!

The Junior vampires unstealthed first. There weren't many of them left, seven at the most. We accepted the fight, distributed the targets and began casting. Then about a dozen Elders appeared on the scene, followed by the Patriarch on top of the already-familiar cliff with his entourage of three high-level warriors.

Zena glanced at them and swore through her teeth, shaking her head. "Kill whoever we can and retreat. We can't fight through them. Team up and try to kill at least a few, we have thirty secs at most!"

I chose an Elder busy fighting with Whizz. The rogue chick was desperately spending all of her abilities and combos trying to destroy an opponent of equal strength. I set both my pets on him and began siphoning off his life hoping that the spell lived up to its promise of ignoring all types of magic resists.

"We're leaving! Freckles, pull us out!" I barely recognized Zena's voice. Targeted by three ancient vampires, she was busy fighting them, sending sparks, blood and f-words flying as the four were swirling around.

My target wasn't going to last long: the others had already forced the vampire's hits into the orange zone. Gritting my teeth with disappointment, I activated Destructive Touch. *Bang!* The Elder lost six-something hundred hits and collapsed onto the rocks. The evacuator popped open. Freckles pulled us out a few hundred feet away from the scene. Trust my luck to land in a crevice in the cliff twenty feet deep, losing half the hits in the process.

I heard her cast a portal spell—a classic group one this time. With a pop, we found ourselves about three miles from the battlefield, just next to the Manticore's Lair. Good job we'd noted its location—well done, Freckles. Saved us the trouble of retracing all the way back. The girls hissed and cussed under their breath and still some sounds were missing. Too quiet. Almost knowing what I was about to see, I checked the group's status. Minus Zena and Charmsy. Oh.

I checked the group chat. Zena was there spitting orders as she changed into a spare kit meting out instructions to the rest of us. I got my share, too:

Relax, dude, this is business as usual. Charmsy and I have respawned at the Guild's, I just need five sec to discuss something with someone, then Freckles will bring us back. Just wait up a bit.

The five seconds lasted a good quarter of an hour. Add to it the teleports followed by buffs and meditation time—the clock kept ticking. I had barely two hours of paid time left and we had covered barely five miles.

Zena came over and crouched next to me. "Keeping an eye on the time, eh?"

I nodded.

"You understand, don't you, that we're not going to make it?"

I nodded again.

"Actually, time isn't the only problem. We won't be able to make it past the vampires. We've got to either hire more people, at least the same again, or take another road past the nearest city, but that's 150 miles with no guarantee of success."

I shook my head, "Two teams for another twenty-four hours, that's fifteen grand. Too much. I'm not some oligarch picking dosh from money trees."

Zena lay her minute green hand on my chainmail gauntlet. "I understand. We've been getting the measure of you. You're all right. You're not bossing anyone around. You're not tight with money. And you're not an idiot. Summing it all up, we've got a counter proposal for you."

I looked up at her with interest. All sarcasm was gone from her intelligent eyes.

"We'll switch to an hourly rate. Strictly as a private offer: the guild doesn't list this kind of service. This way, you're happy and we can skip the 20% guild tax. Just do keep your mouth shut about it, okay? I've already had my first warning. Four hundred an hour, will that be okay with you?"

That was a good offer. In fact, it was perfect. My freshly-gained authority was starting to bring in its first dividends. I needed to tell my inner greedy pig to take a leaf out of my book. Not everything is measured in money. Good contacts and healthy relationships can often do more than any amount of gold.

"Agreed," I said. "But that's not all. You've just said we can't get through."

"I did. But I haven't finished talking yet. Now, I have a friend. She collects those numbered vials. She has seventy-one of them already. Whenever she hears about a new vampire spot—especially a fresh nest like this where they may drop rare numbers—you can't stop her. I've had a word with her. She can bring her team to join us if they get the loot and you don't claim the nest and promise to keep the information under wraps for a week. What do you say to that?"

"I say, awesome! Thanks, Zena! You're the best!" unexpectedly for myself, I leaned over and pecked her snub little nose. Then I drew back blushing as I realized what I'd just done.

Zena burst out laughing. The girls' faces blossomed with unsure smiles. It wasn't often their leader laughed so wholeheartedly, especially without a good reason. On the contrary, this was some serious brow-wrinkling time.

Zena looked up at me, her eyes moist with cheerful tears. "I bet you thought I'd drop my frog skin and turn into a princess?"

Taking in my embarrassed face, she laughed some more, a happy laughter as she blotted the corners of her eyes with a promptly-materialized hanky.

We spent another hour waiting for the other team. I relaxed, trying to enjoy the fact that my money was flowing away, direction unknown. I had a funny feeling everything was going right. Everything was as it had to be. So I dozed off on the grass under the gentle sun.

I awoke as Zena gently shook my shoulder. "Get up, commander. The reinforcements are here. Time to clip the vampires' fangs."

Astra's team was a cut above my own. Although her ladies belonged to the same Sullen squad, all of them were a good thirty or forty levels above Zena's team. Plus vampire-tailored gear. Much to their disappointment (and to my quiet joy) we crossed the vampires' territory without a glitch. The bloodsuckers just didn't dare attack a group twice as big. Astra kept looking this way and that, indignant, as her two rogues branched out a few hundred feet, trying to encourage the cautious vampires, but they'd apparently thought better of it. The tough chick pursed her thin lips, promising to sieve the area and dig it all up as long as she found the wretched nest. At least she stuck to her part of the deal, taking our team all the way to the Bone Fortress. There, she shook our hands reminding us about her exclusive rights to the farm. Impatience glinted in her eyes as she shifted from one foot to the other, impatient to bolt off and add to her vial collection. True collectors are all like that. I remember reading about some rare stamp or other leaving a bloodied trail of collectors' bodies, too weak to fight their obsession.

The fortress protected the narrow—and, more importantly, the only—passage leading to the boulder-locked Valley of Fear. Its startling architecture had a bad effect on my head. The unknown builders had used giant dragon bones as building material. Twenty-foot high vertebrae formed a massive wall from one end of the passage to the other—the wall highly resistant to both steel and magic. The towers were put together from ribs, the enormous skull serving as the gate tower, about fifty feet high, its fangs as tall as myself. No idea if it delivered on its promise, but the visual effect definitely did.

We were already about five hundred feet away from it when a heavy steel spear sank into the ground not far from us. We got the message and stopped watching the fortress defenders appear on the walls: a good couple hundred skeleton archers and warriors carrying shields and short broadswords. Among them we glimpsed the stooping silhouettes of Liches wrapped in their gray cloaks. Considering that every skeleton was way over a 100-plus, trying to storm the fortress without a small army for backup was madness to say the least.

Zena stared at me with interest. "Here we are. The contract's closed. You owe us eight hundred for the two extra hours. But honestly, I wouldn't mind spending it on a few front-row tickets to see you charge it."

I was riding a wave of reckless courage as sensing the end of my long-winded journey gave me added strength and nerve. I readjusted the Crown of the Overlord on my head. "Agreed," I gave her a wink. "Choose your seat and go get some popcorn. And don't you tell anyone you haven't seen anything."

At least that way I had someone to resuscitate my arrow-perforated body, I added mentally. I also wanted to leave some lasting impression on the girls. I liked them. It would be a good idea to catch their interest with some intrigue and some prospectives. Our clan's combat section was desperate for a few battle-wise warriors.

I left the group and waved my hand to them. Slowly I walked toward the fortress.

"Make a death wish..." one of the girls whispered behind my back.

When I passed the spear that was buried deep in the ground, I ran my hand along its shaft as if I owned it, my insides shrinking in anticipation of yet another one already in the air, about to pin me down like a large beetle. One step. Then another. A bead of sweat slid down my face. My feet raising clouds of dust as birds sang in the sky, I walked, moving my wooden legs, until I entered the shadow cast by the skull. I stopped right in front of its grimacing face and tilted my head up, peering into the dark void of its eye sockets. Slowly, its jaw opened, allowing me access to the fortress. Looked like I made it.

Chapter Ten

*F*rom the Analytics Department report made at the AlterWorld Corporation's last board meeting.

Agenda: The tendencies in AlterWorld's self-induced development.

Recently, we've been witnessing a new and rather frightening tendency as AlterWorld seems to be switching to perma mode all by itself, not only acquiring more and more independence but also gaining depth, recreating and generating its own past and present.

Just one example. During our worldbuilding phase, we came up with a multitude of myths and legends for our game concept. One of them was the story of Centaurs that had populated the world's prairies from ocean to ocean, then disappeared in as yet unknown circumstances. The gaming community kept pestering the admins to create an event that would bring the Centaurs back into the game. A week ago, the forums exploded with the news of their return, complete with videos and screenshots, even unique loot items that suited the new four-legged mounts. The sole problem being, we hadn't introduced any Centaurs, not even at a design draft stage! The world had created them on its own accord.

We won't even mention little details like the discovery of the Cursed King's lost sword or the grave of the legendary hero Sadaus, etc., etc., that we the developers have nothing to do with!

J. Howards, Director of the Analytics Department

* * *

The dragon skull's massive lower jaw dropped open, thudding against the ancient cobblestones. Its mouth was at least fifteen feet wide—big enough for a wagon to pass had it not been barred by a row of teeth, perfectly white and straight. So how was I supposed to squeeze through?

The problem resolved itself naturally. Noiselessly, the front teeth folded in, exposing a dark cavity behind. I caught a cool whiff of lavender as air escaped from inside. Did they have an aircon there or something?

I stepped in quite willingly, especially as the darkness proved not as pitch black as I'd thought. The skull bones emanated a greenish glow making movement inside quite comfortable. I had barely taken a dozen paces when the teeth shut close behind my back. The glow turned crimson; my head felt as if clasped by a steel band. My vision darkened. I dropped to my knees. The heavy boulders of someone else's thoughts stirred in my mind,

What an interesting sample of a sentient microorganism. He thought of using the Crown of the Overlord as a white flag, manipulating the lower organisms' primary instincts. Oh vain creature, you can't even start to comprehend what it is that you're wearing on your empty head. Heaving said that, who am I to accuse anyone of having an empty skull? And you seem to collect astral marks. The mark of a newborn god, three High Spell cooldown bars, the mark of a Dark Princess and of my little Bone Dragon brother. Next time you reincarnate, don't forget to thank him for the few extra moments of life his mark has granted you. And now, prepare to part with your power willingly. That would considerably simplify and quicken the process of killing you whilst giving me a few extra bits of energy, allowing me to drag out my miserable existence for a short while. I still might see the Titans come back; even Ophion himself might turn his regard to his prostrated servant...

The alien conscience tolled in my head, suppressing my own will. Thinking was a struggle: I just couldn't force myself to resist the dragon's will, let alone do something against it. I just couldn't have cared less. If only I could take a nap in this cool numbness...

I don't know what gave me new heart. It could have been the Fallen One's power forcing its way through the magic-absorbing ancient bones. It could also have been my inner greedy pig throwing a wobbly in my head as he realized we were at the point of being not just killed but also robbed.

"Wait," I forced my lips to move. "What's the point of killing the golden goose? You need strength, don't you? I can arrange for hundreds of sentient beings to scale your walls and dozens of volunteers to cram into your mouth for you to chew on."

The pressure on my chest subsided somewhat. I could finally take in a lungful of air.

"You sound interesting, o micro sentient. Speak on."

"Have you ever heard about the First Temple?"

"Have I?" the glow around me flashed as a wave of crippling aggression assaulted my consciousness, sending me reeling back to my knees. Blood trickled from my nose and ears as my life bar blinked, shrinking rapidly.

"Have I!" I heard as if through a layer of cotton wool. "I was the first to take the impact of the astral breach! The lands around the temple were littered with my scales and the bodies of the slain metal giants and their steel-shelled servants. It was after that battle that the Scarlet Hills had turned into the Dead Lands and their beautiful poppy meadows had become the Valley of Fear. All life had turned into dust and those who possessed enough magic to combat the invisible death had become the walking dead. Look at the proud freemen crawling my spine in the shape of skeletons! Arise, o sentient one. No one dies here without my permission."

A refreshing surge of life coursed through my body, returning me my sight and hearing. I shook my head. "What happened after the breach, then?" I managed. "Did they close the astral portal?"

"The Titans never left enemies behind. Once they'd squeezed them back into their own realm, they followed them, intending to teach them a lesson and find their true rulers. None of them have ever come back, though. The Temple was destroyed, the Titans were gone, and all life was terminated by the invisible force: in the three days that followed, all the flesh came off my bones which still glow until this very day. Here I lie now, feeding on crumbs of micro energies. Now you've raked it all up... so much so that I even wasted some of my precious energy on healing you, you miserable piece of protoplasm. Now the time of my rebirth has been moved another twenty-four hours. If it keeps going like this, I'll only need to hold out for another hundred and eighteen thousand years. Plus another day which you owe me now. Speak up!"

Jesus. How's that for blackmail. First he tried to strangle me, then he poured some cold water over me and fixed me up with a bill.

"Ahem," I cleared my throat. "I can restore the First Temple."

Bang! It was like being stuck inside a giant church bell hit by a howitzer. In an already well-practiced motion, I dropped to my knees, opening my mouth in a silent grunt. As I clutched my ears, blood poured down my hands.

"You bastard dragon! You're gonna kill me before you have a chance to really learn anything from me. Can't you keep your emotions in check?"

The riot of colors died down as the swirling food processor in my head had finally stopped its maddening rotation. Bony idiot, the killer of the immortals—trust him to scorch my brains and pretend he wasn't even there.

"Say it again."

"You bastard dragon-"

"No! Not that. What was it you said?"

I squeezed one eye shut in anticipation of a new bell toll. "I can restore the First Temple," I blurted out, shrinking, waiting for a new *Bang!* It didn't come, phew. My new dragon friend had somehow restrained his primary instincts.

"Go on."

An inkling of an idea scratched the surface of my mind and I caught it just in time. "Eh, Sir Dragon-"

"I'm *Tianlong*, you moron! *Long* for friends."

"Pleased to meet you. I'm Laith. Max for friends." I just hoped that our exchanging names meant more to him than the proverbial *'Pudding—Alice; Alice—Pudding'*. "So, Mister Long. I heard that the First Temple had been destroyed five hundred years ago by the forces of the Alliance of Light."

The Dragon snickered. "It's easy to claim someone else's glory when the true owners ain't home. Not five hundred, even: almost eight hundred years ago. If you do a bit of digging, you can still find the invaders' steel bodies buried in our sands and moors. I've done my fair share of crushing and grinding, I tell you. Again you've got me sidetracked! Now, the Temple! Speak up!"

I nodded, deciding not to annoy this mighty creature any more than necessary. Instead, I didn't spare any lipstick to dress up the pig of my imagination.

"Thing is, I can restore the First Temple. The moment the creatures of Light learn about it, they'll be quaking at the knees, desperate to destroy it. First it'll be lone scouts, followed by small groups, then by raids until one day they might bring in an entire army. And you get to meet them all! Think of all the energy—kilotons, no, megatons of mana! Shortening the time of your languishing here to mere centuries!"

I stopped to check the effect my words had produced. Long didn't say anything.

"So can I go now?" I ventured.

"Wait. War is never bad. But my strength is limited at the moment. I might not have enough. Besides, once my true nature becomes known, the armies of both Light and the Dark will beat a path to my door. The Temple! Potentially, it's a wealth of energy. I will let you go now and I will close the opening. In return, you must redirect one tenth of the altar's mana flow to me. Deal?"

"Agreed," I shrugged. "If the altar allows me to do it, you'll get one tenth of all mana it generates."

Softly a gong rang, sealing the deal. A whirling sign flashed before my eyes and disintegrated in a cloud of dust: the picture of a curled red dragon.

"What was that?"

"Just another mark for your collection," the dragon chuckled. "This way it'll be easier for me to control your whereabouts and your contractual obligations. It can help you, too, if it comes to a big scrap. Now go. The creatures of the valley will leave you alone."

The skull's occipital bone screeched, jolting to one side, blinding my eyes with sunshine. Rare were those who entered this place; those who exited it must had been rarer still.

"Good luck to you, Tianlong!"

"You too, micro sentient one. A fly diving into a pot of honey will need a bit of luck."

How's that for dampening one's enthusiasm? Never mind. Not the first time. I stepped toward the exit.

Damn! I collapsed, tripping over a piece of old iron junk buried in a century-deep layer of fine sand. As I scrambled back to my feet and brushed the sand off my clothes, I peered around in search of the treacherous obstacle.

I saw it and froze.

"It's dead iron," Tianlong commented. "It must have stuck in my teeth when I munched on the steel invaders and their servants."

It sure looked as if he'd been munching on some tanks and airplanes, I thought, brushing the sand off a rather rusty and chewed-up tommy gun. A man of my generation couldn't mistake it for anything else. This model was unfamiliar, its strange proportions betraying its alien origin. Its pistol grip was strangely long, designed either for a very large or a seven-digit hand. To get a comfortable grip of the stock, the shooter's arms must have been at least half as long again as mine. Besides, the weight of the thing was more like a company machine gun. The cartridges, strangely green with silver-and-purple bullets, snuggled inside a small spring-assisted chamber. Well, well, well.

"May I?" I asked hopefully, already knowing I wouldn't surrender the gun even if he tortured me.

"Help yourself," Long agreed, nonchalant. "Now hurry! I've already come up with a model for rebuilding both my spine structure and energy channels. All I need now is energy!"

Clasping the precious trophy to my chest, I finally walked out into the fresh air. Once the shield was lifted, my mana bar immediately began filling up while my PM box pinged incessantly with missed messages. Jesus. This cute little dragon didn't seem to even start to realize his own value in this world. His skeleton could make a perfect prison for the digitized. More dark secrets to keep! Then again, I wouldn't say no to borrowing one of his smallest bones to fashion a nice little coffin for somebody called Tavor. You squeeze the customer inside, fasten the lid and bury it, then go on drinking until you forget its coordinates.

And what if I tried Astral Mana Dispersal on him? I looked back at the skull, scared it could be reading my thoughts. But the skeleton, polished by both wind and time, remained silent, deep in his dreams and calculations. He probably missed flying. Dragons had to be a bit like birds: without the sky, they would pine away.

I shoved the gun down my bag for future reference and opened my private messages. Zena was spamming me, anxious to find out how I'd done it and furious because the moment she'd ventured after me, she'd been peppered with arrows until she resembled a porcupine. Women and their curiosity!

I had to play the man of mystery, explaining it away with some class quests and my personal charisma. Zena didn't sound convinced, too desperate to get to some new unexplored lands. I felt uneasy. Trust that little fool to walk right into a dragon's den—literally. That could complicate everything. So I warned her against trying to ram her way through the skull where she'd be stuck, spread-eagled, in one of the numerous clever traps while her teammates stormed the castle trying to get to her shriveling frame.

I closed the chat windows. Finally I could have a good look around. The inner court of the fortress had been marked with the imprint of the dragon's enormous wing bones. If you looked at it from above, you could see clearly the position the dragon had been lying in when his heart had ceased beating.

The undead stopped ambling around and began gravitating toward me, even though they didn't dare overstep some invisible line that only they could see. They would come close and stop dead in their tracks, their empty eye sockets staring at me. Should I summon my zombie to keep them company? Having said that, I'd rather not. I could be the proud mark-bearer thanks to my secret supporters, but I couldn't predict the local skeletons and Liches' reaction to my humble pet.

I walked through their ranks, expecting the strong stench of dead flesh, but time must have picked their bones clean of meat, so they didn't smell at all. I kept going until I'd left the piles of bones behind me. Here the canyon split, revealing a rather green valley specked with wild flowers. Whatever monster inhabited it apparently didn't lay claim to the green bit. I glanced at the white expanse of the map which was rapidly filling with schematic hills, brooks and other special signs.

Then I saw the first specimens of what passed for the local fauna: a level 160 zombie grizzly bear and a mutant reindeer, his antlers glowing the same acid green. He wasn't radioactive, surely? A Geiger counter would have come in handy: I didn't wish to share the dragon's fate.

The reindeer noticed me and froze just like the skeletons back in the fortress, apparently unable or unwilling to flee. Gingerly I approached him, running my hand along the beast's warm side, as he snorted, shuddering, his berserk bloodshot eyes squinting at me. I reconsidered and stepped back. No need to upset the critter. His upper lip rose, exposing some definitely non-herbivore canine teeth that added conviction to my decision.

I walked along a barely discernable road reduced to a trail by earth deposits and a riot of greenery. Occasional ruins studded my path: watch towers atop of some strategic high points; the crumbling shells of inns and taverns clinging to the roadside where they'd once promised shelter and food to tired wayfarers. All the buildings were in various stages of decay. And if you shook your head, switching from high-fantasy mode to today's realities, you could discern the stitches of automatic weapons that had once ripped through the walls and the petals of shrapnel left by every caliber shell under the sun.

I walked over to the pockmarked ruins of a tower and rummaged through a heap of rubble at its base. Soon a piece of shrapnel lay in my hand, silver and purple, its edges ragged and incredibly sharp. It didn't look as if time had any power over this once-deadly piece of metal. Once I had rubbed it free from dust, it glistened in the sun just like it must have done eons ago. I attempted to read its stats.

Mithril Ore. Metal content: 8%. Weight: 0.22 Lbs.

Jesus. May I have two, please? So those steel invaders used depleted mithril to knock up their missiles? That was rich! I thought I knew why the Titans hadn't been back yet: they must still be sitting next to a mithril Everest even now, smearing the desperate tears from their greedy faces knowing they couldn't stuff it all in their pockets.

If you remembered that mithril was ten times the price of gold, my little find could easily cost anything up to eighty gold. I liked this kind of math. I stood on the hilltop, looking over the unfolding panorama of several busted ruins and a few promising shell holes, long collapsed and overgrown with grass. For all I knew, it could have been a tree uprooted a hundred years ago, having shifted a good dozen cubic feet of earth in its fall. Then again, the bottom of the hole could conceal the mithril tail fin of a five-hundred kilo bomb...

The gold rush got the better of me. I spent the next half-hour crawling on all fours at the foot of the tower. Finally, I slumped onto a cleaner strip of grass and poured out my finds in front of me. Eight glistening fragments, sharp and angular, weighed in at about six hundred grams: a Klondike times Eldorado. They didn't happen to have a fifty-ton tank buried here somewhere, did they? Had I had a dozen diggers complete with spades, I'd be driving a Ferrari by this time tomorrow. Having said that, I wouldn't have changed Hummungus for any kind of Rolls Royce. But then again, there had to be some mithril bear item recipes around, surely? It was about time I got myself a cool set of purple armor, too. Having said that, it all depended on the resulting item's stats. Probably, I'd be better off finding some way to use mithril to upgrade the already existing items. In any case, with my negligible forging and enchanting skills, I'd have to pick the experts' brains.

I carefully poured my finds into my bag, added a placemark to my map, cast a concerned look at the sun and started out for the valley below.

After another hour of watchful walking, I climbed another hill. A breathtaking view opened out before me, revealing a huge fortress, apparently very ancient—older than the dragon and in about the same state.

"Holy cow. Stalingrad, January 1943," I muttered.

The outside walls formed an octagon three stories high, each of its eight sides about half a mile long, studded with towers every two hundred feet or so. I estimated the total length of the walls at about two miles, times the density of the soldiers needed to defend the fortresses' seventy towers under attack. The resulting figure made me feel sick. This fortification had been designed to accommodate one hell of a crowd. That's not even counting the second row of walls that showed behind the first one, while the third and final line of defense loomed up at the heart of the castle.

The road snaked downhill toward a small fort that arched over the once-busy trade route, covering the access to the main gates against any potential enemy. At close range, the fortress turned out to be in an even sadder state: the proverbial Reichstag building after the storm. The once-unscalable walls grinned through their missing teeth exposing dark gaps and crumbling drops. I passed the fort and dived into the gateway. The walls' sheer thickness was astounding.

Congratulations! You have discovered a castle!
Class: Super Nova
The capture of the castle is impossible due to irreparable damage to the Control Room.

I paused, imagining myself to be the proud owner of that behemoth. The Black Lord in his gloomy citadel. While it sure tickled my vanity, I had my doubts I'd be able to keep such a juicy morsel. I dreaded to think of the sums the Admins would demand just for buying out the land and buildings.

The road took a ninety-degree turn, taking me to a littered passage between the two walls. That was clever: in case the attackers did break through, they would have to cover another few hundred feet under crossfire, losing speed, manpower and enthusiasm. Did I say a few hundred feet? I had to walk well over a mile tracing the 180-degree curve of the wall until I finally saw the gates which led inside the second line of defense.

That must have been some blood-bath, I tell you. I stared at two-feet deep chips in the walls generously pockmarked by automatic guns and streaked with molten stone—the latter, if the truth were known, could have been left by the defenders as well as the attackers. The picture was complete with a couple of petrified mountain trolls. Their massive bodies, perforated by some large-caliber quick-firer, had frozen the moment death had looked into their glazed eyes.

One of them held an interesting weapon. Collapsing on one knee as he died, he leaned against his club, trying to regain his balance. Even now the club still glistened purple. Most of all it reminded me of the torn-out barrel of a tank turret with its recognizable fat thermal sleeve and a rather battered loading mechanism that the troll must have used to bash the enemy with.

A prompt popped up:

Depleted mithril ore. Metal content: 1%. Weight: 1628 Lbs.

Visibly disappointed, my inner greedy pig poked at his calculator. The resulting figure sent him into a stupor. Seventy-four thousand gold! Immediately that raised a lot of questions. I didn't for one moment doubt the existence of various ore benefication methods that would leave me with a nice neat fifteen-pound ingot of pure mithril. The questions started with the costs, the losses of the valuable ore, as well as logistics and shipping. And how I was I supposed to cut it up or shove the ten-feet barrel into a furnace? Besides, it was breaking my heart robbing the beautiful death statue. No sculptor in the world could recreate the tragedy of the piece, the last exertion, the forehead wrinkled with effort as the troll attempted to force himself back to his feet and onto his enemies. It commanded so much compassion and respect... As far as I was concerned, it would be the last item to end up in the furnace.

I nearly broke my legs scrambling through the debris before I got to the gates of the second line of defense. The third wall loomed up about a hundred feet away, taller and even more impregnable than the first two. I turned my head this way and that, looking for the gate. WTF? Was I supposed to go on another two-mile hike? How had whoever'd lived here managed to get in in times of peace? There had to be something there that I didn't yet know. This was logistics' worst nightmare. They had to have had some magic elevators or teleports.

It looked like the mysterious invaders had shared my indignation, unwilling to traipse another half-hour in the walls' artificial shade. A few hundred feet further up, I stumbled across an artificial mound of broken stone. The whole part of the inner wall lay in ruins. Still, climbing it wasn't as easy as walking up the stairs to the third floor. I had to work hard getting to the top of that manmade hill secured by deformed lengths of construction steel.

The top offered an excellent view of the citadel which was the reason for the complex defense structure. The First Temple. Even now, with one third of it destroyed and its top stories collapsed, its tower spires molten, its wall gaping with a huge breach instead of a doorway, it commanded reverence and admiration. Its almost-Gothic style blew your mind away with millions of distracting little details. I know it sounds weird but it felt as if I stood below an enormous organ suspended high in the air, its keys transcending the sonic barrier in their solemn prayer. Eight spike-shaped wings emanated from the central building: some little more than fragments of the bearing walls, others perfectly unscathed. The whole architectural group could accommodate thousands of people. A truly enormous potential.

Gravel rustled underfoot as I gingerly slid down the slope, grasping at the rusty steel bars and braces. After five minutes of picking my way through the debris, I approached a gap in the Temple wall that opened up the way deep inside. I just hoped that the altar was somewhere other than the destroyed roof or top stories: most likely, they housed the catapults and the fortress control room. Which made sense because any invaders would storm the building from bottom to the top, not the other way round. So the altar had to be downstairs. All public religions shared the same logic.

I stepped in and gasped. The interior of the Temple looked like an open-hearth furnace laid up for maintenance. There had been a quality fire burning there for a long long time. I got the impression that, once the fire had exhausted all the combustibles, oxygen included, it had made a real effort and kept going for another couple of days, melting granite by the force of its pride alone. The vitrified floor and dripping walls had fused, wax-like, revealing a pristine slab of the altar barely shimmering in the center of the Temple.

My steps echoed flatly across the empty hall. I ascended some one-time steps, molten into the semblance of a volcanic staircase. The altar. A half-inch crack ran across it from corner to corner. The stubborn stone had chipped in the middle, the shape of the chip vaguely familiar. Without looking, I reached into my bag for the Large Fragment. It seemed to fit perfectly. Should I do it? I made a mental sign of the cross and, holding my breath for no known reason, placed the fragment onto the slab.

Gong! My ears rang; my knees hit the ground. My entire field of vision became cluttered with admin messages,

Universal alert! The Fallen One is back! The Dark Ones have restored the First Temple, allowing the Fallen God to break his fetters and regain control over a part of reality.

Effect 1: +7 to XP bonus to all worshippers of the Fallen One. The bonus is calculated by the formula of 1% per each level of the First Temple plus another 1% for every temple consecrated to Dark gods.

Effect 2: The possibility of restoring the Dark pantheon and summoning new gods to serve the Fallen One.

Effect 3: The Dark One is back in power. Now his worshippers will have the option of dedicating themselves to one of the pantheon's junior gods by offering sacrifices and receiving religious ranks. Every god has his or her own choice of gifts and skills available for their followers.

Warning! People of Light, to arms! In a month's time, the First Temple will lose its immunity. By that time, you will need to find and destroy the spawn of the Dark!

Warning! The Dark Ones, to arms! In a month's time, the First Temple will lose its immunity. By that time, you will need to unite as one man to protect the heart of your religion!

Quest completion alert: Knowledge Breeds Sadness IV. The First Temple Restoration. Quest completed!

Congratulations! You've reached Level 66!
Congratulations! You've reached Level 67!
Congratulations! You've reached Level 68!
Congratulations! You've reached Level 69!
Congratulations! You've reached Level 70!
Congratulations! You've reached Level 71!
Congratulations! You've reached Level 72!
10,000 points fame received!

Fame alert!
Your Fame has exceeded 11,000 points!
You have reached Fame level 4: Ballads are written about you.

Fame alert!
Your Fame has exceeded 17,000 points!
You have reached Fame level 5: Children are named after you.

Your relationship with the Dark Alliance has improved to: Friendship!
Your relationship with the Alliance of Light has deteriorated to: Hatred!

I had barely skimmed the messages and closed them, intending to reread them properly at my leisure, when yet another gong resounded in my ears.

Gong!
A unique position available: The First Priest of the Dark God.
Accept: Yes/No

Oh, great. Wasn't life just weird? Why did it like to break us, forcing us into the most uncomfortable positions? Me, a lone player, had to shoulder a clan. I had nothing to do with religion and now I was offered a unique priest's job. Should I decline? Then again, I couldn't predict the Fallen One and the Dragon's combined reactions to my act of social protest.

My internal interface cursor jumped from *Yes* to *No* and back, following my glance, and even pressed them a little without sinking them in properly, the way a gunman strokes the trigger squeezing it, then releasing it again, all the time keeping the bead on the target. *Yes* or *No*?

Chapter Eleven

I closed my eyelids to relieve the information overload. Then I got to thinking. A quick Wiki search had produced nothing: apparently, there could only be one First Priest whose post was currently occupied by a Light NPC. I hadn't found any further info on his rights and responsibilities, apart from the fact that he could appoint new priests, consecrate new temples to their respective patron gods, listen to an occasional plea and pass it on to the head of the Pantheon.

Now what would a high post like that have in store for me, then? Would it mean the forces of Light hunting down my precious hide? Having said that, sooner or later they were bound to find out the name of the person who'd restored the Temple. I had left quite a trail, starting from my unusual escort request and ending with Zena and her team who'd seen and heard their fair share and probably second-guessed a lot more. My relationship with the races of Light had apparently plummeted, too, reaching the levels of pure unadulterated hatred. I only had my mysterious quest reward, *status: unknown*, to thank for that. Actually, they should warn players about tricks like that. The only way back to the City of Light for me now was at the head of an army, ramming our way through the gates and razing the city walls to the ground. Considering that the ranks of my enemies and ill-wishers kept growing at a frightening speed, accepting the post sounded like a better alternative. For me, any gain of physical or political strength was the call of the day.

What else? Was the Fallen One going to burden me with nightly vigils, fasts and shaman dances around the altar? Why would he need to? He's a young god; he needed deeds and actions, not symbols and rituals. He could set you up with a quest or ask of you something you wouldn't be able to refuse. At least as far as gods went, he was all right. He wasn't a grabbing god, on the contrary: until now, he seemed to be the one who protected and nurtured us while he could have easily fixed us up with some vicious debuff you couldn't remove until you either prayed or paid your way out. No, AI 311 knew everything about motivation. I didn't think he was capable of any dirty tricks.

Now, the responsibilities overload could be a problem, sure. What was it Lena's mom had said? It was the retinue that made the king... Few kings were brilliant economists, generals or sociologists. They didn't need to be. As Comrade Stalin used to say, *cadres are key*. And for once he was right.

Responsibility, that's what scares us. All our lives we're trying to avoid it, wriggling our way out of school and college commitments, afraid of starting a family or business, unable to start a conversation with a girl or break an overeager bully's nose. Wasn't it time we stopped running?

Besides, the Fallen One had granted me one advance too many. And I had indeed promised him to help and restore the Pantheon. I gave my word to the Dragon, too. To quit now you had to be a thankless ingrate with no self-respect. Time to stand up for one's principles.

I opened my eyes, bit my lower lip and exhaled, pressing the button:

Yes.

Congratulations! You have been successfully promoted to a unique post: The First Priest.

Being the First Priest, you are entitled to additional skills granted to your position as well as those granted by the High God of your religion and from each of the Pantheon gods. Unlike the Fallen One's regular worshippers who are required to choose a particular patron god of the Dark, the First Priest has default access to all of the Pantheon's skills and blessings. The number of available skills depends on the First Priest's level which is always equal to that of the First Temple. Current level: 3.

New positional skills acquired:

Ordination. The First Priest has the authority to ordain any Dark worshipper. The maximum number of the world's priests cannot exceed the number of temples multiplied by 10. Current figures: 10/50

Excommunication. The First Priest has the authority to anathemize any Dark worshipper. Duration of excommunication: from 24 hrs. to eternity. Cooldown: 24 hrs.

Appeal to Gods. The First Priest has the authority to appeal directly to any of the Dark Gods who will always hear his plea even though he won't necessarily reply.

Outcast. The First Priest has the authority to proclaim any of AlterWorld inhabitants a Religious Outcast who will then become fair prey to all Dark worshippers, to the point where anyone who kills a Religious Outcast will receive a considerable amount of Faith points that are necessary for religious rank growth and choice of skills offered by their Patron God. The Mark of Outcast disappears after its bearer's death at the hands of a Dark follower. Cooldown: 24 hrs.

Blessing: a raid buff

Effect: +25 to all types of magic resistance, 10% to physical damage resistance

Duration: 12 hrs.

Ingredient: Spark of Dark Flame. Can be acquired by a lump sum donation of 5,000 gold to the Altar.

Congratulations! You've learned the spells:
Personal Portal to the First Temple
Cast time: 6 sec
Mana expenditure: 300
Group Portal to the First Temple
Cast time: 9 sec
Mana expenditure: 1100

Congratulations! You've learned the skills:
Patron God: the Fallen One
Shadow of the Fallen One. Allows you to conceal your name, religion and clan affiliation, temporarily changing your relationship with all races to neutral.
Duration: 1 hr.
Cooldown: 24 hrs.
Shield of Faith. Gives complete mana regeneration and 30-sec immunity to all types of damage.
Cooldown: 24 hrs.

Congratulations! The First Priest has taken his place by the Altar! 5,000 points Fame received!

Fame alert!
Your Fame has exceeded 23,000 points!
You have reached Fame level 6: Your name is written in the history of the world.

Oh. I exchanged glances with my inner greedy pig as we reached out to feel each other's virtual biceps. That had been a generous downpour of freebies indeed. Even though not all of the skills gave you a permanent boost, my character's sociopolitical importance had grown manifold. I still couldn't clearly see all the prospects and potential scenarios for using these particular skills, but my gut feeling was telling me I had been dealt a handful of trumps, not of dribs and drabs.

I looked over at the altar. The cracks in the shimmering stone had resealed, the air around it humming with a powerful energy flow. It felt a bit like standing under an electric power cable of, say, five hundred kilowatt. You could almost see the surge of its physical power rush up to be swallowed by the grimy ceiling, then disappear into some unknown astral plane. Was it the Fallen One siphoning the channel, enjoying a quick mana high? I was going to close the tap on him in a moment. I had my own plans for that mana fountain, not to forget the greedy dragon demanding his share of the mana pie. I just hoped that I was the First Priest not in fancy name only; I had to be able to control the Temple when needs be.

I lay my hand on the altar, highlighting it and activating the interaction regime. It exploded with cascades of opening windows. That got me thinking. I'd just done what any regular player would have, highlighting an object, then right-clicking it. That was my old gaming reflex getting the better of me. Still, the Fallen One was my witness that I'd done so for the first time in the last week. The rest of the time my interactions with game objects hadn't differed from real-life ones: you pick it up—you study it—then use it, no interface crutches involved. Which meant that all the little buttons and menus kept integrating into my new reality, commonplace actions and skills replacing gaming elements.

I studied myself, looking for anything different from the default layout. Anything unusual, anything missing? Immediately I noticed the first thing out of place: the quick access menu. The ten little slots in the corner of the screen had disappeared—don't even ask me when or where to—and these days I instinctively reached for the tiny pockets on my belt without even looking, feeling for the right vial in the heat of the fight.

I counted them: eight. Well. Where were the remaining two, then? Let's try it.

I pulled a new vial out of the bag and tried to shove it down a non-existent pocket in my belt. My fingers touched the hard leather, pushing against the steel rivets, then finally felt the opening and shoved the vial into the little pocket. Nine! It worked!

I peered at the little loop suspiciously, then pulled the vial out expecting the opening to disintegrate. As if! Its bandolier-like dark eye kept staring at me, showing no intention of disappearing. Disappointed, I looked away and blinked, detecting a blurred motion out of the corner of my eye. I stared back at the belt. Eight. Funny that.

Now another test, even more important than the first. I pulled two more elixirs out of my bag and brought the amount of little pockets to ten. Then I relaxed, trying to concentrate on other things, and without looking shoved the eleventh elixir down my belt. Wasn't it great? Well done! Now that could give us a considerable advantage over regular players. That was something to consider and to look into—a new direction to take.

Further inspection had shown that the quick spell access slots had equally disappeared. Now I simply remembered the ten quick access spells without having to leaf through the magic book or transfer them to operative memory. The potential of this was much more serious than just an easy access to an extra vial. Increasing the number of available working spells could give the perma players a considerable advantage whenever they battled monsters or other chars. More spells meant more tactics; more chances to get an extra gram of experience or survive a close shave.

At the moment, it wasn't a good time to look into this mystery, so I left it until later. I had a funny feeling there was more to it than that. My hair was already standing on its end as I'd come too close to the altar—so close I was getting little shocks. A high-voltage transformer isn't a good place for thinking.

I concentrated on the opened interface windows. I'd have loved to rip the arms off the bastard who'd tested the interface's ergonomics and usability. It was as clear as mud. Actually, how sure was I that it had been tested at all? I was looking at the inner workings of the NPC admin panel. More than likely, both the post of the First Priest and access to the altar hadn't been meant for real players to begin with. Very well. There's always the good old method of trial and error. I just hoped the system was foolproof and wouldn't let me do anything stupid to this mind-blowing nuclear kettle. With any luck, I'd stay in one piece.

Naturally, I exercised the utmost caution. I didn't touch any settings, just studied the menus, my absolute memory soaking up their multiple branches. Once I checked all the options, I shook my head, trying to put the puzzle together and build a complete map of altar control. After that, it was time to proceed with caution and understanding.

Consecration to a junior god.

For your information: Every Dark Temple automatically boosts the Fallen One's strength. In addition, it can be consecrated to a junior patron god of your choice.

Pantheon alert! The Pantheon of the Fallen One is empty! You can't consecrate the Temple to an existing subgod. Would you like to summon a new god?

You bet! I pressed *Confirm*, triggering an enormous list sheet. Hundreds of names flickered before my eyes. I had to sort them all out into some kind of system. Why, for instance, would I need all those Indian ones, all those Agni, Brahma, Varuna, Vishnu et al? It wasn't as if I was on the Hindu's pay roll. I fiddled with the list until I finally managed to get rid of all the unwanted ones and arrive at the list of ancient Slavic gods. I also kept the Greek and Scandinavian ones: I had a soft spot for them for some reason. Both Aphrodite and Odin appealed to me more than Guan Di or Hanuman.

The triage resulted in about thirty ancient Slavic names: the likes of Perun, Belobog, Hors and Svarog. A quick prompt popped up when I highlighted the first of them, complete with a list of bonuses for the god's worshippers. That did it for me. Gods, let me tell you, are seriously cool. Take Perun, the god of thunder, patron of warriors. The skills he could shower onto his worshippers made me want to prostrate myself in awe.

Heavenly Thunder: a powerful discharge of electricity that deals the target 2,000 pt. damage. Cooldown: 12 hrs.

Chain Lightning: targets several creatures standing next to each other, starting with the chosen target. Every new target halves the damage: 1500, 750, 350, 200, 100. Cooldown: 12 hrs.

Sky Guard: allows to summon a warrior from Perun's numerous retinue. The summoned creature's level always equals that of the summoner. Spell duration has the minimum limit of 5 min. with no maximum. However, the number of the Thunderer's warriors is limited causing the summoned Guard to leave the summoner at any time in case of a shortage of available retinue warriors when somebody else is casting the same spell. Cooldown: 24 hrs.

Blessed Steel: a weapon buff adding +25% to magic fire damage.

Spell duration: 2 hrs.

Cooldown: 24 hrs.

There is an off chance of the buff never wearing out, leaving the weapon forever enchanted by the divine word.

And so on and so forth. The skill list was long: the god was trying a bit too hard to push the worshipper into earning Faith points, elevating him through the ranks and offering him the chance to choose yet another uber freebie. Wonder if it was the result of the god's already being forgotten once? Meaning that now the divinities would appreciate their earthly following, hurrying to get them out of trouble and showering them with skills.

It looked as if I was in it for the long haul. I lay my shield on the black sooty floor and sat cross-legged on top of it. Let's have a look!

The next dose of shock I received when I made my way down the list to Morana's name. The goddess of winter and the wife of Koschei—the Slavic god of death. The very first ability made me sit up:

Life Cycle: by using this skill, a player will gain one level per second, including all respective racial and class bonuses. Upon reaching level 200, the character's life cycle comes to an end and he receives an XP penalty as he would have in the case of death at the hands of a mob. Cooldown: 24 hrs.

How very unusual. I wasn't even talking about its combat properties: they required quite a bit of combined thinking from me and my calculator. Still, the fact was that this particular ability was my long sought-after suicide button. Plus giving you a couple extra minutes to beat the hell out of your adversaries who wouldn't know what had hit them. As somebody who'd done my time suspended from a hook in the Cats' torture cellar, I knew the true potential of it.

Still, it was never a good idea to bet on a dark horse you'd never seen even though you might have heard that yes, it's a horse and yes, it might be able to run.

I queried the Internet service for everything they had available on Morana. I had barely made my way through half of her skills when they contacted me. Did they have an AI in their customer service or something?

I opened the file and started reading, my heart sinking with every sentence. I really, really didn't like her. Not a good deity at all. Very vicious. Her symbols: the Black Moon, a few skulls and a scythe that she used to cut the thread of life. Holy moly. How sure was I that summoning her wouldn't be a blunder to end all blunders? What if my name would be cursed for millennia for summoning the goddess of death into a deathless world? Laith the Traitor, the Immortality Thief. Did I like the moniker? Not really. Couldn't I find just one out of these hundreds of deities with similar skills and a nicer temper?

I spent the next few hours scanning hundreds of pages of fine print. My head was buzzing on the same note as the mana flow: either from the information overload or from the proximity of the altar. And I couldn't even move aside as I still needed to be in direct contact with the stone. All discomfort aside, I had to admit that few things were more gratifying that studying the skills and abilities of the average Pantheon, especially in a world where gods weren't just manipulation tools in the hands of corrupted priests. Here, they were a force to be reckoned with and the knowledge of them remained a vital tool indeed.

I kept turning page after page. A god, a goddess, a Titan, a dragon...

Zhelia, the goddess of sorrow, sympathy and weeping. Logically, she could do: lots of interesting skills, like blocking pain sensations in battle. To my chagrin, she didn't have what I needed most: voluntary death.

Karna, her sister. Mourning the dead, eternal grieving, greeting the fallen ones on their way to the world of the dead. Same thing: lots of bells and whistles but not the one I needed most.

Finally, when I'd made my way through not only Slavic gods but also Scandinavian, I found it!

Macaria. The daughter of Hades and Persephone. The goddess of blissful death. In Greek mythology, hers was a bit part: apparently, she sacrificed herself at the altar in order to win victory in battle for her brothers. As a goddess she didn't account for much, her skills being mainly passive, but they all dealt with one thing only: an easy death, beneficial and even enjoyable.

Second Chance: a passive skill giving a 10% chance of immediately respawning on the spot in full armor without any XP losses.

Always At Hand: a passive skill giving a 25% chance of your grave teleporting with you to your bind point.

Smile of a Goddess: a passive skill giving 1% chance of receiving extra XP in case of death, equaling five times the XP penalty in case of death at the hands of a mob.

Grace of God: a passive skill giving 10% of not losing experience in case of death.

And, finally, that was it:

Blissful Death for Another. The skill grants and easy and painless death while sharing the experience lost equally between the Goddess, the Fallen One and the player of your choice. Cooldown: 1 hr.

Bingo. I sent another Internet request for more information. The answer was quite reassuring: the girl had no backstory of any scary or questionable actions, a perfect faceless prospect, virtually a new skill tree with no Hades, Morana or Koschei lurking behind it to pull any strings. Or so I hoped. True, it was unlikely the girl would strengthen the Fallen One, but that wasn't the idea. The sheer voluntary death option would preclude any kidnappings or forceful imprisonment, bringing all perma players—at least a hundred thousand people—under the Fallen One's banners. That was even if you didn't count some totally cool passive skills that could cut your experience losses a good 25%.

I stole a look around, making sure the Fallen One wasn't listening in. He could well have his own ideas about his Pantheon, and there I was, suggesting Macaria the Blessed as his sidekick. I highlighted the line I needed and pressed *Yes*, whispering,

"This is none of my fault. You should have let me in on your plans."

Bang! Once again, the floor shuddered. The shield I'd so comfortably been sitting on slid from under my backside like a dog on ice. I dropped onto my back, noticing a cloud of a thousand lights appear under the dome and thicken into a luminescent figure.

Pantheon alert! A new force has entered the world! Macaria, the goddess of easy death, has joined the Pantheon of the Fallen One.

Dark worshippers! Now you can choose your patron god. In order to do that, visit the temple of your chosen deity or address yourself to one of the Fallen One's priests.

Too bad. I would have thought that clicking a god's name on the menu would be enough. But apparently, religion was sold piecemeal. What now, then? Was I supposed to set up a portal right in the Temple or bless every worshipper personally? Wonder how much the Olders would fork out for private protection against kidnapping? And did I really want to offer them that option? That's where my interests could potentially clash with those of the Fallen One. He needed worshippers while I didn't want the skills to disperse around the world. Having said that, I was his First Priest, so any growth of the Temple was also my personal growth. A mind-boggling prospect.

I waved the message windows away and froze. A pretty girl's figure hovered in the air halfway from the ceiling to the basalt floor.

I jumped up, brushed my clothes and lowered my head. "Goddess..."

Macaria turned her face to me, her eyes curious but still trance-like. "Priest. How long did I sleep?"

Oh. Suppressing the desire to scratch my head, I flexed my math muscles. "Over two thousand years."

"That's a lot. Where are the Heraclidae, my brothers?"

How was I supposed to know? She liked asking uncomfortable questions, didn't she? "In the legends," I managed.

"And this," the girl poked the molten stone with a squeamish finger, "is this my Temple?"

"Actually, this is the Temple of the Fallen One. He's the highest god here. But it's yours as well, my lady," I tried to sugar-coat the news that she'd have to share.

She frowned, shaking her head. "Never heard of him. This awful place just can't be my Temple. Everything has to be white!"

Following a wave of her hand, the streaks of molten stone shifted on the walls, acquiring the whiteness of the finest marble and the sheen of mountain snow caps. In a flash, gone was the dirt; gold mosaic patterns ran across the gleaming white. Slender stucco columns reached for the ceiling sparkling with the finest frescoes.

I stood open-mouthed, watching the Temple's miraculous resurrection. Had anyone ever witnessed something like this in real life, they'd have stopped wreaking havoc on earth and sought redemption under the banners of faith.

"It's just like back home," the goddess whispered. She clutched at her chest and burst out coughing, blood fountaining from her mouth. The girl sank to her knees, croaking, then collapsed to one side.

I darted toward her and scooped her up in my arms, swinging my head every which way. What was I supposed to do? She kept coughing, spitting red everywhere, dark streaks running from her ears and nose.

I concentrated on my internal interface and slammed the new *Appeal to Gods* button. Tasting the girl's blood in my mouth, I yelled,

"Help me, O Fallen One, quick!"

You have tasted divine blood! Now you will always retain a divine particle within you. Your skills and abilities will be a cut above the rest of the mortal world. But beware of false pride! Do not consider yourself equal to Gods! The stairway to heaven is long and fragile; according to some, it has no end at all.

Jesus. For a brief moment, I even forgot about the girl who was hosing everything down with her blood. A hoarse croak brought me back to my senses. I swept the message into Junk and yelled again,

"Fallen One, you son of a-"

"Keep your voice down," a calm voice said next to me. "So you're a vampire now, eh? Who is it you're sucking dry?"

He looked pleased with himself like a cat who'd stolen a pot of cream and chased it down with a double serving of valerian. He looked into the girl's face and gasped, his voice sobering.

"A goddess?"

He rushed towards her and ripped her collar open, exposing a voluptuous blood-soaked chest. He lay his hand on it. Groaning threads of energy stretched from the altar toward him, pumping enormous amounts of mana in double record time. The veins bulged on his glowing arm. Shaking all over, he stood there unmoving, scowling, siphoning kilotons of mana into the wasted goddess. As I watched the altar's glow fade, I grew restless. What if AI 311 had botched up the system it had taken me so much to restore?

The old 311 hadn't let me down, though. Soon the umbilical cord connecting him to the altar started to wither. Heaving a sigh, the Fallen One breathed in the last drops of energy and waved his hand, severing his connection with the altar. His legs gave way; he lowered himself onto the blood-soaked floor next to me.

"Stupid girl..." he whispered looking at her, his voice strangely gentle. The girl's face was clear now, her breathing level. You'd think she was asleep.

He turned to me, raising his hand for a high-five. Mechanically I slapped his palm, celebrating our victory. The familiar gesture symbolized the finding of the Temple, the double resurrection of the goddess and our shared closeness on the bloodied floor. But once I slapped it, I quickly retracted mine. Wasn't I a bit too fraternal with a god? We weren't basketball buddies, after all.

The Fallen One smiled, understanding. "It's all right, Max. You've done good. Congratulations on your priesthood. Now you're the first man on earth after God. Make sure you carry your title with honor. My special thanks for the altar and," he paused reading the information unseen to me, "for Macaria. She is much more significant than she might seem. And when millions of players start worshipping her, they'll make her a true gem of my Pantheon or even something much more important..."

He grunted, getting back to his feet, and walked over to where the girl lay, crouching next to her. Then he smiled, listening to something, and took her hand in his, whispering.

In the meantime, my inner greedy pig had come to and demanded my attention. Knocking himself on the forehead, he winked at the crimson puddles of potentially precious waste. God's blood, oh well. I glanced at the Fallen One's back and reached gingerly into my bag. Trying not to make much noise, I felt for the alchemy kit and produced five empty vials. Dunking them quickly into the priceless ingredient, I sealed them tight and shoved the vials deep into my pocket. Why not? It was going to be wasted, anyway. I might end up mopping it all up in a minute. Wiping God's blood away with a dirty cloth, yeah right...

I rose with a sigh and dragged my feet toward the altar. While the Fallen One was there, I still had to sort out one other thing, namely the promise I'd so stupidly made to one greedy ex-dragon.

I lay my hand on the dark stone, glancing at the status menu.

Dark Altar of the First Temple. Consecrated to the Fallen One.
Junior God: Macaria, the Goddess of Easy Death.
First Priest: Laith
Level: 3
Faith points: 12,911
Faith points needed to proceed to the next level: 2,987,089.
Mana flow: 3,000 per sec. Already accumulated: 180,341. Maximum capacity: 30,000,000
Access levels to mana flow:
Fallen One, 90% control
First Priest, 10% control

I broke the connection, cursing. He'd been smart, hadn't he, that clever bag of bones! And I'd wondered why he'd only asked for ten percent considering my rather hapless situation. That shrunken lizard must have known from the start that that was all the mana available to a priest. But how about my own little projects? My baby dragons, my castle self-restoration channel and a tiny one for my own personal use? That wasn't the deal!

"Eh, Fallen One? Need to talk."

* * *

To Dave Rubac, Head of Integration and Development Department.

A memo excerpt:

Dear Sir,

In accordance with the plan endorsed by you we are now working on a number of retrofitted deep implants into AlterWorld. As of now, we have generated 24 class A installations, 411 class B installations as well as over 6,000 items, quest triggers, control modules and legal paperwork.

The process isn't as smooth as we'd hoped. Figuratively speaking, we're trying to shoe a running horse using gold nails and an electron microscope for a hammer. At the moment we can't introduce any changes above level 4. Most tasks at hand can't be solved head-on. You can't imagine the lengths we've had to go to in order to create the Battle Golems' bunker. That demanded over five hundred micro actions that discreetly pushed the world in the right direction.

However, to our deepest regret, even this method seems to have developed quite a few faults. The required number of the pressure points keeps growing at a frightening rate, increasing the probability of both our error and of the higher beings' resistance.

Considering all this, the recent loss of three class-A installations looks especially humiliating. I am talking about the closed-off Dead Lands zone, including the 9A installation known as the Super Nova Temple and excellently mapped-out mithril deposits having the total weight of 317 tons (entry 18A in the classified inventory). That's not even counting the roughly hundred lower-class artifacts still in the lands that are now off limits to us.

According to our investigation, AI 4915/E who was officially introduced as the generated territories' secondary tester responsible for the behavioral intellect of the implants' guards, stopped answering our status requests a few days ago. We tend to believe he went perma mode, then transferred his mind into a more powerful entity under his own control. We can only guess how the activated implant affected his own consciousness, but the fact remains that he has granted access to the object to the most undesirable individual in the whole of AlterWorld. No way that could be a coincidence as the player in question had in his possession an artifact that allowed him to restore the First Temple—a game scenario which wasn't at all previewed. And the nearest event that was supposed to solve several strategic problems at once, namely Obtaining the Heart of a Dark God, was only scheduled for the coming Christmas season.

The player has proved to be digitized which prevented us from checking his logs, but at least we've managed to recognize some residual traces of divine influence. It's possible that one of them, unable to restore the Altar on his own, generated a chain of events similar to how we create implants. Those are micro events: a mosquito biting you on the neck, a mob critting you, a waitress' cleavage distracting the object's attention for the 1.5 seconds necessary.

Whether the entity's objectives are limited to restoring the First Temple or they reach much further, we can't tell you right now.

Jan Kaevski, chief of the closed group.

Chapter Twelve

I gave the god a quick update on my adventures, then grassed on the sly-assed bag of bones. "You understand, don't you," I concluded, "that I need some mana flow even if only to clear up this mess," I pointed around me at what I remembered to be piles of junk.

The Fallen One studied the gleaming white decor with skepticism, raising a quizzical eyebrow at all the gilding and artwork. Embarrassed, I showed him my filthy hand smeared with the divine blood. "That's all Macaria's work! Outside, the place is a bomb site. The castle is in ruins and so is the Temple."

I started unbending my fingers. "Firstly, I need to restore the castle walls and the temple grounds. Then I'll need to explore the lands and ensure my own safety. Thirdly and lastly, the baby dragons on the North Tower are starving and need to be fed. There must be more, only I can't think of everything at once."

"That's enough," he shrugged off my arguments. "I know about Tianlong. You can't miss him: his lair is absolutely impenetrable to magic. But one-tenth of *my* altar for eternity—that's a bit thick! Next time you sign up for something stupid like that, at least cross your fingers behind you back. That way your karma cooldown will be less in case you renege on your word. Your contract is questionable in many respects so one could easily circumvent it, especially considering my training: I've made my way through a good hundred thousand manuals of which over two hundred are legal tomes. But... Dragon is our man, if you can say that of a skeletal Elf god. Attracting him to our camp is a number one task. Okay, wait here, I'll see what I can do."

He glanced at the goddess. With a warm smile, he rearranged the ripped shirt on her chest. Perfectionist! He could have restored it had he really wanted to. He snapped his fingers. The girl's body disappeared, on its way to some heavenly chambers awash with the sounds of panpipes. One more snap—and I stood there alone.

I looked around me. The hall was medically clean in its Greek beauty. The god had left, taking all the blood-stained DNA samples with him. What a shame. My inner greedy pig had been pulling at my jacket fighting to attract my attention, hinting that the miserable five vials were nothing compared to a cozy wine cellar stacked up with more of the same.

Okay, what next? I checked my virtual to-do list and grinned. Freebies!

There's a time to cast stones and a time to gather them, I said to myself as I reached into my bag for the Soul Stone containing the Hell Hound. I wiped it clean with my sleeve.

"I've taken good care of you. I haven't wasted you stupidly. So please don't let me down."

I placed the stone onto the altar's mirrored black top and stepped back, just in case. In the nick of time.

My ears resounded with a powerful blast. A portal window materialized over the altar, allowing me a glimpse into the depths of the Inferno: it glowed every shade of crimson, lava flowing unhurriedly amid the strangely formed piles of basalt rocks.

Judging by the flames, the atmosphere there was thinner, causing oxygen to burn faster than the weird-looking Hell flora could produce it. Air gushed into the portal, trying to level out the pressure and pulling in everything within its reach. Like myself, for one. It was a good job the portal had a short-impulse structure. Had it lasted a bit longer, I'd have had every chance to enjoy the afterlife sooner than expected.

It all finished very quickly: with a double popping sound, the portal opened then closed again, with me clutching at thin air, my back a strangely convoluted shape. Talk about a lucky miss.

I switched my focus to read a new quest message:

Quest completion alert: Hell's Temptation. Quest completed!
Reward: Access to quest Hell's Temptation II.

Oh. My inner greedy pig opened and closed his mouth, speechless with indignation. Hadn't he had enough freebies? They kept coming faster than we could sort through them. A new quest was a very good thing: the further the unique chain of quests took us, the heftier the prize at the end of it. Consider the lost stone an investment, I told my greedy alter ego before closing the message. Underneath it, I discovered another one:

Congratulations! You've learned a new skill: Portal to Inferno.
The connection between a necro wizard and an imprisoned soul is so great that the stone that holds it becomes a flashing beacon calling him. The portal, this smoothed-out fold of matter that covers the rupture to a different plane, cannot conceal from you the crystal's true light. From now on, you can always open the portal leading to the dark depths of Inferno and keep it open for as long as is needed.
Ingredient: a Soul Stone of a level identical or above that of the caster.

I tipped the crown onto my forehead and scratched the back of my head. Curiouser and curiouser. The uberness of the skill directly depended on the degree of the portal's inaccessibility by the usual means. A quick Wiki check showed that no such means existed. Only the planes' respective bosses could occasionally drop portal scrolls; even less occasionally, you could receive them as rewards in some truly mean quests. These kinds of skills only existed as fandom rumors and vague official hints. It couldn't be otherwise, considering the frequency with which a few top guilds raided their respective planes. Having said that, the answer to the question was now right in front of me, so you never know, I might one day lead *my* guild against some Infernal Arch Demon's castle. Not today, of course, not even next Friday. But it was good to know I had that option if I needed it. I could also earn a quick and quite hefty buck on the side as a gate keeper for some serious customers. This I could also keep in mind as a potential and relatively kosher money spinner.

So where was the promised access to the new quest? I stole a look around, then tapped the altar with a sacrilegious finger. Hell Hound, hello?

A new gust of wind forced me to spread-eagle in an attempt to keep my footing on the slippery floor. Once the artificial tempest subsided, I ventured a look around. The hound stood not far from me, looking quite the worse for wear. She was heaving, her back streaked with blood, holding one paw gingerly in front of her. In her teeth she held a still warm lump of flesh, its severed muscle fibers twitching. She downed it in one forced gulp, spat out a bloodied clump of hair onto the white marble and limped toward me, her glare unkind and unpromising. Her pack—or should I say, whatever was left of it—froze in a thin line behind her back. Three were rather in a bad way— males, as far as I could tell by their impressive size and wide chests,—and over a dozen females of various sizes and ages, each of them holding a puppy struggling half-heartedly in their mouths.

The Hound approached, her neon glare burning a hole in me. A familiar voice resounded in my head,

"Thank you for doing what I asked of you. And doubly so for laying the soul stone onto the First Temple Altar. Its sacred power alone allowed me to survive and save the remains of my pack who were already cornered at the nest's lower level."

"What happened? Why were you attacked?"

"You weren't in a hurry, were you?" she gave me an accusing look. "In the land of the Inferno, it's survival of the fittest. Our hunting grounds are poor. Even the best of our trackers can only find fresh meat but once a week. So once our pack had lost its leader, everybody and their grandmother were after our hunting grounds. I was nearly too late to help—and still my attack from the rear had surprised the enemy and allowed me to break through to rejoin my pack—or rather, the third of it that's still left."

She raised her hackles, her voice accusing. Obeying her non-verbal command, the other pack members stepped forward, baring the deadly needles of their fangs under their threateningly shaking lips.

"Hey, wait!" I recoiled in a rush to activate the shield and locate the new ability that gave me 30-sec immunity. "It wasn't a pleasure cruise for me, either. First I was in jail, if you remember, after you'd left me there. Almost as soon as I was released, I got kidnapped and jailed again. I tried to restore the temple in the City of Light's catacombs which was how I found this altar fragment that allowed me to restore the First Temple. Which I did precisely two hours ago! So what's your problem? Had it not been for me, you'd still be pining away on that chain, looking at the world through prison bars. As an alternative, you might have become a zombie hound serving some Necro summoner," I dropped by way of a hint.

She squinted at me, her intentions unclear—they could have been political as well as gastronomical. Then she tilted her head toward the pack, growling. The hounds stepped back, dropping to their skinny backsides. Their thin ratlike tails, covered in fine armor scales, still brushed nervously across the floor.

Finally, she made up her mind and raised her head to me, her stare hypnotic. "We need a new home."

New quest alert: Hell's Temptation II.
The remains of the once-powerful pack of Hell Hounds have been forced to abandon their nest and are now looking for a new place. Help the creatures of Inferno to find a new home.
Reward: up to you. The Hounds are strong. It's not often they accept somebody's superiority. Whatever happens, do not corner them. Even a rat is capable of attacking a man who's cut off its escape routes.
For your information: The divine particle reacts at the first sign of aggression that targets its bearer and dissolves in his aura granting him a near-absolute immunity. You can now enjoy maximum protection from mental control spells.

Bummer! How was I to know that? I wished she'd have swiped me with her claws, then I'd have gotten some physical damage immunity instead. That way I'd have been a true monster killer. What. A. Shame. Never mind, we'd simply have to work with what we had. I glanced back at the Hound who was studying the effect the news had had on me. I smiled, shaking my head.

"Sorry, babe. That's not how we're going to talk."

She shrunk and dropped to her ass, dumbstruck, jerking her bad paw with an involuntary yelp.

"I'm afraid you don't seem to know who you're trying to manipulate," I said. "I am this Temple's First Priest and the God's personal friend. If you need something from me, then we'll have to discuss it on equal terms, no mind games. Let's try it again."

The hound shook her head in disbelief. She gave me an unsure look and repeated haltingly,

"We need... a new home. This area abounds with game. My pack could regain its old powers soon; potentially, if we could find a way to stay here for long enough, we could become the strongest clan in the Rocky Wastelands. What we need is an official permission from the landlord. Somehow my gut feeling tells me it's you. Do let us stay. At least until our pups shed their baby armor."

All that unclaimed power sitting there doing nothing, waiting for my decision. No idea why they'd mistook me for the landlord but something in her words struck a chord besides the usual kind of compassion that we feel for homeless pups. Did she say a clan? We could try, I suppose...

"I've heard your request," I said. "Still, you are a force too threatening to remain a wild independent pack living in the shade of the First Temple," seeing the hound stand up about to say something, I raised my hand, gesturing for her to let me finish. "As the First Priest and clan leader, I am responsible for lives other than my own. It is possible that soon this place will be crowded with people, some of them my own. So what do you suggest I do when you start slaughtering each other? Wait! I'm not finished! So I suggest an alternative solution. You and your clan will swear me your oaths of allegiance. That will automatically change your status to allied which will allow us to join forces against our mutual enemies. That's the only proposition you're getting. Here, catch!"

I clicked on the contract template that I'd thrown together earlier on, securing their junior-partner position in my freshly-baked alliance, and pressed *Send*. I'd wanted it to cover all the relevant rights and liabilities that marginally resembled a liege oath. The contract wasn't meant for NPCs, of course—only for existing clans of real human players. Then again, no one had ever tried to argue with a Hell Hound before, let alone negotiate.

The Infernal creature stared at me trying to second-guess the weird human's motives. For the first time, someone offered her friendship and protection instead of demanding gold or services. I could almost hear the game's gears crunch as it adapted itself to accommodate another piece of their newborn world puzzle that was forced into its mechanics. It must have, because the Hound had accepted my proposal.

Congratulations! The NPC Clan Hell's Fire has joined your Alliance of The Guards of the First Temple as a junior partner.

You can now summon the Clan's warriors to your service and claim your share of their taxes.

"Excellent!" I gave her a wink as the Hound concentrated on her own feelings, surprised. "Now try to add the Alliance tag."

Answering her bewildered stare, I decided to give her a demonstration. "Watch the name," I poked the imaginary halo over my name where with a minimum amount of willpower a player could conjure up some basic information about the person.

Laith

I ticked the menu,

Laith, Level 72.

More clicks:

Laith, Level 72, Death Knight <Children of the Night>, <Guards of the First Temple>.

I unticked the extra information. "Your adversary doesn't need to know your particulars," I nodded to the Hound. "See now?"

The Hound wrinkled the only line on her forehead, all her muscles trembling with the exertion. Once again I could hear celestial gears crunch. Finally, another piece of the world puzzle fell into place.

Hell's Hound. Level 151. <Guards of the First Temple>.

I glanced at the mini map and smiled. The red dots that had marked the hounds as *dangerous and aggressive* were now glowing blue: the color of regular NPCs like the guards that used to patrol the Vets' castle walls.

Throwing caution to the wind, I approached the battered animal and patted her armored neck level with my chest. The pup must have been hanging on by the skin of her teeth. Only now had I noticed that her life was deep in the orange zone and virtually not regenerating. Was she so hungry? I studied the pack again—this time not as a victim but as a proprietor. Fugitives any way you looked at them. Deadly dangerous, still seething with the heat of the battle and the agony of their loss. Their puppies were their only salvaged possessions. Time to bring the pooches under control: this was not the right moment to breed anarchy.

I rummaged through my ever-lengthening ability list for the God's gift. Help of the Fallen One. I selected the pack's leader as target and activated it. In a flash of special effects, the Hound sprung back on all four feet. Tilting her head this way and that, she studied herself, disbelieving. Then she turned her massive head to me, slouching in a grateful bow.

I nodded and shrugged her gratitude off: *don't mention it.* I'd better double-check my control of the pack, outline a few tasks and try to solve a few pressing problems in the bargain.

"Think you could use the Temple cellars for your quarters?"

The Hound glanced at the altar. A greedy spark flashed in her eyes. Looked like I wasn't the only one profiting from my close relationship with an artifact of this caliber. It had plenty of goodies to go round.

"Very well," I said. "Now listen here. Make a quick check of the cellars. Purge any insentient creatures. Leave the sentient ones for me, I'll sort them out later. Find yourself a good place to make a den, preferably in the furthest reaches. If it needs a bit of work, just let me know. The whole place needs quite a refurbishment so it won't be a problem digging a couple extra rooms or exits."

The Hound stomped and shifted her feet, impatient to dash off in search of fresh food, experience and a new home. I hurried to finish,

"One last thing I want to ask of you. If you find any big lumps of metal like this one," I reached into my bag for a handful of the purple fragments, "bring it to me here, will you? You can leave it... say, over there," I pointed at a far corner, gesturing in the air to show them the size of the anticipated pile of wonders.

The Hound leaned forward, sniffing the fragment, and recoiled. "The true silver! The cursed metal. Very well, my Dark brother. We'll keep our eyes open."

Turning her armored muzzle toward her pack, she barked a short command. The females looked relieved as they laid their puppies on the floor, shepherding them expertly together. Three of the more battered ones stayed on to supervise the nursery while the rest followed their leader who had already dashed off, disappearing into the depths of the Temple.

Quest completion alert: Hell's Temptation II. Quest completed!

I dismissed the rather useless message and wiped the sweat from my brow. Phew. Looked like I'd just settled a potentially stinking situation and even emerged with some decent prospectives. I glanced at the tired hounds sprawled on the cold floor watching the puppies crawl about, their blue tongues hanging out.

Remembering my school years and mom-packed lunches that I used to feed to our local feral dogs, I pulled a dozen sandwiches out of my bag: I had plenty left after leveling my culinary skill. I walked over and crouched next to the immediately tense animals. I removed the cover and took a bite, demonstrating their edibility. Thank God, they started eating, casting grateful glances my way. I patted a puppy behind the ear and returned to my position by the altar.

It was probably a good idea to invest into a couple of Sparks of Dark Flame. Useful ingredient, you should never be without them. Wonder how much I could retail them for? There was a chance that the auction crowd had no idea how to get them and was therefore prepared to pay a King's ransom for them. In that case, they could be a veritable cash cow. I clicked an auction window and basked in anticipation as I typed in the key word. Then I froze. It wasn't that the Sparks weren't available—on the contrary, a good couple dozen had been languishing at the auctions for several months. Even though raid bosses dropped enough of them, no one had yet thought of a way to use them. And as for NPC priests, they weren't interested in goods-for-money exchanges. Still, it was a freebie even though of a different kind. The offers were for fifty gold, you couldn't complain about that. I activated the auto buy with a mental raspberry to all the priests (whom I admittedly hadn't appointed yet). Those would quickly catch up on the item's true value but by then I'd cream off all I could.

Only then I noticed the Inbox flashing. Oops. Two PMs, one from Zena, the other from Dan. In different wording, both said the same thing:

Is this your work? We need to talk.

Zena I could understand. But how could our cloak-and-dagger have figured it out? I understood, of course, that they were obliged to keep tabs on me as an important figure, a patent holder and a universal lockpicker. In other words, the clan's mysterious friend that they were obliged to keep an eye on so that he didn't stray to the wrong side of the barricades.

I paused to think, then typed off a quick note explaining I was awfully busy but ready to speak once I had a free moment. Told them there'd been some interesting developments—asking them not to make their speculations public just yet.

A portal popped open, bringing me back to reality. The Fallen One hummed something, looking pleased with himself. Catching my quizzical glance, he gave me a wink. "You'll be paying the Dragon five percent of mana flow for next year. I'll add the rest. We need to resuscitate that bag of bones double quick. Shame to waste mana, of course, I could use it myself. I need to grow too, and in my case simply killing monsters won't cut it, I'm afraid. That's it, gotta dash. I have some plans for tonight."

He gave me a meaningful smile, then glanced over the nervous hounds and gave me a thumbs-up. Apparently, he was already in the know. Had he kept an eye on the Temple all the while?

"Ahem, Sir... O Fallen One, I wonder if I could have these stupid marks removed? I'm all covered in medals like a champagne label."

The god tapped his forehead, remembering, then snapped his fingers, materializing a bottle of champagne. "Why? Do they itch or something?" he guffawed, turning to me. "That bag of demented bones must have forgotten that a mark works both ways. The astral link that connects you is his own doing. You have a long life in front of you; you might still cross paths with the Titans and talk them into granting you a couple of skills—Rider, or even Tamer. Then the boot might be on the other foot: the dragon will be yours to ride and travel on! Okay then, got no time to chat, sorry. I've got business to attend to," he lovingly stroked the bottle as I came up with some last-minute advice,

"Don't forget some flowers for the lady, you Romeo. And a box of chocolates."

The god nodded, preoccupied, before disappearing down the portal.

"Wild nights, wild nights! Were I with thee, wild nights should be our luxury," I commented into thin air.

Chapter Thirteen

Well now! I'd done everything I could to make everybody happy. The only thing left for me to do was to prioritize the order of the Temple's regeneration. Then I could finally set off on a marathon along the castle walls in search for the dragon's eggs. Last time I checked, the three defense walls counted at least a couple dozen northbound towers. I knew I didn't have to have contact with the altar in order to control the mana flow but I couldn't very easily send mana to someone I didn't know: it would be like looking for a needle in a haystack. I needed to know enough of the item's or character's stats to prevent any mixups—as my own crude way of placemarking its astral position. Even that wasn't so important as long as I could give instructions to the altar to redirect the mana flow.

I touched the stone's glossy black surface, receiving a status message of the five percent available. It looked as if the Fallen One had already redirected the mana flow overrunning my earlier obligations. I opened the utility menus. I had no idea how long it would take me to restore the entire castle and how much time I'd have to spend afterwards adding the finishing touches by hand but at the moment, the control hall regeneration was my top priority. I had to have total control over the entire castle, otherwise the Temple would become a defenseless standalone building, however pretty. Personally, I was looking forward to meeting the hordes of Light armed and prepared once my fortifications became something more serious than piles of debris.

Jesus. What a mess of options, menus, submenus and dropout lists. Had the developers outsourced the creation of this interface to some Indian sweat shop? My unfocused stare fell on a section entitled Summoning the Temple Guards. This might be interesting. I decided to check it out.

Apparently, I had 30,000 level units available, calculated as the temple's rank times ten thousand. You could cash them in, summoning the widest range of creatures, both sentient and mobs. This exchange rate wasn't linear, either: the ratio remained at 1:1 until level 100, then began rapidly growing. In the most irrational scenario you could waste your whole 30,000 on one level-900 uncategorized entity. To give you some idea, I could summon a giant Cerberus the size of a five-story house and properties to match. Wonder if the Hell Hounds would rejoice at seeing their big brother and appoint it their high canine deity? In any case, I wasn't going to hire any guards at the moment. They demanded payment on a daily basis: one gold per point spent. By doing some simple math, you could see that full-scale hiring would cost me three grand a day. In case of a guard's death the spent points returned into a common pool and became available for repurchase after twenty-four hours.

After some hesitation, I decided to hire a few status guards for the Guard of Honor who would also prevent the mobs' access to the donjon. After five minutes of fiddling with the settings, a dozen orcs in heavy armor took their posts by the Temple's doors and gates, led by a Lieutenant in a suit of armor embellished with silver. The pleasure of having them cost me fifteen hundred gold. Actually, was I supposed to keep the Temple army all on my own? Again I buried myself in the menu, finally discovering the finance section which said that the First priest had access to 1% of all donations to the Fallen One. At the moment, the sum was negligible as the sheer motivation to earn Faith points hadn't even existed until less than an hour ago: hardly enough time for anyone to have found a Dark priest and dedicated themselves to the only available deity, i.e. Macaria. I was worried, though, that the digitized community had already sussed out all the advantages involved and was now at boiling point and threatening to explode. They didn't need consecration rituals to appreciate the entire range of services offered, so quite a few people had to be ecstatically looking for a suitable priest or altar.

While I was at it, I looked into their faith point catalogue. To receive one Faith point, you had to either donate 1000 mana, 100 XP of 1 gold. Considering that the first religious rank called for 1000 Faith points, you could easily work out that it would cost the buyer exactly one hundred bucks. Of which I was getting one miserable dollar bill. Still, this was a numbers game. I multiplied one dollar by the number of potential followers, multiplied by eternity. Immortality was a good thing any way you looked at it. The resulting figures were impressive.

Finally I got to the upgrade and rebuild menu and opened the submenu tree. So! Macaria hadn't wasted her time! Apparently, she wasn't one for half-measures, having reanimated not only the Temple hall but also all of the central donjon. I was pleased to see that the First Temple's potential allowed the use of its self-restoration facilities also for rebuilding other castle structures. I could see now that the entire complex had been conceived as an organic unity whose defense and regeneration functions often overlapped or even merged with only one objective in mind: the enhancement of the Temple's defense potential.

Even on their own, both the castle and the Temple must have cost tens of millions. But their combined value was tenfold. A dream goodie, as precious as it was useless. I had to be careful not to choke on it. The only chance I could have in this new game was due to my freshly-acquired post and celestial support. Had I been just Laith, even a clan leader, I'd have already auctioned the castle's coordinates, creamed off my couple of million and washed my hands of the whole thing. But as it was now, fate had dealt me half a pack of trump cards so I'd better use them while I had the chance. Another one like that might not present itself for a long time.

As somebody said, luck is what happens when preparation meets opportunity. Fate may keep opening doors to new opportunities, but how ready are we to jump at them? When you get a dream offer of a job abroad— is it time to regret you never got down to mastering your language skills? When you are confronted by a zombie towering over the body of a policeman who'd just emptied his AK (rather uselessly) in it, is it time to regret you don't know how to change the spent clip? Well, in that case it's no good blaming your luck: you're your own worst enemy.

I leafed through the castle plans, storing the schemes and building's statutes in my memory.

The main flight of stairs. I placemarked it on the map. Status, green: fully functional.

Arsenal. Status, yellow. Partially functional. Restoration time: 28 days using the current configuration, 6 hours if assigned top priority and all available resources.

Underground dungeons, communications and cellars. Status, red. Decay level: 81%.

And so on and so forth. Macaria had poured her main effort into refurbishing the Temple hall and façade, restoring the rest of the facilities to their minimal functionality levels.

Finally, at the donjon's fifth level, I discovered the Control Room marker. Status, yellow: partially functional. Did it mean I could just walk in and take over the castle? My inner greedy pig was throwing a fit threatening to rip the place apart if I didn't go there now and claim control over the abandoned property. For a brief moment, he gave me the creeps as I remembered an ancient Alien movie where the monsters ripped their hosts open from inside. You hear that, porcine face? You'd better not upset me, buddy, or I'll upgrade you to a toad and pretend you'd had always been like that.

Actually, I was curious too. To stumble across an unwanted Super Nova-class castle was cooler than finding an abandoned car transporter loaded with unclaimed brand new Bentleys. I checked the map for a shortcut and had a good look around, adjusting the visuals to the freshly-digested maps. Then I closed the menus, severed contact with the altar stone and dashed under the archway above a far-off flight of stairs.

My corridor run brought me equal doses of disappointments and new discoveries. What had Macaria been thinking about? All the rooms I passed were immaculately clean, their functional granite tiles sparkling. Clean being the operative word! Whatever happened to all the technogenic debris? Where were all the spent shells, empty clips and broken ammo belts, precious mithril shrapnel and fragments of armor? Where were all the heaps of rubble

I had counted on in which to unearth a couple of slightly soiled Warmechs? This wasn't cleaning, this was plain sabotage.

I felt like a husband who had unlocked his garage expecting to face the familiar mess where he could find every screw blindfolded, only to discover that his wife had given it a surprise spring clean, sweeping out all the precious bent nails, torn elastics and bits of wire creating a clean, neat and absolutely useless space. What had Macaria done with all the trash? Had she unthinkingly shoved it all away in the astral depths? It might have been worse: she might have processed mithril into energy, no wonder she'd pulled off this sixty-minute makeover single-handedly. What a bummer. I just hoped she confined herself to a surface clean which left me the hope to find a few stashes. And I still had the cellars. I just had to pray her obsession with cleanliness hadn't stretched that far.

The fifth level. A long spiraling corridor circled the windowless donjon, taking the potential attackers past rows of barracks and cutoff zones peppered with gunslots. Massive slabs of basalt stood ready to collapse creating an impenetrable barricade. All you needed was access to the control artifact or even a mere key that could open the intricate Dwarven locks.

The last corridor was angular, its sharp bends getting narrower with every turn. The last thirty feet or so could be successfully defended by just a couple of soldiers who could easily block the passage. That was clever, like everything here. Shame the restoration wasn't on a par thanks to one hasty young lady. This Macaria of Milo by an unknown sculptor deserved having her arms pulled off.

With a sigh, I examined the pale tiles lining the corridors. It looked as if a team of cowboy builders had hung cheap suspended ceilings over the Hermitage frescoes.

Shivering with anticipation, I finally heaved open the small but unmanageably thick iron-oak door, entering the castle's sancta sanctorum. I felt sorry for the castle's potential attackers who had to fit into the ever-narrowing corridors, leaving behind first their battle golems, then ogres, and finally trolls. The defenders wouldn't have any such problems, especially considering their monopoly on portals. The high ceilings—twenty feet at least—allowed the defenders to use a whole variety of AlterWorld races, including the latest in golem building. The power center was located behind the fenced-off battle grounds. The walls were lined with empty sockets meant to house accumulating crystals. How many could they hold, a hundred, two hundred? Considering each cost about a million gold, the castle builders had to have been quite ambitious.

I walked down an L-shaped passage between two fenced-off areas and found myself in the castle's heart: the control room.

Almost all of the space inside was occupied by a white U-shaped marble desk gaping with dozens of empty slots for artifacts of truly unknown purpose and nature. It looked rather like the control desk of some high tech submarine or nuclear power station with its empty mountings and ripped-out units. Some mysterious panels—once mirrored and now dented—looked suspiciously like monitors.

In the desk's center, the control panel of the castle artifact glowed a subtle green. The exact location of the artifact itself I was yet to determine; its unknown makers could have cemented it into the room's foundations for all I knew. I crossed my fingers and lay my hand on the imaginary keyboard.

Welcome to the Super Nova Castle control panel!
Your access level: Guest
Information output mode: video-assisted telepathy. How can I help you?

I shook my head, amazed. This didn't look like your ordinary menu options.

Are you sentient? I asked, just to be on the safe side.

After a second's pause, a faceless voice answered,

"Not exactly, even though I am closely approaching that idea. The control crystal contains a dissected soul of one of its mage creators, its freedom of will suppressed and all unnecessary emotions removed. My desire to serve and obey orders has been increased—the only thing that brings me satisfaction. What else can I do for you?"

I could hear a badly concealed plea in his voice: *Do ask me something, anything at all!*

"Current status?"

A Super Nova Castle. Decay level: 68%. Last authorization: 790 years ago. Last important event: 43 minutes ago, the restoration of 11% of its structure.

"Whose property is it?"

Question unclear.

"Who owns this castle?"

Since the restoration of the control center functionality, there were no registered ownership requests. Would you like to submit one?

You bet! "Yes!"

Forced activation of a one-off script. Establishing connection with the financial center as of instruction 82a.

This is AI Bordeaux7 stream 155. Congratulations! You have discovered an unclaimed castle. Class: Super Nova. As of clause 59 of EULA, you can claim ownership by paying the price of the real estate and repurchasing the land. Would you like to complete the transaction?

Yes! My voice broke. I swallowed. I'd never owned as much as a studio, let alone a castle.

The price of the 3 sq. mile plot is two million gold.

The price of the Super Nova Castle, including the unique Temple Complex with 68% wear and tear is 23 million. For your information, the castle has been recently restored.

"I know, thanks. That's twenty-five million..."

All that was left to do was bite my lip and tap the control panel. Over two million US dollars, an enormous amount even in real life. But more importantly, I just didn't have it. I simply had to wait for some Olders or others to buy the castle, then be cloistered in the Temple Hall without much right to anything else.

If you thought in terms of eternity, there was always the possibility of earning this sort of money. But right here and now? Then again, why not?

"Would it be possible to pay in installments?"

What monthly amount could you afford?

Did this mean it was possible? That's the solution, then! "How about ten thousand gold?" I added a pleading note to my voice.

The installment plan is limited to one year. Considering the state of your bank balance, we suggest the following solution: a down payment of one million gold which would secure your ownership of the castle, followed by twelve monthly payments of two million gold each. This is our best offer.

Oh. Where was I supposed to find two million a month? True, I had indeed managed to raise a similar amount in my first month in the game. The question was, how sure was I I'd have the same kind of luck for a further twelve months? Sure, I possessed a number of unique opportunities, but turning them into cash quickly and error-free was not going to be easy. In case of success, it would indeed consolidate my position in AlterWorld. If I failed—well, I would lose all the cash I'd paid. That was bad but sufferable. Should I go for it? What would my greedy pig say?

For the first time in my memory, he didn't react. Was the million in hand better than a castle in the bush? No answer. How I understood him! I had to do it.

Switching off all self-control and sense of reality, I said in a stilted voice, "Agreed."

This was how I'd always reacted whenever a situation called for inane determination, like doing a high-board dive or approaching a stunningly beautiful girl. I switched off all emotion, shrugged and stepped forward.

"Agreed," I repeated in a more confident voice.

Congratulations on your acquisition! I thought I heard a hint of amazement in the AI's voice. *An invoice and standing order request have been sent to your address. Upon confirmation of payment, all deeds will be sent to your Private Message box, signed and sealed by the official AI of the Cayman*

Islands offshore zone. A copy of the deeds will be forwarded to your official registered mailbox.

Indeed, my Inbox flashed with a new message. That was Drow Bank informing me of the requests received. I heaved another sigh and confirmed the transaction, burning all bridges. Sorry, Mom, sorry, Dad. I know you'd spent a lifetime hammering into me that credits were evil. You knew better, what with your Second Great Depression experience and all. But this thing was completely interest-free. So I just prayed I hadn't made a fool of myself and hadn't just become the winner of the How-to-Lose-Your-First-Million race.

More messages flashed before my eyes.

Congratulations on your acquisition! You are now the legal owner of a Super Nova Castle.

Updating the virtual property register... OK

Sending form H:244 to the tax authorities... OK.

Control of the funds' provenance... in progress.

For your information: As of 2029 Law 5011 on virtual property, the yearly tax rate of your property is 1.5%. The nonrecurring virtual property tax for amounts over 1,000,000 is 4%. Notice of payment has been sent to your bank. Please note that non-payment within ten days will incur a late-payment surcharge of 5% on every 24 hours.

They didn't mean it. I had barely signed the freakin' thing and already I owed the Feds one million gold. Talk about conjuring money out of thin air. If you closed your eyes and turned round, then pointed your finger blindly, whichever object you pointed to would be taxable. All those excise and customs duties, direct and indirect taxes—the entire society was entangled in a golden web, its precious threads wound into gigantic balls somewhere in the depths of the state machine. How many months a year did it leave you to work for yourself? Two or three? Four max. The rest you were supposed to surrender. I remembered reading that every loaf of bread included over a hundred various taxes. AlterWorld wasn't like that yet.

I imagined a monster dropping one gold and dozens of greedy hands reaching for it. Before you blinked, you were left with a handful of coppers you'd then take to the shops and pay VAT on top of everything else. The Tartar Yoke with its negligible tithe paled in comparison—a true tax-free Golden Age.

In any case, I had nothing to pay their taxes with. My rainy day million had already cleared my account, leaving me with a miserable twenty grand and over two million in monthly payments. Without the six-digit bank account, the world had changed its colors. The debt load burdened my shoulders, breaking my fragile wings and dissolving all my opportunistic plans. From now on, it was nose to the grindstone for me, only raising my head in order to look around for more work to do and someone willing to give it to me. Mom had been right, after all.

No. They weren't going to do it. No one was going to break my wings. What doesn't kill us makes us stronger.

I'd find the money even if I had to eat dirt.

By then, I was a bit fed up with standing bolt upright, but this sterile box of a room had no seating facilities. I slapped the desk. It reacted so fast I didn't have a chance to speak.

Master! so much passion and barely suppressed joy was in that voice that I felt ashamed.

"I'm Max. Call me Max, okay?"

As you say, Master.

Yeah. "Listen, Castle..."

There's no need for tactile contact. You ownership entitles you to a copy of the control artifact which allows you to stay in mental contact with the castle at virtually any distance.

With a pop, the control desk created an octagonal charm on a thin platinum chain. I weighed it in my hand. It was heavy. I put it on and addressed the Castle AI mentally. *Can you hear me?*

Yes, Master.

Yeah. Never mind. *So what's with the lack of soft furnishings?*

Allow me to explain. The castle generates three hundred universal points an hour. You can spend them on restoration, building works or upgrading the existing facilities, including interior design. At the moment, six universal points are available. This will only be enough for the simplest of all devices meant to support a human body in a seated position.

A chair, I presume? I don't need a fancy one, just something to rest my backside on. Go ahead and generate it.

I'd suggest you wait another seven minutes. That would allow you to order a Gothic Chair #52 from the Miserly Knight collection I have just finished downloading.

It sounded a bit suspect. I frowned, "Don't tell me it was a pop-up ad. You're not going to hang the castle walls with banners and promote panty liners via the intercom? I hope not. And please, none of those oak chairs with high straight backs. Let the designers themselves get numb bums from them. I personally prefer ergonomic soft furniture. Now, where's my chair?"

The emotion the Castle AI sent me was the mental equivalent of a shrug. The air quivered with a snap and I realized I should have waited. On the floor stood a handmade stool, rough and wobbly. Oh, well. Haste makes waste. Now I had to keep this contraption out of principle to make sure I didn't forget that particular old adage again. I crouched gingerly and swayed on it trying to balance myself. At least I wouldn't fall asleep on it. I had too many things to take care of.

"AI, do you hear me? Is there a master suite in the donjon?"

Yes, there is. The entire sixth level.

"How much time would it take to restore it to a medium comfort level?

Castle AI paused for a moment. *Approximately ten to fourteen days depending on the chosen design.*

Too long. "How about guest rooms, then?"

Yes, Master. Fourth level. Six detached suites.

"Excellent. I want you to restore one every couple of days. Just a bed, a table, a chair or two and a fireplace. Look up a few ready-made designs and send them to me, I'll choose one. You think you can do it?"

Yes, Master. I will start now.

Excellent. That would give him something to do. In the meantime, Master—myself, that is—would get busy cashing in on his skills and statuses.

I opened the auction and checked my auto buy's anonymity settings. Full-blast paranoia, that's my boy. The vendor is only known by his number, all correspondence redirected, no way to identify him. So—what did we have to offer the world?

I opened a new window and generated a new auction. A few minutes later, I entered the first lot:

A unique raid buff for sale. Effect: +25% to all kinds of magic resistance, +10% to physical damage resistance. Duration: 12 hrs.

The success or failure of your raid is in your hands!

Offered on condition that the buff will not be used in raids targeting worshippers of the Fallen One, their clans or castles.

Price: 30,000 gold

Not too expensive, especially considering the price of the Spark. Still, this was a reusable offer so it should generate a trickle of steady money my way.

Next one:

A unique offer! A raid portal to Inferno! Hurry before your rivals beat you to the ancient castles of their demon lords!

The offer includes a one-way group portal. Return is done under one's own steam, via respawning or teleporting.

Price: one-week's public auction, bids start with 1 gold.

Good! What next?

Only a perma player can appreciate the choice of Macaria as their patron deity. Unique offer: her priest will personally dedicate you to the Goddess of Blissful Death.

Potential buyers are invited to teleport to the point given by the vendor. The dedication rite is 100% anonymous.

Price: 10,000 gold

The next lot—or rather, my pack of trump aces:

A unique offer for big clans or connoisseurs: the First Priest will ordain you as a Dark Priest. Bring your clan under the protection of the Fallen One and secure your people's immortality.

Price: 1,000,000

I reread it and paused, thinking. Was it the right thing to do, really? The price was high, but in all honesty I could add another zero and still our oligarchs would cringe and pay it. And what was I supposed to do with that clique of professional schemers with their security services, analytics departments and cellars full of gold? How sure was I they wouldn't cut me out and start their own game that wouldn't do any favors to the name of the Fallen One, his religion or his First Priest? Those gentlemen were the opposite of cute and cuddly: those were sharks who'd survived the Second Depression, the Dictatorship of the State and the New NEP. They'd swallow me whole without even noticing.

That wasn't the way to do it. Hadn't I said myself just lately that cadres were key? And was I really going to apply the trial and error approach to this crucial step? Next thing I knew, I'd have a quiet modest man sitting in one of the Temple rooms under a sign, *First Secretary Comrade Stalin* who would start placing his own men in all key posts. Before I knew it, he'd hold a re-election campaign which would demote me to the post of junior carpet sweeper. No. I had to think it over, then think again and again some more. I blinked, sending the finished description into the Recycle Bin and made a mental note to deal with it later.

Next. Deactivating a castle shield. The altar's help allowed me to cast a High Spell while the Shadow of the Fallen One secured my anonymity. Still, I wasn't going to auction off something that scandalous. I'd have to look for potential buyers myself.

I opened the long-forgotten news feed, the section of war conflicts. Most clans were constantly in a state of smoldering vendetta with each other. I was sure I could find someone interested enough.

The OMON clan has besieged two central castles belonging to the Gold Net trade clan. The latter have hired large mercenary units which makes the outcome rather unclear. If you remember, OMON members have taken and resold three standalone castles in the last few months, all belonging to second-division clans.

The Pratz clan has been besieging a private castle on the border of No Man's Land without success. The point of their activity is dubious as they don't seem to have the potential to breach the shield.

The Korean farm alliance has completed a raid on the human city of Humas. Within the last twenty-four hours, they have taken and destroyed four nearby castles and a dozen mansions. The persistent Koreans seem to be quite happy with the twenty percent profits paid out for destroyed property. Insurance companies are said to have raised their premiums.

Last night, a blitz operation carried out by the Ninja Looters resulted in the taking of Silver Citadel, a strategic point covering access to the mines of the same name. An anonymous source claims the success of the operation was the result of treachery by a senior guard officer who had apparently leaked the portal access codes to the attackers. Reportedly, the officer in question is a professional spy specializing in this kind of one-off operation. It had taken him over a year to prepare the mission. Having joined the clan after a period of express leveling, he excelled in his duties, enjoying a quick career growth which culminated in a lump sum of over a million gold for the valuable intelligence. Consequently, he deleted the character concerned.

Oh. I scratched my head. These guys played big. The Looters now had a half-a-million dollar castle. And the patient spy, a hundred grand for a year in the game. Now he'd go to the Maldives for a well-deserved month in the sun before registering a new character. So how were we supposed to protect ourselves against his type?

I remembered the incident with the tobacco smoke turning into soap bubbles, giving away the nondescript individual who'd been trying to worm his way into the Vet's clan. Wonder if my invention had saved the Veterans that day from professional infiltration like the one above?

I had gleaned something, anyway. Now I had some idea of the prices people were prepared to offer for breaching a castle's defenses. In all honesty, I didn't feel like offering my services to any of the clans involved in current military actions. I had an idea, though. It looked as if most of the OMON forces were drawn to the besieged castles. What if I offered their victims the possibility to counterattack? I could remove any shield from any of the castles mentioned by the vendors. All they needed to do was assault it which would probably allow them to alter the situation and save their property, making a nice few bucks on the side. I could also make a similar offer to the ex-owners of the Silver Citadel. I had a funny feeling they wouldn't say no to the opportunity to bring it back under their control.

Very well. A quick search brought me the names of clan leaders of both Gold Net and Minediggers. I created an anonymous mail address and sent them my offer. They could forward their payment via official middlemen who, for a mere two percent, would make sure that all parties respected the fine print. All I had to do was remove the dome shield of a specific castle at a specified time. Price quoted: one million. That was it. Now I could sit back and watch the sharks and whales swarm into my net.

A double clink of gold informed me of the first bite. Sold: one dedication to Macaria and one raid offer. I was forty grand richer. Things were moving!

Clink, clink! Another bite!

Chapter Fourteen

I spent the following three hours networking non-stop, sifting through the messages that were pouring into the anonymous box. While the bulk of the letters were from the doubting and the curious and didn't merit immediate attention, those from serious buyers I had to answer on the spot as I tried to come up with the logistics of the impending operation. It looked as if it was going to be something truly extraordinary. Already I had over a hundred fifty people on the dedication list and more kept coming every minute. When two messages were dropped almost simultaneously into my inbox—two leading clans wanting to know the details—I finally realized I was losing my grip on the situation.

I closed the virtual keyboard and, forgetting, tried to lean back, losing my balance on the wobbly stool. Damn their cabinet makers!

AI's soft voice resounded in my head. *Master, I've taken the liberty of saving 29 American dollars. May I offer you something to replace this sorry excuse for a chair with an ergonomic six-setting adjustable recliner bed?*

What was it he'd blabbered about his emotions having been removed? His voice was rife with sleek sarcasm. I should have taught him a lesson of course, by refusing his offer and leaving myself to suffer in silence. But my heart was craving some comfort.

"Deal, you smooth operator. Where's your chair now?"

Name the desired color, please.

"Fucking purple!"

What kind of upholstery would you prefer?

"Whatever! Suede!" My annoyance started to affect my struggle with the stool's four uneven legs. Why would anyone make something like that?

The closest local analog would be the skin of a sand lizard. Unfortunately, it will increase the price of the desir-

"Chair—now!" I snapped. I didn't care anymore.

The air parted, materializing this marvel of modern design and medieval technology. With a yelp, I plonked myself onto its suede cushions and groaned with delight.

"Well done! As a reward please accept your new name: Lurch! I hereby allow you to use one percent of all the units generated for your own needs, on the condition that your activity doesn't hurt me or the castle's functions. Use it as you see fit. You could get yourself a gold weathercock or some fancy railing, you get the idea.

AI paused. Finally he spoke, his voice shaking with emotion. *Thank you, Master. You've no idea how much this means to me. Thank you.*

"You're welcome, Lurch. How about a bit of celebration? Some lemon tea, how about that? No chance of any cookies, I suppose? What's the situation on the kitchen front?"

Al's voice was filled with drama and regret. "The kitchen unit is status orange making it impossible to prepare dishes of over 80 difficulty. But that's not the problem. We're completely devoid of kitchen staff. Unfortunately, I don't have access to the kitchen interface. I would recommend hiring eleven sentient beings as castle staff in order to secure a bare minimum of habitability."

Bummer. More expenses. Still, he had a point. He might be a bit greedy but a castle needed some staff. I fiddled with the settings, and after five minutes the room filled with voices. First thing I hired three human chambermaids with cute faces and random-generated characters. It was more fun that way. I didn't quite get why a pretty face cost five hundred a month while the same character with the same functions but looking like an old hag was two hundred. I just hoped Taali didn't find out that I'd had choice, or she'd demand I replace all supermodel types with helpful old ladies.

Next I created a corpulent cook with +500 Culinary skill. She cost me more than all the chambermaid chicks put together, but once I'd studied the list of her skills, I gulped in expectation and pressed *Confirm* double quick. The portly lady's bloodline counted at least five different races endowing her with all the secrets of the numerous Elven, Dwarven, and human cuisines as well as some special meat recipes à la Orc. She also had direct access to the ingredients auction and her own bank balance which was the first thing I filled when I'd created her. Now that I had the food department out of the way, I told her to get some tea ready and went back to my work.

The incoming messages had been flashing at me for ages. I opened my inbox and hiccupped with astonishment. The auto broker balance had already exceeded three million, the number of those willing to surrender themselves into Macaria's gentle hands had reached two hundred eighty. But what made my day was the letter from the Vets where General Frag personally was asking the anonymous priest about the terms of having a seven hundred-strong clan dedicated. The General put it plainly that seven million was a bit thick and that two million would do the job nicely plus the dubious addition of their gratitude. The Vets didn't change, did they? They were still not averse to trading their friendship and pressurizing everyone with their authority. Two more similar letters from other clan leaders were still awaiting my answer.

That wasn't all. There was also a flagged letter from the auction admins informing me they had temporarily blocked the assets in my account until I fulfilled all commitments to my customers. They had assigned me a personal manager as a controller who'd just sent me another letter, introducing himself and asking about the time and place of the upcoming ritual. I clutched at my head, groaning. I needed more staff! I wasn't made of steel. Having one head had also proved pretty inadequate. But I had to make do with whatever I had at hand.

I concentrated, trying to remember my bind point. It had to be the Vet's portal hall. I sent a message to my mini-clan (Cryl and Lena, that was the extent of it) telling them to meet me in my apartment. Then I wrote to Frag asking him for an urgent meeting of paramount importance to the Vets, ideally in the East Castle. Two minutes later, the General replied saying he was expecting me in his office and that I had better be quick as 'it's like Israel and the end times here; the arrival of the Fallen One has changed the lay of the land and the clan is delirious with excitement'.

Clear enough. I looked around, checking if everything was under control, and wistfully canceled the tea break. I was about to teleport when something in my newly-acquired environment caught my eye. I gave the room another scanning glance. The unhappy cook, purse-lipped, was placing her pretty china teapots and cookie plates back onto their tray; one of the chambermaids fussed about arching her back and darting her vibrant eyes as she polished the newly-materialized table with a pristine white cloth brushing away the non-existent crumbs. Crumbs. Fragments. That was it! Yes! I needed to hire a hundred cleaners to sweep the entire space inside the inner wall, collect all the scrap mithril and pile it into neat little piles.

In my mind's eye, I reached for the charm on my neck, activating the castle control menu. I scanned through the unfolding submenus until I got to recruiting. Non-combat staff, cleaning services. Chimneysweeps, plumbers, various moppers and sweepers. The latter were exactly what we needed, including their foreman. His wages were three times those of his workers but he allowed me to delegate the task of running his brush brotherhood. In total, they cost mere peanuts even though they admittedly took up a lot of staff positions.

A troop of little goblins filled the room, armed with brooms, dustpans, buckets and some totally arcane cleaning tools. Immediately I realized quite a few of the mistakes I'd made. Firstly, I didn't really need to hire this cartload of chimpanzees for a month. I should have paid ten percent more and just kept them for five to seven days. My second mistake was ticking the 'character: random' box. Already those green monsters were making a sparrow-like racket, pushing and shoving each other, a few of them rolling on the floor in disagreement.

"Out, everyone! Out into the court! Line up!" I yelled, confirming my command with an almighty kick that sent flying the two goblins who were fighting over some especially good broom.

I hurriedly summoned their foreman, ran through his options and increased his strength, aggression, diligence and desire to please his patron.

That was another fifty gold a month gone, but I had to be sure he was able to run his menagerie with an iron hand.

The ash gray goblin was middle-aged and covered in old scars. His stance commanded respect. He studied the surroundings and stroked the bamboo stick he carried as weapon.

"What can I do for you, Master?" he lowered his head.

I glanced at his stick. "You'll be Harlequin," I said remembering the Italian *commedia dell'arte* character whose job was meting out blows to the ever-sad clown Pierrot.

The goblin stood up straight. His eyes glistened, his back bending lower in a bow. "Thank you, Master."

They all seemed to have funny reactions to the name-giving procedure. Could it have something to do with the divine spark the Fallen One had mentioned? When we singled someone out, raising them over the homogenous faceless crowd by giving them a name, were we not breathing life into them? I really had to find out my Hell Hound's moniker or present her with one.

"I've got here fifty cleaners to put under your authority," I said. "Your task will be to clean up the castle. All the non-standard debris has to be collected and stored in the inner court, sorted out where possible: metal and ores into one heap, artifacts into another, unidentified miscellany into a third one. What else... yes, no dismantling any compound objects. You'll see two statues of trolls, please don't touch them but try to transport them into court if you can."

"What's the surface area?" Harlequin asked, all businesslike.

"Everything up to the outer walls. In case of any danger, address the head of castle guards. Let me know when you're finished. I'll need you to arrange a work party to the fort. That's it. Get on with it!"

As he dashed off, eager to apply himself, I had one belated idea. "Wait! One more thing. On one of the north towers," I gestured in their approximate direction, "there's a Bone Dragon's batch of eggs. You need to find it."

He scratched his head. "What does it look like?"

I very nearly did a facepalm, amazed at his stupidity, when it dawned on me: did I have any idea myself how the eggs—whether bone or phantom ones—looked like? Not good.

"Eh, a nest and, you know, two eggs, yes, sort of round ones," I made an OK sign with my finger and thumb. "I think. Just play it by ear, dude. I don't think the place is packed with dragon eggs."

He shrugged, as if saying, *the boss is always right*. Obeying my nod, he finally dashed out of the room. Right he was, too. I could bet my bottom gold piece his subordinates were already at each other's throats, busy ripping each other's overalls.

I suppressed a smile and activated the portal spell. Bang.

I greeted the Portal Hall guards, one of them a very bored Eric who roared like a happy bear as he descended on me with an equally bear hug. Immediately he began telling me about some really cool piece of bear gear he'd seen, if only-

There he was interrupted by a messenger—the sergeant who'd been shifting his feet by the door as he waited to take me to the General's office. I shook Eric's enormous paw and hurried down the stairs after him.

The NPC guards saluted me indifferently, showing no reaction to my *hatred* relationship status. By then, I already knew how easy it was to change the guards' friend/foe settings from the castle interface. The Vets' clan didn't differentiate by race or faction, they had plenty of players of both Light and the Dark. You couldn't surprise anyone here with a Blood Orc whose face otherwise graced all the quest boards elsewhere in the Lands of Light.

Finally I reached the carved oak doors of the General's office. The sergeant knocked and opened one side of the door, letting me in.

Inside, Dan and Frag were choking on their coffees. You can't really enjoy the poison of your choice twenty cups in a row. Dan squinted at me, tired but cheerful. The General's poker face didn't change; he nodded and beckoned me to approach.

"Come sit down. Take the weight off your feet."

I obeyed. Both stared at me expectantly. Pointless beating about the bush with two seasoned sharks like those. So I moved straight to the point.

"General, as far as I know, you were considering the possibility of dedicating the clan's entire contingent to Macaria, offering two million for the rite. Is that correct?"

Frag raised an eyebrow, soundlessly enquiring about my information sources but neither confirming nor refuting my words. Dan gave me an encouraging smile.

I took in a lungful of air and said with a TV-soap actor's lilt, "The Dark Priest you wrote to is me."

I wasn't prepared for their reaction. Dan guffawed, clapping his hands. Frag shook his head, unbelieving.

"You didn't believe me, did you?" Dan turned to him. "So you owe me one more staff member for my seventh department. Sorry, Sir, a bet is a bet. I want Brown's Lieut, please."

"You want too much. Find someone from your kindergarten group and train them up yourself," Frag turned to me and lay his heavy fists onto the fragile tabletop. "Report," he ordered, boring me with his glare.

I scowled. "General," indignation was welling inside me, "I have come here as a clan leader, First Priest and your friend. But not as your subordinate."

"First Priest, I knew it..." Dan muttered, ignoring my escapade.

Me and my big mouth. These sharks had me just where they wanted. I was fed up with their rotten tricks. "Please. I know very well you have guys like myself for breakfast every morning. But I'm afraid, I'm the only First Priest you have, at least for quite a while. I may be a bit simple but there's no need to rub it in. Let's just work with what we have."

Dan grew serious. He raised his hands in a peace-making gesture. "Stop grumbling, Max. We're all friends here. We're only laughing because we want to make you see it's time to tie your simplicity up in a few knots. You're flying way too high these days, and still you're trying to remain Laith the simple guy playing a new and funny game. They'll scoff you up before you can say *Ding!*"

Poor Fallen One. How I understood him right now. This wasn't life: this was some stupid downward escalator, its steps sweeping you right down into a sea of lava, its top riding high in the thunder clouds, and you keep running up the stairs simply to avoid being swept into the fire.

I took a deep mental breath and looked Dan in the eye. "I've heard you. I really appreciate your advice, thank you. But my life has long ceased being a leisurely walk in the park. It has since taken me up and down all sorts of funny little trails. Just give me some time. I might end up such a smartass bastard you'll regret ever saying this to me. You'd better knock on wood it doesn't happen soon."

Dan chuckled and tapped a bony knuckle on the wooden tabletop.

"So, First Priest," Frag cut us short, "what can we do for you and what can you offer us in return?"

Taking the bull by the horns, very well. I concentrated, lining up the items I was going to discuss with them. "The First Temple will need protection. Its restoration will also demand a considerable injection of funds. Although the official version of the Temple's devastation is not exactly correct, its outcome is the same: the place is in ruins. I don't think you're going to question the importance of having the Temple properly defended. The advantages of Macaria's gifts are too obvious."

Dan's eyes had glazed over the moment I'd mentioned financial problems. Now he sat up, offended, "Not everything is as rosy, I'm afraid. Our clan's siding with the Fallen One might bring us some serious pain in the butt."

"So what?" I said. "We'll still have our XP bonuses plus the Goddess' skills..."

Dan and Frag exchanged glances. "How many deities are there in the Pantheon of Light?" Dan asked softly. "Your guess?"

I frowned. "Dunno. I was sort of too busy to find out. My life has been a bit hectic in the last few weeks. I thought you knew that."

Dan shook his head, refusing to accept my excuses. "Six—six gods, each with his or her own specialization. It's true that they don't have the

High God or the First Temple: they've got some democracy there, or anarchy, whatever. But they're quite generous with their skills, not to mention their fourteen temples and their respective XP bonuses to all the worshippers of Light."

I slumped in my chair. How could I ever have missed it? True, I'd given their temples a wide berth, unwilling to worship one particular god: my chosen class cast plenty of shadow as it was. But how come no one had told me that? I desperately needed an analytics department of my own.

"So I hope you don't think," Dan went on, "that all the players will now march to join the Fallen One's ranks? True, the smarter among us—those who are either capable of independent thinking, have the necessary information or possess good self-preservation skills—will ignore the Light Ones' toys and will be more than happy to dedicate themselves to Macaria. Over time, we might look at a figure of several tens of thousands. Add to that those who'll follow him out of conviction or racial solidarity—there're bound to be a few. But those of the players who choose their religion by dumbly comparing the available bonuses will all remain on the other side of the barricades. And what do you suggest we do when, after a few tentative attempts, the Admins call for an event and a hundred thousand-strong crowd will arrive at the First Temple's walls? Who's going to face them—you and I and ten thousand die-hard permas? Because that'll be all the force we'll have."

He kept speaking, probably trying to bring me back down to earth by making me see the sheer vastness of the task at hand. And I—yes, I guess you could say I *was* a different person already because the problem's scope didn't scare me any more. To each of his arguments, my mind came up with a possible solution and a potential counter measure. Too many temples of Light?—we could always thin them out. Not enough manpower to defend ours?—Well, humans weren't the only AlterWorld's inhabitants. Gnolls and Hell Hounds were prime examples of the opposite. Our Pantheon too modest, the XP bonus too small?—It only meant we had to summon more gods and build new temples.

Had I bitten off more than I could chew? But that was the only way to do it. You had to have ambitious goals. Saving enough for a new couch would hardly motivate one to move his backside. But if his objective were to buy a Porsche Cayenne in three years' time, that might motivate him to move it and be proactive, seek so he could find.

I nodded to Dan, "I appreciate the sheer scope of the problem. But we'll make it. What solution do you suggest, personally? I'm not going to charge my allies seven million; I'm not even going to accept the two the General has already offered. I need friends and allies more than I do trade partners. I intend to make one of the Vets a priest so he can dedicate the entire clan to Macaria. I also invite you to sign up for my alliance, The

Guards of the First Temple, in order to join our defense forces. I don't seek a commanding post. There are some people here who deserve it more than I do."

Again they exchanged glances. Oh yes, I was full of surprises: first my new confidence that seemed to defy the complexity of the situation, then my rejection of a very lump sum, and now the news of the alliance I'd created. They froze, apparently discussing their decision through some closed private channel.

I had told them the truth. I needed allies more than anything. Money, too, but judging by the auctions' trends, I had staked a gold mine with plenty of potential to pay off my castle mortgage. And one more thing. By refusing their money, I hoped to reset my clan obligations to zero. Because if one day they had asked me for a service in return, I'd have had to drop everything and comply. This way, I was debt-free with them.

Clink, a money transfer dropped into my inbox.

You've received a money transfer: 100,000 gold.

Sender: The official Veterans clan account

I raised a quizzical eye to Frag.

"We appreciate your proposal," he said. "We're more than happy to accept it. We also give our preliminary approval to joining your alliance, but this will need more discussion and working through all the agreement details. As a gesture of allied good will, we return to you the sum you paid us for helping to solve Taali's little problem. We'll pay our men from our own resources. Moreover, we'll monitor her problem closely: I can already tell you that we're going to replace her gun. The civilian Tiger is good enough but a Vintorez will suit her purpose better. I'll also make sure some of my men will cover her at the most difficult stage: a retreat."

At that point I couldn't keep my emotions in check any longer. Taali's problem was something I couldn't help her with which worried me quite a lot. These old dogs knew my weak spot, cleverly manipulating my nicest points. But I still had something up my sleeve to rub into their poker faces.

"I can't thank you enough for this," I said. "But as you've mentioned the guns, I think I've got something for you."

I reached into my bag, pulled out the steel invaders' heavy shooter and slammed it on the table. Nothing was going to happen to it. Mithril could take much more than that. One-nil, guys. I would claw through the Valley of Fear for another technogenic artifact just to see their expression again.

The General jumped from his seat and grabbed the gun. He studied it in disbelief. He unlatched the clip, pulled back and cocked the hammer a couple of times, then ran his sensitive fingers along the embossed frame. Still unbelieving, he exchanged glances with Dan and pressed the gun to his chest like a father who'd found his long-lost son. Was it my imagination or his eyes glistened moistly?

"Where-" his voice gave. He cleared his throat. "Where did you get *this*?"

"Just an echo of war," I answered in my best indifferent voice, enjoying the pun.

"Fuck the echo of war!" Dan exploded.

Frag gestured him to shut up. "Wait. Max, I hope you understand what it is you have here. Firearms can radically change the balance of power in the game."

"Actually," I said, cutting their greed down, "the game's definition of a gun is a lump of mithril ore ready for recasting. Secondly, ammo is a bit of a problem, especially as I doubt that gunpowder or whatever it uses to generate the gases has retained its properties after eight hundred years. And thirdly and mainly, where do you see this imbalance? Are you sure that bullets can be a stronger argument than a regular level 1 self-guided firebolt? I don't even mention the Meteor Shower Spell or Armageddon which is easily comparable with a volley from a multiple rocket launcher."

Dan shook his head. "I don't intend to start a flame war on whether firearms are cooler than magic. Wait till you get a fifty-gram slug up your ass from a sniper about a mile away. Or when your castle takes a direct hit from the aforementioned rocket launcher—then you can compare them to level-1 firebolts all you like. Magic and firearms are two unique tools at opposite ends of the same branch of evolution. If someone manages to merge them, the Universe will shudder. Then everyone who doubted our peaceful intentions will drown in the resulting bloodbath."

That got me thinking. He could be right. He had to be. I definitely wasn't going to look into all of the consequences of, say, all of our players going back to the real world while preserving their characters' abilities. What had Frag called it, 'Israel and the end times'? It could well be. Actually, the former risked being the first to disappear from the world map. No amount of security walls or breakthrough technologies could save you from a stealthed nighttime 'well-wisher' smothering the sleeping streets and houses with clouds of Choky Death. I shuddered. God forbid.

"Imagine that?" Dan asked, watching the sequence of emotions run across my face.

"Yeah. A different scenario, actually, but it doesn't change the facts."

"So it looks as if you got it. How much of this stuff do you have?" he nodded at the gun in Frag's hands. The General had already ejected the contents of the magazine and lined it all up on the table in front of himself. "Have you unearthed the Ancient Ones' storeroom or just broken into some gaming millionaire's armory packed with made-to-order artifacts?"

So! I paused, trying to take in his random suggestions. This guy had some sick fantasies.

"Apparently not," a faked disappointment in his voice, Dan kept watching my face. "I will never believe that you've given us the only gun you had."

I'd have given everything for a shot of botox to paralyze my facial muscles. His soul-searching stare was getting to me. I wasn't a TV, after all.

I shook my head. "You don't need to believe it if you don't want to. This shooter is a real echo of war. With compliments from those technogenic dudes who tore the Temple apart eight hundred years ago. Oh, I got this thing, too."

I rummaged through my logs for the two screenshots of the dead trolls with a tank barrel as a club and forwarded them to the two.

"Holy shit," Dan whispered. "That's impressive. That's them just standing there? You think you could sell them? These are proper warriors, you understand, and they have this... firearm. This way the soldiers will have something to worship."

I shook my head. "They can worship Macaria if they want. Sorry but I have my own ideas about them. You can take the screenshot and have a painting of it made in the City of Light. If it inspires you that much."

Dan nodded, deadly serious. "I will. I need a copy of this for myself."

"Two!" the General broke his silence.

This was how it happened that the two unknown heroes had shed the dust of time, their act of desperate bravery acquiring a new lease of life before my very eyes. In another five hundred years, some Drow boy scouts would stand, open-mouthed, before the painting in some local art museum as the Troll guide would shed an involuntary tear, narrating the ancient legend.

Chapter Fifteen

As my associates recovered from their art appreciation experience, I rose and, searching their eyes for their permission, poured out a generous cup of coffee for myself. It was almost two in the morning; the accumulated exhaustion was weighing my brain down, I was sleepy as well as hungry. I looked over the conference table: nothing edible, only piles of paperwork. With a sigh, I slumped back into my chair. Dan who'd never lost control of any situation, read me with ease and snapped a couple of commands into the castle's control console. He really should play poker: he'd make millions. Having said that, he wasn't that poor: take the recent scheme with the two brokers at the tournament when a good hundred thousand US greenbacks wriggled their way into his pocket. I already had a funny feeling he'd creamed off more from the cigarette boom than even I had. Well, I didn't mind. Having good role models was never a bad thing. Being the smartest guy among idiots may be flattering but it didn't get you very far. Becoming part of a good team so you could profit from the old dogs' experience, now that was well and truly useful.

Soon, the table was laid with several platefuls of cold cuts and starters. After five minutes of laborious chewing, life was looking up even though now I was even sleepier. Both Dan and the General welcomed the pause as they got busy making changes to the clan's prospective roadmap in view of the intelligence received. I even forgot about the rabbit pie I was holding as I watched their master class in strategic thinking and solving mammoth tasks. How do you eat a mammoth? Easy: you keep nibbling until there's nothing left of it but bare bones. Same here: the seemingly unmanageable task could be broken down into smaller segments that could be delegated to actual workers or relevant administrators.

Finally, the General raised his head to me. "Are there any requirements for the position of priest? Their level, their relationships with other factions? Do you have someone in mind?"

I checked the list of priest abilities. Formally, there were no restrictions. Macaria hadn't made any particular demands, either—having said that, she could have been too preoccupied. That wasn't my problem, anyway. But as for the candidates, my first thought was Dan, he was made for the job with one exception: he was completely unreadable and uncontrollable. *That* could be a problem because the priests were supposed to be my helpers—subordinates, even. I just couldn't imagine him in that role. But I hadn't yet met many Vets—none at all, in fact, apart from Eric. Eric... well, why not?

I looked up at the General and shook my head. "Currently, no restrictions. As for candidates, I believe Eric to be suited best to the post. I'd like you to keep in mind that if a priest is proven to be unsuited to the job, he can be defrocked or even excommunicated. This rule applies to everyone," I said as gently as I could hoping they didn't interpret my words as a threat.

They exchanged smiles. Those bastards just refused to take me seriously. I had my work cut out for me, authority wise.

"We could in fact agree to your proposal," Dan said, adamant he'd milk the idea for everything it was worth. "As a return favor, we'd like to help you carry your pot of mithril from the other end of the rainbow. For a few pennies, of course."

Yeah, right. Looked like they'd outsmarted themselves this time. Had they not been flexing their thinking muscles in front of me, I might have said yes. But now I could smell rats everywhere I turned. In any case, how were you supposed to give someone access to your own bank vault without supervision? No metal detector would find the gold stuck to their sweaty paws: the game's mechanics allowed you to move a tank into your bag with a single silent command. Okay, maybe not a tank—I hadn't yet met anyone with a thirty-ton weight carrying capacity here. Then again, you shouldn't forget about those artifact bags which could diminish or even nullify the item's weight. But pilfering something like a mithril tank barrel from a petrified troll's hands, I wouldn't put it past them. Soldiers! They can't resist temptation. There isn't even a word for stealing in the army. Instead, they say "appropriated". No, guys, sorry, but the gun is mine and you're not getting it.

"I have an offer, too," I said. "For a few pennies—say, a million gold— I'll sell you the coordinates of an alternative rainbow with a field of gold at the end. Mithril I can't promise but what I can guarantee is about twenty hectares of the best Gigantic Fly Trap."

Dan sat up. He swung his head round checking a place for unwanted ears, then mumbled, trying hard to look disappointed, "One million—don't you know any other figures for a change? How about a hundred grand? Any piece of intelligence is worth that!"

I grinned, shaking my head. "Sorry, chief, that's non-negotiable. You'll reap ten times more from that field. A couple of weeks working the land, and you'll have your million. I would have done it myself but I don't have any spare hands to guard and harvest it. Besides, I'm too busy as it is. It will also allow you to level up your farmers a bit. The area is unexplored with plenty of untamed game for them to tackle. By the same token, their presence will protect them from some overeager PKs."

Dan glanced at the General who nodded. He then heaved a sigh, his character begging for more haggling, but obeyed the unspoken order, accepting my conditions. "Very well. You have our preliminary consent. I'll forward you our standard contract for the acquisition of information regarding class A objects. You need to fill it in attaching all the screenshots and coordinates of the field, then seal it with your digital signature. We'll send our men to make sure the place answers your description. If it does, the money will be on your bank account the next morning. Please don't think we don't trust you. We just want to make sure you're not mistaken. It can be a different type of Fly-Trap or some visual illusion... ever heard of mirages?"

"Very well," I said. "When's Eric coming?"

Dan checked his internal interface, "He's on his way."

The General raised his stare at me as he rolled a dozen purple cartridges in his wide hand. "One more thing, Max. I really hope that if you happen to find more of the same, your findings won't spread uncontrollably over the entire cluster. You must understand the dangers firearms bring into our world. But personally, we would greatly appreciate having more samples... for research purposes."

Now what was that for logic? What's yours is mine and what's mine is my own? I decided against making an issue of it, giving him a noncommittal nod. He was welcome to interpret it in any way he wanted. By then, my inner greedy pig had smeared his venomous drool all over my heart, ogling the gun I'd just parted with. I shouldn't gift anyone another one of those in the near future if I didn't want to finish Mr. Piggy off. And what would I be worth without my resident treasurer? I'd splurge all my riches before I knew it.

Hurried steps resounded down the corridor. The door swung open, letting Eric in. He sprang to attention in front of Frag.

The General nodded. "As you were."

Eric slumped in the chair. Then he saw me, grinned and poked my shoulder with his giant fist. "That's what it is! I couldn't understand why they'd want to haul me over the coals. Sorry, Comrade General!" he glanced over the table groaning with various leftovers and twitched his nose, doglike. "May I?"

Not waiting for an answer, he scooped a few cookies.

"I thought the guards had eaten half an hour ago?" Dan asked.

"Ah!" Eric waved his objection away. "That was then!"

"Very well. If you can listen while you eat, you'd better do so. Command has confidence in you," Dan raised a meaningful finger. Eric frowned, surprised. His type wasn't used to command's confidence.

"You're about to fill a unique post. You'll be the clan's priest. Quit looking at me like that. You have Max to thank for that. But remember that the posting isn't interminable. One slip-up, and I swear on my immortality I'll make you swallow dust twelve hours a day as a second ammo carrier in an NPC gun crew of the defense ballista of the seventh tower of South Castle. I'm not joking. What with your level and your track record, you're long overdue for a promotion. If you really can't overcome the perma mode euphoria and if your healthy body and your immortality mean so much to you, you'd do better joining the Pratz. They love goofs like yourself. Is that clear?"

Watching Eric was breaking my heart. His drawn face paled, his doglike expression miserable and begging forgiveness. He jumped up, pressing his hands to his chest.

"Sir! I'm sorry, I mean it! It's like the devil's playing with it all the time. I feel like a teenager on his first night of boozing, I can't even walk, I can only hop and run! It gets better, though. I can control it. I still clown around, but it's more out of habit now. I really appreciate your confidence in me, Sir!" he jumped to attention and reported, saluting, "I won't let you down, I promise!"

Dan fixed him with his stare, then rose, adjusting his shirt like one would uniform, and crisply saluted. "Go to it, Lieutenant!"

"'Yes, Sir! Permission to leave, Sir!"

"As you were," Dan nodded, then turned to me. "Your turn. You'd better dedicate your protégé before he loses patience and races off not even knowing why or where to."

Impressed by the change in my best friend's behavior, I looked up the necessary skill on the priest's abilities list, selected Macaria as patron god and pressed the virtual button.

Millions of little bells filled the room with their gentle chimes. A cloud of glittering sparks swirled under the ceiling like a snowstorm, creating an opening into some other plane that revealed Macaria's happy and (I think) tipsy face. She peeked out, studying Eric, then gave him an encouraging smile, nodding. The opening collapsed, sending the colored snowflakes flying all over us. As Eric stood there open-mouthed, my internal interface reported a growing number of priests. Now we were already eleven out of the fifty. I'd love to know where the other three Dark temples were. I had big plans regarding them. We had to expand the Pantheon as soon as possible. The more people I could enlist, the fewer besiegers we'd find one day under the Castle walls.

Eric heaved a sigh. "What a woman!" he clearly couldn't forget the celestial apparition.

I just hoped that this was a temporary adolescent crush and not the ritual's side effect. I still felt obliged to warn him, just in case, "Eric, she and the Fallen One are an item. So you'd better keep your ideas to yourself before you get him on your case. You won't like that, I assure you."

"You think?" the freshly-baked priest glanced warily upwards. Shaking the heavenly snow off his shoulders, he went into reverse, "I said it from a purely esthetic point of view, you know. The Fallen One needs it more than... I mean... finding a broad... er, a goddess can't be easy in his situation."

Dan shook his head. "Eric, I think it's a good idea that I cast a silence spell on you a couple times a day or so. That'll do you a lot of good, trust me.

If I don't do it, some unhappy god will one day. All right, Your Holiness, you may continue with your duties and dedicate us to the beautiful Macaria.

Eric zoned out for a bit as he tried to figure out his new skills. He must have found what he'd been looking for as he cast an unsure glance at Dan before activating the ability. A pillar of white light veined with black and green enveloped the secret agent, still shimmering when we heard him whisper as he, too, was studying the menus,

"There... I see... patron god... skills... that's the one... One point is worth a grand gold, so! Oh well, here's my donation..."

A string sang softly as another wave of light, pale green this time, poured over Dan. Faith level 1? It sure looked like he'd done it.

"Yes! We'll live!" he exclaimed.

I knew how he must have felt at that moment as the unbearable load had fallen from this immortal's shoulders: the fear of captivity, eternal and torturous.

The mother-of-pearl snow was melting under our feet. Curious, I peered at its stats:

Sparks of Divine Presence. An extremely rare crafting artifact that allows you to transfer any kind of magic to a scroll and seal it, creating a one-off spell scroll.

So! I scratched my head. I'd never heard of anything like it. Having said that, it didn't change anything: the very expression *extremely rare* pointed at the item's high value. It was worth taking.

Stepping closer, I scooped a handful of vials out of my bag and crouched, sweeping in the colored flakes.

Dan cast me a puzzled glance which then glazed over as he scanned the messages on his interface. Then a miracle happened. What else could you call it when Dan made an almighty leap across half the room while reaching into his pocket for a vial, then plopped down onto his stomach next to the shrinking pile of snow. Paying no attention to the damage sustained, he was stuffing the melting sparks into his vial.

Casting me a wild stare, he shouted, "Shut the fucking lid before it evaporates!"

True, the air over the vial hovered, misted. I hastily sealed the vial and checked the contents. The vial was nearly full. Eric and the General had already joined us, but still our combined trophies weren't that much: we'd barely filled five vials.

I surveyed our team sprawled on the floor amid iridescent pools of gaslike liquid. That made me smile. The informal meeting of the clan's religious leaders with its administration. I shared the thought with my friends and the office shattered with their guffawing.

The air over the conference table thickened, materializing the White Winnie. Casting a puzzled glare in our direction, he made the screwy gesture against his temple, grabbed a couple of meat pies and reached for an open folder. All documents in it were lying text down (that was Dan and his professional vigilance). Dan growled a warning as a throwing knife glistened in his hand. The weapon glowed crimson, dropping sizzling sparks onto the floor.

Winnie snatched his paw back, baring his teeth, then kicked the folder off the table right into the pool of water. The room echoed with a simultaneous popping of a teleport and the sound of cold steel piercing wood.

"How I hate him," the agent groaned, fishing out the waterproof pages. "I dream of the day when I retire to my rocking chair by the fireplace, sipping brandy and relishing my cigar, admiring two white ears nailed to the wall."

Eric added, apparently missing the two pies, "I just hope that by then it'll be the only unique pair of ears ever available. Let's pray this creature doesn't propagate. In that case, you can forget about a quiet retirement. These teleporting monsters will pop by every two minutes to borrow a cigar or to help themselves to a shot of brandy. Privacy will become problematic, even for matrimonial purposes."

"Touch wood," I whispered, knocking on a table leg. Everybody followed suit. Soldiers are superstitious by definition, and the above prospect justified a couple of rituals just to be on the safe side.

The General leaned forward, groaning and forcing himself back to his feet like the old man he in fact was, then jumped up effortlessly: the mental inertia of an octogenarian in a young healthy body. This is how inexperienced astronauts use their entire body weight from their back muscles to their ankles in order to get to the space station's dome instead of just sending their body there with one well-directed nudge.

"Now, Dan, you owe me an explanation," the General said. "What's this stuff we've been filling the vials with? You jumped at it like somebody dying of thirst seeing an oasis."

"Haven't you copied its stats, Sir?" Dan asked innocently. "My educated guess would be that this ingredient is AlterWorld's long-sought Holy Grail. It allows one to create spell scrolls. Any spells—Unique and High Ones included."

The General raised his eyebrows. He grabbed a vial and brought it up to his eyes. "Holy shit."

"What about it?" I asked. "Would you like to create a one-off teleport scroll so that magic-deprived players could use it in case of emergency?"

"You might," Dan answered. "You could use a gold shovel to clean the snow off your driveway, too, I suppose. You could also use it for more appropriate things. Teleport scrolls are already on the market—expensive, it's true, as they call for some unconventional ingredients, but it's simply a question of money. But locking a High Spell in a scroll..." Dan gave me a meaningful look as if estimating how many Astral Mana Dispersal scrolls he'd love to have in the Vets' arsenal. "Or a unique spell like the Inferno portal that has recently been auctioned by some painfully familiar auto buy..."

Oh. Apparently the Sparks, while solving a lot of problems, were at the same time generating a whole new bunch of the same. A Dome Shield Removal scroll, if auctioned, would win the People's Choice award and fatten up my wallet no end. But it'll also bring new headaches. First, someone would suss out the principle behind the dome removal and the scroll itself might later resurface in some truly unsavory place, raising a lot of dirt in the process.

Dan was watching my face, apparently pleased with seeing my furrowed brow and not the idiotic joy of a tramp who'd just found a suitcase full of heroin and was now celebrating his good fortune. In any case, the Sparks created new opportunities: a new tool for my workshop that I was sure I could use to solve a multitude of problems. I did get his message about the auto buy. It was time to ignore my inner greedy pig and hire a new one-time vendor for every risky transaction.

This was something I should have remembered a long time ago. There's no such thing as anonymity any more. Neither online nor in real life. It's only the question of how much the interested party is prepared to pay for the information. While you're small fry, you've nothing to worry about: you'll remain anonymous simply because you're not worth the trouble. Just remember that when the time comes, all your cyber trail will come to the surface. All your phone records, your entire web surfing history, all your bank card transactions, all the CCTV footage with your face on it and lots of other things.

Under Dan's greedy stare I placed two of the vials—those I'd filled myself—into my pocket. He then cast a meaningful glance at the remaining pots and gestured over his head imitating a whirlwind. "Think we'd better discuss it."

"Not now," I cut him short. "I'm desperate for some sleep. I still need to have a briefing of my own."

The General turned to me. "Do you think you could ordain me personally?"

I nodded. That wasn't a problem.

Ding! A flash of green light colored our faces an alien tinge.

"Heh, I've already done half a Faith level," the General didn't really sound surprised. "It looks like the starting point depends on the ordainer's rank. There was something I heard about a year and a half ago, if my absolute memory is anything to go by. I met some dude who'd done this quest that entitled him to be ordained by the First Priest. A Light NPC, naturally, but it's of no consequence. So when I met him he was in the process of celebrating all the gold and time that he'd saved."

Dan didn't say anything, his glare indignant. He wasn't a cheapskate and still the fifty dollars that he'd just wasted on the experiment he could have spent on a bunch of flowers for his wife and an armful of chocolate for his rugrats.

The General gave me a pleading look. "You think you could dedicate my men, as well? It's still a lot of money, you know, we could save almost forty grand."

Exasperated, I was about to protest. What kind of attitude was that? He wanted all the gain without any of the pain. I didn't have time, that was exactly why I'd given them a priest of their own. The Temple had to grow! Actually, that was reason enough. Eric could do with a rank boost, too.

I shook my head and pointed at a hesitant Eric. "Even not mentioning a whole host of other problems, it's in your clan's interests to level your own priest. If you think about it, Eric will only get a percentage of Faith points from those he dedicated personally, while he's desperate for some growth simply to be able to tackle the clan's problems. Which means that on top of his personal skills like Voluntary Death, he'll also need to invest into everything the clan might need, like raid buffs and all sorts of curses and anathema spells. So my advice to you would be not to skimp on his services."

Catching Eric's grateful glance, I gave him an inconspicuous wink. He must have already looked through his skill list and—knowing his appetites—must have already chosen a dozen abilities he could use had he not been nearly stripped of referral XP from a good seven hundred of already-dedicated players. Thank God I didn't depend on these parameters, otherwise I'd have been running around like a headless chicken doing other people's jobs instead of my own farming bit.

The thoughtful General nodded. "Very well, Max. Now go and get yourself some rest. You look like a vampire with those bloodshot eyes."

I exchanged handshakes, waved my goodbyes and left the room, heading for my apartment.

There, Cryl and Lena were happily lounging in the soft chairs, all bright-eyed and bushy-tailed, talking over each other as they exchanged their last farming experiences. They'd very nearly done level 30 in just a few days which admittedly couldn't have been too hard for people who'd invested real money in the game. Lena screamed with delight when she saw me. As she fell around my neck, I felt something warm inside as if hugging my little sister after a long separation. Cryl didn't seem to be jealous. His eyes betrayed his pleasure at seeing me. This was my family, the Children of the Night.

Once we've had our hugs, I sat them down and gave them a summary of the last few days' events. The news of our own castle, with its First Priest as their leader and Macaria as their patroness brought my authority to a height previously unknown. That's why they enthusiastically accepted my request of joining the ranks of religious workers. Even the Help of the Fallen One didn't automatically make Cryl a priest but rather defined his religious preferences and offered him some unknown freebies.

The kids jumped up and pulled some serious faces, preparing for the ceremony.

"Not so fast," I stopped them. "We need to get everything ready first."

As they stared at me, uncomprehending, I scooped a couple handfuls of vials out of my bag, lining them up in strategic rows that ensured prompt grabbing, filling and closing.

"Now listen," I said. "I'm pretty sure the goddess will come to have a look at her new disciples. Her arrival will be accompanied by the natural phenomenon of the Sparks of Divine Presence, which will be the first pillar of our upcoming financial well-being. Once the celestial window is closed, grab the vials and scoop the Sparks into them."

I looked around the room choosing a relatively empty corner. Pulling the rag aside, I pointed, "Come and stand here."

Casting one final glance at their deadpan faces, I stuck my tongue out and gave them a wink. It wouldn't do greeting the goddess looking like a funeral procession. Young people are naturally giggle-happy and they don't need much prompting. When, to the jingling of the bells and the glittering of the snowflakes, Macaria's face peeked out of the celestial window, all she saw was two happy geezers grinning from ear to ear. Herself blushed with (I suppose) the Fallen One's energetic advances, she nodded and gave me the thumbs-up.

The portal window glazed over, shrouding her face. With a pop, the air thickened, revealing the bastard Winnie standing right in the middle of the precious sheet of celestial snow. Cringing, he wiped his filthy paws and sloshed across the puddle toward the fireplace, kicking and stomping out the precious Sparks.

"You pig!" I selected him as target and slammed a mental fist on the priest skills panel.

I really don't know what I meant by doing this. It all happened too quickly. Either I meant to cast a curse over him or report him to the gods for getting in the way. Instead, Winnie got ordained.

The bells jingled again, anxiously this time, and the goddess' annoyed face—her lips slightly bee-stung—didn't promise a joyful rite. Seeing the would-be priest, she raised her eyebrows, her eyes fixed on me in surprise. I shook my head, shielding myself with my hands, gesturing I had nothing to do with him. The white bastard finally awoke from his momentary confusion and was now trying to make himself scarce. As if! Panicking, the creature launched a string of unsuccessful teleport attempts rattling like a machine gun while Macaria, having blocked his teleport skill, turned round and said something to somebody behind her back.

Could it be I'd been too cruel to the white monster, I thought seeing the Fallen One's scowl. As his glare fell onto Winnie, his face cleared; tilting his head to one side, the Fallen One chuckled in surprise.

"That's funny," I heard him mutter. "I could use that..."

Reaching out of the window, the Fallen One grabbed Winnie, pulling the creature toward the portal window. Have you ever heard a wounded hare scream? Probably not, otherwise the ranks of animal protectors would have soared into millions. That was the kind of scream Winnie had emitted. Meeting Lena's begging stare, I nodded and activated my Appeal to Gods ability.

"Listen, AI 311, make sure you treat him well, okay? He's not bad at all..."

The Fallen One glared at me, his voice pounding in my immediately-sore head. "Don't you talk back to me. It's my business what I do to him. And one other thing. I'd appreciate it if you gave your dedication shit a rest for tonight. Otherwise I'll be forced to make sure you don't enjoy your own matrimonial state for the next hundred years or so."

The window slammed shut. My two friends grabbed the vials, hurrying to pack away the glittering carpet of snow.

I just stood there scratching my head and thinking of an appropriate answer.

* * *

An economic evaluation of the Happy Dreams private virtual prison model.

The first private for-profit correctional facilities were officially introduced in the USA in February 1983.

The Act of Congress 6133 approved April 203X makes provision for the digitization of long-term inmates.

Social advantages:

Complete elimination of violence, drug trafficking and escape attempts in digital mode following the procedure recommended by the Department of Corrections.

Psychological testing shows that digitizing increases the first-time offenders' chances of successful reintegration into society 19%. This figure is 5% for repeat offenders.

Financial advantages:

A six-fold increase in prison population density;

Guard staff decrease 75%;

Payback period of 11 months;

Expected profit: $9000 per convict per year, depending on the virtual world, the more popular and populated ones being the most desirable in regard to their farming and crafting potential.

Chapter Sixteen

I congratulated the two on their priestly status. Then I lectured Cryl on the importance of the Voluntary Death skill and meted out their responsibilities for the next few hours. I gave them access to the auto buy, entrusting them with the pen-pushing task of sifting through the messages and answering them using a few templates I'd jotted down. All the really important stuff they had to forward to my PM box. I scheduled the dedication ritual for one p.m. the next day. With one final umpteenth yawn, I motioned them out of the room.

They couldn't have been more understanding. Chirruping like sparrows, they made themselves scarce. Funny how the dissociation of visual and behavioral patterns can affect brain functions. On the outside, Lena was the epitome of an Elfa, sophisticated and sensual: the AI-perfected idea of male doom. But that was visually. My brain was boiling over her childish hopscotch gait, her open-mouth curiosity and bright-eyed enthusiasm. So while my mind was screaming, *she's only a child!* it was unable to stop the drool from running down my virtual chin. I just hoped that Cryl understood it, too, and was able to postpone any heavy-duty courtship for another couple years.

It looked like the day, however crazy it had been, was finally over. I had to admit I'd already started to regret getting caught in the stream of events that had taken me to the top of AlterWorld's political life. How much nicer would it have been to sit by the Gnoll Hill smoking the gentle monsters. It had to be the proverbial fear of responsibility speaking for me, the unwillingness to step out of my comfort zone.

Thus sympathetic with myself, I headed for bed. Time to catch a few Zs. Time to dream of a beautifully fat female pig... oops, that was my inner buddy raising his own sleepy head. Would be funny if he developed into a separate being, then materialized- oh, no, giving him a name probably wouldn't be such a good idea. It was probably better to only mention him allegorically, the way cavemen did when they spoke of the world around them. We still have no idea how they called their totemic animals—the bear, for instance. All we know is that they tried to disguise his true nature somehow, for fear of the animal hearing his name and answering the call. Their superstitions fit our reality so well they must have known something important. My little piglet would have made a fine majordomo! Having said that, I needed his services too much to part with him. Nightie night, Piglet!

The next morning was late. After a big breakfast, I began sorting out our financial situation. I checked the auctions and discovered over eight hundred potential followers willing to part with a grand to get dedicated by the hand of Macaria. Holy moly, this priesting job seemed to be more lucrative than even the tobacco business. Then again, the tobacco thing had a future while this was definitely a one-off, a quick gig on the side akin to stealing the collection box.

The customers kept paying, their money clinking into the auto buy account where it sat, frozen, until the deal was consummated. Either the Admins were playing safe or they just jumped at the chance to make money out of thin air. If you thought about it, there had to be about a billion in frozen assets on various accounts at any given time. The accounts and their owners changed but the sum, on average, remained the same. So nothing really prevented the Admins from depositing it at 3% annual interest, that's thirty million a year. Nice and polite, the way these things are done in a democratic society: "Sir, would you be so kind as to face the wall, hands behind your back, please, feet wide apart. Please allow me to fit you with a pair of handcuffs, for your own protection, Sir, thank you very much for your cooperation." Bastards.

The Inferno portal auction was especially gratifying. Over a hundred grand there, plus lots of questions from raid and clan leaders. Interestingly, it wasn't necessarily the same person. Managing a clan and taking it on raids were two entirely different skills. I could understand their impatience: I still remembered the news feed mentioning a raid to another plane where the total value of auctioned loot amounted to millions. It definitely made sense for top clans to be involved. And as for all those Chinese and Korean entrepreneurs, it was a gold mine. Their labor camps had switched from making T-shirts and license plates to farming virtual items long ago, their sweatshops thriving all over AlterWorld.

I decided to create a scroll with the Portal Spell written on it, then hand it to the auction winner. This way it secured his and my anonymity plus gave me some time advantage. Time was what we needed right now, its absence grabbing my throat, dictating me its will, controlling my actions. Do you really think I'd have sold the Vets the coordinates of my Gigantic Fly-Traps field for next to nothing had I had one year of quiet life in front of me? Never.

My only two clan members had already woken up—if they'd even gone to bed at all. The auto buy's unread messages counter kept clicking, growing and decreasing as the kids worked their way through them. I rummaged through the PM box and discovered a report from the security agency complete with their standing order receipts. Their fees paled into total insignificance next to the auction purchases and impending earnings. The thought that I spent less on my mother's security than I did on the Temple's guards of honor made me physically sick. Under my inner greedy pig's unexpectedly approving stare, I sent a request to treble the security, adding to it a hired help I'd found through some recruiting agency. It was about time Mom quit busting her hump doing her own cleaning, cooking and shopping. She needed to get some rest. She also needed to get a medical checkup and maybe go to some health spa or other. Knowing her, I knew she wouldn't do it, but then again, I still hoped I could talk her into going perma mode sometime soon. It wasn't as if AlterWorld needed many primary school teachers, but then again, why not?

Thinking about the health checkup made me remember my own miserable frame, apparently still comatose in the capsule's snug interior. According to the bodyguard's report, Mom returned to her old flat twice a day to perform some life support procedures such as replacing the glucose IV drip, changing my diaper, wiping my body with a damp sponge, all the while talking to my motionless body which was apparently on its very last legs approaching the red line foretold by the doctors.

I paused, thinking. It wasn't nostalgia alone. My body and I, we had much in common. We'd been through a lot together. And if there ever was a chance to preserve it—don't even ask me why—I had to use it. My mind was apparently immortal which meant that one day I might come back, albeit temporarily, to that joint-creaking frame, even if just to have a stroll along the streets of Moscow—if Moscow still existed, of course. Seventy thousand dollars didn't sound like a lot of money any more. I wrote a lengthy letter to Mom, giving her Olga's Chronos number and asking her to mention the code phrase, *Laith, Level 52 High Elf*, in order to make an urgent cryonics contract. She'd already had a power of attorney to act in my name, and as for my death certificate, soon it wouldn't present too many problems. The new expense did smart, but I had that feeling that I'd done something very right.

Mom would never agree to go perma while I was still alive. But Taali— she would need a capsule of her own very soon. It was never a good idea to use one of those underground digital parlors as they were all regularly raided by the Feds who pulled the naïve idiots out of their paradise of choice and blacklisted every one of them. Those who were suspected of suicidal or digitized behavior were ordered to visit the nearest ID center for a retina scan—apparently, it made digitizing much more difficult. Absolutely voluntarily, of course. Alternatively, they were sent for compulsory treatment in a closed medical facility.

So what I needed was a second-hand capsule. I already knew how to hack one and where to get all the rigged gear and jailbreak chips. This was one shady market the authorities would have a hard time cracking.

AlterWorld was buzzing with all sorts of operators offering real-world services. The auction was flooded with their offers:

Only for perma players: assistance in family reunion.
A FIVR capsule for daily rent, completely renovated.

Bugs for sale, hard and soft! Entomologists don't need to apply.

This last offer interested me the most, especially because the vendor had been in business already for over a year, his profile boasting tons of positive feedback. Once he checked my digitized status against some arcane database of his, he promptly answered my PMs, agreeing to find a capsule, do it up, then deliver it to the address given. With all the bells and whistles plus his commission, it cost me three thousand dollars. I could live with that. If everything went as he'd promised, they'd deliver a functioning FIVR set to my mother's in the next two days. But the vendor's unobtrusive offer of 33% off if he could have his capsule back once I didn't need it any more made me realize another thing. It looked like I would end up with two more bodies in need of cryogenic procedures. Burying them would be sacrilege. At this point, my inner greedy pig gritted his teeth at the prospect of parting with another hundred and forty thousand bucks. Yeah right, who said the rich had it easy? I cost more in maintenance than some goddamn aircraft carrier.

I'd have loved to text Taali, even if just for a quick smilie exchange. But I couldn't. She was already lying low, avoiding any eventual electronic trail. No phone calls, no logins nor bank card transactions, moving around only in covered transport. She had to be cussing under her breath as she was adjusting to her new gun. Then again, she could be enjoying its quiet report and gentle recoil. Her shoulder must be all black and blue from her old Vepr. From what I'd heard, this was how they'd detected women snipers during the Chechen war.

We'd planned her to act in five to seven days. Fingers crossed. I knocked the bedpost. Good luck, old girl.

The clock showed past midday. Enough spending! Time to make some dosh. I contacted the auction controller, confirming our meeting in a café on the town square. I'd made the reservation well in advance to provide for any eventualities. It was a good thing I'd done so, too: the central square of the Original City was bustling with eleven hundred and forty would-be disciples awaiting dedication matched by about the same amount of bystanders. Ten auction representatives were already working hard for their 3%, keeping order and separating the onlookers from the customers.

Next to the auction controller sat a sturdy man in an unknown uniform, his clan tag in full view: *Virtual Police.* All right... The use of this word combination was prohibited when naming any clans or characters. So this had to be a true to life virtual pig, the real living and breathing thing, if you can say so about a cartoon avatar. Actually, the likes of him weren't regular characters—they used special accounts that gave them rights similar to the Admins', allowing them access to databases, internal control consoles and lots of other important things. A law passed seven years earlier obliged every virtual world developer to create this kind of puppet for Federal needs.

The auction controller rose, offering his hand. "My name is Chris. I'd like you to meet Officer McDougall, Chief Inspector of the Virtual Police Control Department."

The cop wasn't particularly courteous. Glancing in my direction, he gave me an excuse for a nod.

The controller explained guiltily, "The law demands the Virtual Police monitor all deals between players that exceed one million dollars. The balance of your yet unsecured account exceeded that limit an hour and a half ago."

Yeah, so the Feds thought it gave them the right. "You'd make much better use of your time if you tried to monitor all instances of forceful imprisonment," I scowled back at the cop. "Any idea how many people are stuck in cells and cages? How many are bound to torture posts?"

He didn't deign to answer, just squinted at me and spat on the paving stones. The agent gritted his teeth and commented,

"The digitized individuals still don't have any legal status. You are either a game character belonging to a legally incompetent comatose individual or a piece of uncontrollable binary code."

Now it was my turn to squint. I took a step toward the cop and waved my hand in front of his face. "Hey, fancy communicating with a sequence of zeros?"

Unperceivably, he grabbed my hand and squeezed it in his iron grip. My life bar blinked, reporting damage sustained.

"I suggest you don't move if you don't want to spend the next week in a FIVR Police Department cell for assaulting a police officer in the course of his duty. Understood?"

I yanked my hand, indignant, but he didn't budge. "Understood?"

What was that now? Even here these Federal bastards could get at you. Well, they could try! The long arm of the law wasn't long enough to haul me out of the First Temple.

"Not, it's not understood!" I yelled. "Your department won't stand for much longer if you keep people in cages on such petty charges!"

The officer grinned, reaching for a pair of handcuffs gleaming purple. "Threatening, well. Article 119 of the Anti-Terrorist Act doesn't require an arrest warrant and allows to keep a suspect in custody for up to three years, including third-degree questioning and the use of special interrogation techniques."

"Officer," the agent butted in, "I'm afraid I'll be forced to file a complaint about an unprovoked arrest on personal grounds."

The cop looked at him. His glare glinted with promise. "And you're his associate, I presume?"

The agent wasn't easily frightened. Meeting the cop's stare, he said, "I've videotaped our exchange. I'm authorized to do that. Based on the video, our legal office AI predicts 96% probability of the arrest being ruled as illegal."

The cop grinned. "Well, if it makes you feel better in the cell. You really think we can't stand up for our own? So you'll have plenty of time to repent while waiting for the case to go to court. You might even hang yourself with guilt. These things happen, you know."

"Is this an official statement?" the agent snapped, his gaze vacant.

The cop paused theatrically. He cringed and shoved me aside. "Very well, you may live... until the next time."

Rubbing my arm, I walked over to the agent in awe. This was the kind of man you could go to war with. What was his name again? Yes, Chris. I needed to get his office's address. One of the first things a man of means has to obtain is his lawyer's business card. It helps solve a lot of petty everyday problems, everything from falling victim to bumper crime to successfully discouraging police sharks.

"Thanks," I said.

He shrugged it off with a smile. "My pleasure. That's racism. Some hate Africans, others can't stand Jews. And this is a new trend, disliking perma players. They say the permas cause the economy to collapse by embezzling loans and siphoning off funds into the virtual world. They apparently become contract killers because they can get away with it. It's easy to blame those who have no right of voice. It's like with self-defense: you really shouldn't leave any enemy alive. Funnily enough, that gives you a better chance to avoid a prison sentence. So that's what turns virtual cops into digiphobes. Your unclear legal status drives them up the wall."

"I'm recording it, too," the cop said icily.

Chris smirked and nodded: like, he was welcome. Paper can't blush. "There is a 99.8% probability that my words can't be qualified as insulting a Virtual Police officer."

The cop growled. The agent grinned: he must have enjoyed annoying him.

I lowered my voice. "You don't seem to like them, do you?"

"Well, you know. We were two brothers. One was a lawyer—that's me, actually. The other was a typical underage bonehead. The lawyer once took on a case you may have heard of, David Cuffman Vs. New York Precinct #47. He was defending someone. First he received a couple of subtle warnings followed by an open-text threat. The lawyer was too young and too ambitious to see reason. Then his brother was arrested with nine grams of coke in his pocket. What a coincidence, don't you think?" he raised his voice turning to the cop who ignored him pretending he was monitoring the crowd.

"I had to give the case up," the agent went on. "I did manage to get parole for my little brother but I wouldn't have been able to save his backside from prison, that's a fact."

He fell silent, reminiscing.

"And then what?" I reminded him. His story seemed to be getting quite educational.

He smiled. "He couldn't attend the hearing. His body had apparently been hospitalized in a comatose state. One of those family dramas," he gave me a wink.

Curiouser and curiouser. I pointed a meaningful finger at the crowd and rounded my eyes in silent question. Chris grinned and nodded, pleased with himself. He was too much! I gave him the thumbs up, causing him to frown in puzzlement. Yeah, right, he wasn't Russian, was he? He probably didn't know this sign. I made a circle with my thumb and forefinger, gesturing an OK. Now he understood it!

The cop stirred unhappily. "It's time."

Yes, of course it was time to start. The chat was boiling over with impatient customers. It wasn't a good idea to cross them: these were short-tempered people quick to pigeonhole you. I highlighted the clan chat. "Let's start!"

Cryl and Lena had all this time been mixing with the onlookers. Now they chose the first random pair of customers, checked their list and activated the dedication spell. The first flashes of light caused the crowd to shrink back, but then the freshly-baked disciples screamed with joy, attracting everyone's attention. The crowd surged forward, trying to get a glimpse of them and shower them with questions. The screams of joy promptly turned to half-smothered squeaks. A new dose of holy light saved my nearly squashed converts as the crowd abated, drawn to newer attractions.

The auction workers were screaming at the top of their lungs in the chat, begging those already served to leave the sacred zone.

With a faint smile on my face, I could almost physically sense my wallet getting ten grand heavier with every flash of light. I could almost see Macaria in her opalescent wrapper painting her eyelashes at a fancy dressing table in the Fallen One's once-ascetic bedroom. She froze, taking in the significance of the moment as her first followers started flooding in.

A portal popped open behind my back. I didn't think I'd pay any attention to it under the constant gun rattle of ins and outs. The familiar little bells made me prick up my ears. Talk about the devil. What if the goddess herself had decided to take a look at what was going on?

I turned and my jaw dropped. Okay, some transparent Greek robes were barely covering her body—I might have guessed as much. I didn't think the two gods had got out of bed before midday. But why did she wear makeup on one eye only? Was it my clairvoyance skills or was it the Divine Spark influencing reality?

She either didn't notice me or ignored me completely. Instead, she touched an onlooker's shoulder who stood with his back to her, apparently enjoying the little squabbles flaring up within the crowd. "Excuse me? Could you please tell me what's going on?"

The man glanced back. Appreciating the inquirer's appearance, he hurried to share the news, "It's a dedication ritual. They've all paid to become worshippers of the Goddess Macaria. Have you bought it, too? You think it's worth ten grand? Then you'd better move under that arch over there. You see, where those two priests are waiting."

Holy shit. It's possible that at least half of all world's secrets had remained secrets simply because no one had bothered to tell their owners the truth. Don't people just love to leak information? They just can't keep anything in, happy to tell everyone whatever they've seen or heard, with this proud I-know-it-all message.

I had a funny feeling the goddess wouldn't appreciate my clever money-making idea. Well, I couldn't have been more right. She squinted, her eyes fast becoming slits. Her nostrils flaring, she swung her head round, looking for the culprits. I stepped aside, concealing myself behind the agent's back. He looked at me, puzzled, then traced my stare back to its source and tilted his head in the most ironic manner. The goddess was bursting with fury. The crowd around her was dissipating, pushed away by a strong wind borne from her slim frame. Even the sight of her weightless robes fluttering in the gusts didn't challenge anyone to make a pass at her, so strong was the pressure forcing them to stumble back over each other.

A mini portal flashed. In a swirl of opalescent snow, the goddess teleported to the center of the square, hovering high above it. Her legs were amazing. The Fallen One was one lucky guy.

The crowd stared up, enjoying a miracle and a free striptease show. Then the goddess' voice thundered down making them duck and cover their ears,

"Sentient beings of all races! I, Goddess Macaria, now tell you that from now on, a sincere prayer is enough to become my follower! And so be it!"

The earth shuddered. The world around me quaked as the new law of magic elbowed its way past the universe's unyielding constants, making itself at home.

I must have been the only person who, instead of admiring the goddess' voluptuous charms, peered hard at her young face praying she didn't hurt herself. Indeed, two red streaks showed from her nose, threatening to ruin her snow white robes. Her eyes rolled back.

I slammed the Appeal to Gods button. *Macaria needs help! She's strained herself!*

"I can see that," the skies rustled.

Already the goddess had lost control of her levitation and began sliding down onto the paving stones when a portal noiselessly opened under her feet. With a flash, Macaria was gone. The Fallen One had made it just in time. I don't think anyone realized what had just happened. Dumbstruck, people stared at each other, at the now empty sky, at the few colored snowflakes floating away in the wind. Flashes of bright light enveloped the crowd as some of the smartest disciples checked their dedication gift.

Women. It was so like them, ruining a perfect money spinner on a mere whim.

"Well," the virtual cop's sarcastic voice broke the silence at our table. "I can attest that services have been rendered to seventy-three customers. The rest are advised to cancel the deal as unnecessary and unavailable. A notification from the Control Department has just been sent to the customers' addresses.

"What do you mean, cancel the deal?" I demanded. "The services were rendered in full. All the customers were dedicated to Macaria at the stated time and place."

The cop shook his head, smiling sweetly. "My investigation has shown that the paid dedication took place in violation of the goddess' will. I have in my possession a video corroborating this conclusion. Macaria publicly denounced any and all middlemen and personally dedicated everyone who so wished. You had nothing to do with it, which renders your charges unjustified."

What was that now? I cast a helpless glance at Chris who made a helpless gesture.

The cop beamed, suddenly very pleased with himself. "What will your office AI say to that? What's the probability of a successful appeal?" He wasn't upset by not getting the answer he wanted. With a sarcastic salute, he disappeared in a portal flash.

Life was a bitch. First it sent you a cop who could be Tavor's big brother for all I knew. And then it sent you another female canine, no names mentioned for fear of her sensing the full range of my emotions.

Talk about gratitude. I pulled her out of oblivion, and the first thing she did was sweep the Temple clean of tons of mithril and other artifacts. And in less than twenty-four hours, she graced me with another blunder, this time for a million and a half bucks! This woman had a talent for being a nuisance.

I opened the auction and stared at it with a silent groan. The number of automatically processed complaints had already reached seven hundred and counting. The consumer rights protection worked without a glitch, making mincemeat out of the dodgy auction vendor.

What a bunch of jerks. Good job that the first seven hundred thirty grand had already been released into my account as was the Vets' million. Some of the unlucky first seventy customers were cheeky enough to contest the transaction but they had no chance in hell. Some consolation, I suppose.

The financial question had once again raised its ugly head. I just had enough cash to pay off the federal tax and all the current costs, but there was no way I could pay my first installment on the castle. Oh, well. Easy come, easy go. I still had a couple more ideas up my sleeve. I could still cook something up... provided Macaria didn't interfere.

Women. Having said that, she did look a sight. Taali, my sniper girl, where are you?

Chapter Seventeen

The morning of the new day came late, largely due to the rain that hadn't stopped for the last twelve hours. The heavy clouds scraped their bellies against the flagpole over the donjon, their grayish haze enveloping the Vets' clan banner that hung off the rooftop like a wet cloth. Looked like I was grounded.

That was actually the first rain I'd seen here. At least they didn't have seasonal changes in this land of eternal summer laced with occasional instances of sunny autumn and blossoming springtime. If you happened to fancy snow or scorched desert, that wasn't a problem, of course: plenty of desirable locations here in every stage of exoticness. AlterWorld had something for everyone provided they paid for it: from a mammoth safari in the tundra to those wishing to add a lava-living salamander to their trophy cabinet.

I stumbled out of bed and ordered some breakfast, then pushed open the wide mosaic-pane window and, pulling my soft chair closer, began watching the raindrops' incessant play. Water and flame, the two things that hypnotize you allowing you to relax and forget your mundane troubles—be it the monotony of the surf washing over a sandy beach or the quivering dance of a candle flame.

With a cautious knock at the door, the servant girl rolled in the breakfast trolley. Wonder why they had set her character to being so humble? Was it that their majordomo was a Victorian type who believed that domestics should fade into the woodwork and be neither seen nor heard?

I lifted the heavy silver lid and flared my nostrils in anticipation. An enormous plate of Russian salad and some saucers containing extra cream and mayo. Yes, Russian salad for breakfast, so what? The castle chambermaids could see right through me: they knew very well what breakfast choice guaranteed them a tip of a gold coin and they weren't going to overlook my weakness. No idea what NPCs would need money for but their joy at seeing gold was genuine when they stashed the coins away into their little secret pockets. Were they saving money for buying themselves out? Which was why I was on a Russian-salad diet to a degree. Even when I ordered a barbecue dinner, I was bound to find a little bowlful of the salad lurking somewhere on the tray, the servant girl's stare watchful and just a tad hopeful. I had to live up to every pretty face's expectations: the coin would disappear into the depths of their cleavage, and the salad, into the depths of my dependable digital stomach.

Having finished off the main course, I poured a hearty dose of cream and sugar into my coffee and habitually turned to my morning mail.

Two raid buffs had already sold making me a hundred grand richer. Bids for the Inferno portal had hit two hundred grand. Excellent. I also found some responses to my shield removal offers. Predictably, what the vendors wanted from me were guarantees, evidence and discounts. Among them, a letter from the *Minediggers* clan breathed anger and hatred. They didn't seem to worry much about the money. Their message read:

Agreed. Will close the deal via the auction through an agent. When can you remove the shield?

This was the kind of businesslike approach I liked. But in any case, before risking my own skin and anonymity, it might be worth trying to transfer the spell to a scroll. That would considerably limit my chances of blowing my incognito, at the same time removing most of the customers' questions. A scroll was exactly what it was: a scroll, no personal factors and no dirty tricks. So I decided against answering them on the spot. Instead, I opened Wiki in search for a skill that had suddenly proved to be so useful.

Glory be to the gods—calligraphy turned out to be a skill and not a profession. That saved me dozens of hours and thousands of gold I'd have had to spend in order to be able to create my own High Spell scrolls. In this case, they had used another restricting tool: the rarity and high cost of the ingredients necessary. The skill itself you could learn for a symbolic fifty gold from the Chief Scribe of the King's Library in the City of Light. Whom I could go and see straight away.

I walked downstairs to the Portal Hall hoping to hitch a ride to the city. The guard on duty turned out to be Porthos the Wizard who sat there in a long-suffering pose, hiccupping, his stare fixed on a mana vial. On the wall over his head hung a newspaper cutout saying,

The first case of heartburn among the perma players: How long till we get toothache?

Porthos raised the eyes of a sick cow. "Where to?"

"The Original City. The City Library."

He shrugged. "Couldn't do it even if it were the red light strip. It's the basic portal to the main square. I'm not the Porters guild impersonated. Don't expect me to have five thousand exit points."

"The square is all right," I didn't want to argue. The main thing was, he didn't have any questions which meant my right of passage was still valid. Which was good news.

I transported to the city, got everything settled in under twenty minutes and teleported myself back to the castle as the proud owner of a new skill. At first I wanted to go straight to the First Temple and spend some quality me-time staging some visually impressive hazardous experiments. But then both Lena and Cryl began PM'ing me demanding to take them along so they could explore our clan's new home. Nothing prevented them from going there themselves using their Journey Home ability, but they were understandably wary of showing up there in the absence of the owner.

'Porting, grouping in, 'porting again. Home, sweet home. Inside the Temple, a Hell Hound was busy shepherding their litter. She'd all but jumped at us barking when she noticed me and cooled off.

"They're with me!" I pointed at the freshly-baked priests. Then my eye happened on a heap of scrap metal as high as I was tall. The heap gleamed purple, promising great returns once it was smelted down. Good dogs! Not only had they got hold of the moon silver: they'd retrieved it and somehow dragged it back to the Temple.

"Where's the pack's leader? Call her for me, please."

"Aww, puppies!" Lena squeaked behind me and rushed fearlessly toward the guarded nursery.

I winced, closing one eye, expecting the dog to lunge and the girl to scream, followed by the thud of a tombstone against the marble floor.

But apparently, the girl wasn't as simple as she looked. The Hound stifled a yelp, snatching back a trodden-on paw, then froze again in a Sphinx-like pose as the girl got busy cuddling the pups. Cryl and I exchanged glances, breathing a sigh of relief. What was it the Fallen One had said about her *phenomenal immersion*? Looked like it. At least the hounds seemed to have accepted her.

Then the Temple's reverential silence was disturbed by the screeching of metal. Claws scratched against the paving stones. I heard some familiar grumbling. A weird procession opened up to our eyes.

My good old Hound friend headed the group. I'd have recognized her anywhere after our combined stretch in the pokey. In actual fact, I think it was my new absolute memory that fixed the unique combination of the dog's features, from the shape of her scars to the pattern of her irises. Actually, I wasn't so sure any more. The idea of absolute memory had started to erode somewhat. Talking about her irises, I wasn't at all sure that I'd be able to draw an identical picture of them if you asked me to. To a degree, it sounded logical and even soothing: it meant we remained human with all our weaknesses, not some cyborg types with their memory crystals stored behind their belly armor panels.

A zombie dwarf was shuffling his feet behind her. He was pulling an improvised sledge loaded with mithril junk. The zombie didn't really look like an undead, more like a dwarf in exile who'd spent the last ten years in the mountains. A shabby cloak concealed a kit of full armor. A bandana covered signs of recent burns on his hairless skull. A beardless dwarf, now that was an oxymoron. Struggling under his heavy load, he grumbled almost voicelessly,

"According to the Haroun Convention, Article 6, Clause 4, the use of prisoner of war labor by private individuals is considered a third-degree crime and is punishable by..."

I didn't get the chance to hear the rest as one of the convoy hounds growled, driving the absent-minded lawyer forward.

The procession drew level with us and stopped, obeying a commanding bark. I gave them a friendly nod and turned to the chief bitch. "Great to see you again. It looks like the new lands are abundant with prey?"

Indeed, she seemed to have gained weight since I'd seen her last. Her once-dull armor gleamed with a mirror-like finish.

"Greetings, O Dark One," the Hound lowered her head. "We thank you for your permission to settle in these lands. Not an hour passes that we don't sing a song of joy. I don't remember ever having such an easy and glorious hunt! Our pups are bloated like the lazy gastropods in the Lord of Fire's own herds. They refuse to eat bones and cartilage, all they care for is freshly-killed meat!"

To show their agreement, the whole pack raised their heads and howled like some mad orchestra of chainsaws when they hit some hard gnarly bits. Their voices hit the supersonic waves that sent shivers up your spine.

I fenced myself off with my hands. "That's great! I'm so happy you like it! I can see you haven't wasted your time. Does it mean you've cleared the cellars and done what I asked you to?" I nodded at the mithril heap that was calling my name.

"We have, Priest. We've mopped up the cellars destroying over four hundred beings who believed the place to be their own. Many of them were indeed dangerous. But not many can still stand after my pack finished with them!" a note of smug boasting rang in her voice. "At first I thought you'd been mistaken. For a long time we couldn't smell a single crumb of the cursed metal. Then we discovered a whole heap of it piled up in one of the dead-end corridors. There we found this zombie, greedy as a dragon, crawling on top of it."

"I'm not a zombie!" the dwarf objected. "I am Durin the Smart, the Master of the Mithril Smithy, one of the defenders of these lands which suffered the steel invaders' ire. I was saved by the Element of Metal which I'd served all my life and which didn't let me die the final death."

"His greed didn't let him die," the Hound explained. "His soul couldn't leave his body after it obtained riches beyond the mountain kings' wildest dreams."

"Yes—greed!" the dwarf exploded. "The greed for knowledge! In all these hundreds of years I've studied every inch of the cellars collecting every crumb left by the steel invaders. Do you have any idea how deeply they'd delved into the secrets of metals? Can you fathom all the wisdom and the high secrets concealed in this heap of depleted ore?"

The dwarf boomed louder and louder, his voice reproaching: finally he had a chance to voice all the silent arguments he'd generated in all those lonely years of inner monologues. "You have any idea what this is? You really think it's a rock?"

Untangling himself from his harness, he sank his arms elbow-deep into the heap of junk, producing a smallish egg and shook it in front of my nose. The egg had a very recognizable body complete with a detonator and ring pull.

I shrunk, mechanically pushing Lena behind me, shielding her. "I believe I do," I said in a suddenly hoarse voice. "This is an offensive grenade. Looks remarkably similar to the famous RGD5."

"Pardon me?" the dwarf managed, speechless. "Offensive? Who would want to offend it? Actually, I called it the egg of the fire salamander. Have you ever tried to break one?"

I peered at the unfamiliar markings and fluorescent stripes that coded the grenade's type. "All you need to do is pull on the ring without letting go of the handle."

The dwarf sort of shrank in size. "I shouldn' have let go of it, should I? I didn't know that."

He opened his shabby cloak revealing homemade mithril armor plates peppered with ragged holes.

"Good job you kept your head attached," I sympathized.

"I didn't," he sighed. "Nor my arms. I respawned twenty-four hours later lying on a mithril heap. Your hound has a point. The Moon silver draws me and won't let me leave."

"Don't worry. We're going to melt it into nice neat ingots and lock it in the treasury. Maybe then it'll set you free."

The dwarf shook, hiding the grenade behind his back. I cast a meaningful glance at the empty space where it had just been. "How many of them have you got?"

He hastily shook his head and stepped back, stumbling against the hounds' noses. They growled; the dwarf recoiled, mumbling, "That's the only one! The only thing I have! You're not getting it!"

Greedy guts! He'd make a nice friend for my inner pig. I had to give it some thought.

"Sir Durin, I'm afraid you don't understand," I said. "I'm the Temple's First Priest and the owner of the castle. I have my men here with me and our alliance representatives. We can't allow zombies to roam these corridors unattended, nor can we let them sneak our mithril and ammo. As the castle's owner, I have the right of ownership to everything in these lands."

I almost felt guilty expropriating him. The dwarf was a sorry sight. He started shaking, recoiling this way and that with a haunted look in his eyes, stumbling against the hounds' bared teeth. Finally he froze, scowling like a cornered rat.

I reserved my compassion for the old idiot. It was time to make him an offer he'd find hard to refuse. "You could, however, stay in the castle. You don't even need to part with your treasure."

The dwarf pricked up his ears, looking at me expectantly. I screwed my face into an appropriately official expression. "Durin the Dwarf, Master of the Mithril Smithy, I hereby invite you to join the Children of the Night and accept the post of the clan's steward and treasurer!"

Why not? I didn't have enough people, did I? So I had to think of something pretty quick. At least he wouldn't be able to run off into the real world with our money. Nor would he fritter away the funds to the first so-called friend or honey trap.

"Your job will be to guard and increase the clan's property. Which doesn't mean I'll have to run after you begging you every time I need a nail to drive in the wall! You are the guardian; I'm the owner. You have a minute to consider my offer."

The ex-Master didn't hesitate. I don't think he expected to get a second similar offer from somewhere else. The alternative, however, was sad and unenviable.

He nodded. With a metallic click, he drew his hand from behind his back and offered it to me, palm up. On his thumb hung the pin ring he'd pulled from the grenade.

"Don't move," I said to him calmly. "Show me your other hand, very slowly, and please don't unclench it!"

Impressed by the seriousness in my voice, the dwarf pulled the other hand from behind his back, showing me the primed grenade. I lay my hand over his wizened fingers and squeezed it to prevent him from letting go of the safety clip. Gingerly I removed the ring, pinched the two ends of the split pin in my teeth and rethreaded it into the hole. Breathing a sigh of relief, I much more calmly let go of the clip handle. What a kamikaze. Had he just tried to blow us all up or was he really so clueless? I didn't ask. I motioned him to open his shovel-like hand, caught the deadly pineapple and cautiously put it in my bag.

The dwarf's greedy stare followed the disappearing treasure. "Do you understand the steel invaders' mechanics?"

"Sort of," I mumbled as I scanned the heap for any more hazardous junk. Trust them to unearth some tactical nuke so that this smartass could try to take it apart with a sledgehammer. How was I supposed to rebuild the Temple after that?

I wondered what the Vets would think when they noticed an atomic mushroom on the horizon? Would Dan and Eric immediately think about me? I seemed to be their prime suspect for lots of things.

"And who are you?" the dwarf squinted like a cop and—inconspicuously, so he thought—reached under his cloak. "Are you their servant or something?"

"Don't worry. It's been eight hundred years since anyone heard about them. Few still remember they existed at all. The world has new inhabitants now: the Immortal Ones. Millions are just visitors while hundreds of thousands have settled down here for good. I'm one of them. So please stop searching your pockets for whatever it is you're looking for, just surrender it to our ammo depot. Pointless trying to kill us: I've just told you we're immortal. So are you with us? Here's the invitation."

I selected him as target, crossed my fingers—no clan had ever hired a zombie before—and sent him an invitation to join. The Universe didn't shatter—apparently, the world's mechanics had been sufficiently changed the last time—but our clan counter grew by one.

Now that's a motley crew! Should I invite the Fallen One to join, too? Or Macaria, talking about the devil? Had she already realized she was now sitting on a time bomb? How did she expect her priests to level if she'd pulled them out of the food chain between her worshippers and herself, stripping them of the necessary referral XP? Never mind Eric: I was sure the Vets wouldn't let him down by seeking another priest for their own initiation. Actually, hadn't they invited me to some official 'do or other this coming Saturday? That was in their own interests: the priest's raid tricks and special abilities could add their two cents to the clan's power making it stronger and more competitive. But what was I supposed to do with the other Temple priests? Did I have to pay them for every initiation? Suicidal little cow. First she'd made a real botch of things, then she disappeared and left me to clean up her mess!

I stirred and glanced at the zoned-out zombie who must have been digesting his new status, saying goodbye to his eight hundred years of solitude.

I mentally reached for the Castle-controlling artifact. "Lurch!"

"Yes, Master!"

"What do we have in the way of a treasury? Know any?"

"Three!" AI reported with a note of pride in its voice. "One is official, used as bait for burglars and as decoy for an attacking enemy. Lots of traps and very few real treasures, mainly costume jewelry. The second one is the owner's personal treasury, an artifact strongroom with floating coordinates. It's currently on standby buried deep in the foundations and can be moved closer to your suite at your first request. Finally, the secret vault used to store real treasures. Status: yellow, borderline functional. Unfortunately, the regenerating wave that occurred sixteen hours ago has caused forty-one tons of the vault's contents to mysteriously disappear."

Bam! My virtual greedy pig collapsed, unconscious. I gave him a mental slap on his fat cheeks, wiped his large tears and sighed, "Oh, well. No use crying over spilt milk. Now listen: on my orders, Durin the Dwarf has been appointed castle treasurer. He is granted access to the last treasury you mentioned. His initial task will be to store the mithril ore and other valuables. Notify me of all instances of him carrying out more than 1% of the vault's contents."

With a smile, I turned to the dwarf and slapped his wood-hard shoulder, shrinking as I imagined him crumbling to the floor with my hearty endearment. But by now he was too dry and wizened to fall apart. Good.

"Welcome to our ranks! We are few but we do have potential—a Super Nova castle, the First Temple complete with a priest, and the promise of support from two gods. Potentially we might be looking at a major war but you can't scare a dwarf with a good fight, can you?"

He grinned in agreement, exposing a row of perfect white teeth marred by a couple of impact gaps. His jaw must have suffered a few quality punches in its time: to the best of my knowledge it took a good horse's kick to make a dent in Dwarven teeth. And not just any kick but a fractal one involving some twists and turns. Dwarves could gnaw on rocks without as much as a toothache.

I was about to send him back to the cellars for a new dose of mithril when I remembered the point at which we were interrupted. "How many grenades did you say you had stashed?"

He tried to play dumb but now it wasn't so difficult to put the squeeze on him. If he were a clan member in an honorary post, he had to get used to discipline and hierarchy. He seemed to have realized it as he mumbled,

"Seven with rings. And two crates without, that's another forty."

Logical. They had to store the grenades without fuses. Finding them was another thing. I told them to go through the place with a fine-tooth comb and deliver the steel invaders' treasure to me personally. And gently, on tiptoe! I couldn't really say that the discovery of the grenades shifted the balance of power, reversing the course of history. How much explosive would they contain in total, a hundred grams? That wouldn't exceed the destructive effect of a level-90 Shooting Star spell. And that's in an ideal world, considering the weird markings. It could be a gas grenade, a signal flare or a thunderflash for all I knew. You tried to use it as a last argument in a critical situation only to discover you'd just lobbed a smoke bomb at the charging enemy. That wouldn't help you bring the world to its knees. Now if I had a whole factory of those, I could in theory give them to any number of zero-level characters, essentially arming them with the equivalent of a near-100 magic. But now all I had was a new tool, a trump card up my sleeve and I needed to make sure I used it promptly.

I turned to the two other clan members. "Lena, do leave the pup alone, will you? His mom can't wait for you to go, you've been treading all over her paws, I'm surprised she hasn't bitten you yet. Let's go outside and check on those ruins. I want to see what those mad goblins have done."

I lay my hands on their shoulders and led them toward the exit to demonstrate the whole grandeur of the Super Nova ruins. We stepped out, blinded by the piercing sun after the Temple's majestic gloom. Then we cried out: I in surprise, Lena in awe. The inner court looked as if it had been worked over by a talented landscape designer. Colored mosaic paths ran amid rich flowerbeds that climbed some of the walls forming hanging gardens. I didn't know any of those billions of flowers and plants that swayed in their pots, each humming its own note that weaved into beautiful melodies. Fruit trees offered their shade, all in different season: cherries budding and in blossom, and those bearing fruit from pale yellow to deep burgundy, all clinging to the same lace pavilion. Jesus, it was beautiful.

"Lurch?" I whispered into the artifact, unwilling to break the spell of the moment. "Got something to tell me?"

AI was smart enough not to ask me what I meant. "You did allow me to use 1% of all the units generated for my own needs, didn't you? So I thought I'd make myself pretty, the façades at least. Lying in heaps of debris for eight hundred years was intolerable. I used to be a painter once, you know..."

"I don't want to know! What 1% are you talking about? Have you done anything inside at all? I can see at least five gardeners here! Where do you think you got the money from?"

"Sir," Lurch's voice filled with injured dignity.

"Don't sir me! Okay, you can call me Master if you really have to..."

"Master, didn't you authorize me to hire extra staff with the automatic payment option? Indeed, the final version of the design you see now cost a hundred times more than I could afford. But I only paid for the project itself, plus the seeds and the enhanced-growth seedlings. The rest was all done by the staff hired as of your orders."

"Was it?" I didn't like the way he said it. "Who did you hire, then?"

"Ahem," Lurch paused. "Just some gardeners and diggers, a few stonemasons, carpenters and interior decorators, plus a couple handymen here and there..."

"How many?" I groaned.

"A hundred and seventy nine sentient beings," Lurch answered in a sunken voice. "But it's only for twenty four hours! And then I did send you a full expense report!"

"Where is it? Where the f-" I stopped noticing my friends' scared faces. "It's all right. Just the Castle's AI exceeding his authority. I've got to show him who's the boss..."

I finally trawled the message from the depths of my overflowing inbox. I opened it and groaned. "You butthead! You only sent it to me two minutes ago, didn't you? Jesus... An Elf designer, fifteen hundred a day. Total, forty one grand? Lurch?"

"He's the King's personal designer, Master. An award-winner. He used to decorate the palace of-"

"Fire everyone! Once their twenty-four hour contract is expired!"

"We can't!" Lurch protested. "All this will die!"

I looked at the glorious beauty around us. At Lena who was sitting amid the flowers that seemed to cuddle up to her, stroking a huge violet blossom that curled up in her lap ringing like a silver bell.

"Very well. You can leave the bare minimum of staff to care for all this splendor."

"You really like it?" Lurch asked timidly.

"Of course I do. But for future reference, all expenses over a hundred gold have to clear my desk. This is official, effective immediately."

"Yes, Sir!"

I heard what sounded like the chirruping of hundreds of sparrows coming from the direction of the mosaic paths. Then a screech of metal. This felt like some sick déjà vu.

I turned my head and my blood turned to ice. Squalling and quipping, a dozen goblins were dragging across the paving stones the enormous egg of a 500K GP bomb, its stabilizing fins bent.

Chapter Eighteen

"All freeze!" I squeaked, watching the metal spark against the stone. "Where d'you think you're taking that?"

Apparently relieved, the goblins let go of the bomb which thumped to one side, crumpling its fragile fins. I shut my eyes and shrunk my head into my shoulders. A second passed. Nothing. Phew. I could live without this sort of surprises.

One of the cleaners—no idea where he'd got hold of his grubby bandana—wiped his sweaty forehead. "Well, eh... You said eggs, didn't you? We're taking this thing over there," he nodded at some designer art in the shape of a hill two stories high covered in flowers and veined with blue streams.

I stared at the hill's rounded sides. Then one of the flower beds stirred, letting out the shabbily clad skinny backside of a goblin crawling out from under the amber moss. The creature cast a furtive glance around and began studying his stolen trophies. Raising his left hand to his nose, he sniffed what on closer scrutiny turned out to be another grenade. With a screech of metal against metal, he tried to bite a bit of it off, snorted his disappointment and cast the inedible thingy aside. The grenade thumped up and down on the uneven ground, rolling toward us.

By then I was quite used to the sight of ordnance being dropped. Stepping on the dirty-green sphere, I stopped its chaotic journey. The same as the one I'd taken from the dwarf, only the markings this time were a sickly glittering acid green. Good thing, anyway. Waste not, want not.

In the meantime, the goblin was already appraising another trophy. This time he was in luck. An enormous egg the size of that of an ostrich—at least—promised him a hearty meal. The goblin sniffed it greedily, bit the top off, then began swallowing the contents. I, however, was studying the handmade hill with a different eye, recognizing the familiar shapes of various ammunition in its bumps and mounds. If the whole thing detonated, holy mother of God...

As if answering my thoughts, a dull explosion echoed not far from us. The earth shook quite tangibly.

"That's nine," Lurch commented.

I peered at the cloud of smoke rising over the castle walls. "A sapper only gets to make one mistake. And that's when he chooses his profession."

Only then I noticed the goblins' foreman. He was running past us, his stick shredded, one eye twitching.

"Harlequin? Where do you think you're going?"

"Eh? What?" he looked about him. Finally noticing us, he ran right toward me. "Master! Forgive me, Master, but we need more hands!"

"Really? What have you done with the old ones, then?" I upped the sarcasm in my voice.

He hung his head. "It's that damn nest. Once I told those idiots we were looking for eggs, they keep tasting everything they find. Also, sometimes the shells break when they drag them. Then we had this big boom..."

"Casualties?" I grew serious. It was all right laughing at it, but every blown-up goblin was costing me.

Harlequin made a helpless gesture. "I can't be everywhere at once, Master. These are their clans' castoffs, they have no brains, only instincts. If I could have some warriors or craftsmen, or even free artisans... Those guys over there are junk. All they're capable of thinking of is food, sex and the fear of punishment."

Oh well. Hint taken. Penny wise and pound foolish. But how was I supposed to know you needed brains to collect junk and sieve through stone debris? True, I'd accepted the cheapest offer available... and a cheapskate always pays twice. "What are our losses, exactly?"

"One mighty big egg, three medium ones and lots of small ones. They just swallow them whole, the bastards..."

Illustrating his words, a new *Boom!* assaulted our ears, much more powerful than the previous one. The earth tried to shake us off. A gray cloud of dust rose to the sky over the outer wall.

"That's *four* medium ones," the foreman corrected himself.

"Actually, I meant workers. And how about this egg, does it count as 'mighty big'?" I looked at the bomb which by now was gradually integrating into the garden's design. The flowers' tendrils climbed its rough sides, generous touches of colored moss streaking the sad metal. Quick job. Better not to drop anything of value here: before you could bend down to pick it up, the lost gold piece would be forever buried inside the trunk of an ancient oak tree. No joke: it looked like the gardeners had overdone it on the growth promoter.

"That one? That's a medium one," the goblin snickered at the bomb. "The real mighty big one, that was a different story. I was a hundred paces away and my eye is still twitching. So I'm afraid we don't have many workers left, Master! A dozen-plus at most. You've got to hire a few new ones."

Holy cow. I dreaded to think what it was that they'd detonated over there. No, I couldn't leave it like that. These little goblin rats were certain to blow us all to hell and back. Besides, it was a shame wasting our supplies so pointlessly. Every explosion made my inner greedy pig sob as he mourned, crossing it off his list, every bit of the loot we could have taken off the great dragon Nagafen had we used all that ammo to blow him to smithereens.

"Lurch? Do we have somewhere where we can store hazardous artifacts? Someplace well protected, preferably underground?"

"We do indeed," he answered. "The lowest level of the basement, Alchemy Laboratory #2. Before, it was occupied by some spider-like monster and now it's Hell Hounds living there. Master," he hurried to complain, "the hounds disturb the walls' integrity! They're digging two tunnels, one of which is coming out behind the exterior wall!"

I glanced at the hound next to me. I had little doubt that her mental magic skills were more than enough to listen into our conversations, so openly she sneered and wiped her feet on the grass as if removing the non-existing cobwebs. Actually, I wouldn't want to be the spy who used the tunnel to walk right into the Hell Hounds' lair. Besides, I had indeed promised I'd let them choose any room they wanted so it wasn't quite kosher to backpedal now, not to mention the harm it could do to my reputation. Head tilted to one side, the hound followed my thinking process with some interest. Jeez. I really didn't need another cloak-and-dagger specialist to haunt me.

"No, Lurch, I don't think we need this kind of time bomb right under our backsides," I told him. "If something goes wrong, God forbid, the First Temple will be blown to kingdom come. At least my friends and I can go back to our respawn points, but the NPCs have no such luck. You'll be reduced to nothing. Hound?" I halted, not knowing how to address her. It really was time I got her a name. "Excuse me, Hound, if you find it too personal, but actually—are you male or female?"

The pooch glared at me, tensing up. Her mental message hit me like a slap in the face—literally, judging by the Divine Immunity prompt that popped up. I ignored the attack. Sorry pup, I didn't mean it.

"Female," she mumbled, indignant. "Males are incapable of mental speak. They can't lead the pack," she snorted, bathing me in another mental wave of indignation that sent the squeaking goblins scampering away. She was one powerful bitch.

"Sorry, babe. It's just that I don't know how to address you. I'm fed up with calling you hound. What if I call you... eh..."

I rummaged through my memory, trying to think of something nice as I hurriedly discarded various Ladies and Lassies. Inferno creatures were fast and deadly. Lightning sounded about perfect, but for me it was more associated with the cute Disney car than a dog, and in this world of wishes coming true you had to be careful about any subconscious slips. I didn't think the Hound would grow two pairs of wheels but nor would she appreciate a postbox-red lick of paint. Oh well, if not Lightning, what then? Spark? More modest but also fast, it too could hurt or even lead to a fire or an explosion.

"Spark! How d'you like that?"

The Hound started. Her nostrils flared, her claws crumbling the path's precious mosaic as she retracted them. She tilted her head to one side, apparently listening to herself, appraising her new status. Her eyes glistened with intellect, acquiring a new unusual depth.

Finally, her heavy armored head lowered in a bow. "Thank you, Priest, for your priceless gift..."

Aha. There seemed to be a pattern here. Apparently, for all monsters a name was something much more important than just a sequence of sound waves. "It's my pleasure, Spark. I'd really appreciate it if you told me what makes this gift so valuable."

At the sound of her name, the Hound rolled her eyes and, forgetting herself, grunted with pleasure. "By distinguishing me from amongst thousands of others and rewarding me with this unique mark, you use your power of creation to enter me into this world, giving me a soul and a chance to be reborn. The name is what shields us from oblivion and its ocean of shapeless biomass that forms thousands of creatures every second only to be destroyed in a matter of hours by the death-hungry Undead Ones."

Oh well. These monsters seemed to have pretty grim afterlife ideas. Now I could understand their unwillingness to die. Wonder if the developers had introduced this behavioral algorithm on purpose in order to improve their combat qualities, or was it some secret knowledge that had surfaced on its own?

I turned to the foreman faltering nearby, "Harlequin? What do you think?"

He silently pointed at the gaping holes in his clothes, reached into his pocket and produced a handful of purple fragments. He lowered his head.

What was that now? Had he already blown himself up somewhere? Then how come he hadn't disappeared like the faceless cleaners had? Did it mean he'd respawned?

"Lurch?" I called.

"Master," his voice broke. "Only yesterday I was a mixture of cold logic and a desire to serve. And now I take in the flowers and colors, I feel tickled when the Hounds dig their tunnels, and drool over the mosaic roof tiles in the designer catalogue. Also, there's a couple of starlings made their nest in the donjon's Southern gun slit. The way they sing, it's something..."

The mind boggles. Who were we, then—toddler Creators, playing with tin soldiers in some celestial nursery? Were we building worlds then destroying them without even realizing it? No. We were still a long way from becoming creators. We were, at best, some Godlike larvae, their gestation period stretching into hundreds and thousands of years. Only then, provided you hadn't lost your soul on the way, did you receive the chance to turn into a butterfly.

I turned back to the Hound. "Do you think it would be a good idea to give names to all the dogs in the pack?"

Spark paused, thinking. Then she shook her head, "No. I don't think it's a good idea to grant one a soul casually. Besides, your powers aren't boundless; on the contrary, they're infinitely limited. It's one thing to add one final stroke to the unique portrait of an already-extraordinary creature, finalizing its creation by breathing life into it. And it's quite another to create a unique personality from a faceless outline. I don't think you're strong enough to do it. You need to wait for a particular situation—an event, a deed of courage—when this member of the pack steps out of the ruck. Only then the precious seed of the name you give her can sprout into a fully developed soul."

That made sense. It felt—how would I put it—it felt *right*. I had this sense that this was how it was supposed to be. Well, all the more reason to accept this explanation as a working theory until proven otherwise.

"I see," I said. "Okay, back to our problems. Harlequin, I'm going to hire you twenty top class workers. As for the eggs, you shouldn't drop or drag them. You need to carry them with caution and on tiptoe."

I paused, comparing the goblins' frail arms and legs with the half-ton contraption. Well, well. What you really needed here was a troll trained in ballet dancing so he could carry stuff around for them. I had to check the hiring board, they had all sorts there. If push came to shove, I could always create my own staff using the manual generation option. True, it was more expensive and had its limitations: you couldn't, for instance, create a vampire hobbit as strong as an ogre. But it probably could build something like a super-cautious and balanced troll.

"Lurch, I've got a job for you. You need to clean all the stage scenery from the hill. You can add all the props later. Let the goblins do their job first."

"*Both* hills!" the foreman demanded.

I looked around. Which both? Were there two of them? Why didn't I know anything about it? Indeed, at the back of the court lurked another rather enormous heap partially concealed by the first one. Hadn't I told them to put all atypical junk aside? Wasn't that what I'd told the foreman?"

Greed got the better of me. "Clean it up!" I snapped.

As Lurch sighed, protesting, the cleaners began pulling apart its colored moss and fragile flowers. I noticed a few of the more intellectual plants that, scared by the prospect of total destruction, tucked up the skirts of their leaves and scurried off the hill all by themselves. So! I'd seen fly traps and I'd heard of cannibal vines, but I'd never come across anything like this.

In the meantime, the goblins acquired a taste for pulling things apart. "Easy!" I shouted. "We'll still have to restore it all. I've paid for every handful of humus with my own money!"

"Absolutely," Lurch agreed. "I had to buy everything here, even the earth worms, and these goblins gobble them down like there's no tomorrow! You can't just stick the Singing Bluebells in the ground! You need to provide them with a proper eco system."

"Very wise," I winced. "Listen, I just pray to God you don't buy any more worms or whatever without asking me first. Are you a responsible building or a market stall? I'll tear you down and build some outhouses instead! That's a promise!"

"Eh, I-" Lurch faltered. "Root worms, they don't propagate, you see. You need to buy new ones every month..."

"How many?" I groaned.

"Only a couple thousand. If no one starts eating them, of course."

"How much?"

"Peanuts! A hundred gold," Lurch pleaded.

I stared at the plants, their jingle anxious now. They were beautiful, nothing to say. Besides, it would be a shame if they died... "Very well, then. And not a penny more. Also, I'd like to ask you to move one bluebell to a pot. I need to make a gift."

Finally, the second heap bared its sides gleaming in the sun. I poked at it with my virtual cursor, selecting objects as targets to read their stats.

A ragged piece of metal, the side of a good serving dish, must have made up part of something seriously heavy caliber, judging by the remaining markings and the recognizable curve of its shape:

Mithril Ore. Metal content: 8%. Weight: 13.4 Lbs.

About a dozen neat rectangular plates like those used in bulletproof jackets:

Enriched Mithril Ore. Metal content: 64%. Weight: 0.7 Lbs.

Oh. It looked like the steel invaders used an octal number system: too many of their numbers were divisible by eight. The length of the gun handle, too, suggested a much wider hand—definitely not a five-digit one.

I walked over and stuffed the plates into my bag. That was a near-pure ingot of Moon silver that might come in handy anywhere—whether for crafting, selling or representation purposes.

I paused wondering which one of our technogenic metals it was equivalent to. Something light but robust that you could use to create heavy-duty alloys for making armor plate and things like that. Titanium? Could be.

I looked over the heap trying to second-guess its size, then shoved a couple more handfuls of frags into my bag. The whole lot probably wouldn't be enough to fill in the financial abyss but with any luck it might cover at least one third of it. The thing was to enter the market wisely, making sure I didn't bring the demand down by flooding it with offers. In that case, even my children might have to sell the strategic mithril reserves one piece at a time.

I turned to check on my team, still faltering in the courtyard, goofing around as they waited for my orders. That wasn't the deal. We had more work than we could manage and no initiative offered to get it done!

"Durin," I began spitting out orders, "make an inventory of everything. Then sort it by metal content and anything you find worth noting. Lock all the valuables in the vault and set all the weird objects aside. I'll check them myself later."

"I'll manage," the zombie grumbled. Rolling his sleeves, he headed for the precious hill.

"Spark! Check the area quick and find me a cave or a cellar, somewhere to keep all this explosive shit in. I'll give you a troll to move the stuff and a few guards. It should be at least..." I estimated the size of our arsenal, "no less than two-thirds of a mile from the external wall."

"I'll send someone in a minute," the pooch said, childlike. She was busy trying to shift the armor plates on her neck and scratch it with one hind leg—a very doglike gesture. Lena felt sorry for her. Coming over, she began scratching the dog nice and hard. The pooch groaned in ecstasy.

"Lena?" I said.

"I'm busy, sorry. My Dad has just sent me a message. He'll be logging in in five minutes. I need to go and get him. I want to show him the castle."

Okay, Dad was an important enough excuse. Besides, I wanted to meet him myself if he was going to become a new clan member.

Lena seemed to follow my thoughts. "You *are* going to accept him, aren't you?"

"I am. I promised, didn't I? But you're an officer yourself, so you have the right to recruit whoever you want. Bet your Dad will be pleased to see you in a serious post of authority. It's probably better you do it yourself."

"Thank you, thank you! Dad's coming, how cool!" Lena gave the indignant hound a flick on her nose and burst out laughing as she disappeared in the radiant portal.

What a kindergarten. I turned to Cryl, about to find a job for him, when a panting goblin came running from the direction of the outer wall.

"The eggs! Master, we've found the phantom eggs!"

"How d'you know it's them?" disbelieving, I asked the cleaner.

"They're phantom ones, aren't they? You can't bite through them!" the goblin's voice trailed away as he took in both his foreman's glare and his raised fist.

I pretended I hadn't seen it. "Come on, then. Let's just hope you're right."

Ten minutes later I was climbing up the rickety steps of an inner wall tower. I walked out onto an open platform to an energizing breeze. The place was littered with all sorts of junk.

I found it straight away—a typical bird's nest, only instead of twigs it was made with a whole plethora of AlterWorld minerals. Marble and stone, iron and copper ores, and a scattering of scrap mithril. An ancient silver toll bell lay next to a huge chunk of quartz veined with a fat streak of gold. This nest alone could buy you a brand new Mercedes. Was its purpose purely decorative or did it conceal some hidden message?

The eggs were hard to notice in the hotchpotch gleaming with metal. But once you saw them, you couldn't mistake them for anything. How else, do you think, would a Bone Dragon's phantom clutch of eggs look like? Translucent to the point of being invisible, they were covered with the finest web of intricate carvings. They were large, at least three feet high if you or somebody else tried to stand them upright. And when you touched them, your hand sank into nothing as the eggs themselves were only an iridescent hologram—they didn't exist in our material world.

I selected one as target.

An Egg of a Bone Dragon. A unique clutch. Chances of hatching a Phantom Dragon: 97%. Probable gender: female
Mana: 0,081,722... 731... 733... 735... /4,000,000

The last figure kept changing, growing like a gas station meter. Shouldn't it be the other way around? Why all the mana growth? I chose the other egg, identified it and froze:

An Egg of a Bone Dragon. A unique clutch. Chances of hatching a Phantom Dragon: 91%. Probable gender: male
Mana: 0.000.432/4.000.000.
Mana: 0.000.418/4.000.000.
Mana: 0.000.401/4.000.000.
Mana: 0.000.388/4.000.000.

The chick's mana counter kept dropping by the second. Cursing, I fiddled with the settings, trying to locate the First Temple Altar control menu. It looked like the male chick was funneling his own mana to his sister trying to help her survive until their mother was back.

Found it! I pushed the mana flow bar all the way to the right, highlighted the five percent available to me and pressed *Donate*. The barely visible energy cable promptly reached from the Temple, enveloping the egg. It worked!

Mana: 0.000.132/4.000.000.
Mana: 0.000.278/4.000.000.
Mana: 0.000.398/4.000.000.
Mana: 0.000.533/4.000.000.

"That's better," I whispered to the would-be chick. "How did you expect me to face your mom, then? How would I look her in the eye? You don't know about her eyes, do you? They make the hair on your spine bristle. A cross between a floodlight and an eighteen-inch naval gun. Now you can stop sending your mana to your sister. I'm going to redirect part of the flow to her in a minute, I just want to fill you up a bit first."

Not to waste time as I waited, I opened the castle staff menu and hired ten Drow archers whom I immediately dispatched to guard the nest. Safer that way, especially considering its value. I wasn't going to touch it for the time being, but once the chicks had fledged, I fully intended to take all the valuables to the treasury. No shortage of them there: from where I stood, I could see a very interesting ammo belt circling the nest twice. Fat fifty-caliber cartridges promised a healthy profit when melted down. And if I managed to find the original gun...

Oh. I jumped up and began circling the platform, my eyes searching in all directions as I tried to estimate the potential field and flanking fire positions. Over to one side, the space between two walls was begging for a pillbox. You lured your enemy into this fire-spitting cul-de-sac and then... Oh, all the things I could do!

Never mind. Back to reality. I still had to hire a few of the more intellectual workers to move the rest of the explosives. We weren't shifting bricks, after all. I really wanted to preserve at least part of the arsenal.

The developers knew which side their bread was buttered. They charged you an arm and leg for any customized deviation from the standard. Either fit in with the rest of the crowd or prepare to shell out.

I opened the manual character generation menu, chose a troll, maxed out its strength bar, paid double for extra agility, and finally glared at the costs of intellect. One point cost the same as thirty points strength? As my inner greedy pig sniffed his indignation, I raised the monster's intellect from the level of a preschooler to a high school C-student. That had to be it; after that, the numbers went through the roof. Would have been cheaper to carry everything myself.

I saved my creation and confirmed his hiring. The troll was indeed custom-made in everything including his markings: he turned out to be an albino. Immediately I sent him to see Harlequin. As I watched his large white back, I got an idea.

"Hey! I'll call you Snowie!"

I didn't give a damn about what the Hound had told me. This wasn't a 'faceless outline'. This guy was just too unique.

The troll looked back, his red eyes focusing on me, then beamed—a broad winsome smile. He waved his paw to me and, waddling for some reason, set off to look for Harlequin.

That seemed to be it. I redistributed the mana flow equally between the two chicks and, too lazy to walk, teleported to the Temple. Everything seemed to be all right there. The puppies were crawling around, the guards stood their watch, the dwarf sniffed indignantly as he hauled armfuls of mithril deep down the corridor. I had to do something about his temper. I really didn't enjoy all that mumbling and looking daggers. What could I think of that dwarves liked? What would soften him? Beer, gold, a pole-axe, a smoking pipe and a beard—this was all I knew about dwarves. Being a zombie, it was unlikely he was able to smoke or drink—on the contrary, it would upset him further. Gold was definitely inferior to mithril; a war he'd have to wait for, and as for a beard... He didn't have one, his old burns were just too bad. Could it be why he was so bitter? It was probably easier for me to walk around the city in the nude than a respected Master from the Kingdom Under the Mountain could show in public without his beard. Wonder if they had wigs for sale here? Having said that... I got an inkling of an idea.

I watched the bald dwarf leave and walked out into the courtyard. There he was, Lena's father. Time to make his acquaintance. He, too, had chosen default character settings: a human being with a small pouch—was it a conscious choice or just mindless clicking through character generation? Then again, he was supposed to be a chief hospital physician so his IQ had to be high by definition.

I stepped closer and offered my hand. "Greetings, Sir. Welcome to the clan," I paused reading his avatar, "Alexander Nikolaevich." Hadn't anyone told this guy he could change his name?

Guessing my predicament, the doctor smiled—or rather, his lips smiled as his eyes were filled with fatigue, endless and hopeless. "Call me Alec. Or Doc, whatever you prefer. I really appreciate everything you've done for us. You have no idea how much Lena means to us. I can safely tell you that by saving her, you've saved two more lives—at least. Thank you."

I didn't know where to look. "I'm not the one you need to thank, Alexander Niko... Alec. It's Cryl who deserves all the praise. He invested his very heart in it, not just his time and money. I hope you'll get the chance to meet Taali soon. She was very upset about your daughter's predicament. She really took it to heart."

Finally, Doc smiled a real smile: still a tired one but very sincere. "Yes, my wife told me about them. I look forward to meeting them all soon."

"Excellent. Now have a good look around and make yourself comfortable. Choose yourself an apartment and decide on its design. I'm afraid I can't allocate you much but I'll tell Lurch to set aside one percent of all resources to restore and redecorate your quarters."

Doc looked interested. "Lena told me that this castle is the safest place in the entire AlterWorld. Is it really so?"

"It's also the most beautiful," the girl butted in. She was sitting nearby amid the flowers trying to teach them to play Jingle Bells.

I paused, thinking. Then I nodded, "For the clan members—yes, without a doubt. No intruder can get inside. We have our own guards and the Hell Hounds, plus the Castle's AI is seriously paranoid. And we're backed up by the First Temple and the Gods' support."

Doc rubbed his hands. "Excellent! What size apartment can we take? How many rooms?"

I had to admit I was slightly taken aback by his pragmatic approach. "Take whatever you need. There's more space here than we can possibly use. But it does need some TLC."

"And if I ask you to allocate us a whole wing?" he nodded at one of the eight buildings that radiated from the Temple. This guy had some appetite.

"Actually, the place is sheer Stalingrad," I answered. "It's nothing but collapsed walls and other debris, stuffed with explosive surprises more than likely. And I really can't afford to renovate anything of that caliber..."

"I could inject some real money in it. From what I hear, the game does have this option. Do you think I could use that money to buy some redecorators?"

I nodded. "Possible. I could hire a hundred through the castle interface if you want. Stone masons, carpenters. No idea how fast they can work but work they do."

"Excellent! Then, with your permission, I'll choose one of the wings and adapt it to my needs, agreed?"

I just shrugged. He didn't want much, did he? Never mind. Time would tell. "It's not as if we're facing overpopulation here. OK, then. Make yourself comfortable."

I shook his strong hand and turned my attention to other things. What was next on my list? The chicks. I wanted to give them a good boost: not the required minimum of 2,000,000 mana but the whole 4,000,000. I just hoped such a waste would positively affect their stats. If I didn't sleep, I'd know it within fifteen hours. Oh, Jeez, I'd completely forgotten why I'd come here in the first place! I'd wanted to try and create a spell scroll!

I slapped my pockets—good, I had all the ingredients with me: the Magic Parchment and the Sparks of Divine Presence.

I looked around, choosing an open space. Over by the North wall looked about right. Having warned everyone in the chat they were about to witness some loud and visually impressive experiments, I hurried to the chosen area, mentally scrolling through the calligraphy manual as I walked.

The skill didn't let me down. Even though I'd had to temporarily redirect all the altar mana flow onto myself, I didn't think the chicks had time to even notice it. All I needed was patience and enough stamina to withstand the cooldown of the High Spell.

By the end of the second minute my legs were giving way, my neck cracking under the weight of my leaden head. Good enough!

Bang! I finally stopped casting and collapsed onto the ground. Who the hell said it was easy?—magic was damn hard work.

When I felt slightly better, I scrambled toward the parchment on my hands and knees and ID'd the still-warm charter glistening with wet ink.

Magic Scroll
Item class: Epic
Contains a High Circle spell: Astral Mana Absorption.
Effect: siphons 8,388,608 mana from the chosen target.
Cast time: 115 sec
Protect the person who reads the scroll! Any damage sustained will cause them to lose concentration, breaking the spell.

It worked! Okay, so the magic cooldown would only allow me to make one scroll every twenty-four hours, but that wasn't crucial at the moment. What *was* crucial though was that I could create a Portal to Inferno scroll right there and then!

Two minutes later I was blowing the imaginary dust off a fresh scroll before packing it into my bag. The day had been good. I'd done a lot of what I should have done. Now I had every right to finally check my own apartment and hopefully catch a few Zs. I was completely tuckered.

I walked upstairs, following Lurch's directions and listening absent-mindedly to his bragging about his exploits in the field of perfect interior design. I swung my door open and felt like someone from the Million Dollar Decorators TV show. There was no need for me to whoopee for the camera, but I wished I could do it. This Lurch was one hell of a guy.

It merged antique and modern, bent oak furniture the color of ebony and the softest ergonomic chairs complete with a stunning couch. A stuccoed ceiling hung over the marble fireplace and the mosaic parquet in the league of the Hermitage museum. Speaking of which, it was all so beautiful but it didn't give you that 'museum' feeling: just a cozy gloom

dispersed by a live fire, a soft chair by the mantelpiece calling your name...
Yes, I'm coming! I pulled off my dusty boots in the doorway, strode to the
chair and, sighing with delight, began lowering my body onto its cushions.

"Grrrr!" I heard under my backside. I recoiled and groaned.

The White Winnie scowled in the chair. Spikes glistened on his plain
collar that now bore the Mark of the Fallen One.

Damn.

Chapter Nineteen

At five a.m. the next morning the internal alarm clock screeched in my ear. I'd consciously chosen the most annoying ringtone and the most eye-hurting strobe light to go with it. Here, you couldn't cover your head with a pillow or smash the alarm against the wall... it would hurt and cost you a lot of money. Come on now, Mister Cyborg, arise and shine!

A reminder came up, *The chicks!* I shook my head, collapsing message windows, then asked Lurch for a light breakfast complete with a couple coffees. I couldn't think straight. The night before, I'd spent until midnight trying to get the wretched White Winnie out of my bedroom. He seemed to like my reaction to the constant popping of portals. Finally, I'd warned him I'd speak to the Fallen One who'd be more than happy to add a designer muzzle to match his collar. With a painful glare, Winnie growled some kind of four-letter indignation. Then he pissed off, for good this time.

I grabbed a quick bite and filled myself to the brim with coffee. Then I trotted down the dark corridors. My Elven vision didn't help me much. Most of the passages were tucked away in the windowless depths of the building, which was clever security-wise but hard to negotiate, especially at nighttime. The smoking torches did little to disperse the dark: the castle had no free resources available to create some fixed magical lights. Our top priority at the moment was to restore the castle's defense potential.

When I stumbled for the umpteenth time, I sent the economy to hell and dispatched the order to install some proper lighting. I wasn't a ghost, after all, to roam the place in the dark, hurling curses. Those ruins had stood there with their holes gaping at the world for the last eight hundred years, so another half-hour wouldn't make much difference.

I came across some Orc guards by one of the exits. I told one of them to swap his weapons for a couple of torches and follow me. That was better.

The top platform of the tower was gleaming light blue in the dark. WTF? I hurried up the steps. No nasty surprises this time, luckily: the eggs were so overflowing with mana it was leaking over, wasted, melting away.

Oh. It's been awhile since someone took me to task for forgetting to turn the electricity off. About time the Fallen One arrived and knocked some sense into us. Stealing a look around, I quickly pulled the plug on the chicks, redirecting the mana flow back to the Temple. Then I glanced at the eggs and froze.

Well-nourished and properly formed, they had completed their manifestation in our space and time. Their textured surface swirled with two hundred fifty-six shades of opalescent gray forming complex patterns: a mesmerizing sight sending any careless spectator into a deep trance.

A heavy gauntleted hand shook my shoulder bringing me back to reality.

"D'you want me to go get some more torches, Master?" the Orc torch bearer croaked. "These ones are finished. But it's morning now, anyway..."

Morning? I cast a confused look around, then stared at my clock. Morning it was, already past eight. Did that mean I'd been standing there for over two hours bug-eyed and droopy-mouthed, drooling all over the hatchlings? That was a very curious form of defense. Imagine some curious type like myself wishing to filch a taste of the eggs while the mother hen was away—he'd just freeze, hypnotized, until the dragon came back home grinning, having no need to look for a dessert, least not one that had had the audacity to come and the patience to wait.

If I could only cover our dome shield with an egg shell like that! One glimpse of it could send your surprised enemy into oblivion. A dream waffle.

Taking care not to look at it directly, I tapped the shell with my knuckle. It echoed without breaking. Knock knock, anybody home? I selected one egg as target and read its stats:

Mature Egg of a Bone Dragon. A unique clutch. Chances of hatching a Phantom Dragon: 99.9%. Probable gender: female
Mana: 4,000,000/4,000,000
100% bonus to initial stats.
Do you want to break the egg and help the chick get out?

Do I not? I slammed a virtual fist on the button, flooded with relief like anyone who'd just completed a long and tenuous task.

Yeah, right. Keep on dreaming.

Congratulations! You've learned a skill: Broody Hen.
Now you'll be able to instantaneously hatch any egg of your choice, bringing a new creature into this world.

Oh, no. I had to make sure no one found out about this new ability. I didn't look forward to being nicknamed the Broody Elf for the rest of eternity. My sarcastic friends would be constantly pestering me to hatch eggs for them! Wish I had had this ability in real life. At least then I could get a job at some poultry farm and start raking it in!

Quest completion alert: Grief of a Dragon II. Quest completed!
Reward: a new skill Dragon Whisperer.
Once every twenty-four hours, you will have the ability to divine all hidden gold within a thousand paces, boosting your treasure hunting instincts.

I shrugged. This particular ability definitely didn't look promising. Did they think AlterWorld was stuffed with unclaimed gold? Windows kept popping up, obstructing my view; I swept them away and stared at the egg. What are you like, then, a baby Phantom Dragon?

The shell cracked into perfect petals, opening up. A curious head poked out, shattering the air with a deafening screech that defied the sound barrier. The little chick didn't hold her emotions back. A powerful surge of joy and happiness flooded the place forcing your lips to smile as your heart missed a beat in anticipation of something inevitably wonderful. The baby dragon's tiny armor scales gleamed as she tried to change her colors, chameleon-like, or make herself invisible altogether. Her little fanged face glowed with all the colors of the rainbow which occasionally resonated, making the chick disappear for a few brief moments like a faulty hologram.

She looked around, casting a facetious glance my way baring a threatening upper lip. Then she whistled again, only this time emitting an alarm call filled with uneasiness and loneliness, with her desire to cuddle up to a strong bone chest, trusting it to protect her and conceal her in the swirling darkness. Mom, Mommy, where are you?

Unwillingly I recoiled, covering my ears. This little 'un had to stop it pretty soon. She had no idea of her own ability to jack-hammer other people's heads!

Still, her alarmed squeaks rose to a crescendo of hopeless desperation, finally growing into an eye-watering physical agony, pushing me further and further away. Leaning forward as if against a gust of wind, I tried to stay put without letting it force me off the platform. In the clatter of the stones falling behind my back, I heard the Orc scream as he toppled off the tower. His voice gave me the extra motivation I needed. Why wasn't my appeal for divine help working? Was it because this wasn't a conscious mental attack but a simple amplification of emotion? Jesus.

I should probably let her brother out, too. Together they might cheer up a bit.

Pressing my back against a dangerously loose rampart, I selected the second egg and set the chick free.

Weeeeoo! The second shriek, alarmed and inquiring, joined the song of bitter desperation. A brief pause, a rapid exchange of mental images—then a double surge of anxiety and fear hit my momentarily eased nerves. I collapsed to my knees, groaning with the mental pressure and sniveling with my suddenly bleeding nose.

I barely registered the sound of bare feet slapping quickly against the stone when a disheveled Lena rushed onto the wretched platform. Her slim frame was barely covered by a thigh-long T-shirt, her feet bloodied by her mad sprint across the shards of stone that covered all of the castle's floors.

At least she wasn't followed by an equally half-dressed Cryl, saving me from any indecent ideas.

She looked me over, her eyes tearful with sympathy. "Hold on, Max," she gasped, rushing toward the chicks. She struggled to reach and hug both their spiky heads, paying no heed to the blood that started oozing from at least a dozen cuts on her arms and hands, and whispered something very soothing, kissing and stroking the sobbing baby dragons.

The pressure started to subside. The pain and anxiety were still there but at least they didn't make you feel like wanting to jump to your death in a stupid attempt to escape it.

I wiped my still bleeding nose with my sleeve and dried my tears, then struggled to my feet to take a look at the chicks. They were sniveling and complaining, crystal liquid forming in the corners of their eyes. A heavy viscous droplet rolled down a scaly cheek, hardening as it fell.

Ding dong, the vitrified tear rang against the flagstones and rolled toward my feet.

Forcing my cramped muscles to move, I picked up the still-warm crystal.

A True Tear of a Phantom Dragon.
Item class: epic
Effect: +75 to a characteristic of your choice

Holy shit. I'd never heard of anything like it. I didn't even dare to venture a guess at its price. I buried myself in the Wiki pages, scanning the search results, my fingers squeezing the crystal even stronger. Fifty to a hundred grand! The price for a unique object like this floated across a large scale, limited only by the buyer's financial muscle. Not everyone was able to pay the price of a good car for a couple of virtual marbles, but the item's cataclysmic rareness and its properties outweighed any expenses in the eyes of those who understood those things. An item like that could allow you to improve any piece of top gear or create a unique customized set of jewelry tailored to one's particular needs. So for the perma players like myself the stone was priceless.

If you think about it, how many billions, in real life, would a football team owner pay for a tiny diamond which, when pinned to one of his players' shirt, would add 75 points to his strength? How much would an aging millionaire be prepared to offer for +75 to his dwindling life? Or a scientist for an equal bonus to his intellect?

Ding dong, another crystal rolled across the floor, disrupting my fantasies. The baby dragons kept sobbing and weeping, generating a steady flow of artifacts...

How's that for a money mill?

Oh-ow, an especially heart-wrenching bout of despair doubled me up. A tear mill, more likely. How much for a child's tear? And for a baby dragon's? What would I be like, trading in infants' misery?

"Max!" Lena called anxiously. "Where's their mom?"

I gulped. Spitting out more blood from my bitten tongue, I croaked, "Dunno. In a zoo... hopefully."

"You've got to find her! The babies won't last more than a day without her! I can't prevent them from panicking for long!"

New Quest alert! The &#ç$ Priestess' Request!

You have 24 hours to find the Phantom Dragons' mother and set her free.

*Reward: ?&@$*é№*

'xcuse me? Was it that Lena had just sent me on a quest? "How did you do that?"

"What're you saying? Hurry up!" she tilted her head, annoyed. She bit her lip, blood from her scratched arms streaking the chicks' scales red.

"I got a quest from you! To find the chicks' mother!"

"Then go and find her!"

"I am going! Only how are you going to-"

"Master!" Lurch's worried voice broke into my mind. "The goblins are all running off! The guards have been forced out past the outer walls, and I.. I can't stop crying for some reason... even the starlings have abandoned their nest! They're gone."

Here's another one looking for a shoulder to cry on. What was it with me that they all turned to me for help? Can't someone help me for a change, at least to get up and clean my face from all the blood and tears?

"Wait a bit, Lurch," I managed. "Everybody's screwed up at the moment. We've got some new chicks hatched here and their mom is gone. So they're crying us a river. Wait a little, I'll think of something."

Ding dong. What kind of sadist was he who'd come up with that wretched sequence, grief—tears—money? Couldn't they have thought of Crystals of Laughter or something? Disgusted with myself, I picked up the precious tears from the flagstones making myself the solemn promise that I'd do everything it took to set the Dragon Mom free and wouldn't linger for a second to acquire an extra crystal.

"Hold on, Lena. I'll be back as soon as I can."

I scrambled back to my feet, activated the portal and teleported to the Temple. Here the pressure wasn't as heavy but I still found it hard to concentrate, especially considering Lurch's quiet whimpering that had added to the Dragons' duo.

I had to do something about it. This was a real psychological weapon from some governmental agency's arsenal. Like when the secret services hide a tiny transmitter the size of a dime behind your wallpaper. And there it would sit resonating, driving their unwitting customer to such mind-wrenching depression it would only take him a couple of days to step off the balcony. Or swallow a handful of sleeping pills before laying his head back on the pillow with an angelic smile on his face, anticipating a quick end to his misery.

And here I had a couple of grief generators cuddling up right next to me. I personally could scram for a day or two, but Lurch couldn't, and I didn't really need a nutter AI around me. But above all, we had to help the chicks. They were tearing my heart out.

Wincing from the pressure of unwanted emotions, I activated the portal to the Vets. A quick ID check, mutual nods of greeting, a few hundred feet of narrow stairways and corridors, then I collapsed into a chair. It had been a hard day, considering it had only just started, so it was time I made myself some soothing herbal tea. By nighttime, I would sure need some.

Now. Task #1: locate the dragon. A few keyword searches promptly offered the information I needed. Not a minute too soon, though. The administration of the City of Light announced that this very midday, the servants of the God of Light would use the purifying power of sunrays to exterminate the vile spawn of the Dark: the Bone Dragon. Actually, as some independent reporters sneered, the decision had been taken in view of the dragon's explicit unwillingness to live, so that she was about to kick the bucket on her own accord depriving the zoo owners of a stable cash flow. That's why they decided to squeeze the last drops of gold out of the collapsing story: an exemplary execution, entrance fee ten gold. Truly medieval. In another hundred years, they might start burning witches at the stake.

I had about four hours left. Theoretically. The cooldown from yesterday's High Spell would only expire one hour before midday. And I still hadn't got hold of the Reset Potion. Twice had it showed up at the auction and each time the bids exceeded my auto buy's reserve. And in any case, I still had to break into the dome shield as they wouldn't be able to restrain the Bone Dragon with ordinary chains and bars. They did say in the news that she was very weak, the question was how weak exactly. Anyway, we'd have to solve that problem when we came to it. I just hoped she was strong enough to pull her backside off the ground and stay in the air for a few miles.

Task #2: a support group. No one was going to let me deactivate the dome and steal an important dragon in full view from the city square. I didn't want to ask the Vets for help: they would take too much time to get their act together. Besides, I wasn't really prepared to shoulder another moral debt—

that's not even talking about the money which I'd have to pay them anyway. It often happens in life that you end up paying more for a friend's service than what professional mercenaries would have charged you. So mercenaries it was, then. I had a few contacts and faces to turn to. I scrolled through my already-long contact list for Zena's name and PM'd her asking for an urgent appointment.

She replied instantly,

Our secretive Max, finally! It's taken you awhile! What caused you to remember the ladies you dumped in the Dead Lands? Okay, RV: Original City, The Pickled Penguin ice cream parlor. If it's something serious, you'd better make it quick. Ladies don't need much: we'll be as high as a kite after a couple of banana splits.

Scratching my head, I searched for the map I'd bought ages ago and found the café in question, then rushed down the stairway looking for the hiccupping Porthos or whoever it was on duty in the Portal Hall.

The next minute I was rubbing my bruised feet after landing on the square's flagstones: the portal had hauled me too high up. It had never happened before: either the wizard had hiccupped while casting the spell or, God forbid, my magic had begun to play up. Which wasn't a good thing considering this square was about to witness a highly publicized event. Moreover, I hoped that the viewers would get a lot more show for their bucks. How interesting could it be, really, watching twenty servants of Light disembody an apathetic dragon which would then crumble to the ground in a heap of bones? But an attack of the Dark Ones and the following mass slaughter, that would be a totally different scenario.

The place promised to be pretty crowded. Market stalls lined the square already busy with vendors laying out their wares. The city carpenters drove the last nails into the long rows of benches that semi-circled the improvised arena. I estimated the average backside's size, multiplied it by the number of benches by twenty rows and shook my head, disheartened. The organizers were looking at about three thousand spectators. Way too many.

Checking my internal compass, I trotted toward the mysterious café. I located the girls at once: you had to be blind not to notice the massive Troll hugging a bowlful of colored ice-cream scoops the size of a washtub.

"Hello, ladies!"

Zena's purple tongue demonstratively licked her spoon. She gave me a wink. "Hello you too, castle conqueror and dead dragon slayer! What brings you here? What on earth would make you remember our green-faced bunch?"

The Troll gave their leader an offended look. "Gray-faced, too!" she boomed grudgingly.

I waved my hands at them trying to extinguish the first spark of the conflict. "Don't listen to them, baby! They're just jealous. I thought more of you than I did of them put together."

"Did you really?" Bomba the Troll stared at me with suspicion.

Not wishing to aggravate my karma with petty lies, I gave her a reconciling smile. "I've got a really nice troll living in my castle, you know. He's strong and agile as a cat, and—he's quite an intellectual. True, he's an NPC but does it really matter? Fancy meeting him?"

Bomba peered into my eyes trying to work out whether I was poking fun at her. Her face blackened. She lowered her eyes. "Mind if I do? There aren't many of our kind around, actually, and those that are..." her voice trailed away. She made a helpless gesture.

Actually, I hadn't exactly meant it. I *had* been poking fun, to a degree. But nothing prevented me from introducing Snowie to her. Wasn't I myself drooling over Ruata the Drow Princess? If so, why couldn't Bomba meet a single responsible Troll seeking same? You never know how the years spent in the skin of a different race could affect your mentality. I could clearly see these girls had been here for quite a while. I'd have loved to hear their story one day. Their strange racial choice for perma mode made me prickle with curiosity.

An approaching waiter disrupted my musings. To his "What are you having?" Zena turned to me.

"What you mean to discuss, is it serious?"

"A contract," I nodded.

She cringed, her face resembling a pickled lemon, then instructed the waiter, "Two Isabellas for me and a bubbly."

"Eight brandies," Bomba mumbled, looking upset. "Make sure they're all different!"

The waiter marked down three more orders in the same vein, then stared at me, expectant. What kind of ice-cream parlor was that? I ventured a guess,

"A few beers, please. One light, one dark and one Elven."

Nonplussed, the waiter jotted it down and left.

Sensing the quizzical silence, I leaned forward and lowered my voice. "Now, girls. I need a group of Dark mercs for a five-minute gig at the main square. Today. In two hours."

They exchanged glances. "How many are there?"

I gave it some thought. "At least three hundred. They are going to have a big event there today. At least three thousand attendees are expected. Plus staff, guards and some rapid-response people. We need to distract all that menagerie to allow me about three minutes of absolute immunity so that no arrow or stray bolt of lightning disrupts my concentration. Which means that I will need a group or two to cast a Minor Power Dome. The rest will have to create a security ring to keep all the potential assailants at bay," I stopped as Zena shook her head. "What?"

Her tiny reassuring hand lay over mine. "Max. What you're offering is not some boss raid or a clan scuffle. We here call it 'interference in the sphere of interests of a large faction'. Your contract would bring our Guild into conflict with the City of Light and the King's administration, the Light priests and God knows who else: the guards, the King's officers, and other clans who just happen to be in the wrong place at the wrong time..."

"Doesn't the merc contract say it doesn't affect your relationship with factions?" I said.

She nodded. "Not officially, no. But in reality, there will be some bad blood left. With time, it might backfire really badly. Imagine if it was your raid we slaughtered while you were busy dishing out the loot? Nothing personal, just business as usual. Imagine for a second that they also know the name of their employer—let's call him Clan X. Imagine that? So you think you wouldn't change your opinion of those mercs? Cross your heart? Ah, you see. So what we need is the Guild Coordinator to sanction it. I can pull a few strings to make sure he sees you as soon as possible. Would you like that?"

Why was life so complicated? I had no choice, though. I nodded.

She seemed to have expected it. Her eyes glazed over, her fingers trembling as she hit the virtual keyboard wording the message to the mysterious Guild Coordinator.

The waiter arrived and began filling the table in front of each of us with a plethora of bowls containing colored scoops of ice-cream. We sat surrounded by whiffs of the aroma best described as an alcohol-delivery truck accident. Finally, he reached me. Placing a crystal thin-stalked bowl onto a lacy napkin, he commented,

"Your order: a scoop of light, another of dark and," he swallowed enviously, "a scoop of Elven ale, 5142 brew. Enjoy your food."

"Cheers," Zena raised a spoonful of burgundy Isabella.

Chapter Twenty

Moscow. Max's apartment. Current time.

Max's mom Anastasia Pavlovna was finishing her daily manipulations over her son's body. She'd already changed the almost-dry diaper, wiped his skin with a damp sponge, massaged his main muscle groups and replaced the saline bags on the automatic IV drip.

She swept away an unwanted tear and stroked her boy's cheek, dry and scratchy like parchment. He was so gaunt. Not everyone would have recognized him as the once-cheerful young man who could have lost a few pounds. Between his deadly disease and the extended coma, they had eaten his body on the inside and transformed it on the outside.

Anastasia Pavlovna glanced at the dozens of sensors that covered her son's body stretching their bundled cables to a massive console brought into her apartment by the Chronos workers.

It had all changed so quickly. After Max contacted her, she had barely made an appointment when a couple of young and aggressive sales managers stormed into her apartment, pitching to her in the best traditions of neuro linguistic programming. Good job they were followed by a very nice girl called Olga, apparently a friend of Max', who came running after them— very sweet, intelligent and strangely sad. They would have made such a nice couple. Anastasia Pavlovna would have loved to sit with some grandchildren while she still had time.

The girl had easily overrun the two. Under their pained stares, she had crossed out half of the contract's clauses fighting for the best offer plus some extras on top from their VIP reserve. Anastasia Pavlovna had herself heard one of the managers whisper in Olga's ear, "You stupid idiot, what do you think you're doing?" She had very nearly asked the bully to leave her house at once and only the sight of her son's pale face had stopped her from doing it there and then.

She hadn't waited for the money transfer from her boy. She signed the contract on the spot and paid the deposit out of her own savings including her 'funeral money'. That didn't matter so much, really. As long as her boy was all right, money would take care of itself. Besides, hadn't Max told her he was earning a good wage in that AlterWorld of his? He definitely made enough to rent that lovely cottage for her. He also had some very no-nonsense friends: one of them, Vladimir, was even now sitting by the kitchen window monitoring (as he called it) the front door. She'd told him so many times it wasn't worth the trouble, told him she was too old to be bodyguarded like that. But he wouldn't listen, would he? He was always one step behind her, turning his head this way and that, checking the surroundings. A fine young man, even though he'd never offered to help her with her shopping bag. 'I'm awful sorry, ma'am,' he'd say, 'but my hands must be free at all times.'

Recently two more had joined him. Oleg usually stayed in the car. Constantine came late at night to replace one of the other two. It would be a good idea to cook some meat balls for them, you couldn't expect them to stay fit on all those pizza orders and rice cakes wrapped in synthetic seaweed.

The heart monitor beeped, its alarm disrupting her thoughts. On its screen, the neat curves gave way to sharp peaks and scary dips. Her son's heart missed another beat, and again, followed by a long pause. The monitor's anxious whine grew as the peaks straightened into a thin horizontal line. Come on now! Start beating! Hold on, son, keep on fighting!

An emergency call light blinked, summoning a Chronos resuscitation team. The hospital's remote operator hooked himself up to the resuscitation equipment that crowded around the headboard of the capsule. The day before, she'd had to sign a hospital waiver and pay for the VIP-class home care. Without that, they would have taken him away to some hospice where he'd have faded away like any other coma sufferer.

The operator sent the charge command to the defibrillator and activated the pulse generator. The sharp click of the jet injector startled her. An empty adrenaline cartridge rolled across the floor.

"Clear!"

Her son's body arced, convulsing. The autosampler methodically injected the contents of the first-aid container into the IV drip. On the monitor screen, the hospital doctor's face frowned, concerned.

"Clear!"

Whiffs of smoke rose from the capsule's sensitive electronic components. There had to be a cutoff system there that disabled any non-core hardware, but it didn't seem to have worked. Again the jet injector clicked, sending an empty atropine cartridge spinning across the parquet floor.

"Clear!"

The monitor was still whining when the corridor filled with the stomping of many feet. The Chronos men were the first to arrive.

Hope in her eyes, Anastasia Pavlovna looked up at the hospital doctor on the monitor screen. He turned away momentarily, then forced himself to answer her stare, shaking his head. Then the monitor blinked, the picture replaced by a list of the resuscitation procedures. The arriving ambulance crew took over from him. He switched off.

Half an hour later, Anastasia Pavlovna sat at the table, barely responsive, clutching some sedatives in one hand and an official pen with a built-in ID check in the other. She wasn't even looking at what she was signing: the death certificate, the ambulance crew report, the burial certificate that stated her son's body was to be laid to rest cryogenically. She was almost happy she couldn't see or hear much: the last thing she wanted to hear now was the squelching sounds of a machine that was pumping extra liquid out of her son's body, replacing it with cryoprotective solution.

A text ringtone made her jump. She froze. This was the tone she'd assigned to messages coming from her son's number.

Not yet knowing what she was doing, the mother looked up at the comms bracelet. She touched the screen, opening the incoming message. A wide smile lit up her face.

He's alive! My boy's alive! Oh, thank you, AlterWorld, thank you!

* * *

We were finishing our alcocreams when my chest seized up quite painfully. I winced, rubbing what had to be the heart area.

"Whassup?" the ever-observant Zena asked.

"Dunno. Feels like my heart's just played up."

Her eyebrows rose. "You're not going to become the first perma who popped his clogs from a heart attack, are you?"

"I hope not," I smiled back, concentrating on my body sensations. The pain seemed to have subsided, or was it my imagination? My nerves were like live wires with all the recent events, and the shock I'd received that morning could have well added its pound of flesh. I was surprised I wasn't hearing voices yet, let alone suffering phantom pains.

Her stare unfocused briefly, then she was back with us. "He'll see you in ten minutes. Are you ready?"

"Yes, ma'am!"

"Good. Freckles, finish your mojito and give Max a lift to the Guild. And you can show him to the office. He doesn't have much time."

"Sure," the female wizard mumbled, clinking her spoon as she scooped out the last of her soft-green poison of choice from the bowl.

In theory, virtual liquor didn't have intoxicating properties. But in practice... It could simply have been brain chemistry playing up; alternatively, the drink could trigger existing subconscious reflexes, but it was a fact noticed by many: the alcohol did affect you. Some more, others less, but no one was a hundred percent immune to its effect apart for some die-hard teetotalers and rehab rats whose subcortex didn't possess the necessary neural links.

That explained the fact that the girls were just tipsy enough to move to the next stage of the dating game, some quite prepared to skip it and move directly to the inevitable horizontal stage. Yeah, right. Bomba especially could use a strong male hand. The other girls weren't exactly beauty pageant material, either. Having said that, the time spent in AlterWorld had somehow changed my perception of beauty. To my eye they seemed quite cute even if a bit homely, though had I met their team in real life, I was guaranteed a few embarrassing moments complete with a pair of soiled pants and some early gray hair.

Freckles checked her bowl again and, finally convinced it was empty, sat back in her chair. She sent me an invitation to join the group, waited for the acceptance notification and announced with the intonations of the first man in space,

"Off we go!"

I had barely jumped to my feet when a micro port pulled us out of the café and onto the teleport pad opposite the mercs' Guild building.

"After you!" she motioned me into the main gates guarded by a pair of golems.

I forced the last mouthful of Elven beer down my suddenly constricted throat. I pulled the spoon—which could now be considered stolen, I suppose—out of my mouth, studied it in astonishment and hurled it aside. "Come on, then."

The VIP conference room was dripping with over-the-top luxury. Its walls were lined with tapestries depicting the mercs' exploits: the Nagafen raid, the week-long defense of the entrance to the Valley of Gold, and the storming of the Citadel of Gloom.

I sat in a comfortable leather chair. The Coordinator's powerful figure towered across the table opposite. Apparently, the corporate dress code that demanded all minor staff to wear Goblin guises didn't apply to him. Personally, I wasn't sure that a malicious snout with its finger-long fangs sticking out between black lips was a good working image to communicate to his VIP conferees. But judging by the fact that his green mug with its recognizable tattoo on one cheek kept recurring on some of the tapestries, the Coordinator hadn't always been a staff pen pusher. He must have come up through the ranks: his tough-guy appearance must have initially been generated for the battlefield, not office chitchat.

He gave ear to my request, his direct stare unsettling. Then he paused, thinking. He seemed to have made up his mind as he sat back in his chair and spoke,

"You see, dear Laith, there are several problems with your request to begin with. But let me start with a question. How are you going to hack the dome?"

That got me thinking. I really didn't want to expose my ability in front of all that crowd. At first I'd planned on using the Shadow of the Fallen One that guaranteed me some nominal anonymity. Very nominal, because even Snowie was quite capable of putting two and two together and sussing out the ability's proud owner. And I didn't want them to make me do their dirty work for them. But wait—there *was* a solution. Costly enough to make my inner greedy pig clutch at his heart, but a solution nonetheless.

I reached into my bag, produced my handmade scroll and laid it on the table. The orc peered at it. His nostrils twitched greedily; his hand jerked mechanically as if to grab it.

"Hm. Are you sure you want to waste a unique item like that? Why not sell it to me? I'd pay you two hundred thousand in gold. You don't really need it to deactivate the dome. Just hire an extra hundred wizards and they'll do it for you, for less money too. What do you say to that?"

Yeah, right. I'd give it to him, and then the scroll would resurface at the worst possible moment, probably under my own castle walls. Not mentioning the fact that the spell cost at least a million. The merc wizards would take at least half an hour to break through the shield. As if I had that kind of time! I probably could just about handle the guards with their 15-min respawn times, but regular players could step in, too, and they respawned instantly.

No, giving matches to children wasn't a good idea. "With your permission, I prefer to act fast and be sure. So how much do I owe you for hiring three hundred top warriors for a five-minute coup?"

With a disapproving shake of his head, the orc began talking up his prices. "The minimal hire is twenty-four hours. It would take me about two hours to gather the force you need. Five hundred each, that's a hundred and fifty thousand in total."

"That's a lot," I tut-tutted. "No wholesale discount?"

He gave me an encouraging smile, like, there would be if you wait a bit. "I haven't finished yet. As the proposed op has a more political rather than military character which may potentially affect the Guild's relationship with some of AlterWorld's top factions, a risk ratio comes into play, doubling the price. That's in case I give you my permission to proceed. Which I won't because under these conditions, the money is of less interest and can't serve as a means of payment."

"Then what will?"

He gave an indifferent shrug. "Possibly, the return service of a comparable caliber or," he pointed his eyebrows at the parchment, "a unique item of similar value."

Wasn't he cornering me, the bastard? No, Sir, I don't think so! The higher his interest in the scroll, the less I wanted to satisfy it. I just didn't happen to like shady types with unclear agendas.

Under his sour stare I put the parchment back into the bag. I felt for a Tear of a Phantom Dragon and placed it onto the table. The orc's eyes glistened. Tilting his head, he read the stats and beamed. Gingerly he picked up the stone, his sensitive fingers stroking it.

"Very well, dear Laith. The Tear *is* valuable. I think I know what we can do with it," his eyes stealing toward an enormous scimitar on an expensive mahogany stand. "But... I'm afraid it's not enough."

Looking into his gleaming yellow eyes, I slowly reached for the second tear. The Coordinator leaned forward, his cheek twitching. "Still not enough!"

Oh, well. Their combined value was between a hundred and two hundred grand. True, not quite enough, but considering their scarcity... Very well, Sir, take and choke on it. My Lena was probably standing up to her waist in baby Dragons' tears now...

I lay the third tear onto the table.

"Not enough."

Wasn't he a bit too greedy for a senior manager? He could use a lesson. Fuck the whole hire thing—if it failed, I'd just have to try something else. I could always turn to the Vets: I could ask them to give me Lt. Singe's men to cast the Minor Power Dome on top of the 30-sec immunity I got from the Shield of Faith. I just might make it.

Again I reached into my bag and started pulling my hand slowly out. The orc leaned forward till he lay on the table, his clawed hands twitching. Then his stare froze, uncomprehending, first on me, then on the protruding middle finger that I'd produced from the depths of my bag.

"W-what do you sug-gest?" he stuttered.

"What do you think? All finished! No more stones! And those that you have already may just have all run out, too. Some people should keep their greed on a short leash. Now. Three Tears against a proper three hundred squad, fully equipped and buffed to the teeth. Deal?"

I was about to offer him my hand but reconsidered. This dashing armchair warrior made me question his combat past. His brutal looks, his tapestries with his own image lovingly portrayed in the foreground, his scimitar on the mantelpiece... He could just be a militarized office rat—I'd seen his type in real life. They love wearing camos and cropped hair, have a house collection of a dozen knives and burn the night oil at all the relevant forums. Never mind they never did army service. Or if they did, they were on kitchen duty.

But this character didn't quite fit the mold. Too smart, the bastard. A millionaire daddy's spoiled nerd with Harvard behind his belt, casting jealous glances at pumped-up movie hulks? Could be.

In the meantime, the orc was combatting his own inner greedy pig. After a minute's thought, he scooped up the crystals and recapped,

"Three hundred sentients. Average level, one-fifty. Plus the buffs, catalog price forty grand. Combat time: ten minutes, after which the warriors are ported back and the contract is considered closed."

"I thought you said the contract was for twenty-four hours?" I asked. I could always find ways to use all that manpower. I could send them to farm a dungeon or find other ways to keep them busy.

He shrugged. "That's as may be. Still, the conditions remain the same. You've just said it was a five-minute job. That's why you got this price. I can recalculate it for twenty-four hours, if you prefer. Fancy that?"

Scumbag. Never mind. Every dog has his day, especially when the dog has absolute memory. A thousand years later, I'd still remember this day and the way he pulled my strings. Actually, the same applied to me, too. I should really watch my tongue and go easy on making new enemies. This wasn't Kansas anymore. Time wasn't going to heal anything here.

I gritted my teeth and shook my head. "Not really."

"Excellent. I'll PM you the contract template shortly. I'm going to summon my junior coordinator to accompany you for the duration of the contract. This is a compulsory condition in case of hiring fifty personnel and over. Now you'll go to assembly hall six. No, it's not a factory floor but a large hangar-like depot. That's where raid parties are formed, briefed and buffed. You are the raid leader. Choose the teams' leaders as your officers. Try not to split existing groups unnecessarily as it may lower the efficacy of the whole force. The junior will tell you. That's it, then! Thank you for thinking about us. It's your money for our swords. Have a nice day!"

He shouted the last of his speech at my back as he ushered me out of his office and gestured at me to a solemn-looking Barbarian warrior who was waiting in the reception area.

I swung round, sending caution to the wind, about to tell him everything I had boiling inside me, when his office door was promptly closed in front of my very nose. I recoiled. "You piece of-"

"Yes, Sir!" the voice barked behind my back.

I turned around to face the Barbarian. He offered me his hand. "Alorrienar, which stands for Widow Breeder, or Widowmaker as our guys here call me. But for you, I'm Alexis."

He gave me an open smile. I enjoyed shaking his strong hand callused by sword use.

"That one," he nodded at the door, "just forget him. It's the management's protégé, some top dog's son. Lots of attitude and an enormous artifact collection. He lays his hands on everything that's not bolted down. Half our guys dream of busting his stashes. Right then, let's go to the assembly room. I've got the contract details already. Looks like it's going to be fun. It's been a while since we gave the Lighties a rocket. Actually, what would you say to a bit on the side? I'd like to invite a couple of reporters to join the group. They pay quality money for an invitation to a good scuffle. Mind you, it's always better to milk them ourselves because the information will leak, anyway, even if only seconds before we jump. Someone always talks. Happened lots of times. Keeping a large raid secret is not easy, and those hacks will pay anything for a tip.

"Which is how much?"

"Ten grand at least. Five hundred each. Easy money!"

I only shrugged. We dollar millionaires—or I could say debtors—don't care much about half a grand. Never mind.

"Go ahead," I waved in agreement. "Just make sure you keep the details secret. They don't need to know them."

Two hours later, I was standing in the thick of a crowd who wished to gawk at the still-alive dragon, generously cursing everyone and their grandmother under my breath. The wretched Patriarch of the Church of Light had promised to close the event by casting a free mass buff for everyone. Ad gloriam, so to say. Circuses and freebies—that was the explosive mixture that had driven over ten thousand sentients to the square.

My three-hundred strong group that had looked so huge in the hangar had dissolved within the sea of people leaving no trace. Zero hour was almost upon us. Warriors thickened around me, squeezing out all the irrelevant individuals, surrounding my fragile frame with their monolith ranks. Obeying unseen orders, they increased the gaps between themselves, forcing everyone else back and clearing a space in the middle. The crowd grunted and gave way, surrendering the area without a fight.

I caught the junior coordinator's quizzical glance and shook my head. I hadn't yet lost hope of reaching the Bone Dragon's mind. The beast was in a bad way. Her massive skeleton, once shiny, was now yellow and cracked; her once-gleaming eyes two dying embers. Amid the crowd's racket, I barely heard what sounded like a dry branch snapping as one of the Dragon's ribs broke. Awkwardly she slumped to one side. The creature was dying.

Was she so dead she couldn't hear me or what? *Come on, you bag of bones, speak to me! This is Laith, I've done what you asked me to, you've got two lovely chicks, damn them!*

My stare was boring a hole in her as I kept up my rambling, flexing my non-existing telepathy muscle. Finally, her enormous bulk bulged; she raised her head, her unseeing eyes scanning the crowd. The mob roared—apparently, the dragon hadn't entertained them with any signs of life for a while.

Laith?

Yes! Yes, damn you! You've got chicks, you empty skull, a boy and a girl. Phantom ones, just like you hoped they'd be!

With a stir, the dragon forced a feeble wing open and struggled to her feet leaning against it. Crack! Her fragile bones snapped in a whiff of dust as her once-powerful body collapsed back onto the cobblestones. The crowd was celebrating. The priest needed no other encouragement to keep going on about the power of Light and the approaching demise of the Dark.

The dragon raised her unwieldy head. The primal Darkness that once filled her now swirled in barely noticeable grayish spots. But happiness—true happiness—was now gushing out across all band widths. The crowd quietened down, open-mouthed, gawking at the joyous creature of the Dark. Tears welled in the corners of her eyes; then they left her empty sockets clattering across the stones, easily passing through the dome and disappearing under the crowd's feet. A struggle began in the first rows immediately growing into a fight.

The stands protested. Someone especially sensitive jumped up, shouting, "Mercy! Have mercy!"

With that initial impulse, dozens of spectators began chanting,

"Mer-cy! Free-dom!"

Their voices were barely heard in the thousand-strong crowd but still the chief prayer-monger sensed the change of sentiment. He hastily motioned to a thin line of about fifty servants encircling the dome.

"Commence!"

With a jolt, I hurried, *Hold on, we're going to get you out now. I've got mercs here with me. Just don't you dare die on us, your chicks are going mad with worry, they're flooding the location with their emotions! They need their mother! Just wait till I lift the dome, then fly to your castle!*

The dragon audibly sighed. She paused, thinking, and then whispered a decision that didn't seem to have come to her lightly, *Very well, I'll try... At least I can go with dignity, snapping my jaws at them one last time...*

She lowered her head. Groaning with pain and effort, she pulled out one of her own ribs. The crowd gasped. The dragon stuck her head into the resulting cavity and almost immediately jerked it back out. In her teeth she had a huge black diamond.

"Heart of a Dragon," Widowmaker commented in the staff chat. "At least a thousand years old, judging by the size of it. What a loot! That is in fact the main ingredient for a dome shield artifact. A Nova class, even. Half a million gold."

Crack! The Dragon munched through the stone. A wave of energy surged through her from top to toe, restoring the clouds of Darkness and knitting the broken bones. Many, but not all, by far not all. But at least now the creature looked like a rather battered dragon and not a dead bag of bones like she had a minute before.

"*Was* half a million," Widowmaker corrected himself. "So she decided to risk her afterlife..."

"Pardon?" I asked mechanically, too busy assessing the rapidly changing situation.

"It's common knowledge. If a dragon leaves its heart behind, it'll never respawn. Quite rare loot, that. Was. The stone's a goner. At least the holy

Joes won't lay their greedy hands on it. But I shouldn't die any time soon if I were this dragon. She won't respawn anymore."

The Patriarch jumped up from his folding throne. "Get on with it!" he squeaked.

Get on with it! I echoed in the battle chat.

"Once you remove the dome, keep away!" the dragon whispered. "I can't see. I'm blind..."

"Charge!" Widowmaker yelled at the top of his lungs.

"Barrraah!" hundreds of throats joined in.

Things got rolling!

Chapter Twenty-One

Zelenogorsk Highway, not far from St. Petersburg. Current time.

Snowflakes floated in the blue sky landing on Taali's face where they immediately turned into tiny droplets. Sorry to see their beauty disappear, she pulled down the edge of the balaclava, covering her face. After a moment's hesitation, she lowered her large goggles that, apart from their yellow marksman's lenses, didn't differ much from the regular sports ones. Now everybody was happy: the snowflakes as well as the girl who'd become absolutely unrecognizable.

Taali lay on a foam mat spread over the well-trampled snow: the position carefully prepped for her beforehand by her anonymous helper. The spot he'd chosen for her was perfect. A straight half-mile stretch of road lay in front of her—sufficient to shoot as many rounds as she wanted to and at any distance. Then the road made a sharp turn of at least sixty degrees, skirting the forested area where she lay in waiting.

A tiny pink radio—virtually a toy—dinged with a code signal. The target car had cleared the control point. That was the last she'd hear from her unknown assistant whom she'd never be able to identify even if she wanted to.

She rolled onto her stomach and pulled off her warm mittens. Underneath them she wore fingerless suede gloves, soft and thin. She lifted the suddenly heavy Vintorez, pressed the heel of the butt against her shoulder and rested the forestock atop a low ice parapet. The touch of the deadly steel and her favorite smell of gun oil and burnt gunpowder felt calming and soothing. She took several deep breaths to level her respiration. Pressing her cheek to the butt, she looked down the sights.

The car showed up a few seconds earlier than expected. This quiet Saturday morning its police driver hurried to reach her luxury country house. Time to bring her to book. Nine hundred feet. Too early. It took the heavy subsonic bullet a whole second to cover the distance. Its ballistics demanded a considerable adjustment for height and wind.

Six hundred feet. Get set. Taali took another deep breath and began squeezing the trigger softly and gently, millimeter by millimeter. Three hundred feet. The car was within sighting distance. Her optimal range. The one she'd performed best during training.

She aligned the crosshairs on the top button of the corrupt policewoman's uniform and softly squeezed the trigger. Clap. The recoil poked her in the shoulder. For a brief moment, the image in the sights jumped. A small white spot appeared on the car's windscreen, turning into a red blot and generously splashing over the car's insides. Lowering the sights just a tad, Taali fired three more bullets in rapid succession, almost without aiming, into the target's presumed outline. She breathed out.

The heavy car veered to the left, clinging to the central barrier and emitting long trails of sparks as it careered along it, grazing its side. Scaring the few road users with its unpredictability, it pulled over to the other side, crossed both lanes and dove into a ditch.

"One, two, three..." Taali counted the car's somersaults.

Finally, the BMW lost momentum. It stood on its nose, swayed in search of a new equilibrium, then tumbled backwards. Oh well, not a good scenario. According to their plan, the ideal situation would have been for the car to expose its gas tank. In this projection, all Taali could see was the car's reclining front and its creased roof.

Oh well, plan B, then. The last six armor-piercing rounds in the clip could go through an 8-mm steel sheet at three hundred feet. *Bang, bang, bang.* The heavy tungsten carbide bullets ripped through the engine's vulnerable aluminum casting, showering the area with red-hot shrapnel and fountains of sparks. A clap, followed by an almost-white flash and black smoke bellowing from the car as the fire slowly took hold. Passing vehicles were already pulling up by the roadside, commuters getting out, pointing their communication bracelets at the gory scene in search of five minutes of cheap YouTube fame.

Time to leg it. Dragging all her equipment along, Taali crawled backward a dozen feet. Rising to her knees, she stroked the gun farewell and took a good swing hurling it as deep into the forest as she could. They were going to find it, of course, but not straight away. As her anonymous well-wisher wrote in his message, it was humanly impossible to track the Vintorez to the hitman. The gun was already obsolete, replaced by the state-of-the-art VSS Boor, its production licensed out to at least twenty different countries. Considering all the army depots looted during the Second Georgian war, the Vintorez had long become the most popular and numerous (after the AK, of course) medium-range score-settling weapon— amid pros and amateurs alike. And Taali had every right to consider herself an amateur.

She folded the mat and attached it to her weekend backpack. Then she pulled her skis out of a pile of snow and clicked a switch in her glasses, lowering the mirror filters. Now she had to get to the train station and mix in with the hundreds of Saturday skiers to get home safely. Considering her current mundane appearance, CCTVs wouldn't be much help to the investigators. She'd lie low in the hotel room rented in her dead sister's name. Then in the evening she had to arrive at a second position, directly opposite the casino patronized on Saturdays by those boastful Caucasus-tribal types with their black cars and their young victims.

She had only run for a few hundred feet when a deafening explosion made her look back. A black cloud rose over the little forest. The gas tank had finally exploded. Excellent. Those German rides had big tanks, a good twenty gallons easy. Now they had to wait for the fire brigade and the results of an autopsy which was the only way for them to determine that the policewoman had indeed been shot. Taali hoped it would give her a good twenty-four hour leeway.

Time to go! One more stop, one more shootout, after which she was going to one of those little towns outside of Moscow to meet Max's mother and enter the FIVR capsule's warm womb. Bye, cruel reality; hello, AlterWorld.

* * *

"Attack!" the battle cry gusted across the square drowning out the thousand-strong throng.

About fifty rogues—a popular character choice with mercs—flickered, stealthing. Immediately they unstealthed, only now they stood behind their chosen enemies' backs commencing their tooth-shattering combos. The fun began!

The clap of hundreds of elixir vials popping open all at once signaled the start of the melee. In between hits, hand-to-hand fighters gulped their life potions while mages downed their mana drinks. Wizards didn't bother selecting targets as they bombarded the crowd with mass damage spells, showering the square with meteors and torrential hail. Liquid fire and venom streamed in every direction; arrows, throwing knives and crossbow bolts pelted the panicking crowd. Sheer Armageddon.

Already after the first few seconds of the battle, hundreds of tombstones began to clatter down onto the cobblestones. The crowd recoiled, hurrying to free up the area around us. Low-level players died instantly. The event had attracted lots of newbs: for anyone between levels 10 and 40 a skirmish like that was a one-way ticket to their resurrection point. Indeed, ninety percent of the attendees presented no serious threat to the mercs—with exception to their numbers as grinding through nine thousand people is no easy task. But the remaining thousand were more than enough against our three hundred. Plus the hundred guards on duty who were already elbowing their way through the human sea. In addition, we expected the King's guards to arrive any moment. Time was running out.

"The dome!" I yelled. The team of wizards on duty opened the Minor Power Dome.

I pulled the scroll out of my pocket. Selecting the dragon's transparent confinement as target, I broke the seal. In a clap of fire, a ravenous twister rushed upward to the sky, the familiar bolts of black lightning swirling like mad dervishes. We were on the right track.

Until now the Patriarch had stood frozen, his incomprehensive stare searching the crowd. Now he'd discerned the source of all evil. He pointed his gnarly finger at us. "Kill them!" he squalled.

About fifty of his staff flapped their cloaks wing-like, raising their hands and pointing them at the mercs. The skin on the palms of their hands began to burst exposing, in the midst of the bloodied wounds, large colored eyes. Blinking the blood away, they glared at us. The next moment, red, blue and green blades of plasma began slashing at our dome, Star Wars-style, sparking and leaving lingering scars behind.

"What's with the Jedi shit?" I croaked into the staff chat. The High Spell cooldown was already weighing me to the ground.

"It's the bastards of Light with their God's Glare. Deals the same damage as a bolt of lightning from a level-180 wizard. I can tell you it hurts," Widowmaker commented as he watched the battle unfold.

I cast a quizzical look at the wizard team's leader. He shook his head, groaning without unclenching his teeth, "We won't hold it. Another twenty seconds max. Distract the servants!"

I nodded to Widowmaker who was listening in, "Proceed!"

He rushed through the staff chat in a whirlwind of orders,

"Group leaders Sissy, Absinthe and Duke! Change of priorities. Priority target: the servants of Light. Allocation of targets: scheme 3."

About a dozen of our rogues darted toward the cloak-wearers, stealthing as they ran. The epicenter of the magic cataclysm shifted, covering the area all around the Dragon's dome including the servants of Light and the first rows of the more unlucky spectators. A dozen archers continued to draw their bowstrings, sending heavy arrows deep into the flurry of flames.

As if it could stop the Patriarch. Raising his flimsy fists to the skies, he shook them, begging ecstatically, "Oh our Lord of Light, hear my plea! Give us strength!"

His God did hear him. The skies shattered, sending scared clouds flying in all directions. The God's irate face showed amid the blinding light.

Divine Blessing alert!
The Sun God has turned his benevolent gaze to the terrestrial quarrels, granting new strength to his followers.
Effect: +20% to ALL characteristics for all worshippers of Light.

Thousands of shafts of light reached down from the sky, highlighting the selected figures and granting them the aforementioned blessing. The funny thing was, at least one-third of my mercs turned out to be worshippers of Light, so we got a share of his attentions, too. Nil nil.

The irate little man kept raging. His sharp eyes singled me out in the crowd. "You!" he shook with anger. "You filthy spawn of the Dark! Here's a stamp to mark your blackened brow!"

The Curse of the Sun God's Patriarch!
Daylight causes mana regeneration to drop 90%!
Duration: as long as the High God or the Patriarch are still alive.

You scumbag! Now that hurt. Really. Or rather, it would have—had I not switched the Altar mana flow onto myself just in time. That gave me any amount of virtually non-stop mana bath.

The patriarch just couldn't leave it alone, could he? His glare burning a hole in me, he began whispering something dangerously long and definitely just as unhealthy. Time to wrap up the show. I turned to Widowmaker and nodded at the priest.

"Try to neutralize him. Ideally, kill him."

More order-rattling. The epicenter of the magic tempest shifted once more, covering the Patriarch and his bodyguards. He managed to take cover under his own magic shield. Then his eyes widened in surprise: apparently, the pressure on the shield was much higher than expected. Shouting encouragements to his men, he activated a portal and disappeared in a flash.

We'd managed to neutralize one of the threats, at least temporarily. Still, the change in the focus of the attack had cost us dearly, giving time for the stunned crowd—who hadn't expected to be attacked from inside—to shrink back, recover their breath and grasp the significance of what was going on. Now that they'd determined our meager numbers, the enemy became furious. It couldn't have been much fun to realize that you'd just been hysterically scratching the cobblestones with your nails trying to crawl away from opposition thirty times your inferior.

The situation had turned on its head. The human flood surged in the opposite direction trying to get to our vulnerable bodies and trample them into the dirt. In doing so, the enemy had produced a couple of clear thinkers who introduced some semblance of discipline and control. The small fry stepped back, showering us with arrows, magic and crossbow bolts. It might be weak, but imagine a thousand-strong crowd of immortal first-graders, their self-preservation instincts disconnected, armed with sharpened steel bars. Would you rather bank on them? I would. This was the case of quantity turning into quality.

Our second problem were the hundreds of pets, ghosts, familiars and the like who'd attacked us from all quarters. There were quite a few pet controllers in the crowd, so now they unleashed their beasties while keeping a safe distance, thus dramatically increasing the numbers of our opponents.

But the main danger came from the high-level players who had finally found their bearings and were now rolling in on us, pushing the bravest of us aside, threatening to drown the mercs by their sheer numbers. The sound of opening portals announcing the arrival of the King's guard was just the cherry on the cast-iron cream cake which was heading toward us with a speed of a cannonball.

Bang! The human flood hit the wall of steel shields and rolled back, leaving dozens of bodies hanging from the spikes. *Bang!* Rows of our more impatient enemies lunged at us again, reinforced by the pressure from those behind them. Again the human sea ebbed, losing more of the squashed, charred and pierced human shapes that turned into granite tombstones even as they were dropping to the ground. *Bang!* The third wave pressed into the line of shields so now we were backing up, our ranks serried, the patch of free space in the center collapsing.

Our loss counter quivered and started spinning, faster and faster. But the enemy's casualties had passed the thousand mark, a lot of them slain by their own hands. While we as a raid were immune to friendly fire, the disjointed crowd kept loosing off arrows into the backs of their own warriors, covering them with blanket spells or just selecting wrong targets. How were you supposed to tell friend from foe in a couple of growling paladins jostling each other with shields and spears? Should you smother both in a cloud of Choky Death? This way even if you killed one of your own, you were sure to take out a few enemies, too. And if you managed to smoke someone on the sly, then crawl toward their body amid the fighters' shuffling feet and pick up a precious item from the hapless victim's body—then it was Christmas! This was the only explanation I can offer as for the amount of dead bodies piling up on our front line. We honestly couldn't take credit for at least half of them.

Still, thirty to one was thirty to one. It wasn't as if we were sending a tank against a savage natives' army—we were on a battlefield opposing a matching force. The outcome was easy to predict. We weren't the three hundred Spartans and this wasn't Hollywood.

There were barely half of us left when the dome imprisoning the Dragon split open.

"Change of targets!" Widowmaker shouted without waiting for a command.

Right he was, too. The bonebag wasn't part of our group. We could easily smoke him or at least do him some serious damage with our friendly fire.

Now I could finally see why you needed a raid to capture a dragon. Spreading her wings and breathing venom, this spawn of the Dark began her deadly dance, striking her enemies down with direct emotional hits. Green peaks of poisonous gas spread around us turning the air into a viscous tide of swelling emerald. Not counting on her own accuracy, the blind dragon showered the area with acid rain and fragments of bone, guided by her hearing and glimpses of emotional echo alone. Still, somehow she managed to single out our group in the crowd, restraining her murderous surges whenever one of our mercs happened to cross her path. Thank God for that!

"Go away! Fly to the castle!" I yelled, realizing there were barely a hundred warriors left.

But the dragon was on a killing spree—alternatively, she could be dancing a sacral dance of death for all I knew and couldn't stop it halfway—I'm not big enough on Dragonology to know. The bone lizard kept swirling around like the harvester from hell, grinding thousands of sentients in her wake. I even got the impression that the battle had done her some good. Her eyes blinked once, then again, and lit up—the two pale-green search beams as I remembered them.

"I can see," a thunderous whisper swept over the battlefield.

"Go, now!" I yelled. "Your chicks are hungry! Go home! Shoo! Shoo!"

"Just a moment... A few more life sparks—then the primal seed will rebirth in my chest, the seed of a new heart!"

Pop, pop, pop, portals opened one by one, disgorging the white-clad sea of servants of Light. The unhappy Patriarch had sent in reinforcements although where he'd managed to find so many was a different question entirely. There must have been at least two hundred priests; most likely, the temples all over the cluster—if not of all AlterWorld—stood empty now. Had I known that, I would have asked Cryl to check out their treasury. Then again, they wouldn't leave their assets unattended even on Judgment Day.

The cables of sticky light sprang swirling upward from the servants' hands, entangling the dragon. She tore through them with ease, simultaneously counterattacking, eliminating the priests nearest to her. Still, her speed kept dropping until finally another power line entwined the dragon's bone body and, ringing like an overstrung string, resisted her attempts to break it. Another one lay next to it, and yet another... In less than a minute, the dragon was struggling in a powerful net, breaking her bones, entangling herself even further.

Shit! I bit my lip surveying what was left of my army. Fifty at the most. That was it, end of war. Some general I was.

Ding, the skies rang. The jingle of a billion little bells drowned out the battle.

Macaria! Today more beautiful than ever, in full makeup this time, shining like a Super Nova with divine energies.

"O the Sentient! I am giving you your reward and a purpose on the day of this glorious and equally pointless battle! Accept it as a sign of the gods' gratitude for your faithful service and this exceptional show!"

Ding! The goddess disappeared, leaving behind a few snowflakes floating in the sky. The players' interfaces flashed with a quest message:

New Quest alert: The Glorious Battle.
Divine Macaria will bestow her gifts on anyone for any victory in this battle! Take a look around and bury your blade into any enemy survivor.
Reward 1: 100 Faith points for every Light follower killed.
Reward 2: 200 Faith points for every guard or officer killed
Reward 3: 300 Faith points for every Light priest killed

Silence fell, replaced by cautious sideways glances. Then, simultaneously, the clashing of thousands of swords meeting swords. There were no idiots there. The new quest was exactly what the crowd needed. There were hundreds of mortally wounded lying around begging for the coup de grace, their bodies a promise of rich reward. Allies only a moment ago, now they turned to face each other, slaughtering everyone who still moved. For ten bucks a frag plus loot why wouldn't they?

"Hold the ranks!" Widowmaker shouted, still alive, bringing the remaining mercs into some sort of formation.

"Thank you, Macaria," I whispered soundlessly, activating Appeal to Gods.

The last thing I wanted to hear back was something along the lines of, *You owe me one.* But today was a day of surprises. With the gleam of her kind smile in the air, I heard a soft, *I hereby pay part of my debt.*

I shook my head in surprise but immediately switched my attention back to the battlefield. No one seemed to pay much heed to the mercs' thinning numbers anymore. Everyone was busy choosing easy targets: the already wounded and the low-level players, trying to earn themselves as many points as possible before they themselves fell prey to a stronger opponent. In any case, it looked like we'd lost the dragon. The priests had split into two groups, one of which made an outer defense circle, fighting off the attacking crowd while the other group kept tightening the net, breaking the unfortunate creature's bones, pressing her into a gigantic sphere.

"Dragon," I groaned, unable to stop myself.

"I'm sorry," I barely heard her. "Take care of the chicks..."

"Fuck you!" I exploded. "What's wrong with all you, people, everyone bossing me around? First it's those newborn gods, then it's that underage newblette telling me to go and get you, and now you? You're not just trying to die on me, you're giving me more tasks again?"

I was ranting and raving, all the while leafing through my by now quite considerable skill list trying to find something at least remotely relevant. Wait-wait-wait, what was that? The Help of the Fallen One? Completely restore health of any creature in AlterWorld?

I hastily selected the bonebag as target and gasped. 2% Life!

Activate!

Bang! The tangled mess of the white threads exploded, freeing the furious dragon. With a crushing sound, white-robed body fragments went flying. Attacked from both sides, the priests' ranks staggered and broke into helpless individuals. Slaughter had set in.

I glanced at the clock. Fourteen minutes since the start of the action. But the mercs were still fighting. I touched Widowmaker's shoulder. "Why are you still here? The time's up. The contract's closed."

He flashed me a grin. "It's personal now. Well, the dragon is free. You still need us?"

I shrugged. "I don't think so. Thank you for everything!"

"Well, then," he turned to the remains of his army and bellowed in a practiced commanding tone, "Formation type four, arrowhead, direct at the priests! Three, two, one! Barrraah!"

Ten minutes later, I stood amid a sea of tombstones roamed by occasional bediapered human shapes looking for their graves. Even more occasional armored ones studied each other suspiciously, not sure what to expect from the opponent. They'd soon discovered, by trial and error, that the repeat murder of a player brought no faith points, so those flashing their naked butts were mercifully left alone which made me wonder how many of those were genuinely smoked and not just being clever by removing their clothes and stashing them away in their bags. Either Macaria had shown some mercy or even the gods couldn't afford to allocate millions of extra faith points to the prize fund. Had it not been for that particular restriction, the place would have been Armageddon in the flesh. As it was now, it rather resembled a village cemetery on a Saturday morning.

I couldn't see anything past the forest of tombstones. So I summoned Hummungus and gave him a hearty smacker on the nose. I'd missed my Teddy. Pushing pens in the office had done me no good.

I climbed into his tall saddle and had a look around. Far on the other side of the square the Dragon was still chasing single players. A few tight groups were mopping up their areas of responsibility trying not to cross paths with each other.

A few hundred feet away I noticed the shape of a virtual policeman who was studying the battlefield with disapproval whispering something into his communications line. A nasty chill ran through my veins.

The cop sensed my stare and turned round. He flashed a smile full of promise. Then he shook his finger at me, pointed at his own eyes and made a clenched fist—meaning, he was keeping an eye on me, prepared to crush me the moment I stuck my neck out.

'xcuse me? What did *he* have to do with it? Okay, so a few players engaged in hand-to-hand, slaughtering each other and boosting their PK counter which was an acceptable way to have some fun in the game. The virtual police only dealt with either explicit crimes or money but even so, they showed no interest in sums under a million. Or could it be something personal? AlterWorld seemed to have been exceptionally generous in creating enemies for me. I really, urgently, had to grow: in power as well as in influence and connections. I had to gain some weight and security if I wanted to finally be able to ignore petty ill-wishers.

The cop gave me a mock salute and disappeared in a portal flash. Excellent. You have nothing to look for here.

I shrugged and went on surveying the battlefield. One of the organized vulturine groups seemed to be heading toward me. Sorry, guys, that's the last thing I need. I was about to activate the portal—the bonebag didn't need me to show her the way to her own castle—when I recognized, in the crowd of warriors, the familiar outline of LAV. Whom you could call Hummungus' brother, I suppose.

I nudged my bear, directing him toward Eric. So! This looked like the bulk of the Vets' entire combat section. I knew virtually all of them, so no problems there.

How's that for a meeting on the Elbe! The two bears brushed their sides as Eric and I hugged each other.

"What brings you here?" I asked.

He was about to speak when I heard an unstealthed Dan's voice, "Just checking to see who it was painting the town red this time. The General even refused to bet it was you. Listen, dude, you're getting a bit too predictable!"

Fed up with talking with his head tilted up, Dan pulled an artifact whip out of his bag and cracked it in the air. I liked his mount—a proper knight's charger, gigantic and powerful. Not as impressive as Hummungus, of course, but still.

Once he mounted it, I offered him my hand with a smile. "And seriously speaking?"

"Seriously speaking, we were in town so we thought we'd check out the event they were having here. Eric out of curiosity and me, to level my new pickpocket skill. Might come in handy in my line of work. And there you were, as large as life and twice as ugly. Once the tea party started, we announced a yellow alert over the castle and pulled in a few guys so you shouldn't think you've been battling them all on your own like a Biblical lion. And once that celestial beauty had kindly offered us more of her bottom views, no amount of God's—let alone Goddess'—wrath could keep them back."

"Thank you very much, guys. So what's the score?"

Eric shook a proud fist in the air. "Seven, I got seven of the bastards!"

Dan gave him a pitying look. "I have sixteen. Overall for the Guild, three hundred eleven frags, plus some gear and Faith points. All in all, not a bad day."

With a start, the Vets shrunk back, drawing their weapons and raising their shields.

"WTF?" I turned round to take a look. It was indeed impressive—the dragon, glistening in the sun, was heading in our direction. I waved to the Vets—no worry—and rode out to meet her.

"Priest, I'm ready! Thanks for your help. I owe you. But now I'd love to see my children."

No, I definitely wasn't a dragonologist. Was she a boy or a girl? After the dressing-down the Hell Hound had given me, I didn't dare ask. Or maybe, her skeleton didn't have gender by definition, but once it accumulated a bit of energy, it could start laying again?

In any case, she didn't need to yell. I shook my head restoring my hearing. "Don't mention it. And turn the sound down, will you? My brains are about to explode. In any case, how do you expect us to travel? You're a bit too bulky to teleport."

"We can fly!" the dragon bared her teeth and lowered one wing to the ground as an improvised boarding ramp. "Put your critter back into his artifact and climb up. The sky's the limit! There you can find the ultimate freedom!"

Oh, well. Teleporting would be faster, of course, but who was I to resist the invitation of a dragon ride? That wasn't some Boeing-manufactured aluminum tube shared with a hundred sweaty bodies. This was an honest-to-God, wind-in-my-hair, earth-the-size-of-a-handkerchief *flight*. Yes!

With a pat on Teddy's neck, I folded him back into his artifact and ran up the bony steps. So! The game developers had thought of everything. A reclining bone chair with anatomic armrests was just as comfortable as your office one. I had barely sat down when the dragon took a quick run and kicked herself up into the air, spreading her wings. A flying mount, the first one in AlterWorld, had taken her rider to the sky!

My inbox pinged. *Need to talk*, Dan PM'd me, followed by a new message, from Eric this time,

You're too much, dude! Can I borrow your dragon for a ride?

Chapter Twenty-Two

As we approached the castle, I didn't sense any of the chicks' emotional pressure. Below lay the Valley of Fear, rather sad and boring, striped by ancient roads and pockmarked with ruins. All that I diligently marked on my map. You can say what you want but air recce is a great thing. From the ground, you don't notice one tenth of what I copied from half a mile's height.

The dragon emitted occasional broadband impulses, scanning the horizon and listening in to the echo. It was probably why the chicks had quieted down, their sensitive hearing detecting their mother's sonar.

Finally, the Castle. Now the outer walls looked much more presentable than the sad picture of bombed-out desolation that had been revealed to me a week ago from the top of the hill. The sleepless Lurch had done a great job. His hands were oozing magic. The inner courtyard had been transformed, too, and now looked like a botanical garden set amid a field of flowers. And the Castle! I nearly fell off the dragon when the clouds parted and the sunrays illuminated the once gloomy stones. The donjon's gray towers erupted in billions of colored sparks that glistened rainbow-like as if some upscale interior designer had studded them with countless handfuls of precious stones.

Precious stones? Lurch!

"Lurch!" I yelled into the communications artifact. "Why are you sparkling like a diamond factory on steroids?"

"Greetings, Master! It *is* beautiful, isn't it?" he asked rather timidly.

"You can say that! Now answer my question."

It haltered while I was hurriedly leafing through his access levels. Where had he gotten the resources for all this magnificence?

"Master, when the chicks were crying, everything here cried and wept with them. These are Tears of Stone. They seeped through thousands of its pores until they hardened and turned into perfect crystals. I must be the most beautiful castle in the entire AlterWorld now. I wonder, Master, if you wouldn't mind me taking part in this year's exterior design contest? I'm more than sure we'll get first prize."

"Wait! You and your contests! The crystals, do they have stats?"

"Random ones, from +1 to +20 depending on their caliber. But please don't start ripping anything off, I beg you!"

"Or what?" I teased him, repaying him for the moment of anxiety. "You gonna cry too?"

"Dunno..." Lurch whispered.

His voice was filled with so much sadness I felt like a real piece of work. "Not to worry. It is very pretty. You are undoubtedly the nicest castle in the whole of AlterWorld. Just in case, could you please calculate your square surface and the average quantity of gems per square foot? I'd love to know how many gems you've got stuck to you. And if you think you can grade them by size, that would be-"

I shut up midword and grabbed at the bone armrests as the dragon banked in a steep turn and began to land. She zoomed down onto the tower and flapped her wings, damping the speed with their power field. Softly she landed onto the ancient stones.

A powerful surge of emotions threw me out of the saddle. I switched off. No idea how long I was out. When I finally came to, I was sitting on the flagstones with my back against the rough rampart. Lena was fussing around me, shouting, about to raise her hand for an encouraging slap on my cheek. I caught her hand in mid-air and shook my head, returning my thoughts to their usual places. I must have missed something, anyway. The dragon sat on her nest brooding like a chicken, the two fat-bellied chicks squawking happily under her wings.

"How's it going?" I asked, my throat dry and coarse.

"Fine! It's you I was worried about. You just collapsed flat out."

I tried to swallow. "It's all these phantom emotion generators assaulting my brain. I'd love to know why those idiots don't classify emotion amplification as mental attack."

"Excuse me?"

"Never mind. I was talking about an ability I have, a very useful one, too, shame it only works when it wants to."

I pointed at the baby dragons. "Did they cry a lot when I was gone? And by the way, where are all the Dragon's Tears? I thought the tower would be knee-high in them by now?"

"Almost none left!" she beamed. "A couple still left in the corners, maybe. I found how to calm down the chicks so they didn't cry any more!"

"Eh? Oh, shit. You really shouldn't have. So they'd have sniffled for another half-hour, big deal. That was millions in gold which," I glanced at the cutest chicks, "which we'll never have now."

Lena shrugged, disinterested. "At least they didn't cry. They forget everything when they eat! So I remembered you normally gave baby chicks the egg shells for calcium or whatever, so I gave them some. They gobbled it down like there was no tomorrow!"

"Eh? The egg shells? The gray ones with a funny pattern?"

"Yes! They ate every single bit of them and licked my hands afterwards. How's that for a waste-free production?"

I groaned. "Lena, sweetheart. I had plans for them myself. Really, really big ones."

She shrugged again. "You should've told me. I'm not a mind reader. You should be grateful I've kept your gold and silver. They very nearly ate that, too. It was a good job there was a lot of scrap metal in the nest, so I distracted them with that."

"Which scrap metal?" I grabbed at my head with a groan. I already knew what she meant.

"Sort of purple. Some bent helmets, pieces of tank tracks and a handful of cartridges—they kind of explode in their mouths with those little flames going everywhere, it's so cute. I called the chicks Draky and Craky. You'd never think those tiny things could go through two tons of metal. Only then I noticed that they'd grown double in less than five hours."

I fumbled around me for something to satisfy a sudden urge. The gods in their eternal kindness had sent me exactly what I needed: a long rod (no idea what stray wind had brought it up here). Grabbing it, I scrambled to my feet and offered Lena a knightly hand to help her get up, then gave her a hearty lash across her perfect backside.

"Ouch! What's that for?"

"For those stupid quests of yours!"

"Ouch!"

"And this is for your lack of subordination and attempts to take control!"

"Ouch! Uncle Max, that's enough!"

"For those goddamn eggshells!"

"Ouch! I'll be angry with you!"

"And that's for the two remaining Tears and for the millions lost!"

Shhh, one of the chicks opened a purple eye watching us. A powerful surge of emotion—that felt more like a baseball bat—knocked me over.

"You see, Uncle Max? Now you hurt yourself. You could have fallen off the tower, you know."

"Come here, you! I still owe you for that silver. And another one for the scrap metal. And I'm not your uncle!"

"No way!" she stuck out her tongue. "Don't be so mad, Max," she added with a nice smile. "We all know how kind you are. Thank you so much for finding their mom, we were worried about her."

Quest completion alert: Request of a &#ç$ Priestess. Quest completed! Reward: a new skill %*#@$#@$$@ ##@$$# @@$$%

"Er, Lena, how do you do it? What kind of skill is that? I can't read a thing."

She shrugged. "No idea. It just happens. I'm off, anyway. Dad needs me."

"Wait!" I managed but she activated her bracelet and was gone with an artful glint in her eye.

"Spare the rod, spoil the child," I whispered. "Discipline is gold."

Enough for today. Time to crawl back into my castle. Bedtime. The rest had to wait till tomorrow. Okay, collecting the Tears probably wouldn't. So collect them I did.

I teleported to the Temple and rushed up the stairs to the inner rooms. Soon I was back in my apartment. Peeling my armor off and stuffing it into my bag, I staggered to the bed and collapsed on top of the comforter.

Weeeeeoooo! the wretched White Winnie squeaked from under my backside.

I jumped straight back to my feet directly out of the prone position. The wretched creature lay in a tangle of sheets, blinking his sleepy eyes at me. Oh-kay. He couldn't have found a better time.

I lunged forward and, not believing my own luck, managed to grab the scruff of his neck. I flung him in the air and gave him an almighty kick that sent him flying like a sleepy football through the window. There! I didn't miss. I'd never managed to do this trick in real life. The receding stream of interjections was broken not by a slap against the flagstones as I'd hoped but by the popping of a portal. Apparently, he'd woken up in midair. Shame.

Was he really hoping to become an unwanted lodger in my bedroom and sleep in my bed? I didn't think so. My picture-perfect idea of family life didn't include any peeping fluffballs. It was time I brought him down a peg.

The clinking of coins dropping into my account awoke me the following morning. I'd forgotten to mute the internal interface. Actually, I found the sounds of gold rather pleasing. I might install them as the alarm clock tone. And in any case, who was it sending me money at 6 a.m.?

Apparently, it was Doc: *Here's a hundred grand gold for the Wing Two repairs, plans and drawings attached.*

Who did he think I was, his foreman? I forwarded the message to Lurch: *Rebuild and refurbish according to the cost sheet. Hire whoever you deem necessary, you know, carpenters, masons, decorators and electricians... What do you mean, what are electricians? Ah, never mind. Were those children ever going to shut up?*

Wait. I sat up in bed, listening. Children? That's right. Their thin voices and occasional laughter were coming through the narrow window—so narrow it had been a miracle how I'd managed to hurl Winnie through it last night. The walls' stucco moldings in combination with abundant foliage prevented me from seeing what was going on at the foot of the donjon. I donned some clothes and rushed down the steps.

I walked out into the yard and froze.

About a dozen quiet children between two and five years old were walking, crawling, running and rolling around amid the lush greenery of the inner court. Some were chasing butterflies while others sat quietly studying a flower or just listening to the gentle song of the colored bluebells. One especially brave boy was cuddling a puppy that he'd somehow—no idea how exactly—taken from its Hound mother. Surprisingly, the Hell mother was nowhere to be seen.

Lena's father sat on the porch, chin in hand, smiling vaguely as he watched the children. I sat next to him. We shook hands. We didn't say anything. Finally, I asked,

"What's that, Doc?"

He shrugged. "Not *what*—it's *whom*. It's children."

"I had a funny feeling they were not gnolls. Why? Where from?"

He glanced at me. "Did they tell you what kind of doctor I was?"

"No. Does it change anything?"

"I'm the chief physician at a children's hospice."

If he was waiting for my reaction, he didn't get it. "Sorry, I don't know what that means."

"That's good. I just wish fewer people had ever heard about them. A hospice is a place where people come to die. Not all diseases can be cured. Some have a definite prognosis that comes with a rather limited life expectancy."

I shuddered. It was so alike my own story.

"We accommodate terminal patients from all over the country. All we can offer these children is love, care and attention. Then they die, usually quickly. Our mortality rate is over 98% and average life expectancy, two months. These kids are some of the worst cases. In real life, most of them are hooked up to IV drips after all the radio. The're given pain killers and antidepressants by the handful. Legally, what I'm doing now is a crime. But I'm sick of burying children. First thing when I arrive at work every day, I ask the doctor on duty, "Who is it?" And almost every day he gives me a child's name. You probably heard it before that every doctor has his own personal cemetery of the patients he's lost. Mine has twelve thousand one hundred forty-three graves. You might not believe it, but I still remember every single name. I'd love to forget them but I can't. That's the funny way that the mind is wired. Even brandy doesn't help me switch off. Soon I might start pilfering their morphine."

I looked at them with different eyes now. Quiet and clumsy, so amazedly happy. Doc was completely different, too. What a giant of a man. How was he even pulling this load?

"My wife and I, we sold our apartment and bought ten FIVR capsules with the money. I installed them in the hospice cellar. Our admin is human, too. He helped me hack them. This is all I can give these kids—one last chance."

"But how are they going to live here? They're only two or three years old! At least you could have chosen older bodies for them."

He squinted at me. "Would you be prepared to take their childhood away from them? I'm not even talking about the potential mental problems of a three-year-old in an adult's body. I'm only talking about their chance to have the happy childhood they've been deprived of. All they know is a chain of hospitals and operation theaters. I did my research. I know there're children here. Not many, a few, but they do exist and, more importantly, they do grow. Provided they want to, of course. So will my kids. Once they're fed up with being so small in a big world where they can't even reach the door handle, they'll start inching up. Where there's a will there's a way."

I wrinkled my forehead trying to grasp the enormity of what he'd just told me and all the potential scenarios it implied. I needed to decide what to do with the whole nursery. "But what about their names and stats? How did they manage to create their characters? And how are they going to choose their skills if none of them can even read yet?"

""Well, Sasha over there can. And Jana knows the alphabet and can count to ten."

My face must have turned crimson because he gave me a reconciling smile. "Calm down. Our admin has tweaked the settings allowing us to control the capsules remotely. I sat at the server computer helping them to generate their characters. I trusted my hunches to choose their classes. I chose the human race to limit any psychological discomfort. I deposited their characteristic points into endowment accounts until they reached level 100. By then, they will all learn to read."

I shook my head in confusion. "What endowment accounts? There was no such option available when I created my character."

He shrugged: *lots of things that weren't available then are available now.*

I rummaged through Wiki looking for the answer to this rather vital question. I quickly located the section I needed and started reading. And once I'd read enough, I couldn't help swearing.

For some reason, the AlterWorld admins had limited the number of upgrades to a bare minimum and switched their focus to non-gaming initiatives: things like offline activities, gaming merchandise or more initial character-generating options. The bank service mentioned by Doc fell into the latter category and was now aggressively marketed as a hardcore pro option for those who've outgrown standard gaming challenges and were quite prepared to put their balls on the table today for a vague promise of potential future bonuses.

Now they could save some of their characteristic points and store them in a bank until reaching the level of their choice. The level number was the actual percentage bonus. For instance, if you banked 10 points for the duration of 20 levels, you earned yourself +20%, pocketing 24 points. Not much but still. Naturally, it made starting off that much more difficult so a money injection was a must. But he'd blocked all their points till level 100!

"Doc, tell me you only banked the starting 25 points."

He shook his head. A bad premonition clutched at my heart.

"All of them, level 1 to 100. Call it a junior savings account, if you want. I ran a simulation, and the dividends were mind-blowing. And most importantly, it'll prevent the kids from making stupid mistakes like investing everything they have in useless agility."

I groaned. A hundred levels without any growth! Potentially, it gave them a monumental advantage: about 350 free points to play with. But how were you even supposed to ever get to them? You could easily get stuck for life somewhere at level 30. It was too obvious the Admins had come up with a nifty way to milk millionaire players forcing them to inject real money simply to keep their handicapped chars in game.

One of the kids waddled toward us. He had the most piercing blue eyes. "Doctor, can I have a puppy too? Sasha won't share his with me."

Doc nodded, pointing at the Temple doors. "Go through that big gate over there past the big toothy men with spears. Inside there'll be a big bald doggie. Ask her to give you a puppy."

The boy waddled off. I knitted my brows in disbelief. "She won't!"

"Oh, yes. The Hounds are all emos. They don't sense any threat in the children. I believe they view them as puppies."

Still, I had my doubts. "I'd rather we went there and kept an eye on them. I don't want the Hell Hound to scare the boy into becoming the first virtual stutterer."

He shrugged. "Go ahead, then. I have to admit I'm afraid of them myself. When they see me—the Hounds I mean—they start shaking. They line up and bare their teeth at me. They can probably sense all those thousands of graves behind my back."

His gaze glazed over. Stooping, he stared into space. I had to shake him back to life before it was too late.

"Doc, wake up! What's wrong with you, man? You've finally got the chance to save a good dozen kids! This isn't a hospice any more! This is somewhere totally different!"

He seemed to have bucked up a bit. His eyes brightened up. Reaching out, he caught a tiny girl running past, her clothes generic, her eyes beaming with joy. He tousled her hair and let her go. Laughing happily, the little mite ran off to chase a butterfly. The children seemed to be perking up. Their voices grew louder, their laughter more frequent.

"Okay, Doc. Yours is a holy cause. I'll do what I can to help you."

He shrugged. "You will, no question about that. Accept them into your clan, enter them onto your books and let's start raising them. If this year we manage to digitize two or three hundred, then my life is complete. No matter how long I live, I'll never do something as good as this.

I shrank back. "Doc, what are you saying? What clan? These are Dead Lands! This is the Valley of Fear, not some Little Lambs Nursery! These children need saving, I agree. But we need to do it collectively, all of us—not drag this millstone all by ourselves! We could buy a house in the city or introduce some kind of non-mandatory tax for the clans."

Doc forced a smile. "Didn't you say that this was the safest place for your clan members? Go ahead, then, grow the new generation of AlterWorld denizens. My wife will soon move here permanently to join our daughter and her friend. I'm laying the groundwork now with some of the parents. I'm sure that after the initial shock of losing their child, then realizing that it's alive and well even if unreachable, many of them will be able to understand and help us. Some financially, others might go digital themselves.

"Doc!" I groaned. "In another three months this place may be sheer hell. It's war we're looking at!"

He stared at me, uncomprehending. "Who would dare attack a children's home? On the contrary: they're the best guarantee of the castle's safety."

I shook my head. "What planet are you from? When did it stop big kids from trampling the little ones' sand castles when they ran around playing at war? Also, I'm not some scumbag to hide behind toddlers' backs."

Lena came out of the Temple gates leading the boy who was already clutching a puppy to his chest. She clapped her hands, attracting the others' attention,

"Children! Who wants to feed the baby dragons with me?"

Screams of joy and a forest of raised hands. She smiled. "Then we'll go now to that big heap of purple scrap metal and each of you may take a tiny piece. Baby dragons love it. Then we'll all line up and march on to feed Draky and Craky."

I couldn't take it much longer. "Lena! Stop wasting mithril. Can't they just eat some normal metal, there's plenty lying around?"

She shook her head sternly. "Steel gives them colic. What difference does it make, anyway? It's either us or Vertebra brings them a whole tank turret again."

I clutched at my heart. "Which Vertebra? Which tank?"

"The big dragon, I mean. She's a Bone Dragon, isn't she? So I called her Vertebra. The tank—well, I don't know much about them. She brought them this turret with two really delicate guns. It's really nice... was. Vertebra says mithril is very good for them. They're at that age when their bones and scales are forming. They grow them out of whatever they eat. Vertebra said they're going to be the first mithril dragons in the world, imagine!"

Oh, no. Some people had rats in their grain barns. I had dragons. What the hell was going on?

Lena clapped her hands again, "Attention, everybody! In a moment, you will see a small square window right in front of your eyes. In it, you'll see two buttons. You must will yourself really hard to press the one that's on the left. Everyone remember where your left hand is? That's right! Are you ready? Press it!"

I was watching, slightly dumbfounded, as system messages flashed before my eyes,

Alexandra Kovaleva, Level 1 Druid, has accepted your invitation to join the clan!

Jana Novac, level 1 Cleric, has accepted your invitation to join the clan!

Sergey Tischenko, level 1 Warrior, has accepted your invitation to join the clan!

Chapter Twenty-Three

Their heartrending voices had long died away but my lips were still moving as I repeated Doc's last phrase,

"Who if not us?"

A very uncomfortable question, once again raising the subject of responsibility. Instead of playing and having fun, I kept sinking deeper into local problems, lugging the load of other people's hopes and struggling in a net of responsibilities that hadn't been mine to accept.

Of course I understood Doc, at his wits' end with frustration, overwhelmed by the never-ending chain of deaths. He was like a cat saving her kittens out of a burning house: her hair smoldering, her eyes swollen with blisters, diving back into the flames time and time again to pull out her wailing babies one at a time. Doc, too: once he'd seen a ray of hope in the dark, he followed it, throwing caution to the wind, selling his apartment, exposing himself to blows from all quarters, all to pull his babies out: not so much *where to*, but more importantly, *where from*.

How could I not understand him? How could I have said no? True, he hadn't warned me; he hadn't asked for my advice. Probably, in the light of his objective it all seemed petty and irrelevant. Like a lip-biting kamikaze pilot pointing his plane at the deck of an enemy aircraft carrier, he saw no problems, only his goal and his duty. In his mind he was already there, burning alive on the mangled deck amid crumpled metal, taking hundreds of enemies and their powerful machine with him.

I had no idea how it was going to work out with the children. In case of war, we could always move them somewhere safe—say, to the Vets to begin with. No human being would object to offering shelter to a child in danger. Besides, they wouldn't have to walk the war's endless roads as refugees. Here, reaching safe areas was as easy as activating a teleport. Wish we had this skill back in 1941 when millions of people had perished in blockades and ambushes. The siege of Leningrad alone had cost us way too dearly...

In principle, given another ten to fifteen years, these kids who knew no other home but the world of sword and sorcery could become its strongest warriors. They would have no inkling that it was all a game. They'd have no doubt that magic is real, invisibility is normal and healing someone is as easy as waving your hand over them. They would be the ones to invent new spells and bring magic under control. There had to be a difference, making knights and wizards out of thirty-year-old office rats and housewives or raising them from two-year-old toddlers. Which of them would I bet on in the long run? Quite possibly, he with enough intuition to foresee this trend now and take the young wolf cubs under his wing could be looking at a considerable jackpot sometime in the future.

Still, I had to do something about Lena. This was a classic case of cognitive dissonance causing me to expect more from her: more responsibility, more help and more maturity. I kept forgetting about the barely teenage girl locked inside that voluptuous adult body, her hormones raging (if that were at all possible here). So I really had to put my foot down before she derailed us all. And seeing as we had a kindergarten in the making, it would be a good idea to introduce a similar hierarchy in the clan itself: we'd have a junior group, a senior group, pre-school, primary school and so on.

I spent a few more minutes distributing some basic rights between the groups, making sure that senior clan members had a few more options than the younger ones. With a vindictive grin, I removed Lena from the clan officers' list and moved her to a new group, *Junior High*. After a moment's thought, I added one final touch. Poking out the tip of my tongue with zeal and satisfaction, I wrote: *Valley of Fear Junior High*. Now, baby, you'd have to prove to me you merited a promotion! Best regards.

Excellent. I slapped my knees and jumped to my feet, scaring a butterfly and earning a disapproving glance from the Hound pup busy hunting it.

Enough digressing. I reminded myself of a steam engine pulling an enormous freight train packed with goods and people clinging to car roofs as I dragged it directly into the financial abyss. I had to force myself out of it. Actually, that was exactly what I'd been doing those last few days. The cigarette business wasn't bringing in any profits yet: all the proceeds were immediately invested into its development, building premises, buying supplies and hiring more staff. Judging by what my analysts had gleaned from my business plan, in just one year we were looking at five hundred grand gold a month to each alliance member. Nice as it was, I needed money now—preferably fifty times that.

I started by creating a new High Spell scroll, put it up at a private auction, then sent an invitation to the Minediggers impatiently waiting for it. In less than ten minutes, they bought the precious parchment. True to their word, they transferred the million into my account adding a polite letter where their ill-concealed impatience and hopes for quick revenge shone through their words of gratitude. I had a funny feeling they weren't going to stop at that. They would keep going, destroying the greedy offenders' castles one after another. They were yet to learn that sooner or later—sooner rather than later—their happy bubble would burst. Everybody in the square had witnessed the scroll in action. All the interested parties had gleaned everything they needed from that demonstration and were probably busy working on countermeasures. Which were quite simple and obvious. It was enough to break the dome down into a few smaller segments or levels. Then the scroll would only be able to remove the first layer, presenting the attackers with an unpleasant surprise: a second protective sphere.

I was afraid that very soon, when discussing a castle's defense levels, everyone would allude to the number of layers in a dome. The scrolls would still be used but their price would fall tenfold, if not hundredfold.

Too bad. I had to squeeze as much out of it as I could while I still could. I had to churn out a scroll a day: the Vets' arsenal could wait no matter how many hints Dan and the General would drop.

Another money-making idea had been burning a hole in my brain for the last twenty-four hours, ever since I'd received Thror's message. That honorable Dwarf, the patriarch of Thror's Gem House, informed me that the work on both altars had been completed. Which made me remember our last meeting and the way he complained of the greedy priests of Light who didn't want to add a new god to their pantheon—one that would answer the needs of both Dwarfs and miscellaneous crafters. Actually, he'd chosen the right shoulder to cry on. Was I the First Priest or just a pretty face? Granted, I only knew the location of one Dark temple out of the remaining four: the one in the Drow capital. But that was plenty to summon a new patron god. Ruata, the Drow Princess doubling as the deserted temple's Priestess, was unlikely to mind. And even if she did, so what?

In other words, I had enough to offer the midgets from Under the Mountain to make them untie their purse strings and dig up their grandfathers' pots of gold. The unique service of custom-summoning a patron god was going to cost them.

A couple of hours later, having rummaged through the available gods lists and having discovered, to my joy, an additional box saying *include deities from literature, fantasy and gaming,* I was knocking at the massive gate of Thror's Gem House with my most enticing smile.

The clan's patriarch knew better than to make me wait. Almost straight away, the receptionist invited me in. He wasn't particularly pleased with the speed with which I accepted my finished order—apparently, he'd been looking forward to explaining every flourish of the intricate design and painting a picture of the task's inconceivable difficulty. Now he sniffed into his beard, apparently betrayed in his best expectations.

Unwilling to alienate him, I hurried to rectify my mistake. "You'll have to excuse my haste, Sir. I didn't want to hurt your feelings by inspecting your perfect work for non-existent faults. The stamp of your House is all I need to justify its quality."

My sugar-coated flattery had the desired effect. The dwarf relaxed, accepting a stance of haughty arrogance. Oh well, end of fine tuning, time to engage the primary caliber.

"Besides, I wanted to save our time and energy for a much more important private conversation," I rolled my eyes meaningfully at the guards behind their firing slits.

The Patriarch gave a kingly nod and began making a complex sign combination with his fingers. Steel trapdoors clanged. The Dwarf's time-ridden face expressed a patiently polite attention with just a tad of skepticism.

"*Absolutely* private," I repeated.

He stared at me with suspicion, chewing his lower lip. Finally, he made up his mind. He made another sign, dramatically more complex than the first one, and froze, listening. Then he made another sign and finally shook his fist at somebody unseen. Another doortrap clanged—hopefully, the last one.

The Patriarch looked up at me from under his bushy eyebrows. "Speak."

"Does the name of Aulë say something to you?"

Crack! A steel pencil in the dwarf's hand snapped in half. With a thump, one of the guards collapsed behind the wall. So he should. The blacksmith god, the lord of earth and metals and the Maker of the Dwarven race who'd passed onto them his love of creations in metal and stone.

"Speak," the Patriarch repeated. He leaned forward, virtually lying with his chest on the table, his hopeful eyes looking into mine.

Four hours later I walked out of his house, not quite stable on my feet due to the amounts of Dwarven Extra Dry consumed, and breathed a sigh of relief. It probably would have been easier to come to a business agreement with an electric kettle than with those skinflints from Under the Mountain. They hadn't given me twenty million. Nor ten. I'd only managed to squeeze seven out of them. Plus five hundred Dwarves deployed for the restoration of the castle's defensive capacity including four external bastions.

And if someone says it's not enough, then I hope they have to deal with a dwarf vendor in every scruffy shop they ever visit on their crooked life's path. And if six months of such pain in the butt doesn't turn him into a gibbering walking skeleton gray before his time—then I'll eat humble pie and admit I was taken for a ride. But at the moment, I was entirely proud of the deal I'd just struck.

According to the Dwarves, they could have seven million in a week in exchange for my keeping my end of the bargain: summoning their much-anticipated deity. Actually, without even mentioning anything else, such summoning would bring thousands of Dwarves under the Fallen One's banners. True that whenever the question was raised, Honorable Thror had turned rather pale and sad—so it looked as if the event could lead to a rift in the Dwarven ranks. Not everyone was prepared to denounce their new gods returning to their original element that technically had found itself on the side of the Dark.

But for me personally, such a Dwarven exodus from the army of Light and their allegiance to the Fallen One was in some respect even more important than the money itself. This was a very hefty weight added to the balance of future confrontation.

Having received a boost from the admittedly decent brew, my mind was already painting countless steely ranks of Dwarf squads lining up at the foot of the Temple, waiting for my command. Then the world shuddered.

Booom, the gong reverberated all over AlterWorld with a system alert. I peered at the opened message and froze in the middle the road.

Pantheon alert! A new force has entered the world! Lloth, the Dark Mother of the Drow, Weaver of Chaos and the Lady of Spiders, has joined the Pantheon of the Fallen One!

A Drow Goddess? Still hopeful, I rummaged through the Altar menu only to confirm that the Dark Temple of the Original City had regained its patron deity. Ruata, you stupid woman, what was that now? How on earth could you have done the dirty on me?

I was like a taut string, unable to restrain my anger. What a cheek! Who did they all think they were? When I needed them to help me restore the First Temple and sort out the problems it had created—no one seemed to be interested. They were all too busy lining up for the freebies! Not just lining up—they were taking the place apart, pilfering everything that wasn't screwed down! Destroying valuable ammunition, stashing away mithril and gobbling it down, even denying me my right to summon a patron god! The Temple's High Priestess was the only person who could have done it, and that's exactly what she did, jumping at her chance. Everyone was busy tugging the blanket while I was alone lying here freezing my butt off.

Sorry, guys. This isn't the way the cookie crumbles. I'd do whatever it takes—excommunicate, anathemize, disembody whoever deserved it.

I found myself running on the cobbled pavement not really looking where I was going, colliding with unhurried players or ducking out of their way. They shouted at my back something about those Elven tykes who should all be put up against the castle wall or hanged on lampposts. I only smirked. Yeah, *no foreigners allowed*, wonder where I'd heard that before? Sorry, guys, bad timing, duels would have to wait.

Finally I reached the massive wall of the House of Night residence. The guards were respectful but unyielding. "You'll have to wait to be taken inside." For five minutes I paced the yard by the front door, working myself up and getting more and more agitated. Finally the majordomo, unhurried and majestic like the Queen, invited me to follow him. I was running rings around the well-fed NPC, struggling to refrain from goading him on with a hearty kick in the butt. The only thing that stopped me was the thought that the guards would interpret such an action as a direct assault, resulting in my respawning a few seconds later in the Vets' portal hall. So I had to grin and bear it, notching up interest on the bill I was about to present Ruata with.

After fifteen more minutes of marching through a series of opulent halls I was already almost sure they'd been walking me in circles. Then the majordomo finally swung open another pair of doors and stepped aside, allowing me to enter.

Yet another luxurious hall, its thirty-foot ceilings heavy with stucco and frescoes depicting the Drow's exploits. A soft 'the Princess will see you shortly' followed by the inconspicuous sound of the closing doors made me swing round. He'd legged it, the bastard. Very well, I could wait. Ignoring the soft couch and the side table laden with delicacies, I began pacing the hall making the guards of honor by the doors jump to attention every time I went past them.

The hall was sixty paces long and forty wide. Just when I started thinking I'd already worn a groove in the marble floors, the world shuddered again.

Boom! The guards bowed deep as the inner interface flooded me with messages,

Quest completion alert: The Prince of the House of Night. Quest completed!

Reward: a new social status, The Prince of the House of Night.

Congratulations! You've received Achievement: you've become the third person in AlterWorld to occupy a Prince's throne.

Reward: +10,000 to Fame

Congratulations! Your family status has been updated! Princess Ruata has become your wife!

Holy cow. That wasn't the agreement! What was that about the Prince? And his spouse? Didn't I have to make another 100 levels for a successful completion?

I opened my quest logs and looked for the record I needed,

Level above that of Princess Ruata (current level: 71) (met)

Gosh. How had she managed to drop a hundred levels? Taali would kill me and she'd be right. Why would I need this stupid princedom, what for? To be perfectly honest, I'd already bitten way more than I could chew. I was looking at at least another couple of years of simply gaining experience in running my own clan and the castle. All I needed now was a couple of thousand Drow and all the problems they could bring.

Having said that... I cast a patronly glance over the surrounding splendor and the guards with their doglike expression. What was it Ruata had said? A hundred fifty cutthroats and three hundred guards? Yeah, right—I gently shut my inner greedy pig's dropped jaw—plus a whole shedload of other people's problems. Including a marriage I couldn't care less about. Sure, Ruata was fire and ice incarnate, the peak of passion and beauty, totally mind-blowing, forcing you to think with completely different body parts. Still, finding myself licking someone's feet, looking up in devotion waiting for their command to fetch their slippers—that was something I really didn't look forward to.

I shook my head and pursed my lips, thus hitting the right note for my upcoming exchange with the Princess. With a decisive step I approached the bowing guard. "Take me to the Princess, *now*!"

"Yes, Sir!"

That's better. For the next five minutes we kept winding and unwinding down the stairs, descending deeper and deeper into the bowels of the residence's dungeons. The number of guards at intersections grew, pointing at our approaching an especially guarded object. Finally we arrived at an old archway of black marble intricately carved with archaic pictograms of a long forgotten tongue.

The guard pointedly stepped aside and saluted, making clear his mission was completed. Very well. I could manage on my own now.

In centuries past, countless feet had trodden a groove in the eighty-eight ancient stone steps that led me to an enormous hall, its size concealed by the True Darkness. A barely noticeable walkway was marked by braziers filled with smoldering embers and crimson sparks. It led to the iridescent soap bubble of a magic dome.

I stepped onto the walkway. It crunched and rattled underfoot. This wasn't the right time to enjoy the divine Darkness, so I rummaged through my bag in search of the Torch of True Flame. Yanking it out, I activated a third of its power and recoiled. The entire floor was littered with bones and ancient weapons. Crossbow bolts that sat deep in crumbling skulls, chestplates that spilled loose ribs, helmets crushed by powerful blows and shields smashed into pulp. It appeared to be the remains of a great battle that had once raged under the Temple's walls. The defenders and attackers lay randomly on top of each other, their bodies piled high in some places. The flesh had long been reduced to ashes and the smell had worn off; there was nothing left but bones and steel.

And artifact jewelry, my inner greedy pig pointed out, spying the glimmer of bejeweled rings on a skeleton's fingers that were still clutching an expensive-looking sword. The ruby in its hilt was enormous. True, there was plenty of loot here but we weren't grave robbers, were we? Still I crouched over the body and lowered the torch wishing to read the stats. I didn't want to miss something epic, something lost in the dust of time, capable of moving mountains and shaking the earth.

I brought my face closer, then recoiled. The skull stirred and swayed. A huge hairy spider forced its fat belly out through an eye socket. His beady lavender eyes stared at me with hatred as he waggled his mandibles, a little drop of cloudy yellow venom forming on them. No, thank you very much. Could never stand those eight-legged creepies. I spat in his direction and barely dodged when he spat back, the venom missing me and landing on a massive siege shield that almost covered a dwarf's skeleton. The metal spumed and smoked with corrosion. Ignoring my pride—no one could see me, anyway—I darted out of the creature's range.

Finally, the dome. I probed it with my finger, afraid of poking through the fragile bubble. As if! Not a trace to be seen on the surface as strong as concrete. My attempt to punch it equally failed as the weird material was absorbing my blows without as much as a vibration or sound. I looked around for something more effective and found it: a mace with a top of meteoritic iron.

I'll teach you to have doorbells! I took a swing and bashed at the dome, falling through it, weapon and all. The mace clattered over the floor while I found myself in a position unworthy of a warrior, standing on all fours with my hands flat on the flagstones. You didn't expect me to break my fall with my nose, did you? Grunting, I scrambled to my feet and looked back. The opening had already sealed as instantly as it had opened.

"Liquid steel, UFO technologies," I commented under my breath as I studied the Lloth altar unit in the braziers' uneven light.

"The Impregnable Dome Shield," Ruata corrected me, emerging from the shadows. "The Great Goddess can learn from her mistakes. She'll never allow for another eventuality to submit her to oblivion. Hundreds of years ago a group of warriors of Light forced their way into the Temple through deceit and treachery, conducting the Banishing Rite. None of them lived to see the sun again but as the First Temple had already been destroyed, we couldn't summon the Great Mother back."

Ruata's voice changed. She lowered her head, sinking on one knee in front of me. "Greetings, my lord and my husband."

A shiver ran along my spine, my head foggy, my mind ringing with desire. I gulped, taking in the aroma of wild strawberries, unable to force my eyes away from the velvet of her bare neck.

Mental attack!
You've been exposed to some dangerous frequencies!
Pheromone attack!

We are taking measures to block and purge your organism of them.

A wave of freshness ran over my body, washing out any unnecessary hormones and giving my mind a jolt. "Stop it, Ruata. You don't need magic crutches: you're beautiful in your perfection as you are."

She raised her head, looking at me with surprise. Then she stood up, a promise in her smile, and stepped toward me, smothering me with the aura of her perfume: forest and strawberries and a woman's hot body.

She shook her hands, flicking eight purple sparks from the tips of her fingers. They darted aside, burying themselves in the small heaps of incense that were piled up in golden bowls. Smoke swirled toward the ceiling. That was something I could relate to—hadn't I doubled up as an incense maker? I quickly scanned the stats,

Submission Potion... the Powder of Bliss... Ecstasy Mix... the Brew of Desire...

Ruata's soft hand lay on my cheek, forcing my head away from the bowls and toward her own eyes, dragging me into their purple vortex. Her eyes locked with mine, she rose on tiptoe, her lips reaching for me. The taste of wild strawberries and mint, of absinth, of cannabis...

Repeat mental attack!
You've been exposed to mind-altering substances!
Pheromone attack!
An unidentified alchemy attack!
We are taking measures to completely block and purge your organism of them.

My taste buds shut down. It felt akin to a dentist's anesthetic shot, the layers of smells replaced by a long-forgotten high school memory of a gas mask on my face: rubber and coal dust. My eyesight glitched, blinked and switched to black and white mode. Thank you, Macaria, thank you.

Gently I prized her off me. "Another manipulation attempt, Princess, and we'll part enemies."

"I'm so sorry, my Lord. I only wanted to be desirable for you..." she cast me a confused glance, lowering her head in guilt.

My eyesight blinked again. The picture glitched and switched back to color. The magic of her lavender eyes didn't oppress me any more.

Only now could I finally see her in a true light which instantly made me want to revert back to monochrome. The Princess looked, er, quite seductive. The torch flames behind her back shone through the thin silk, outlining her perfect shape. The dress's left chest pockmarked with hundreds of holes did little to conceal the perfect hemisphere of her breast. I gulped again. Even without using her mental magic, Ruata exuded the very essence of femininity, an unrestrained hurricane of passion. Wait a bit. What was that for a dress style? Covered in hundreds of cuts and spotted with rusty red from neck to its hem? Blood. It was everywhere: on the fine silk, on her hands and the floor, covering the altar and the plain steel dagger that had been thrown nonchalantly onto its black polished stone.

"You... you sacrificed herself to Lloth?"

She gave me a tired smile. "It's not about Lloth, really. I needed to do something to become equal in strength with the man I liked. He wasn't in a hurry to gain power. And tomorrow... tomorrow the Council of Elders was going to force their own choice of husband onto me."

There was just a hint of reproach in her stare, but it was enough to make me want to apologize. "I'm sorry. I had too many things on my plate. The castle, the clan, that wretched Temple..."

Stop! I shook my head forcing myself to shut up. It looked like even Divine Immunity wasn't able to completely block out her pressure. Still, I'd never been a henpecked doormat and wasn't going to become one any time soon. This kind of behavior just wasn't typical for me. Which meant it had been forced onto me. Another reason to stay away from this femme fatale. I braced myself as if about to take an ice dip, and spoke,

"Ruata. This is about Lloth. How could you summon-"

She raised her hand to stop me. A spider the size of a dog crawled out of the shadows and scurried toward her. Ruata lovingly scratched its bristly back, making the creature roll two of its side eyes with delight. Still, it didn't prevent the thing from watching me with the seven remaining eyes, a drop of toxic spittle forming on its jaws.

She gave the spider a good scratch calming it down. "You should never mention the Goddess' name in her own temple. This way you address her directly, attracting her gaze. She is not particularly fond of men. And as for the Temple... Please do not be cross with me, my lord. For centuries have the Drow been guarding these walls. Thousands of our warriors have died defending its sanctuary. Other gods have no place here! This is our altar. But I don't want you to be ridden by anxiety, so I'm going to tell you about a place where you can find an untouched altar of a Dark god. Take it to any temple, then summon a god of your choice.".

I nodded. Her offer made sense. The deal with the Dwarves might just go though, after all. Very well. Time to take a deep breath and move to the main subject.

"Thank you, Ruata. I'll be more than happy to take you up on your kind offer. But there's another thing. I'm sorry, but I really can't marry you. I already have a girlfriend and I'm happy with her."

And she makes me feel like a man and not a doormat, I added mentally before going on, "Consequently, I can't be a Prince, either. And I don't think I could be one even if I tried. Look at me! I'm struggling to control my clan, its castle and the First Temple. It really sounds very tempting what you're saying but I'm afraid I have to say no to both counts."

Large tears welled in her eyes, then spattered on the flagstones. Ruata sank to her knees, plea in her stare. "Prince! Please don't give me to the Elders! If you reject the throne, the Elder's son Ulgul will take it. A dumb, fat, lecherous pig that can't wait to lay his greedy hands on the title and my body! I shudder when I think of him groping me..."

She grabbed at her virtually bare breast and squeezed it tight mimicking Ulgul's greedy hands. I gulped again, perfectly sympathetic to some Elder's son urges, and registered a surprising pang of jealousy.

The Princess raised her tearful eyes to me and pointed at the blood spots, the dagger and her lacerated chest, disrupting my concentration,

"Have I done all this for nothing? I have died two hundred and seventeen times today, hoping that the late Prince's throne would go to one who's worthy of it..."

She broke down, dissolving in tears. I sat next to her and stroked her hair. What was wrong with her today? Never before had she been so tearful— she used to be a true iron lady. Were things really so grim?

"Try to see it my way," I said. "I have a girlfriend. She would never understand this."

"Very well," Ruata snapped. "I agree. We can perform the divorce ritual now in front of Lloth while we're still in the Temple. It's possible. We'd have had to go to her anyway to seal our marriage... or our divorce. But Laith, I beg you! Give me one year! Take the Prince's place while I find another worthy suitor. You won't have to do anything. Everything will go as it does now. I'll occupy myself with my clan's needs and you can continue doing your own thing. You will have full access to the treasury and the artifact vault. You will also be able to take command of my cutthroats whom you like so much. I just hope," she forced a sad smile, "that you'll be fair and just and you won't leave the clan without money or warriors. The House of Night will never forget your help. We'll forever remain your friends and allies of your clan. Please. I beg of you..."

Again she buried her tear-strewn face in her hands, her shoulders shaking. I stared around me helplessly. This was a very generous proposition. In essence, she was offering me to bear the Prince's title for a year with full control of their troops and finances. What could you not do, having five hundred elite Drow warriors under your command? Just by sending them on an Inferno raid, you could get hundreds of thousands in gold worth of loot on a daily basis.

I mulled over her offer and couldn't see a single catch. Any way you looked at it, it was all pros and no cons. Wasn't it about time, really, I got lucky without having to worry about being set up? I glanced at the weeping girl and shook my head, making up my mind. "Okay, Ruata. I can take the Prince's throne for a year. I promise to treat the clan's warriors with care and won't abuse my access to the treasury. But," I looked her firmly in the eye, "on the prerequisite that we get a divorce."

She nodded submissively. "Very well, Prince. Our marriage was attested by the gods so only they have the right to undo the knot. We need to die here in front of this altar, in order to face the Great Mother. She will separate our lives. After that, you'll be free from this marriage."

With a quiet smile, she pointed at the altar where the dagger still lay in a pool of blood. "Are you ready?"

I flinched. "Is it the only possible way? Stabbing oneself, you know... Besides, from what I hear, your goddess is quite a piece of work..."

She shook her head reproachfully. "The Drow have themselves a timid prince. Look at me!" again she pressed her hand to the round perfection of her breast. "I died hundreds of times today, all for you! So find the courage to sacrifice your life but once, even if only in farewell! Do not fear the goddess. I'm her priestess, you're safe with me. Just don't look her in the eye. Keep your head low and add some respect to your voice. It won't cost you anything and she likes that sort of thing."

She came to a small mithril chest and opened the lid, scooping out a generous handful of gems and flinging them into the red black flames that burned at the foot of the altar. The fire flared up, consuming the disappearing gems, even those that had missed their target. Lavender smoke swirled around, forming eight circles. Ruata grabbed the bloodied dagger and shoved it into my hand.

"On the count of three! We'll strike together. You strike me and I'll strike you. But wait! You're going to resurrect at the other end of the world! Immortal-" she spat out an expletive.

"Quickly!" she hurried. "We have less than a minute. I've just spent two hundred grand worth of gems so I'm not doing it again! You must change your resurrection point. I know you can do it. Why this hesitation? You're the First Priest in a temple of Darkness and a Prince in your own house. There's no other place in the entire AlterWorld that's safer for you. Come on, now!"

Succumbing to her logic and pressure, I scrolled through the magic book, found the necessary spell and activated it.

Ruata was watching me closely. "On the count of three," she nodded. "Close your eyes if it makes it easier for you. One," she reached behind her back for a second dagger. A very multifunctional dress she had on. "Two!.."

No idea what made me open my eyes. I saw her hand raised over my head and the dagger she clutched within it. I froze. The dagger was shaped as a spider, its eight pointed legs contracted together to form a scary-looking blade. I instantly looked up its stats,

The Spider Dagger of the High Priestess Lloth.
He who dies from its blade spilling his blood onto the Altar, dies a final death, his soul forever cast into the Halls of Gloom.

"Three!" Ruata barked, taking a swing.

I caught her hand in full flight, barely stopping the fragile wrist. "What do you think you're doing? Are you out of your mind?"

She looked at me with pity. "You little fool. I wanted to make it easy for you. You wouldn't have felt a thing." She forced a smile and ordered someone, "Immobilize him!"

The enormous spider went for me, sinking its jaws into my hip. I yelped, burying the dagger I was holding into its back. The blade went right through not sensing any resistance. I pricked my hand on the spider's bristles as the dagger's blade slid back into its handle without hurting the monster.

Ruata laughed. I flung the useless dagger at her. Numbness spread over my body, paralyzing my limbs and forcing me to fall on my side.

"Lay him on the altar!" she ordered.

I heard the shuffling of many tiny feet. Something lifted me and threw me onto the icy-cold stone.

The priestess came over to me and looked into my eyes, stroking my cheek in sympathy. "Dear boy, did you really think that I could be interested in you? That you were worthy of taking the throne of the House of Night? Had you once seen our Prince, you'd have known that compared to him, you're like a mouse next to a dragon. My Prince..." her eyes misted, her lips opening in excitement. "Very soon, my lord," she whispered, "you need to wait but a little longer. Soon..."

I was frantically searching for a way out. Magic was out of the question. No good trying to cast a spell when lying on a stone—and paralyzed, too. Blindly I slammed the Shield of Faith button: 30-sec immunity, now think, think! I didn't know how high the risk of dying was from that scary artifact of hers but somehow I didn't want to find out. Fear clung to me, paralyzing my will and thought. All I wanted was to curl up, cover my head, and pee in my pants, whimpering with fear.

No way! I scowled, grinding my teeth until the enamel crunched. I bit my tongue that just happened to be in the way, clearing my mind with a flash of pain and hatred. There had to be a solution! I had to find it!

In the meantime, Ruata lowered her hand, menace in her stare. "So you want to suffer before you die? Then you can listen to what awaits you. My lord and my husband was slain in battle. The Fallen One did not show him mercy. My beloved couldn't respawn and stayed forever in the Land of Shadows. How I begged! How many sacrifices did I offer! The Fallen One turned a deaf ear to my pleas. But the Great Mother didn't! A new soul of the same status and potential can replace my husband in the Halls of Gloom—you! A naïve little idiot marked by the stamp of the powers that be, one that failed to live up to their expectations! A perfect substitute. Lloth will be pleased with the sacrifice. She will accept your soul and send the Prince back to the world of the living. She has the power to do that. I have sealed our agreement with the blood from my eighty-eight voluntary deaths!"

I barely listened to her, busy going through my list of skills. Wrong, wrong, all wrong... how about the Destructive Touch? Take that! Ruata jerked with the charge. A dozen red-hot mandibles sunk into me, admittedly unable to deal me any damage as immunity still worked.

"Heh! Don't touch him. It's more fun this way."

Oh, well.

How about Macaria's Voluntary Death? But what could it give me apart from the loss of experience and a few gained seconds? I was going to resurrect right here anyway, and it had a one-hour cooldown... Why, oh why had I changed the resurrection point? In the future, I should never, but never bind in places I had no control over. Whatever could I do? If only I had a hotline to God! Having said that... Appeal to Gods!

"Help me, O Fallen One! It's urgent! It's too fucking urgent!"

Max, his unhappy voice boomed in my head, *if this is about... Wha-what? Who? Who dared to-*

Bang! The outer dome resonated with a blow. *Bang!* A drop of sweat rolled down Ruata's temple. She narrowed her eyes, catlike.

"So your petty little god has decided to bring on the cavalry? Well, tough! This is the Impregnable Dome Shield!" she stuck out her arrogant chin.

Bang!

Not Impregnable, actually, the Fallen One murmured. *But it'll take some work. Fifteen minutes at least. The weaving is too complex, you can't just break it open, we'll have to push through it. Macaria babe, help me!*

Bang! Boom!

"I don't have five minutes!" I shouted, panicking, watching Ruata's hand taking another swing, the scary blade within it.

I'm very sorry, the Fallen One whispered.

Triumph glistened in her eyes. Eight sharp needles pierced my heart.

The pain took my breath away. The picture blinked and went out. Darkness enveloped me. Only my hearing still allowed me to clutch at reality. I heard the fabric of the universe rip apart. Heavy steps and a strong loud voice,

"Here I am, my love!"

Silk rustled. Ruata's voice whispered, filled with submission and a happiness not known to me, "Greetings, my lord! The Prince's throne and his marital bed await their true master."

The sounds dissolved, disappearing. In the pitch darkness, the lonely window of my internal interface kept flashing a message of doom:

Death alert! You've died a final death! You're about to be transported to the Halls of Gloom!
Teleport in: 5... 4... 3... 2... 1... 0...

End of Book Two

MMORPG Glossary[i]

AFK
Away from keyboard

Aggro
As a verb, it refers to a hostile mob that has noticed a player and is actively trying to attack that player. As a noun, it refers to the amount of "hostility" the player has generated on the mob. In typical combat strategy, the fighter tries to take as much aggro as possible away from weaker players such as healers and mages.

Alt
Short for "alternate". It refers to the alternate character a player has from their main character. This is not a stable category as sometimes alts can outlevel mains and sometimes mains become moth-balled.

Alt Tab
The act of using the ALT+TAB keys to jump from application to application

Bind
In certain MMOs, characters are teleported back to a safe spot when they die. This spot is predetermined by the user. The act of determining the safe spot requires an explicit action by the user. That action is known as a bind. The spot is typically referred to as a bind spot.

Bind on equip
This term refers to items that become soulbound to the player after they have been equipped. In other words, the item can be traded as long as no one equips it.

Bind on pickup
This term refers to items that become soulbound to the player after it has been picked up from a monster. In other words, the item cannot be traded once a player picks it up. BoP items commonly cause looting conflicts and disputes during game-play.

Bokken sword
A wooden training sword

Buff
Temporary boost to character attribute or combat ability

Camp(ing)
The act of waiting in an area to hunt a specific mob or a specific spawn

Caster
A mage or a wizard

Char/Toon
A player or their character.

Class
Professional archetypes. In D&D games, these would be warrior, healer, rogue and mage. The most typical class types are: close-range damage, ranged damage, healing, crowd control, support.

Cleric
Typical healing class in D&D style games

Combo
A combination of hits, especially causing severe damage like paralyzing or bleeding

Corpse
In certain MMOs, a corpse appears where the player died. Sometimes all the player's items and money are left on the corpse and the player is teleported back to their bind spot. Corpses typically will decay after a certain time proportional the character's level.

Corpse Run
The act of retrieving your corpse after you have died. This is typically a dangerous thing because people tend to die in dangerous places rather than safe places.

Crafting
A general category of skills that allows players to manufacture objects from raw resources

Crit
"To crit" refers to landing a critical hit either with melee or spells. Effective damage is usually increased from a base of 150% to upwards of 250% with extra talents/skills/buffs.

Crowd Control

Refers to a set of spells / abilities that temporarily paralyze or stun other mobs or players. Crowd control is an important group support ability when fighting multiple mobs.

DD
Direct Damage. Used to refer to a class of spells and abilities that allow players to damage enemies from a distance. The firebolt is the archetypal DD.

DD/DPS
A character whose primary role in a group setting is to deal damage to the opponents.

Debuff
The opposite of a buff. An offensive spell cast on enemies that weakens an attribute or combat ability.

Donator
A player who invests real money into virtual gear

DoT
Damage over time. Refers to a class of spells that deals damage over a period of time. These spells typically do more damage than DD spells overall.

DpS
Damage per second. Used when figuring out weapon speed and damage.

Drow
A Dark Elf race

Druid
Hybrid class in D&D style games—part healer, part support, part fighter.

Enchanter
A mage specializing in buffs

Epic
An extremely rare item or quest. Has come to mean something exceptionally cool and hard to get.

Experience

A quantity gained when completing tasks/quests, killing mobs, or various other achievements in games. When enough experience is accrued, characters often "level up" and become more powerful.

Familiar
Same as pet

Farm(ing)
The act of accumulating currency or a specific item by repeatedly killing a mob or repeatedly performing a series of actions

Gnoll
An NPS (AI-controlled character) race of humanoid hyenas

Guilds
Semi-permanent player groups. In typical games, players must use a substantial amount of capital to start the guild.

Health
A base attribute of characters

LFG
"looking for group"

Lich
A race of the undead

Loot
Currency or items that are dropped by a mob when it is defeated

Mana
A commonly-used pool of magic potential (magical analog of health points)

MMORPG
Massively-Multiplayer Online Role-Playing Game

Mob
An AI controlled monster. 'Mob' originally comes from the MUD era, where it was short for 'mobile', to differentiate monsters that would patrol a set of rooms as opposed to monsters which would stay in one place until killed.

Mount
Any riding animal from a donkey to a dragon

Newbie
A new inexperienced player

Newblette
A new and inexperienced female player

Noob
The pejorative form of newbie or an unskilled arrogant player

NPC
Non-player character (ie. controlled by AI)

Nuke
Refers to casters, to cast the highest damage spell or spell combo to effectively pull or finish of a npc. Mages usually are the most effective class in highest burst damage.

Nuker
A caster who throws a lot of damage spells on a target.

Perma
Permanent, permanently

Pet
A creature that can be summoned to help and defend a player

PK
Player Killer—a derogatory term—as in a person who primarily plays to kill other players

PK counter
Shows the number of players already killed by a PK and allows to calculate the chances of his dropping an item if killed by another player

Port
Short for teleport. Used as a noun and a verb.

Powerlevel
Same as rush. When a higher level player tries to help a lower level player level faster. Most games have mechanisms that prevent power leveling.

Pull

A standard hunting strategy where a player lures a single or a group of mobs to the group so that the group can hunt from a safe area instead of hunting in areas where new mobs may spawn.

PvP
Player vs. Player combat

Quest
A set of tasks of a player to complete

Quest item
An item needed to complete a quest

Race
Typically fantastical creations, such as Elves, Trolls and the like.

Raid
A more substantial engagement involving a large organized group of players typically set in a dungeon and involving difficult mobs

Regen
Short for regeneration (of health, mana, or other replenishable attributes)

Resist
A parameter showing one's chances to resist a spell, whether partially or completely

Respawn
A character's resurrection after being killed

Rogue
A game class used for scouting and spying

Root
Can refer to a class of abilities as well as its effect. A root spell immobilizes a target. The target is then said to be rooted. Early versions of these abilities involved references to plants, hence "root".

Rush
Same as powerlevel

Server

Due to technical reasons, each server can only support a limited amount of players. Each MMORPG typically has several servers. Players cannot interact with players on other servers.

Slot

A storage unit, especially in a player's bag

Snare

An ability which slows down a character's movement speed, but they are still capable of moving.

Solo

The act of playing alone, hunting mobs alone.

Soulbound

An item-control mechanic where an item cannot be traded. In other words, only one person can own the object and it cannot be traded. See also BoE and BoP.

Spawn

Resurrect

Stealth

A type of invisibility that lets stealth characters sneak up on others for large critical strikes or for scouting.

Stun

A typical form of crowd control ability that immobilizes an enemy

Tank

As a noun, refers to character classes that can take a lot of damage. As a verb, refers to the act of drawing aggro from mobs before other team members strike with their abilities.

Uber

Slang form of super

Wonder Waffle

From German *Wunderwaffe*, a wonder weapon

WTB

"want to buy"

WTS
"want to sell"

Zool
Cool

---

[i] Sources:

The Daedalus Project. The Psychology of MMORPGs

alteredgamer.com

mmoglossary.com

omegaknights.com

mmoterms.com

45125331R00144

Made in the USA
Middletown, DE
25 June 2017